THE COLOR OF FAMILY

By Patricia Jones

THE COLOR OF FAMILY
RED ON A ROSE
PASSING

THE COLOR OF FAMILY

a novel

•

Patricia Jones

AVON
TRADE

An Imprint of HarperCollins*Publishers*

Designed by Elizabeth M. Glover

ISBN 0-7394-4954-0

Printed in the USA.

ACKNOWLEDGMENTS

•

Patricia Jones passed away from lymphoma at the age of forty-two before this book was completed. With the help of family and friends who loved her, we were able to pull together Pat's notes on the novel and bring the book to publication.

We gratefully acknowledge all of those who helped with this truly inspiring effort: my mom, Pat's greatest source of comfort; sisters Bettye, Annette; brother, Tom; my son and Pat's nephew, who was more like a brother to her, Mark; my husband, Kenneth; Cousin Sylvia; my nieces and nephews, whose encouragement was endless; and her friends, who were so supportive of Pat and continue to offer support to the family, Millie, Debbie, and most of all, Daryl.

The publishing community who have supported Pat's career through three books: her literary agent, Eileen Cope of Lowenstein-Yost Associates, Inc.; her editor at Avon Books, Lyssa Keusch; and the talented HarperCollins Publicity, Marketing and Managing Editorial teams. As well, we'd like to thank Lou Aronica of Fiction Studio for helping to shape the manuscript.

Most of all, if Pat was writing this, she would like to single out Alexandra, her "Angel Girl," about whom she often said, "You are the most perfect thing I have ever made." Their bond of love will always be remembered and it will always be strong. Pat lives on in Alexandra.

Velma Adams
June 2004

PROLOGUE

•

Just inside the wrought-iron gate that wrung around the last house on the rue stood the only willow tree along the street. Its leaves dipped so low that they looked like the long slender fingers of a lady caressing the ground, making a canopy just right for hiding. It laid a dramatic drape in front of the Dupreses' house, only one of the finest colored homes in New Orleans. Antonia sat beneath the tree's canopy, where no one could see her but she could see all, sucking on crawfish and munching down pralines, both of which she shared with her old yellow cat that she carried everywhere in a yellow basket that was far older than she. And in the sleepiness of this New Orleans midsummer afternoon, she'd been passing the time eating and stroking and feeding Tippy, for the better half of an hour waiting to see what she'd suspected all along.

She could hear her mother calling for her, from way down at the other end of the banquette, wanting to know where her crawfish had gone to. Antonia had cunningly stolen them from the sideboard next to the stove where they sat after her mother had boiled them for some étouffé, and then Antonia darted from the back door like a flash of lightning running for a rod. But she knew that the pilfered crawfish wasn't the half of what had made her mother so cross. Antonia had wrapped those crawfish up in one of the family's good linen napkins to get them out of the house surreptitiously in the pocket of her dress. Well, what was she to do, with the crawfish being just about her favorite food in the entire world, next to pralines? *"Antonia Claire Racine, you get your-self back here with my crawfish, gal!"* she had heard her mother yell. But Antonia had only taken a few—four or five or ten—just enough to beat back the craving that wouldn't let her loose. Besides, there was no point in answering her mother's angry calls, since she and Tippy were savoring the very last one.

And anyway, she couldn't get up now, even if she'd wanted her mother to find her. She was just about to find out the truth about her brother, once and for all, and in her green dress, just the right shade of green for blending into the boughs of a lazy willow, Antonia was not about to miss her opportunity; all she knew for sure, which was simply not enough, was that some-thing was definitely askew. They say that twins have a connec-tion when it comes to each other, that transcends the physical five senses, and that's how Antonia knew that her twin, Emeril, was up to some kind of slyness. And his mischief was not just about some missing crawfish—of which she was certain he had taken a few before she'd snatched her stash and then gotten blamed for the whole missing lot. He was sneaking around town with that Agnes Marquette, and Antonia could only pray that he had not given his first time away to a woman who was most unworthy.

The thought of Agnes making her brother a man wouldn't have been so bad for Antonia if it were not for one thing: Agnes Mar-quette had more tracks on her than a field of freshly planted corn. And when a seventeen-year-old white girl in New Orleans in 1957 had a reputation so bad that it had snaked its way over to the col-ored side of town, well, it was about time that white girl started thinking about heading out of the city. Yes, old Agnes, with her hair as black as brand-new tar and her eyes as green as the money her family lacked was so well known by the boys, and not a few men, that she had been around the block and parked. This truth vexed Antonia far more than the fact that in the South of 1957, where a thick and intractable line separated Emeril from white women, Agnes's whiteness put his life in a certain jeopardy.

Antonia licked the remnant of praline she was munching from her fingers and looked at the wristwatch she'd just gotten last month for the seventeenth birthday she shared with Emeril. Still, though it was only a month old, it sometimes worked and sometimes didn't, even when it was wound to the end. Now, though, she believed it was keeping perfect time, since it was nearly three o'clock and she could hear Agnes's heels tripping down the banquette, *clickety-clack, clickety-clack*. Right on time. Every Tuesday and Thursday at three, Emeril would mysteriously slide away down the banquette headed for the Dupreses' and then nearly an hour later, there was Agnes Marquette, her face as scarlet as a cut beet, her clothes loose, her hair flattened by wherever she'd lain, rushing by the Racine house as if a fire were nipping at her bottom to make the four o'five streetcar. And now here she comes, rushing to her swain for their afternoon of lust.

Antonia's heart quickened as Agnes pushed open the wrought-iron gate and clicked her way down the path leading to the front steps of the Dupreses' house, her face bright with apparent expectation as she veered off and then disappeared behind the willow toward the back of the house. "Where's she going?" Antonia whispered to Tippy. Just as she was about to get up from where she'd knelt to follow Agnes, she saw Emeril coming through the gate with a haste that said he just couldn't wait. He followed Agnes's trail around the side of the house to the back.

What a puzzler this all was for Antonia. Yes, Emeril worked in the Dupreses' house from time to time, fixing this and that, and old Mr. Dupres thought so highly of her twin brother that he gave him free run of the house with his own key when there wasn't a soul at home. But would Emeril be so stupid as to risk the esteem of a colored man like Mr. Beau Dupres for a few moments of carnal pleasure with someone like Agnes Marquette? No, he just wouldn't be that stupid. After all, everybody traipsed through everybody's yard to get to one place or another. Maybe they went down to the cemetery, and this was the quickest path to where they would meet. That was it, she thought. They were most definitely doing it, and that thought would never be quiet in her mind, but at least they were doing it in the cemetery and not in the Dupreses' house.

So Antonia got old Tippy back in the basket and tucked the pralines in her pocket. Getting to her feet, she peeked from between the droopy boughs to make certain no one had spotted her and then followed the trail where Agnes and Emeril had gone. And when she reached the back of the house, she heard, but could not see, the ruckus of pure unadulterated covetousness that was bawdy and loud enough in its disgrace to make her keep her secrets forever from a man. But for now, she had to stop it. She had to throw cold water on these animals, and fear, the best cold water of all for this un-Godliness, would be a great big old ice bucketful for those two. Antonia ran around to the front of the house and up onto the Dupreses' front porch and just as she was about to lean on the doorbell, someone called to her.

"Fou-fou Antonia! Hey, what you doin' there, cher? Don't you know they ain't home right now. Why it's the middle of the day, fou-fou Antonia. What ya thinkin'? And what ya want with them anyways?" It was Jackson Junior Jackson, whom she always called Junior, since to think of him as Jackson Jackson was simply too much to take even in New Orleans. Junior was the bane and pain of her life, but he could stop her heart with just one look.

"It's none of your business why I'm here, Junior Jackson. I'm mindin' my business and leavin' yours alone," she said with a flirty flit of her head. Then she leaned on that doorbell anyway and took off down the steps and through the gate. She looped her arm inside Junior's and walked in a haste that forced him to pick up his pace.

"Hey, what's the rush, there, cher?"

"Never mind, Junior. Like I said, it ain't none of your business."

Tippy let out a roar of a meow meant only for Junior, which prompted him to say, "Well, you better tell that old yella cat of yours to stop lookin' at me like he's gonna scratch out my eyes."

And just then, Antonia heard her brother yelling up the street, "Antonia? Antonia what do you want?"

"Isn't that your brother down there on the Dupreses' porch, Antonia? He's calling you," Junior said, trying to slow down.

But she quickened her pace nearly to a trot now, and said, as if she hadn't heard Junior, "Never you mind about Tippy, and she's a she, not a he."

"Don't you hear your brother?"

"I don't hear nothin' Junior. I think you must be hearin' things," she said as her name rang down the rue once again. She clutched tighter to Junior's arm and pulled him into a yard and made him hide with her behind a bush. Then she whispered, "Junior, I'm tryin' to keep my brother from makin' the worst mistake and ruinin' his life forever. Besides, I'm in the right, because the Bible says, Keep thy brother from sin and danger." Antonia stared Junior down with the firmness of what she believed with everything in her will to be divine words.

Junior squinted his eyes to ponder the supposed quote, then said, "Antonia, the Bible don't say nothin' like that. What're you talkin' about?"

Antonia didn't hear her name anymore, so she got to her feet, then tugged Junior to his feet. She threaded her arm inside his again and pulled him along with an urgent gait, saying, "Just keep walkin', Junior. Just keep on walkin'."

CHAPTER
1
·

Antonia shrugged on her furry coat. That's what she called it, not a fur coat, but a furry coat, because to her that made it sound truer to its vanity. But she wore it because it was warm and just right for a day like this when the wind and cold seemed to be an entity with heart, mind, and spirit. She hooked the coat closed all the way down to her knees, gathered up the Thermos of hot chocolate with one hand, and then wrapped that arm around the Tupperware container of fresh muffins she'd just gotten from her weekly food shopping at the Giant. Those girls out there on the boulevard need to eat something on a day like today, she thought as she positioned the container more comfortably in the crook of her arm. Antonia just knew they couldn't possibly be eating right and keeping themselves up, given their sleep-around life. They had been run off of Baltimore Street and somehow found their way to Garrison Boulevard, landing practically on her doorstep. She'd fed them every now and then, ever since the day she saw the first of these wayward strollers two years past shivering on the corner nearly in her bare bottom.

With her free hand, she opened the front door, fixed the latch so as not to lock herself out, then stepped across the threshold, closing it behind her. She hurried down the porch steps and along the pathway to the street with a quick short gait that made her teeter from side to side.

When she got to the end of the walk, she looked one way, then the other. "They were just out here," she mumbled to herself.

Then she looked across the street as the number nineteen bus passed by, and there was Jackie. So she waved her hand in the air and yelled, "Jackie, honey." And when the woman looked over to where she stood waving, Antonia descended the three steps to the curb and said, "Come on over here, honey. I've got something for y'all."

Jackie darted across the street as fast as she could in four-inch-high stilettos and a stretched-on swath of fabric that was actually a skirt. When she got to the sidewalk, she trotted over to Antonia with an innocence that, in that moment, seemed to peek out from behind the naughty-girl business of fulfilling the carnal pleasures of men. And almost like a giddy girl who'd just seen her mother, she asked, "How're you, Miss Antonia?"

"I'm fine, honey. Now listen, I brought you some muffins here and a Thermos of hot chocolate." She gave them to Jackie, noticing the girl had no gloves covering her shivering hands. So she scolded, "Where are your gloves, child? You need to have some gloves on your hands or something."

"I've got pockets, Miss Antonia. I'll be all right." She opened a corner of the container that held the muffins, took in their aroma, and smiled. "Aw, man, Miss Antonia. Blueberry muffins. This is so nice of you."

"Well, you take them and eat them. Share them with the other girls if they're around. And keep yourself warm with the hot chocolate." Antonia regarded Jackie for a few seconds with the heartbroken eyes of a mother. She put her own gloveless hands in her pockets, then said, "Now, you know I don't like what you girls are doing out here. You know that. The Bible says that your body is where the Lord lives, you know. But I brought you those muffins and hot chocolate because you've got to keep yourselves up, and keep yourselves warm. And try to stay safe."

"I know, Miss Antonia. You tell us that all the time." Jackie pinched off a piece of muffin and popped it into her mouth, then said, "But you know, Monique went on back downtown. She said it was just too weird being up here near you, since you was her fifth-grade teacher, and all. So it's just me and Gina, but we'll be all right, Miss Antonia. And you know I'm gonna be okay long as I have this," Jackie said as she patted the pocket of her short, some-sort-of-fur, jacket.

Antonia's mind left Jackie as she stood there thinking about Monique and how it was such a futile exercise, the business of wondering what a child might grow to be. When she thought about the bright-eyed, interested child she taught and the woman that child grew to be, it was anybody's guess what happened between those two points that brought her life to prostitution along Garrison Boulevard. And so as Jackie stared into her distracted eyes with puzzlement, Antonia merely hoped that the lost woman would one day find her way back to the promise of her girlhood; and she offered up an instant prayer in thanks for her daughter, Ellen.

"Yeah, well," Antonia said, "that switchblade isn't always going to protect you. You just be careful." And she turned to go back to the warmth of her home. A home, she thought, the like of which these poor lost girls may never know. Bless their hearts. Over her shoulder, she added, "I'll see you later. If you're still out here, I'll bring you some pork chops from dinner. When you're finished with the container and the Thermos just bring them back up to the house."

"Okay, Miss Antonia. And thank you again. You're our guardian angel, that's what you are."

"Well, just remember that this old guardian angel can only do but so much," she said as she climbed the three steps to the pathway.

"Oh, and Miss Antonia? By the way, what the Bible says is: 'Do you not know that you are the temple of God, and that the Spirit of God dwells in you?' It's from Corinthians one, chapter three," Jackie said, grinning with a certain pride.

"It's the same thing," Antonia said with a thin smile of relief, believing that if Jackie had such an intimacy with the Scriptures, then just maybe that's what she held on to to save her life in the abysmal world in which she lived. "And you need to remember that." Then Antonia went on her way at a clip down the grand path stretched out before her.

When she got back into the front hallway, she took off her furry and slung it across the settee. She went straight to the living room to finish the work she'd left when she went out food shopping. Taking the chair by both of its arms, she pushed it in a slow tango across the room, struggling as its feet caught against the carpet. It didn't take her as long as she thought it might to get it the last few inches to the corner by the window so that it could be with its twin, which she had inched there just before she went off to the Giant. It saves money, she reasoned to herself each and every time she rearranged the furniture while her husband, Junior, was away, since reading the paper in either of those chairs by that window in the middle of the day wouldn't require even a speck of lamp-light. She huffed and puffed, tripping over her own legs and the chair's, until she and the chair reached the corner. Then she took two steps back and studied her choice. Smiling with pride, she looked over her shoulder to the place from where it had come. At any other time of the year, when Junior wasn't away, the chairs sat together with a lamp table between them just in front of the couch on the other side of the coffee table, pretentiously waiting for someone to sit for tea or parlor talk. Not very useful by her esti-mation. She and Junior never drank tea, never even bought it. And they certainly didn't entertain enough, she thought, to justify having two chairs and a couch waiting just for small-talk parties. But that's where Junior wanted the seats and lamp table—so that's the way it stayed. Most of the time.

"Ma, we're here," a man's voice boomed from the front hall, snatching her from contemplation over the furniture.

When she hurried with her arthritic shuffle into the hall and found her son Aaron standing there, she could see her daughter Ellen, a perfectly fine name that Ellen liked to shorten to Ellie, hovering behind him. Antonia noted in the deep-cut lines in Ellen's forehead and her frowning lips, that she was none too pleased to be there, but Antonia went against every emotion that made her a mother and decided to ignore her daughter's annoy-ance instead of asking what was wrong. She'd soon show Ellen that coming over would most likely be the most sensible thing she'd do all day. And as Ellen stepped out from behind Aaron, Antonia was stunned into a gape-mouthed stare by her daughter's belly, which had grown fuller with Antonia's first grandchild seem-ingly overnight.

But Aaron, standing between them, held out the Thermos and his mother's Tupperware. "The woman out there asked me to give this to you, Ma." And after he put them in her hands, he gave her a questioning look and said, "Everybody else in this neighborhood is trying to get these women to go away, and you're feeding them. Ma, why do you keep feeding them?"

"Because somebody has to," she said dismissively as she moved around him. "Besides, no matter what their sins are they have to eat, don't they?" So when she finally made her way to where Ellen stood, she reached out to touch the miracle. "Oh my, Ellen!" she exclaimed. "Will you look at this? This baby sure has grown so nicely."

"Ma, what is this about?" Ellen said without acknowledging a grandmother's pride. "I'm between patients and I don't have long." Her voice was saturated with impatience.

"Momma, I've got a meeting with my producer that I can't miss. But you made it sound so important."

"I know you're both busy, and bless your hearts for coming right over. It's good to have such attentive children in my old age. Why I called you here *is* important." Antonia walked back into the living room, and she heard her children follow.

But Ellen stopped before she could come fully into the room, being as preoccupied as she was with matters other than her mother's reasons for calling them there. She looked over at the sofa where the piano once stood, and then over to the piano where the sofa, coffee table and two chairs once stood, and her jaw dropped on its own. She put both hands on her belly as if to keep her baby still while the laughter gurgled up from her depth. "Did you help her do this again?" she asked her brother.

"You mean this furniture? Of course I did. You know I always do," he said in a near whisper to his sister, as if Antonia couldn't hear a word. "You know this is what she does when Poppa goes out of town."

"Ma, when is Poppa coming back from New Orleans?" Ellen asked.

"Oh, some time on Sunday. Anyway, it doesn't matter. All this furniture, even the stuff in the dining room and the bedroom and the breakfast room will be back to the way he likes it by the time he gets back. I just like to have my home set up the way I really like it for a time. This is the way I compromise, Ellen. It doesn't hurt a soul, and it lets me feel like this is my home too."

"Yeah, well what are you going to do when Poppa retires from the board down at Tulane? He won't be traveling back and forth so much. You have to face the fact, Ma, that one of these days you're going to be stuck forever with the furniture the way Poppa likes it without any opportunity whatsoever to change it around," Ellen said as if she were giving her mother a thought she'd never before had to ponder. "And besides, one of these days all your furniture moving is going to take its toll on Aaron's back."

"Not to mention her own," Aaron said. "You should have seen her. And she obviously did more moving after I left, because I didn't put those two chairs over by that window."

Ellen pressed her lips together so that they curled up on each end. Then she blew out a sigh and said, "Anyway, I guess we didn't come all the way over here to talk about the way you move furniture around behind Poppa's back. What's this all about, Ma?"

"Just follow me," Antonia said, stepping around an awkwardly placed magazine rack. When she opened the doors to the dining room, she first made certain they were right there behind her before stepping aside with a dramatic show-girl shuffle to let them see for themselves; the only thing missing was the *ta-da*. And she couldn't understand for anything why Aaron and Ellen, wide-eyed, were gawking like two people caught totally by surprise with nothing intelligible to say. "So, what do you think?" she prompted. "They're all here, pretty much."

The dining room table was spread from corner to corner, edge to edge with newspaper photographs and articles about Clayton Cannon, the concert pianist that Baltimore had claimed from New Orleans. Peeking through the yellowed, frayed edges was the rich cherrywood of the table Antonia Jackson brought from her childhood home in New Orleans to her married-woman home in Baltimore forty-two years before, when she was that much younger and still feeling like a new bride.

What she had there, though, didn't even begin to account for half of the clippings of the concert reviews Antonia had collected on Clayton Cannon over the years. She had friends all over the country sending them to her from wherever he'd played. It seemed that at least one newspaper from every state in the union was represented on that table. If Clayton Cannon was even as much as mentioned in passing in the last paragraph of an article, Antonia had it. And if his picture was in it, it was worth that much more, at least to her. She had them arranged chronologically, spanning his career from the very beginning as a ten-year-old Louisiana prodigy to his days at the Peabody Conservatory, right there in Baltimore, to the very first time he played Carnegie Hall, and every other music hall before and since. She even had the most recent one from the *Sun* papers, "A Day in the Life of the Piano Man," written only three weeks before, after Clayton moved back to Baltimore from New York with his wife Susan, and his twin boys Noah and Luke. Twenty-three years it had been since he'd lived there. But Antonia made it the most important point in her life not to miss one second of his.

Aaron finally spoke. "Ma, you've got these clippings spread clean across what you've always told us was the family's most sacred heirloom. This is the only place in the house where we couldn't even so much as rest a tissue when we were growing up." Then he looked to Ellen as if she had the answers.

"I'm about to do what I needed to do since the first day that boy moved here to Baltimore twenty-seven years ago," Antonia responded, "that's what this is about, and I want you two to take these, whichever ones you want, just in case something happens to me."

There were several seconds of meaningful silence in the room before Aaron spoke. He looked at one or two of the clips, then asked, "Ma, why are you still on this thing? I thought we had all this settled. I thought we had made it clear to you that Clayton Cannon is not your brother's son."

"You didn't make anything of the sort clear to me." Antonia was immediately perturbed. "I know my blood, and that boy has my blood running all through him just as sure as you two do. That boy sitting down there in Harbor Court Towers, the prodigious musical genius brought up out of the great, albeit sometimes backward, yet always musical, state of Louisiana is your cousin. Emeril was my twin. I shared a womb with him and I would know more than anybody when a part of him is still living."

"Okay, Ma, that's it. I don't have time for this," Ellen said. "You either stop this nonsense or, I swear to God, in the morning I will have you committed to Shepherd-Pratt. And I mean what I say." And with that threat, Ellen stormed from the room and walked toward the hall with determined thumps to her measured steps.

"Ellen, honey, please wait. Please just listen to me, sweetheart," Antonia implored desperately. For as much as she knew how the mere mention of Clayton Cannon spiraled her daughter downward into her basest self, Antonia still couldn't help herself. And she thought that without her self-imposed control, she'd be writing to Clayton Cannon constantly; maybe even sitting on the bench at the harbor every day waiting to catch a glimpse of him as he stepped from the front door of those elegant apartment towers. Of course, even now, it was difficult for her to admit to herself without the prickly heat of embarrassment that she'd actually done just that the day after reading that article on him in the *Sun* papers only three weeks ago. It was right there in plain print that he lived in Harbor Court Towers. It was as if fate had given her the go-ahead. Still, if Ellen only knew how hard she struggled against her temptations daily, maybe then she'd understand.

She put the clips in her hand down on the table and followed her daughter into the hallway. She steeled herself against the pain of rejection and said, "Well, you go right on ahead and have me committed. But I'm doing this for you and that grandchild of mine you're growing right there inside you. He or she has got a right to know their kin, don't they? Knowing that that child's great uncle is close to the finest pianists in the world should be that child's birthright, and it will be as God is my witness!"

Then, without waiting for Ellen's response, Antonia took two more steps toward her daughter—but watched as she turned and walked out the door. "And I'll tell you something else," Antonia proclaimed, "I have the truth, and the Bible says ye who has the truth shall be free from the sins of the world!" Antonia's love of quoting from the Bible had yet to leave her since the day it started when she was sixteen years old and carried with her the self-righteousness of having sat for one solid week to read it, book by book, gospel by gospel, chapter by chapter and psalm by psalm. But even though the quotes sounded nearly authentic, they were always her own skewed version of the real thing. She went back to Aaron in the dining room, who looked lost and somehow doubtful of something, and she smiled nonetheless eagerly. "There always comes a point where the children think they know more than the parent. At least you'll listen to me."

"Ma, I'll listen to you, but you have to listen to me, too. What you're doing could affect all of us in a really bad way. We could all be investigated as deranged nuts. I could be taken completely off the air at the station and blackballed altogether in the news business. And Ellen, she's just scared. You know, Ma, this whole thing could compromise her standing at the hospital. This kind of thing could get around all of Baltimore. You know this is a small town at its heart." And in his voice was the crackling desperation one gets when trying to speak reason to the unreasonable.

She wasn't about to budge, though. She shoved two things at him. One was a newspaper photograph of Clayton Cannon standing in front of a sleek black piano and the other a snapshot of her brother. She said, "You can honestly tell me that you don't see my brother through all that white? His white skin be damned, look at his eyes, and then look at Emeril's and look at mine. Those are Emeril's eyes. Those are my eyes."

Aaron obeyed his mother and without looking into the layers of her eyes, he only skimmed over them, saying, "Ma, I've told you before and I'm telling you again, I don't. I want you to stop this now. You have no proof that he's your brother's son."

"The hell I don't! His mother, that Agnes Cannon is a lying snake-in-the-grass. She's made that boy believe all his life that his daddy is that part-Cajun-part-cracker Douglas Cannon. These pictures are all the proof I need."

"And I say you need more. Besides, that's a pretty caustic accusation you're making against Agnes Cannon, and Douglas Cannon, too, because you're basically saying that he's too stupid to know that a half-black child isn't his."

Antonia looked sternly at Aaron through narrowed eyes, then said, "Let me tell you something that you'd better remember for the rest of your life. The dumbest woman can fool the smartest man any day of the week."

"Aw, Ma, come on," Aaron said wearily.

But Antonia was not about to argue this a second longer. She was not going to give up her effort to claim her nephew, and Aaron was never going to believe she was doing anything more than obsessing over her own delusion to keep a dead twin's memory alive. "Are you going to take these things or not?"

"Again, why do you want me to take them?"

"Because I'm about to make my move and I want you to have

the proof in case something happens to me. I don't trust that Agnes Cannon. I believe she'd do anything to keep that boy from knowing he's black."

As if he hadn't even heard his mother's paranoid ranting, Aaron asked, "What kind of move are you about to make, Ma?"

"Why do you care? You think I'm crazy anyway," she said, gathering the clips from the table.

Aaron took the yellowing scraps from his mother and held her hand. He looked deeply into her eyes in a way that seemed filled with a sad farewell. "Momma, I'm really worried about you. Maybe you should see your doctor."

"Just take these and get on out of here. I don't need a doctor, and you'll see that when it turns out I'm telling the truth. Good-bye." She pushed him into the living room and through it into the hallway. She pushed him all the way to the door.

Aaron stopped and turned to face his mother. "Ma, I love you and I'll do anything for you."

"Yeah, yeah, I love you too. Good-bye," she said, giving him the bum's rush. Abruptly, her door was shut and bolted.

She went immediately to her writing table that sat in front of her favorite chair in the entire house. She proceeded to write, writing faster than her mind could gather up the words. She stopped only to study, once more, a picture of her nephew whose eyes as round as marbles of green-speckled honey and head of curls that were just one gene away from kinky made him as much like her as his straight and pinched nose and wafer-thin lips made him a part of Agnes. Yet even though she and Agnes were displayed so prominently in him, he still looked like an all-American, full-blooded white man; just an ordinary white man who turned a deep shade of pink when he laughed too hard or had too much hard drink. Antonia and Emeril, in Clayton, had been completely subdued by Agnes. Damn that Agnes.

Antonia's pen moved across the page as if it were being guided by a much more powerful force than merely her will. It was anger. Anger in its purest. Antonia wasn't going to sit by and abide by this betrayal of her brother a second longer. Over the years, Antonia had written letters to Agnes that varied in the levels of her wrath. They had gone unanswered year after year, after year, and Antonia had long grown tired of waiting. She wanted to know her nephew. She wanted to touch the only piece of her brother's flesh left on earth. So she wrote:

> Agnes,
>
> *I have written so many times I couldn't tell you how many letters I've written if a gun were put to my head, and I often ask myself why I don't just accept that you will never tell the truth, but I persist because Clayton and I are the only parts of my brother left here on earth. I have vacillated between offering you my kindness and offering you my red-hot rage in this matter, but now I am simply resolved. My brother has been dead for the same number of years Clayton has been alive, and before I die, we will settle this because . . .*

Then without warning, her pen just stopped moving, and her mind was forced to the very hour Emeril died. It happened only hours after the exact moment when Antonia knew for certain that Emeril, along with God and that Agnes Marquette, had created a life. It was a hot day in July, and she awoke with the pain of her monthly, but that was only second to the agony of the dream she'd forced herself to leave. Her sleep vision was of Agnes, skipping round and round the Dupreses' willow carrying Antonia's old yellow basket filled not with Tippy, but with fish. There were fish of all kinds, but mostly red snapper and one salmon with a big fishy smile. Agnes just skipped and skipped and smiled as big as that salmon with just as much guile. And Antonia remembered that, when she forced herself awake, she had the sprinting heart that could only be imposed by a nightmare, not a mere dream. This, she knew, had been a nightmare indeed, particularly since her mother's old bayou wisdom believed, and thus made her believe, that a dream of fishes was the certain sign of a birth to come.

So she jumped up and splashed herself with a bit of water, then dressed fast. She scooped Tippy up from where she lay curled lazily at the foot of Antonia's bed and put her in the old yellow basket. As she scurried down the hall, past her brother's empty room, headed for the back stairs that spilled into the kitchen, she heard her mother's call.

"Antonia," her mother beckoned with distress. "Where're you goin'? I'm gonna need you to go down and buy me some corn and tomatas. You done slept half the mornin' away as it is, not to mention the day."

"All right, Momma," she said without really heeding a word of her mother's. "I'll be right back, Momma. I gotta tell Emeril somethin'."

"Emeril's gone, girl. He ain't down at the Dupreses' today," her mother bellowed down the stairs. "Said he was goin' over to the Garden District lookin' for lawn work. Said some friend of his told him 'bout somebody over there needin' somebody to look after their yard."

But this time, her mother's words stopped Antonia where she strode. The Garden District. That's exactly where she was headed, but not because Emeril was down there looking for a job in some white man's yard. What did he need with a job over there with him working at the Dupreses' the way he did and being paid generously to do so? She was headed there because she knew that one of those moneyed families—she didn't know which one, but Cora Calliup from next door said they lived in a house that was the color of flamingoes with lawn jockeys on either side of the porch steps—had let that Agnes Marquette into their home as the charge of their children. Antonia didn't know the name of these misguided people, but unless there was more than one pink house with little black men holding lanterns, finding Emeril and saving him was going to be easy, because something, maybe those fishes in her dream, maybe that extra twin sense, told her that that's where she'd most likely find him. What kind of people, especially of the Garden District variety, would look at Agnes Marquette and not see that she was simply not fit to care for cat or child? And then there was Emeril, sniffing after that girl's secrets, that weren't so secret, with such hunger that he'd put himself in peril by sneaking over to the wealthiest white part of town for sex while the children in Agnes's care skipped rope or played tag. So Antonia asked her mother, just to be certain, "Momma, where'd you say Emeril had gone?"

"He's down at the Garden District, Antonia. What do you want with him, anyway?"

"Uh, I need to tell him that Junior Jackson won't be goin' with him and Junior's cousin Willie up to Jackson, Mississippi, tonight for a visit with Willie's girl." It wasn't altogether a lie. Junior wasn't going, that much was true, but he had told Emeril as much days before.

"Well, you hurry on back here, now," her mother said. "And don't you go messin' things up for Emeril. That's one hard-workin' boy. I wish he could light some of his fire underneath you."

Antonia rolled her eyes up in her head, then mumbled to Tippy, "She would die if she only knew what kind of fire he's got lit under him. And she'd double-die if I had it lit under me." Just before she dashed from the back door, she snatched a square of cornbread from the basket on the edge of the counter and went on her way.

Antonia, with Tippy in tow, got off the streetcar in just one hop. She stopped to situate her cat better in the basket and then went on her way to find the street and then the house that held her brother. She turned onto the street with confidence, but that's when she discovered that there was indeed more than one flamingo pink house on the rue. So she approached the first one, which was the second in from the corner, and studied every inch of the front lawn without spotting one small ceramic black man dressed up for the sport of kings. And just as she was about to walk on, someone called to her from just inside the screened door.

"You lost, gal?" a woman said.

"Yes, ma'am. I'm lookin' for a pink house with some lawn jockeys."

"Well, that could be the DuBoises' or the Laniers'. Which one do you want?"

Antonia hesitated, since she wouldn't know a Lanier or a DuBois if one came up and slapped her on the bottom, so she asked, "Which one has the two young children, a boy and a girl, and a baby-sitter named Agnes?"

"Oh, well that would be the DuBoises'."

"Yes, ma'am. The DuBois, that's who I'm lookin' for."

"Well, you wanna go all the way to the end of the street. They'll be the third house in from the corner down there." And that's all the woman said, as she stepped onto the porch, studying Antonia curiously.

"Thank you, ma'am," and she walked briskly on her way.

But the woman slowed her, saying with a raised brow, "What, you a friend of Agnes?"

"Not really. I just need to bring her a message" was all Antonia said.

"Hmmf," the woman grunted as she twisted her lips into a bow of disapproval. "Well, that's where you'll find her."

"Thank you again, ma'am," Antonia said with a gracious and grateful smile. And in considering the scowl across that woman's face, Antonia believed that Agnes's reputation had reached and singed this woman's ears, and this sent Antonia crossing the street with an extra puff of righteous wind in her sails. And it wasn't until she reached the other side of the street that she took in the magnificence of this neighborhood without the distraction of not knowing where she was headed. The smell is what hit her first. It was nothing terribly distinguishable, but it was definitely floral, smelling like the inside of a lady's boudoir. Then there were the colors that were everywhere she looked. Flowers dripping in strong primary tones from every jutting gallery, and bleeding onto lawns kissed by God's green, and overflowing large pots on every front porch. It put her in mind of weddings, and funerals, and parties, all of which were practically the same in New Orleans. This street was like stepping down the banquettes of heaven. And then she heard the whiny accordion of zydeco gliding faintly through the air. All of it washed over her to put a slight bounce and sway to her gait as she stepped to the beat.

"Antonia?" a young voice called to her from somewhere behind. She turned with a snatch of her head, then looked up and down and side to side, suddenly unsure if she'd even heard her name at all.

"Antonia, it's me Cora," she said, stepping onto the side porch that was darkened under the cover of a low-hung awning. "Hey, cher. What ya doin' round here?"

"What you think I'm doin', Cora?" Antonia said, walking over to meet Cora at the edge of the yard. "I'm goin' down here to stop my damn fool brother from ruinin' his life with that Agnes Marquette."

"Oooo, Antonia, you gonna be startin' some mess, ain't ya?" Cora said with a giddy, secretive laugh as she walked toward

Antonia with the whispery shuffle of her bedroom slippers sliding across the short carpet of grass.

"That's right. And don't worry, 'cause I won't say nothin' about
you tellin' me that they were there."

"Oh, don't you worry 'bout that. Emeril don't know that I seen
him, cher."

"Tell me somethin', Cora. You seen that Agnes sneakin' anybody else in there?"

"Not since June. Back in June it was some black-headed boy,
look like he coulda been from Spain or somewhere. But all of June,
it was Emeril. Nobody else I seen, that's for sure."

Antonia was transported for a few seconds by the zydeco that
she could still hear until Tippy meowed and brought her back to
Cora. "Who's playin' that zydeco?" she said as she began to step
and sway her rear end to the rhythm.

"Oh, that's the lady next door," Cora said, as she joined Antonia in the dance. "She plays it all day long. It's nice sometimes,
but sometimes it really gets on your nerves, you know."

And as Antonia danced, with her dips going deeper and her
swaying becoming more fluid and all her moves coming more
fully into a dance, she laughed, then howled with the joy of a
child and said, "This is my victory dance for saving my brother
from that she-devil." And her laughter nearly drowned the music
until she calmed it down when she asked Cora, "So, you work
here in this house?"

"Yeah, this is it," Cora said, as she followed Antonia's lead in
the dance. "The baby's sleep now. Matter of fact, he sleeps most of
the day. It's pretty easy. He sleeps, I clean up a little, watch some
TV. It's easy as pie."

"All right, Cora, well let me get on down here and do what I
need to do," Antonia said, forcing herself to stop moving.

"Okay, bye now." Then Cora, still bouncing to the zydeco,
slipped her hand into the basket to give Tippy a scratch between
her ears and said, "Bye, Tippy. Y'all be good, now."

Antonia was nearly trotting down the banquette to get to
Emeril. Forget the flowers, forget the heaven-sent scents, even the
zydeco. Nothing was on her mind other than setting her brother
back on the straight path from which he'd veered to follow a

seductress. There it is, she thought, as she reached the edge of the lawn where the jockeys, small and black-faced, stood guard. It was enclosed by a white-washed fence that may have been the purest white she'd ever seen. But as she went to open the gate to step into the yard, she heard tiny voices with giddy summer glee on the side of the house. So she went to the corner of the house and peeked around the corner to find two towheaded children, a boy and a girl, one not much older than the other, splashing and kicking and clapping just as happy as they pleased in an inflated wading pool. She tipped away without the children knowing she was there and climbed the stairs that led to the porch. There was nothing separating her from the inside of the house but a thin screen door, so she knocked on the wooden frame of it, then waited. But then, in the time it took for the sound of impassioned panting to waft out onto the porch and smack her in the face with its obvious lust, she went immediately from cool porcelain to hot steel. And that's when she knocked again, this time louder and with the staccato of a machine gun, and this time yelling, "Emeril Caleb Racine, you get yourself out here right now!"

"What the hell!" Emeril said.

"Come on, Emeril! Come on right now!" she called again. Tippy even let out a call of her own.

Then in no time, Emeril came hopping into the hall threading one leg into his pants. He got to the door and stared at his sister through the screen as he tucked in his shirt and zipped his pants. Emeril drew in his lips, as if to hold back a gusher, then said, "Antonia, are you crazy or somethin'? What in the name of hell are you doin' here?"

"I came to save you from yourself." She looked behind him to see Agnes straightening herself and continued, "And to save you from her."

"What're you talkin' about, Antonia?" Agnes said as she stepped up to the door next to Emeril.

"Y'all think I don't know what you've been up to? I know what you been doin' in there. I know what you been doin' over at the Dupreses', and you just need to come on here and stop it, Emeril."

"We ain't been doin' nothin', Antonia," Agnes protested indignantly. "You just need to get your mind out of the sewer."

Antonia looked at Agnes and said, "Is that why you look a hot mess, girl?"

Agnes looked down and then turned only slightly away from Antonia while she buttoned up, then said, "Okay, so we were foolin' around a little. What business is it of yours? You ain't his keeper, Antonia."

"That's right," Emeril added. "And you sure ain't Momma."

Antonia took one step back in incredulity, laughed haughtily and replied, "Oh, is it Momma you want? 'Cause she'd sure *luuv* to see this, Emeril. Now, are you comin' or do I have to go on home alone and tell Momma what I've just seen here today?"

Emeril stared her down without flinching. But for as tightly as he held her in his gaze, it was clear that she was equally as defiant, so he turned to Agnes and said, "Listen, I'm gonna go on with her. I'll see you when I get back from Mississippi."

"Promise," Agnes said with a pout and an innocent coyness in her eyes cast up at Emeril.

And Antonia rolled her eyes so far up into her head it seemed they just might get stuck there. Then she turned and walked to the edge of the porch, stroking Tippy for calm. Despite her sugary sweet pouts and guileless gazes, Agnes could simply not make Antonia believe her to be chaste. She tried not to acknowledge the wet smacks of their lips as they said good-bye, and when she heard the screen door open, she started down the porch steps. By the time she passed through the gate, Emeril was right behind her.

Taking her gently by the elbow, he said, "You've got two seconds to tell me what's got into you, so you'd better talk fast, gal."

"What's got into me is that you and that wretch of a girl Agnes Marquette just made yourselves a baby," Antonia said, getting her elbow back from her brother's palm. "Now whatcha gonna do, Emeril?"

Emeril's feet simply stopped moving. He took her arm again, turned her to him and said with a dismissive laugh, "Antonia, no wonder they call you fou-fou Antonia. 'Cause you're crazy. Where in the world did you get somethin' like that from?"

"I'll tell you where. I had a dream last night. I had a dream about fish, and you know what Momma says about people dreamin' about fishes."

"No, Antonia, I don't know what Momma says about fishes."

"Emeril, Momma has always said that when somebody has a dream about fishes that means somebody is gonna have a baby. And it ain't me, it ain't Momma, since Daddy's dead. So since you're the only one doin' what it takes to make a baby, it's gotta be you and Agnes."

Emeril let out a big laugh, then said, mostly to himself, "I don't believe this nonsense." He walked in a circle rubbing his head in frustration with the palm of his hand, as if he had not been doing that he just might have punched or thrown something. Then he turned back to Antonia and said directly to her, "So, you mean to tell me that you came down here and . . . well, stuck your nose where it doesn't belong because you believe that some dream about fishes told you I was over here makin' a baby with Agnes?"

"That's right. That's exactly what I'm tellin' you. But I'm also over here because you don't need to be here with that awful Agnes Marquette, Emeril. You're too good for her. That girl's been around."

"That's none of your business, Antonia," he said with a sly smile that told of the memory of something.

"Well, maybe not," Antonia said, turning from her brother and continuing on her path to get him out of there. "But I know one thing, you're my business. You've been my business ever since I came into this world two minutes before you, and you ain't gonna stop bein' my business till one of us dies."

Emeril caught up to her in one stride and said, "Antonia, I've told you before, two minutes does not make you my big sister, so stop acting like you're responsible for me. You ain't never been responsible for me, and you ain't never gonna be, you got that?"

Antonia didn't respond, didn't even act as if she heard him. She walked on like this until they got to the corner and crossed for the streetcar that was on its way. Then, just as the streetcar was pulling up to the stop, she turned to Emeril and said, "You are one selfish somebody, Emeril Racine. You didn't think anything was wrong with me bein' responsible for you when you were failin' math last year and you needed my help. But now that you're failin' in another part of your life, you think you have all the answers and you don't need my help. Well, you go right ahead, ruin your ole stupid life and see how much I care." She stood firmly, her arms quivering with more anger than she could ever remember feeling toward her brother.

The streetcar came to a stop with the door opening right in front of Emeril. He took a step back to allow Antonia to get on first, but when she didn't budge from where she stood, he said, "Come on, Antonia. Get on the streetcar."

"I don't want to get on there with you."

"Well, now you're bein' childish."

"What do you care? I'm not responsible for you, so you ain't responsible for me either. Why don't you just go ahead on."

Emeril blew out a chest full of exasperation, then stepped up onto the streetcar waving his hand dismissively at her and saying, "Ah, just forget you, Antonia."

"Forget you too, Emeril." And just as the streetcar closed up its doors tight and it was clearer than ever that Emeril was indeed going on his way, she yelled, "I hate you, anyway, Emeril Racine! I hate your stupid face!" And now, she shook furiously and angry tears were on the edge of breaking loose and sliding down her cheeks. The last glimpse she had of her brother, as the streetcar pulled away, was of him swiping his hand at her through the open window as he sat down in the last seat. She lifted poor Tippy out of the basket and snuggled against the side of her soft face, and then she wept quietly to appease her own ire at her brother and his lost ways.

"Hey, Antonia," Cora called to her from across the street.

Antonia wiped her face, put on the biggest, fakest smile she could find in her bag of smiles, then went to the bench and sat to wait for Cora to get to her with the cumbersome stroller she pushed. "Cora"—Antonia called to her with a giggle as she approached where Antonia sat—"You're just what I need to get my mind off of how mad I am with that stupid Emeril." Then she got back up from where she'd just sat and said, "Let's just take the baby and Tippy for a stroll."

"Did you find Emeril?" Cora asked as they headed off on their walk.

"I found him all right. He got on that streetcar that just left."

"So you ran him on home?"

"I sure did, and I told him that he was way too good for that Agnes. You shoulda seen her, Cora. She was standin' up there with her breast hangin' all outta her blouse. And I told her, 'You look a hot mess.' "

"What'd Emeril say?" Cora asked eagerly.

"He didn't say nothin' when I said that, 'cause he knew it was the truth. But when we were goin' to get the streetcar, he told me that I wasn't responsible for him, and that made me hoppin' mad."

"I'll bet it did," Cora said as she stopped to make sure the baby wasn't getting a direct hit of the sun, since they'd turned a corner. "He had some nerve."

"Don't you know it. And so I was so mad I couldn't even ride the streetcar with him, that's why I'm still here with you. But I don't know what this is in me, Cora, but I just feel . . . no, I actually know that something is going to happen. Something bad. For the last two weeks, even before I knew about him and Agnes, Emeril has been constantly on my mind along with this funny feelin' all over my body. I guess it's the same way a dog knows when a storm's comin'. In my gut, Cora, I feel like somethin' bad is comin'.' "

"Well, what's it like, this feelin' you have? Is it like butterflies in your stomach, or somethin'?"

"It's somethin' like that, like butterflies, except it's not really in my stomach. It's up higher, more like right here flutterin' all through my chest," Antonia said as she fluttered her fingers across her chest.

They walked on, up one street, then down the next. She and Cora talked and laughed and sighed over Emeril while they munched on the cornbread Antonia had tucked in her pocket. Before Antonia knew it, an hour and more than just a little change into the next had gone by, and Antonia would never make it back, she knew, in time to get to her mother's errands. "I've got to get on home," she said as she watched Cora fuss with the baby until she was distracted by a white woman approaching with the joy of a newborn baby in her eyes.

"Oh my lands," the woman said as she reached them. "Is that Lori-Ann and Charleton's baby?" she asked Cora as she bent down to coo at the baby.

"Yes ma'am, it is," Cora said.

The woman stood with a bearing that had completely changed in its composure, as if it were someone else's giddy face that had come skipping over just seconds before. "You're the baby's mammy?" the woman asked.

"Yes ma'am. I'm the baby-sitter till the end of the summer."

"Well, does Lori-Ann know that you've got this baby out here? This baby's only three months old. Nobody takes a baby out this soon."

"Well, she told me to get him out to get some fresh air and sunshine, ma'am," Cora said nervously, as if suddenly in doubt that she was actually following the right woman's orders.

"Oh, well, if that's what she said," the woman said skeptically. Then she looked at Cora with her head high and her eyes downcast and said haughtily and as if expecting Cora to shrink, "I'll be talking to her, though."

Antonia watched the woman suspiciously with a side glance, then said, "Let's go, Cora."

And just as they were about to continue on their way, the woman said to Antonia, "You look familiar, girl. Who do you work for?"

"I don't work for nobody," Antonia said flatly. Then with her lost anger rising up from somewhere, she turned to face the woman and said, "I'm nobody's mammy, and I'm nobody's maid. And Cora here's nobody's mammy, either. She's a baby-sitter."

The woman's face grew stern, her lips shrinking into their red-lacquered thinness. Then she said, "There was positively no cause for your sass-mouth, girl."

But Antonia just took Cora by the arm and went on her way, leaving the woman standing there in her stew, and once they'd gotten far enough away, she said to Cora, "You see what I mean? You see what they think of colored people? We only good to them for cleaning their mess, burpin' their babies, and fixin' their food. And in Agnes Marquette's case, givin' her sex. We ain't even people to them. What in the world is Emeril thinkin' he's getting himself into, Cora? What in the world." Then before Cora could answer, Antonia heard the rumble and bell of the streetcar approaching from behind, and when she looked up, a stop was just ahead. She let go of Cora's arm and took off running. "I'm gonna catch this streetcar, Cora. I'll see you later when you get home." And off she went and climbed aboard the streetcar just in time.

So by the time Antonia and Tippy had finally found their way home after piddling time away with Cora strolling through the streets of the Garden District, it was already late afternoon. She walked into the house apologizing. "I'm sorry, Momma, that I wasn't back in time to go to the store for you."

"That's all right," she said in the guilt-slathered tone mothers use when it's actually not all right. "Emeril went for me before he headed up to Mississippi."

"He's gone already?" Antonia asked with disbelief. He couldn't have been gone, not with them still mad at each other. "Well, what did he say?"

"It's funny you should ask," her mother said with a bewildered half-smile. "He wanted me to tell you that he forgives you and that he still loves you even though you're fou-fou. I don't know what it all means, but then again I never do when it comes to you two. It's like y'all have had a language of your own right from the day you was born." Her mother went on down the hallway and into the kitchen, chuckling at her children who live in their own world. "I'll call you for supper when it's ready."

Antonia's head dropped with the heaviness of her rightful shame for her unkindness to her brother, then she climbed the stairs to her room. Once she closed the door, she sat the basket down, Tippy's cue to step out and go to her soft spot, which just happened to be Antonia's. So Antonia also plopped onto her bed, as Tippy curled up right beside her, right in the middle. Antonia rolled onto her back and stared at the ceiling and the angst of having been left behind with her last words of hatred filled up every nerve she had.

The nape of Antonia's neck tingled with the same feeling that had lumped up in her stomach and throat and had sent them fluttering so frantically into her chest that sometimes she couldn't know if she'd ever draw her next breath, and it was no emotion she could name. The closest she could come to what it might have been was the sensation she felt when they were ten and Emeril was hit in the head with a baseball and had to get twenty stitches from Dr. Dupres. That day was just not right, because before she'd even gotten the word that he was lying over on the dirt field bleeding from his head, she couldn't shake from herself a desperate need to simply lay eyes on him. And with Emeril gone till Sunday, and with the very last emotion she'd given him having been her wrath, something now was just not right and would never be right until Emeril was back and she could drown him in her contrition. She would make him everything he loved in one meal. She'd make him some monkey bread, and fried catfish, and fried shrimp, and his all-time favorite, fried okra. And by the time he'd find himself completely sated, he would remember none of her anger that made her speak in a tongue of evil.

But even with her plan for penitence, and even though she knew that there was nothing for which her brother wouldn't forgive her, Antonia couldn't swim to the top of something that had taken her completely underneath it. Every breath seemed a struggle. And that's why by the time Junior Jackson had run all the way to their house and banged on the front door like he was half crazed on homemade hooch, she was pacing the floor just as fiendishly. She heard his muffled voice in the downstairs hallway and something had set him beside himself. Antonia grabbed up Tippy and darted from her bedroom and then she sprinted down the hall once she heard her mother moan and then scream. And she didn't even need to get all the way down the stairs before she knew exactly why Junior was there. Still, even though she knew, all she could do was stand in the middle of the staircase and stare through Junior as her mother collapsed to the floor.

"Antonia," Junior said with his voice about to break in two. "I'm really sorry. It was such a bad crash. Emeril and Willie both died. The ambulance had to come way from a colored hospital that was fifty miles away. By the time they got there, they was dead. I'm so sorry. I shoulda been with them! I shoulda been with them!" And Junior slid down the wall that was barely holding him up, and when he reached the floor he sobbed in heaves.

Antonia caught hold of the banister and lowered herself to the stair behind her, and squeezed Tippy to her breast. She rocked back and forth, back and forth, side to side, holding Tippy, stroking her, rocking and rocking, and trying with everything in her will to un-hear what she'd already heard. Then it hit her. This could not be rocked away. That's when she sat straight up, as still as air before a life-altering storm. Something had claimed her, and so she could not be responsible when she pierced the air with a scream that she couldn't recognize as her own, nor could she stop. And then throwing her body prostate and stiff, she slid down the remainder of the stairs, her head hitting each stair with a frightening thud, loud enough, it seemed, to knock her clean out. She spilled partially into the front hall, still screaming as if her mind had just split in two—one part on those steps shrieking with the desperation of wanting to just die right there, the other part on that death road in Mississippi with her twin.

Antonia moaned with the memory of that desperate wail as the pen with which she was writing Agnes Cannon slipped from her limp hand. She slumped onto the desk, resting her head on her arms, and she wept with the shame of her last words to Emeril, but without shame for her tears. And her years-old sorrow didn't let her so much as flinch when her yellow cat, Tippy the Fourth, jumped with its feline surprise onto the edge of the desk and meowed right by her ear, as if to sing her empathy. Antonia sat up and took Tippy the Fourth onto her lap and stroked her head lightly, then put the cat's face next to her own and closed her eyes with the comfort her cat gave her. Then she said to the cat, "I miss Emeril, you know. And I miss Tippy. But I'm glad I have you."

When she went to put Tippy the Fourth back onto the floor to scoot her on her way, she caught a glimpse of the unfinished letter to Agnes Cannon that, lost in her heartrending memories, she'd forgotten she was writing. But when she looked at it, and put it in its proper perspective alongside the memories of her dead twin, Antonia remembered all over again why she vowed, on the day her brother died, to hate Agnes forever. Had Agnes's wiles not lured Emeril to the Garden District that day, maybe Antonia's last words to her brother would have been kinder. She laid her pain at Agnes's feet, and she'd give the woman no recourse but to accept it.

CHAPTER

2

•

The waiting room was filled with the faded echoes of yesterday's voices when Ellen walked in; so unusual for 7:30 in the morning, she noted, when any other day of the week every patient scheduled for the next hour tried to get there to be the first one in and the first one out. But today there was no one.

She rounded the corner to the receptionist's desk to find Nancy, the nurse she was certain she couldn't do without, sitting at the desk in the receptionist's stead.

"Good morning," Ellen said brightly. "Where's Sharon?"

"She went to get breakfast," Nancy said. "She'll be right back."

Ellen turned to look over her shoulder at the empty waiting room, thinking maybe someone had slid in right behind her and she hadn't heard. "So nobody's here, yet?"

"Your eight o'clock, eight-thirty, eight-forty-five, and nine o'clock all canceled. The weather, you know. But Mrs. Simms is here," Nancy said, lowering her head to look across her brow at Ellen.

Ellen returned the look of skepticism, then said, "Don't tell me. She's in there nursing that big boy, right?"

"Yeah. I let her go into the exam room and do it because, remember the last time, she was in here and Dr. Murphy came in and saw her and was too flustered to speak straight?"

Ellen blew out a long, wearied breath. She walked around the desk and removed her lab coat from the hook where it hung behind Nancy's chair. As she put it on, she said, "Don't remind me. He went on for twenty minutes about how odd it was to see a woman nursing a boy that big." Ellen walked to the front of the desk as she buttoned her lab coat. With the last button, she said, "Okay, listen. I'm going to need you to keep her son out here, at least until Sharon gets back, while I have a talk with Mrs. Simms."

"Ellen, you're going to talk to her about breast-feeding that boy?" Nancy asked with eyes that spoke of her shock.

Ellen looked curiously at Nancy, then replied, "Well, I'm going to suggest that she might want to give it up after the new baby comes. But what I really want to talk to her about is her use of these herbal supplements she's been taking."

"She's still doing that?"

"You bet she is. And I don't know how many times and in how many ways I can tell her that she's putting herself and the baby at risk. I've told her time and time again that I strongly do not recommend her doing it, but she just comes back to me with the fact that she does it under the supervision of an herbalist. Anyway, I'll examine her when Sharon gets back so that you can assist." Ellen took the ring of keys that Nancy handed her, opened the file cabinet, and locked her purse inside.

Stepping around the desk, she picked up the manila folder containing her patient's charts and asked, "Exam room A?"

"Yep," was all Nancy said.

Ellen knocked lightly, then entered before the woman could answer. She stepped into the room, then smiled distantly at Mrs. Simms as she watched the woman fasten her nursing bra and pull her top down over her belly full of baby. Ellen became suddenly aware that the woman's blond and gray hair seemed thinner and her face more drawn and sallow, certainly making her look older than she looked just one month before; far older, Ellen thought, than the woman's thirty-five years. "Good morning," she said, with slightly less shine than she'd offered Nancy just minutes before.

"Good morning, Dr. Barrett. D.J., did you say good morning?"

"Good morning, Dr. Barrett," the boy said.

"Well, good morning, D.J.," she said reaching out for his hand. "How's school going?"

"It's good," he said as if he meant it. "I'm in kindergarten."

"I know that. Do you like kindergarten?"

"Oh yeah. My teacher says I'm good at a lot of things."

"I'll bet you are." Then Ellen reached for the boy and took him by the hand and said, "Say, D.J., how would you like to go out and color with Sharon when she gets back? In her drawer she has that basket of crayons."

"The one with every color in the world?" he said excitedly.

"That's right," Ellen said with a giggle nearly as innocent as the look in D.J.'s rounded eager eyes.

"Yeah, I want to color."

"Okay," Ellen said as she opened the door. "Why don't you go right out there with Nancy and she'll get you all set up. Sharon will be back soon. And your mom will be done in a minute."

When the boy left, Ellen closed the exam-room door, then went over to her stool and lowered herself onto it with a pregnancy induced slowness. She looked up at Mrs. Simms and smiled thinly, then said, "I know you know what I need to talk to you about."

"Yes, I do," the woman said softly as she diverted her eyes out the window.

"Mrs. Simms, you simply cannot go on taking those herbal supplements. I have told you this from the very beginning of your pregnancy, yet you continue to use them." Then Ellen's mind caught a memory of the boy who just left—the big boy who'd be going on to the first grade come the fall—and thought to tell this woman that there simply needs to be a healthy cut-off point for nursing, somewhere before he says, *"Hey Mom, I'm going to ride my bike over to Druid Hill Park and toss some balls around; I'll be back in an hour to nurse."* But she thought better of it, and said instead, "I looked at your blood work from the last time you were here and it shows that these supplements are throwing your hormone levels off. Your numbers are fluctuating all over the place and that could cause more harm to the fetus than the nutritional boost you and this herbalist think it's getting."

"Dr. Barrett, I just wish you Western-educated doctors would open your minds to the possibility that there's something to this," she said as if frustrated to no end. The woman then snatched her eyes from the window, looked at Ellen through the armor of her defenses and continued, "You know, I have a good friend who was diagnosed with breast cancer and didn't go the route of chemotherapy, but chose instead a homeopathic course of treatment. That was six years ago and she's still alive to tell the story. I think at some point you all are going to have to recognize that this isn't just witch doctor science."

"Everyone has some kind of story about homeopathy saving someone's life. I think it's incredible that your friend took that kind of gamble and seemed to have success with it, but make no mistake, she was an exception and not the rule. I wouldn't recommend it, and not because I'm trying to push, or have been brainwashed by Western medicine, but because it's the only game in town right now that has been tried and works. And I wouldn't even be having this discussion with you if you weren't pregnant. But the fact, Mrs. Simms, is that your body is naturally producing everything you need to keep this baby thriving in your womb. Everything else you're taking is excessive, and even unnecessary. You're simply taking dangerous chances, Mrs. Simms. That's all I've been trying to tell you."

"How can anybody be against anything that's natural?"

"All medicine is derived naturally, Mrs. Simms. And that's my point precisely. Somehow, you've come to believe that anything manufactured by a pharmaceutical company is poisonous compared to what you can buy in a health-food store, and I'm simply telling you that this is patently untrue. Any herb can be poisonous to the human body."

"Look, Dr. Barrett, my mother drank and smoked when she was pregnant with me. She wasn't a drunk, and she didn't drink heavily, or anything like that, but she certainly drank socially when she was carrying me, and socially in those days sometimes meant a drink a day. To me, that says a lot about how careless she felt about the life she was carrying." The woman stopped as if she were holding some other emotion at bay, then she continued: "And I know you think, just like everybody else, that I'm off the wall for continuing to nurse D.J. I saw the way that doctor looked at me and then turned his head away as if he was witnessing something depraved the last time I was in here. I see the way you look uncomfortable whenever I nurse him."

Ellen looked squarely at Mrs. Simms and replied, "The doctor you're talking about is my boss, the head of gynecology and obstetrics for the hospital, and yes, I must tell you that he was taken aback when he saw you nursing a child far beyond the years of breast-feeding. But Mrs. Simms, since you brought it up, I have to tell you that at his age, D.J. gets more nutritionally from his regular diet than he's getting from your breast milk."

"I tend to doubt that," Mrs. Simms countered with an edge to her voice. "And what about his comfort? His nurturing? He needs me for that, and even if he's not getting anything nutritionally from me, at least he gets that. That counts for his health too, you know."

Ellen lowered her head with nothing to say in that moment, because she knew she could easily get into that slippery area where she just might cross over that hallowed line of telling this woman how to be a mother. So she took in a considerable breath, blew it out, then replied, "Mrs. Simms, I'm certainly not saying to you that you're wrong for having nursed your son for so long, but truthfully, you should be thinking about what this baby's going to need when he or she gets here, because you have to start thinking about the baby's needs now. Even women who give birth to twins more often than not end up having to supplement with formula just because there is not enough breast milk to keep two babies sated and thriving. If you're nursing this baby and a six-year-old boy as well, chances are you're not going to be able to produce enough milk for both. Is any of this making sense to you?"

Mrs. Simms's eyes filled with the fluid of sadness. And just as the first tear fell, she asked Ellen through a quivering voice, "Dr. Barrett, did your mother nurse you?"

Ellen looked shockingly at the woman at first, having been taken completely off her guard, then answered tentatively, "I honestly don't know, Mrs. Simms. That's something that has simply never come up." And then that got Ellen to a place she had not readied herself to go. Did her mother nurse her? She wondered why she didn't know that answer. And would that answer also satisfy so many other questions. "Why do you ask?"

"I ask because my mother didn't nurse me, Dr. Barrett, and I felt that void in every part of our relationship all through my life. I'm determined it's not going to be that way for me and my kids. They are going to be nurtured by me, connected to me; they are going to know I love them." And the woman let her emotions loose so fast they filled the room so that there was scarcely enough space for any other.

This is why Ellen pushed, with everything in her, the question she didn't even know she had in her, back to the place where it lived in ignorance. She had to believe that it couldn't matter, because if it did matter, it would only devilishly taunt her as it played side by side with the shadow of the man who had kept her mother disconnected from the nurturing instincts living inside of every mother's nature. Clayton Cannon. Had her mother nursed the need for Clayton Cannon to be a part of her at the expense of nursing the needs of her only daughter, her only child at the time? She knew that void of which Mrs. Simms spoke. It was vast enough, particularly in the quieter moments of her own pregnancy, to swallow her whole. So in that moment, Ellen had to stop the questions, because one would lead to another and to another until she'd be one more undependable woman in Mrs. Simms's life.

"Mrs. Simms," Ellen said quietly, yet with professional crispness as she listened to the woman sniffle to the end of her tears. "I don't know what happened between you and your mother, but it sounds like something you should work through with her. That's going to be important for you, I think. Right now, though, I'm concerned about this baby you're carrying. You're due in four months, and you want to give this baby as good a start as you can. I'm just asking you, for the sake of the baby you're carrying, to cut out the herbal supplements and perhaps find other ways to nurture D.J. Cuddle him. Maybe snuggle with him at night." She paused and looked down at her own generous belly and rubbed it, then continued, "I don't know, Mrs. Simms. I've never been a mother before, so I can't tell you how to do it. I just know that from the standpoint of your health and the health of your unborn baby, you have to stop the supplements. You have to think about the true needs of the baby."

Then Mrs. Simms said pleadingly, "But Dr. Barrett, Third World women living in villages all over the planet only have what grows from the ground to cure themselves or keep themselves healthy during pregnancy. *And* they nurse their children while they have babies growing in their womb. And some of those children they nurse are as old, sometimes older than D.J. It's natural.

It's the reason we have breasts. And it's the reason why nature put herbs on this earth for us."

Ellen's frustration had wrestled her into a corner where patience had been sucked dry. So she said sharply, "Mrs. Simms, you are talking about women living in abject poverty who have no other choice and no other means of taking care of themselves, or, for that matter, feeding their children if you want to add breastfeeding to this mix. And quite honestly, I find it offensive that you would sit here with the privilege of prenatal care living in a wealthy country with access to the Western medicine that is desperately needed in Third World countries, *and*, I might add, a healthy, well-fed child in the waiting room and dare to equate your reasons for *choosing* herbal supplements and *choosing* to nurse your six-year-old son with the desperate choices those women have to make on a daily basis just to exist. You've got to get some perspective here, Mrs. Simms, and you also must question if the needs you're actually trying to comfort are your own."

Ellen got herself up and went over to the stack of fresh hospital gowns and snatched one off the top of the pile. She stood for several seconds just holding the gown and looking down at the floor, because she had to make certain if what she would say next to the woman was coming from a deep place of professional frustration, or if it was coming from that place of equal depth that was lined with the hormones of pregnancy. But by the time the ultimatum was spilling from her lips, she'd decided that it didn't matter. As she walked back toward Mrs. Simms to hand her the hospital gown, she said, "Mrs. Simms, you have a choice to make here today. You either need to stop taking the herbal supplements or you need to find yourself another obstetrician to follow you through the rest of your pregnancy and delivery. What you are doing could eventually put too much stress on the health of your unborn baby, and I simply will not, I cannot be responsible for that." She let go of the gown once the woman had it in her grip. Ellen went to the door and put her hand on the handle, and just before she pulled it open, she turned and said, "It's your choice. You can let me know when I come back in. If you decide you want to see another obstetrician, I can give you the names of several here at the hospital who are specialists in high-risk pregnancies, because in my professional opinion, that's exactly the category you're putting yourself in as a borderline older mother taking these supplements."

Ellen left the room, pulling the door closed tightly behind her. She stood, not wanting to move, holding the door handle with second thoughts. Then she let her hand drop and walked slowly to her office. Once she'd sat at her desk, it sat right there alongside her with no need for a chair, but there it was, the question of whether or not her mother nursed her. She searched her mind to look for some hazy splinter of a memory that might hold the warm comfort at her mother's breast, but there was nothing. So she went off again in a day-haze of recollection to find a time when it might have come up. When her mother might have discussed the beauty of it all, and the bonding, and the nurturing, and the moment her mother watched her baby grow heavy with the tranquility of warm, sweet mother's milk. Then again, she thought, her mother had never, in any moment she could recall, rhapsodized about anything, with the possible exception being the fantasy where she'd bring her dead brother's son into her bosom to claim him rightfully as her nephew. And even then, Ellen recalled, though spoken aloud, those fantasies were restricted by the way in which they didn't allow anyone else in or around them, and permitted only one man to enter—Clayton Cannon.

Ellen had had quite enough of that thought's devilment. So she picked up her phone and dialed her mother's number. But after only one ring, she slammed it down with the force of her fear, her discomfiture. What would I say? she thought. How do I call up my mother and ask her if she breast-fed me? And the most devilish question of them all, she thought, was what she would say if her mother were to confirm that, no, indeed she had not breast-fed her? Would she then, in protest of her mother's disregard, join Mrs. Simms in swallowing handfuls of herbs and breast-feeding her baby boy from the time he slips from the womb until he leaves her breast for college?

She put her elbows solidly on the desk and cradled her head in the palms of her hands. Fretful thoughts about her mother as a mother swam round in her head. But there were moments, Ellen could recall, when her mother was fully present. She particularly remembered the way her mother gushed over the start of Ellen's menses. And Ellen could even see it in her mother's eyes, soaked with a misty melancholy, as she handed Ellen her first sanitary pad. Her gaze was filled with a longing to get back the years that had gone by. They were the eyes that showed the deepest part of a mother. As Ellen looked back to that day with a clear vision that put a reverence in her heart for the word *Mother* and all its derivatives—Mommy, Ma, Momma, Mummy—she recalled how she stepped from the bathroom and into her mother's waiting arms. She remembered her mother taking her to Security Mall to shop for bell-bottomed jeans and clogs, and lunch at Friendly's, all because her body had changed.

And so now she felt shame. Shame for all those times, past and present, when she'd accused her mother of not completely living up to the integrity of that word because of Clayton. But Clayton was still a force, and his presence had, indeed, stolen something from her. What he'd stolen, though, she wasn't certain of because on that day, when her menses began, her mother was conscious of her in every way.

And there were other times too. Like the night of her ballet recital, Ellen recalled as she took her mind back to her seven-year-old self. It was the night when she, nervous and having completely forgotten the steps to her dance, fell flat on her bottom in the middle of the stage and then did not get up. While some applauded politely to assuage her humiliation and others gasped with the shock of it all, her mother leapt to her feet to give her daughter a standing ovation complete with cheers of *"Wonderful! Beautiful! Bravo!"* and then got nearly everyone else in the auditorium on their feet with the contagion of, or maybe the sheer sympathy for, her devotion. If this wasn't a mother's love, Ellen thought, she would never know the meaning of it. So it was then that Ellen could see, with a distant vision, that her mother had been more than a woman with some part of her emotional life separated, hidden from her only daughter by the distraction of Clayton, a boy and then a man who was as real to Ellen as he was unreal. Even if she had never suckled at her mother's breast, Ellen now had to believe, she would still not end up like Mrs. Simms.

Suddenly, Nancy appeared in the doorway. "Sharon's back. Are you ready for Mrs. Simms's exam?"

Gathering herself with a quick and small shake of her head,

Ellen said, "Yes, of course. Let's go." And she got herself up from the chair with the one big thrust she'd come to perfect.

Ellen followed Nancy into the exam room to find Mrs. Simms in a crying heap on the examination table. At first Ellen simply stood and stared with terrified eyes, knowing it had everything to do with the ultimatum she'd so brusquely thrown at a woman who, like herself, was living moment to moment at the mercy of some extreme hormone-induced emotion. And hormonal shifts might even be more extreme for Mrs. Simms, Ellen thought, because of all those herbs. So Ellen went to the woman, touched her on the shoulder and said softly, with the compassion of guilt, "Mrs. Simms, what's the matter?"

"What the matter is, Dr. Barrett, is that you don't want me to be your patient anymore, and you're the best doctor I've ever had."

"Mrs. Simms, what I said is that if you insist on continuing to follow the advice of an herbalist over my medical advice, then you should find another doctor. The risk of something going terribly wrong during delivery with all these different herbs you're taking gets greater and greater. I'm afraid for you if you continue doing that, Mrs. Simms, and I can't treat you properly if you don't follow my advice." Ellen paused, then went to the stool and sat. "Mrs. Simms, are you trying to tell me that you've decided that you don't want to give up the herbalist and the herbal supplements?"

"I don't know, Dr. Barrett," she said as she sniffled, then blew her nose into a tissue Nancy handed her. "All I know is that I'm trying to do the best I can possibly do for this baby. I'm trying to give it the most perfect place to live while it's in my body. That's all I've ever wanted to do."

"But, Mrs. Simms, don't you see? When I followed you through your pregnancy with D.J., you didn't take these herbal supplements, and he was a healthy baby, and now he's a healthy boy. You ate right and got good prenatal care, and that was it. What I'm trying to say is that you don't need this stuff this herbalist has convinced you to take."

Mrs. Simms brightened with the light of sudden insight. "You know, you're right. D.J. was so healthy he never even had one ear infection. And he never even got a cold until he went to nursery school when he was three. And you remember, don't you, how he scored a nine on his Apgar, right?"

"Yes, of course I remember that," Ellen said with a proud smile that she'd clarified her point. "And so you see, just let your body naturally do its job. You don't need all that stuff to produce a healthy baby."

"What about the ginseng tea?" Mrs. Simms said almost pleadingly.

Nancy wheeled the Doptone across the room and set it up next to Mrs. Simms for Ellen to check the baby's heart. As Ellen got up from the stool and went to where Nancy stood to prepare to listen to the baby's heart, she said, "I particularly want you to cut out the ginseng tea because there's just not enough known about what it can do to a developing fetus. It may do absolutely nothing, but it just may be strong enough to do some damage."

"Okay, well, when I go home, Dr. Barrett, I promise that I'll throw it all out, and I won't go back to see the herbalist until after I've delivered."

"And even then, you've got to be careful because of your breast milk, okay? But by then, that will be the baby's pediatrician's problem to deal with and you'll have to discuss it with him."

Ellen placed the Doptone on Mrs. Simms's belly, then turned it on. Immediately the room was filled with the sturdy beating of the baby's tiny heart. This was the part of pregnancy that always made Ellen feel as if she played a small part in a miracle. As she stood there listening, smiling into Mrs. Simms's face, which was doing the same, she thought of how she'd listened to this astounding sound of life in so many wombs over the years, and each and every one could still put awe in her own heart. That from nothing but a seed and an egg, both unseen by the eye, could grow this beat of life convinced her that the world was full of miracles. Yet why was it, she wondered, that she could never believe strongly enough in her mother's believed miracle, Clayton? And as she stood there reading the baby's heartbeats as they were spat out on a strip of paper from the Doptone, she knew why she couldn't believe. Because two miracles in her mother's life that she'd come to name Ellen and Aaron should have been quite enough. More than enough.

Aaron didn't so much hear the whispers as feel them, along with the stares, when he went into the waiting room of Ellen's office and sat down. One, two, three women, he counted. What he needed, more than anything, was a moment to prepare himself for the eye contact he would not be able to avoid. When he did finally look up, his gaze met the smiling face of a woman not quite as pregnant as his sister, but full enough with child to be obvious that it was more than a beer gut. It was moments just like this one, when he found himself cornered with his fame in a room full of women, that made him aware of the reality that once he stepped from his home, his life was not his own. Most days it was fine. Most days it was something he clearly understood as a part of his job. But then there were days like today when he simply didn't feel like smiling, didn't feel like speaking, didn't feel like being charming or elegant or gracious. So now he was eye to eye with this woman whose grinning glare was as imposing as her red hair that hung right on the edge of nearly being orange. He could see that she was not going to stop until she got something from him—at the least a return smile.

And that's when she said, "Hi, you're Aaron Jackson from Channel Eleven, aren't you?"

"Yes, I am. How are you?" Aaron said with a smile that had miles to go before it would become true.

"I'm fine. And I just love you. I watch you every evening. Of all the places you could be, I can't believe that I'm seeing you here in my obstetrician's office."

"Ah, well, Dr. Barrett is my sister. I'm here to take her to lunch."

"Oh my!" all three of the waiting women said at once.

"I had no idea," the red-haired woman said. "She's just terrific, your sister."

"Oh, absolutely," said the woman sitting next to him, who may have been at the beginning of a pregnancy, or may have just finished with one.

Aaron turned to her, and for no particular reason he could think of, said, "Oh thanks." But then he turned away, because he didn't want to be caught staring at her stomach, particularly if she wasn't pregnant but merely plump.

"Say," the woman sitting next to the smiling redhead said, as if she'd had a sudden thought. "You and your co-anchor Maggie Poole are an item, aren't you?"

"Yes, I guess you can say that we're 'an item.' "

"So are you headed toward marriage?" the red-haired woman asked.

Aaron considered the question at first, rather bold and prying though it was, then said, "Well, aren't we all headed toward marriage?"

And his audience giggled politely, until the woman next to him said, "Well, that was evasive enough."

"Oh, you got that one, huh?"

"I sure did."

"I got it myself," said the woman with the flaming hair, who was now smiling less fervently. "Basically, you think you said nothing, but actually you said no, you're not headed toward marriage, and that makes me sad because I like Maggie. The two of you seem perfect together."

Aaron looked off past the woman for a moment, thinking he'd heard women talk like this before, only it was generally about soap-opera characters, or Ross and Rachel on *Friends.* So how did it come to pass, he wondered, that his life was so invaded by the concerns of people he didn't know, would never know, and most likely would never see again? And why did they care? All he had the presence of mind to say this time was, "She's terrific."

Just then, Ellen showed up to save him from giving away secrets he'd not planned to tell. "Ellen," he said, standing to kiss her, never before so glad to see her as he was at that very moment.

"Hey there," she said, returning his kiss.

"Dr. Barrett, you never told me that Aaron Jackson was your brother."

"Oh, I suppose it simply never came up in conversation," Ellen said. Then she turned to him. "I'll be ready to leave in about forty-five minutes, if that's not too long for you to wait. I got a little backed up even in spite of the fact that I had three patients cancel this morning. Anyway, I've got these three ladies, and then that's it."

"That's fine," Aaron said as he sat back in his seat. Then he leaned over and picked up a magazine from the coffee table without noticing that it was a magazine for expectant mothers. But he flipped it open and said, "I'll just wait here and read."

"Okay," Ellen said as she turned to leave. Then she looked over her shoulder and said, "You ladies can come with me. Nancy will get you set up in exam rooms. I'll be right with each of you."

Aaron continued turning the pages of the magazine until it occurred to him that he should look at the title of the magazine. *Mommy To Be* it said. "What the heck is this?" he mumbled beneath his breath as he tossed it back onto the coffee table. It just wouldn't leave him. That question—"*Are you headed toward marriage?*" Why he answered so evasively was now pressing down hard on him. He could have said yes, since that was what they were certainly expecting him to say. But he couldn't say yes, because that wouldn't have been altogether true. And if he'd said no, well it would have seemed to those women, and even to himself, that he was merely trifling with Maggie, which he wasn't; at least he didn't think that's what he was doing.

What troubled him most was he seemed to recall that just a month ago, he'd given a similar answer to that very same question at a dinner he'd had with two friends and their lovely female guest who'd just moved to town. Tawna was her name. He'd never forget her or her name because he recalled how he'd come to think of her right after the introduction—the tantalizing tawny Tawna. And when she asked him if he had future marriage plans, he remembered now, with a certain humiliation that served him well as he raked himself over his own freshly laid hot coals, he'd said, "*Don't we all have future marriage plans in one way or another?*" The difference between then and now, he realized, was that then, he had a reason for being so evasive—and it lay in the power of an exquisite-looking woman who seduced every one of his senses. But here, in his sister's office, chatting with three married women, two of them very obviously pregnant, why couldn't he have just said yes, I am headed toward marriage with Maggie? It troubled him in a way he couldn't have imagined it ever would, mostly because until now—with that question put to him twice within one month by perfect strangers—the thought of marrying Maggie had never entered his mind. Maybe it was that she was nine years his senior. Maybe it was her college-bound daughter that made him more aware, each and every time he saw her, that Maggie was older. It didn't much matter, though, because he could never say it out loud. Merely thinking it made him a pig, he knew. So why was he with her?

There was something about Maggie that had always made him feel as if he'd known her forever. It was a familiarity that he took with its thorns and its blooms. One that made him as comfortable as it at times made him equally uncomfortable. And the only word that came to his mind when trying to define her was *tenacious*—a quality that, in his opinion, few can carry off with any modicum of grace. Yet Maggie was one who purposely straddled the line between tenacious and insufferable but did not cross it. And that, he supposed, was what kept him with her.

"So there're no wedding bells ringing for you and Maggie, huh?" a voice asked him.

With a sudden turn of his head, he found Sharon smiling at him, expectation and a particular eagerness on her face. He could never be certain, but Aaron thought he knew women and their ways well enough to know when one had plans for him, and this woman, he thought, had rather high hopes for him. So he smiled and replied, "You never know what the future holds."

"That's true enough, but you can certainly have a general idea based on what you want. It sounds to me like you don't want marriage. At least not with her."

Aaron didn't know whether to be angered or offended by the assumption, or dismayed by the accuracy of what she presumed. With this question, that wasn't necessarily a question, he knew he had to respond in such a way that would tell the truth, yet would keep the hopes Sharon apparently had for him lying dormant. "Well, Sharon, the move toward marriage is an organic process, and it takes as long as it's going to take."

"I guess," she noted distractedly. Then she said, "It's just that you're a nice guy, Aaron, and I would hate to see you marry hastily out of some sort of loyalty to the history and comfort you may have with her. Trust me when I tell you, that would be a disaster."

"I believe you," he said plainly, as his attention was pulled, but mostly forced by his own will, back to the magazines on the coffee table. What was it about babies that made them unable to inspire men in the same way they inspired women? But as he gave the question a second pass, he thought it might be best to wonder what it was about men that couldn't be inspired by babies. So he turned back to Sharon, and pointing to the coffee table said, "How does it work for you women when it comes to these babies?"

Sharon giggled and said, "I'm not so sure I understand what you mean."

"Well, what I mean is how is it that a man and a woman can look at a baby, the same baby, or even a picture of a baby and feel entirely different about it?"

"It's in our blood to be maternal, Aaron. That's all."

"So what, men don't have anything in their blood that makes them paternal?"

Sharon looked up into the fluorescent light, as if hoping to find the answer written in the glow, then said as she looked slowly back at Aaron, "I think it's different. I think, for men, the baby has to be born and tangible, and it has to be theirs for them to feel what women feel. And even then, I think it's still different."

"Yeah, I think you're right, because I'm sitting here right now and looking at all these little babies on the covers of these magazines and they're not doing anything for me at all in the way of making me want to have my own kid. I mean, they're cute and all, but I guess men are just able to get over it."

"Yeah, women never get over it." Then she let out a comforted laugh and continued. "You know, my mother had eight of us, and she still says that she has never gotten over the birth of any of her children. She remembers everything, right down to the smallest detail that, she says, most men would forget."

"She's probably right," Aaron said with an ironic chuckle. Then he looked off at nothing in particular and continued rather wistfully, "There are some men who have this whole thing about carrying on the bloodline and the family name and so they get all maudlin and melancholy, or at least as maudlin and melancholy as men can get, about wanting to have a baby. That's never been a thing for me. I figure, if I go the rest of my life without having a child to carry on my bloodline and family name, I think I'll still die without regrets." Then, suddenly self-conscious of the fact that he'd actually said what he'd said aloud, he looked embarrassedly at Sharon and said, "I guess that sounds pretty bad, huh?"

As if she were somehow disappointed but trying to hide it, Sharon answered, "Well, if that's how you feel. I don't know. I just think there's no point to living if it's not for the purpose of carrying on the human race."

A laugh sneaked up on him with a startling intensity and he had no choice but to let it burst forth. "And you see," he said, once he caught his breath, "the way I look at it is that there's always a couple billion people willing to do that, so the human race is going to be just fine without my contribution. I mean, just look at Ellen. If she only has this one kid, our family bloodline will be just fine and she will have given one more contribution to the human race. It all works out in the end."

"And what about Maggie?"

What about Maggie? "Maggie's got a child," he pointed out. "Colette."

"Yeah, but she's almost grown, isn't she? Maggie's still a young enough woman to have another child."

"Quite honestly, Sharon, Maggie and I have never discussed children, so if you want a definite answer on that, I would suggest you go to the source, because I have no idea." And he was so curt and exact in his tone that the room fell awkwardly silent. And as he watched her get back to whatever it was she was doing, her tightened face telling of her uneasiness, he figured it was best to say nothing else since he had peeled back his own scab on his own raw spot. He thought of apologizing for his sharpness, but then he'd have to explain with more words than he knew or, for that matter, cared to speak. Otherwise, he thought, he could simply let it lie, and then when they spoke again the air would be just as undemanding, as if there had never been a breeze of tension between them. That just might work. So he sat and waited for time to do the only thing it knows to do—pass.

As he sat with nothing but his thoughts, the woman with the red hair reappeared. Standing before Sharon to make her next appointment, she turned and offered Aaron a fawning smile, to which he responded, "That was quick."

"All I had to do was have my blood drawn. This wasn't a regular office visit. The doctor needs to keep watch on my hormone levels."

And as Aaron's eyes glazed over with the fear that she'd end up telling him even more of what he didn't need to know, he said, "Oh, I see."

Then the other woman appeared, the one who'd been sitting

next to him with or without a baby in her womb, and said to the woman already standing there, "I had to have the same thing. My hormone levels were all over the place with my last two, and you know I lost a baby between those two, so Dr. Barrett is watching me like a hawk."

"She's good that way, isn't she?" the red-haired woman said.

"Oh, the best," the other woman said dramatically.

The red-haired woman turned to Aaron. "You must be so proud."

"Yes, proud. I am proud," Aaron answered instinctively. And even if there had been time to ponder such an inquiry, he thought, pride would be as good a word as any to describe a feeling to which he'd never truly given much thought.

"Well, I know what I'll be talking about at dinner tonight," the not-so-pregnant looking woman said. "I'm going to tell everybody how I was sitting in my doctor's office and Aaron Jackson from Channel Eleven walks in and sits down, and he's my doctor's brother."

"I know exactly what you mean," said the other woman. "Of all the places to see him."

Aaron smiled thinly and glanced over at Sharon, who regarded him with a certain empathetic smirk. And he thought that it must be more uncomfortable for those like Sharon, observing the fawning, than it was for him at this point in his life as a newsman because, to him, Sharon looked as if she wanted to crawl beneath her desk in shame on behalf of her entire gender. It was an embarrassment with which he could certainly find common ground, as it was no different than his reaction to the men he might see on any given summertime newscast in Orioles caps, or Orioles shirts, or simply dressed from head to toe in orange and black with an Orioles tattoo on their bicep babbling on like star-drunk fools about their devotion to Cal Ripken. But women like these, who will go home and turn a sighting of him into a large chunk of their dinner-hour talk, are a part of his life, and it didn't much matter that, to him, there was very little about their fascination that made sense. All he could do was accept it graciously and be everything they expected him to be—and that, he knew, was something that varied from person to person, perception to perception, fantasy to fantasy.

"Aaron, Ellen said you can meet her in her office." Nancy appeared, snapping him out of his revery.

As he got up and went past Sharon's desk, where Nancy stood with the remaining patient, he smiled and said, "Good luck with your baby."

"Oh, thank you," she gushed. "And it was certainly nice meeting you."

"Likewise," was all Aaron said. And as he turned the corner to go into Ellen's office, he heard the woman whisper to Nancy or Sharon, or both—he couldn't tell—that he was much more handsome in person than he was on the television. He couldn't help but feel the relief of having already passed by before she said this, otherwise he'd have to acknowledge the roundabout compliment.

He stood in the aperture of Ellen's office, waiting for her to look up from what she was writing. There was no doubt whatsoever that she knew he was standing there, but she would simply not respond in any way to his presence. It was as old as his memory of her as his sister, except that when she did it when they were kids, she'd do it with the sole purpose and hope that he would eventually go away, shoo, like the bothersome gnat he was to her. Why she did it now, though, he could only assign to her absolute obstinacy.

But then, without looking up from what she wrote, Ellen finally griped, "Are you going to come in and sit down, or are you going to stand there watching me?"

Aaron walked slowly into her office and over to the chair, and as he sat, said, "Why do you do that—just act as if you don't know I'm there?"

"Why do you just stand there if you know I know you're there?"

Aaron laughed, then replied, "All right, just forget it."

"You brought it up," she said nearly beneath her breath. Then she looked up at last and went on, "So where do you want to eat? I would suggest the cafeteria, but while Johns Hopkins is known for its many areas of medical brilliance, I must say that their culinary talent is no less their Achilles' heel than it is for any other hospital, or airline, for that matter."

"I thought you might want to go downtown, or something. Or Fells Point. That might be nice, huh? Go to Fells Point and eat some seafood. Some catfish, maybe. Or even crab cakes."

"I'm pregnant, remember. I shouldn't eat shellfish because they're scavengers. And the catfish can only be farm-raised."

"Fine," Aaron said, his tone suggesting a mild annoyance with the rules. "I'll ask for the pedigree of the catfish. Now, let's go."

"Okay, but you'll have to bring me back here to get my car this afternoon," Ellen said as she gathered papers and stacked them neatly on the side of her desk. When she was done tidying up her desk, she sat back in her chair and asked, "Aaron, do you know if Ma nursed us?"

Aaron considered the question for a few seconds, shifted with a particular itchiness at the idea, then replied, "No, I don't know, Ellen, and I've really never given it a lot of thought, or any, for that matter."

"You've never been curious about it, you know, about the bonding?"

"Ellen, I said I don't think about it. It's just not important."

Ellen looked at him with incredulity beaming from her eyes. "You could not be more wrong. Bonding through breast-feeding is the most powerful bond in the whole world."

He inhaled a deep breath then sighed it out with a low moan. Aaron wished, more than anything, that he understood all these womanly, motherly changes his sister was going through, and he could only hope that the understanding of it all would give him more patience with her, because he had none now. "Ellie, why are we talking about this?"

"Because I had this patient in here this morning who's pregnant, and she's got a six-year-old son she's nursing. When we talked about weaning him, she said she still nursed him because her mother didn't nurse her, and she felt the void in their relationship for her entire life."

"So, I'm confused," Aaron said with narrowing eyes. "How does this have anything to do with whether or not Ma nursed us?"

"Because, Aaron, don't you see? There was kind of a void of closeness between us and Ma, and if she didn't nurse us maybe that's why we don't have as close a bond as we could have with her."

"I don't know what you're talking about, Ellie. I think we're pretty close with Ma."

"Close, yes, but bonded, connected. I don't think so." She

scooted her chair closer to her desk and leaned forward, toward Aaron. She said quietly, "Aaron, don't you remember when Clayton Cannon won that piano competition? You were ten, I was fourteen, and he was seventeen or maybe eighteen and Ma kept going on and on about him winning that piano competition."

"Tchaikovsky Piano Competition," Aaron said quietly.

"What?"

Then he spoke up. "It was called the Tchaikovsky Piano Competition and he was eighteen."

"So you do remember. Well, I know I'll never forget it because that day when Ma found out that he had won it, she went out and got that record . . . what was it?"

"Something by Beethoven," Aaron said as he listened to the notes that had been bored into his head years ago tinkle through his memory.

"That's right!" Ellen said excitedly. "She played it over, and over, and over again. It nearly drove me insane. It was something by Beethoven. 'Pathétique.' Isn't that what it was called?"

"I don't remember all of that," Aaron said with an impatience born from the annoyance of having to recall those days. "But I do remember that it happened in the same week that Ma found out—and to this day I don't know how she did—that Clayton Cannon would be going to the Peabody Conservatory." Aaron stared off beyond Ellen and looked out the window. Could she have called the school? But he immediately threw that thought out, because even if she had, he was certain they wouldn't have given that information out to anybody just calling up out of the blue. It was too much to think about. And anyway, he didn't even know why he was wasting the time. "Ellen, what's the point of all this?"

"The point is, Aaron, that it was on that day, when Ma kept going on and on about how he'd just won that competition and everything, that you asked her if she didn't love you anymore."

Aaron regarded her disbelievingly. "I did?"

"Yes, you did. And you were more serious than I had ever seen you. You took her hand and then hugged her around her waist as if you would have died if you had let her go, and you asked her that."

"I don't remember saying that, Ellie. But what did she say?"

"She said, 'Of course not, baby. You're my baby and I'll never stop loving you, or you either, Ellen.'"

Well, what else would she say, Aaron thought. "So what are you saying, that I asked her that because she didn't nurse me?"

"Yes. I'm saying that if you had been bonded to her through that experience then it wouldn't have occurred to you to ask her that question."

"How about this," Aaron said as he stood and walked behind his chair, ready to leave. "I asked her that, maybe, because I didn't know why she was getting so crazy about some guy she didn't even know."

"Yeah, I think that's a part of it too. But what I'm saying is that you wouldn't have needed to ask her if you'd had more of a bond with her. And what you did was ask her what I had wondered myself."

"I don't know, Ellie. I think you're making way more of this nursing stuff than need be." And compelled to retreat, to be away from this talk that would only end up spinning them in circles, Aaron shoved his hands into his pockets.

"Oh, what's the use," she said as she got herself up from behind her desk. "You're a man. I don't even know why I bother talking to you about something like this."

"I don't either," Aaron said, as he preceded her out the door.

The minute he turned the corner into the waiting room, he felt as if he'd been slapped in the face with the memory of his mother dragging him across the cobblestones of Mount Vernon Place on the first day of classes at the Peabody. He remembered the day being overcast, with a piercing chill in the air, as they walked to one side of the street, then back to the other, then stood in front of the main building with his mother's eyes searching every face that passed and every young man in the distance. And when she thought she saw Clayton, his mother dragged him, poor unwilling Aaron, by the arm down three steps into a dimly lit cellar with floor-to-ceiling shelves lined with faded books that called itself the Peabody Library and Pub.

Why was he remembering that day, and that place that smelled like old musty books and pipe tobacco? He would never forget the man, the old man who sat in a rocking chair staring straight ahead as if lost in a memory that mingled with the symphony playing low from a small radio by the man's side. That man, with his craggy yellowing gray beard and pipe, his skin as jaundiced and worn as the pages in any one of those old books, could have been made of wax. Or recently deceased, Aaron recalled, because he never moved, never spoke, never acknowledged with as much as a twitching finger that he was aware that two people had just come in and were dashing by.

Aaron also remembered how he so badly wanted to leave that place, yet couldn't until his mother found who she'd come there to see. And as they went into the back where wooden rickety tables sat in no particular order all around the room, there he sat, over in a corner with his head buried in a book that had nothing in it but notes that seemed all jumbled up together. Clayton had his eyes on all those notes as if they were telling him as much as words could and his face expressed pleasure, as if he were actually hearing the music, Aaron recalled thinking with a certain awe. An awe that made him doubt he would ever be that special.

When Clayton Cannon did finally look up, it was only to ask the waitress for more coffee. And when his eyes met Antonia's for seconds that had seemed as long as minutes, and then met his own young eyes, Clayton gave them both a knowing smile but went immediately back to his music. That's when his mother did what he, even now with all the years gone by, could not come to understand—she turned to Aaron and said, "Let's go."

"Let's go," he said aloud.

"Let's go where?" Ellen asked as she pressed for the elevator.

"Let's go downtown to the Peabody Pub," he said without knowing that he would say it.

"It's kind of pricey there, even for lunch."

"It's my treat. I just want to be someplace that makes us feel a little special today." And with that he said no more as the elevator doors opened and he stepped in after his sister, still thinking of the man who was special enough to read the language of music.

CHAPTER

3

•

It was nearly one in the afternoon by the time Antonia got downtown and pulled her car into one of numerous empty spaces. This was one of those days, she thought as she looked around at the parking lot, barren at high noon, that always made her wonder why Harborplace even bothered to open up in the wintertime.

She stepped from her car with care, since the ground was wet with sloshy snow, and headed to the parking meter. Grabbing a handful of quarters from her purse, she began pumping them in, one right after the other. It would take her a good three hours, she thought, to do what she'd come to do. She could be just in time, or have missed him altogether. There was no way of knowing. But when she woke that morning, she was sure she had to satisfy the inkling that pulled her to this place. Just to see him in the flesh, just to hear his voice. It would all be so very innocent. Once she saw him, and heard him, and maybe even had an accidental chance to touch him, then that would salve her until he knew. And he would know. She couldn't tell when and what the circumstances, but just as water can never stop itself from rolling down a hill, truth can never stop itself from, in time, rolling into the light of day.

So as she made her way across Light Street, wondering who she just might run into first—Clayton or Agnes—Antonia thought of how she'd conduct herself, particularly if she saw Clayton. And then, she was there, poised on the threshold of the apartment building where Clayton lived. Once she entered the lobby of Harbor Court, she let out the long breath she'd been holding since she left home and strolled ever so calmly to the doorman's post. Smiling gently, she quietly asked, "So, this is where the pianist Clayton Cannon lives, huh?"

"Yeah, this is it," he said as he looked down at something he was writing. Then he looked up, smiled inquisitively and continued, "This place has really been put on the map, in a way. I mean, it's now a stop for tourists who're fans of classical music. They come in here to the lobby, look around, take some pictures and leave. Many of them even run into him."

"Really," Antonia said as her eyes perked with the enthusiasm of a sycophantic fan.

"Oh sure. He's just a regular guy. Comes and goes, you know. And he always stops and talks to people. He's not in any way stuck up like a lot of those folks are. He's real salt of the earth. That man will talk to a junkyard salesman with the same ease as he'd talk to a king."

"That's nice to know," Antonia said with a distant smile. Then, from the corner of her eye, she caught a familiar movement. Turning quickly, she could scarcely believe that her fantasies hadn't completely conjured what she saw. But, she was sure that no part of her mind deceived her when she snapped her head back to the doorman, who regarded her with an unexpected smile.

"Well, speak of the devil," he said. "There he is now."

"Oh my," was all Antonia could say. Then over her shoulder as she turned to leave with steps already quickened, she said to the doorman, "I'm going to run and see if I can catch him."

Outside, she hadn't caught him, but not because he was out of reach. If she'd wanted to be so obvious, so overbearing, she could have been right up beside him in no time with the way he sauntered. Even in the cold, she thought, he moves slower than molasses pouring uphill. So she dallied behind him, pretending to look for something in her purse then, grabbing a mirror which was the first thing her hands could find, she patted her hair back into some imaginary place. With him moving at the speed of nearly nothing, the halting hand of the traffic sign had brought him to a dead stop before Light Street's passing cars, so she just had to wait and pretend. As the light changed, she exhibited great restraint in staying ten or so paces behind him. When they got to

the other side, a swirling gust of wind picked up nearly everything on the ground that didn't have its own heft to stay put, and
it was so blustery that it nearly felt to Antonia as if it could snatch
her clothes clean off. This, she presumed, was the thing that got
Clayton to pick up his pace, because after that assault of wind, he
was moving along at some clip.

She found herself following him through the doors of the Light
Street Pavilion—or the goodies pavilion, as she'd affectionately
come to call it. Anything under the sun she wanted to eat, she
thought as she followed him through the short vestibule and
through the second set of doors, could be found right in this
building.

On the second floor, she followed him around, wondering
where his final destination might be. With great amusement, she
watched what caught his eye as he passed the peddlers' carts. He
looked at exquisite silver necklaces. He touched a sheer silk scarf
in vibrant shades of blue. And she had to subdue a chuckle when
she saw him look with more than a passing interest at a stuffed
snake in bright primary colors that descended from the top of a
cart as if it were alive enough to strike. It lit something quite
intense in her to know that a part of his little-boy self was still
alive.

When he reached where he was headed, he talked to the young
people behind the counter as if they were long-held chums. Once
he picked up his tray and paid, she followed him toward a table
closest to the window, and then passed by and went to Aunt
Annie's for a pretzel with cinnamon. She fumbled through her
wallet and pulled out a five-dollar bill, handed it to the woman,
and said, "You keep the rest of it. Buy yourself something cute."
She didn't have time to wait for change. There was no telling how
fast or slow an eater Clayton might be.

How fortuitous. Every table immediately around him was
empty. So she went to the one directly next to his and sat, so that
when he looked up he would see only her. The moment she saw
that he was looking in her direction, she caught his gaze and
smiled. Her heart was quick with something very close to fear, but
despite every raw nerve in her body, she managed to say, "You're
Clayton Cannon, aren't you?"

"Yes ma'am, I am," he said kindly, welcomingly.

"I've followed your career for years," she said, amazed at her unintended honesty. In any context, she thought, it was the innocent truth. And so her nerves were at rest now.

"Have you really?" he said, as if he wanted to know.

"I sure have. I'm from New Orleans myself, and so when the buzz about this child musical-genius began to swell, well I was as proud as if I knew you."

Clayton laughed bashfully, then said, "I guess that's how it is back home. We're all so connected that when somebody comes out of there doing something good, we all just claim them."

"That's right," Antonia said as she watched Clayton move his food around, and as he did, it was only then that she was aware that he was eating with chopsticks. "So you eat lunch over here every day?"

"Yes, ma'am, I do," he said, skillfully picking up a salmon roll. "Since I've moved back here, this place has become my favorite spot. But when I was in school here, I never came down to Harbor Place. It was still so new that it was always packed. But now, I guess because I have kids, it's certainly a large source of our entertainment when we want something to do after dinner. We just come over here and get an ice cream or fried dough and sit and look out on the harbor. The kids love it."

"I'll bet they do," Antonia said cheerfully, picturing the smiles on the small faces she could only imagine. "So what made you move back here to Baltimore?"

"To tell you the truth, I'm not exactly sure what brought me back. I guess mostly it's because in our hearts, my wife's and mine, we see our family as a southern one. As the kids got older, the thought of raising them in a place like New York with me on tour for long stretches throughout the year was just too much for my wife. She'd been dying to leave New York since she gave birth to the twins. So since I wasn't about to move back to New Orleans, Baltimore seemed to be the most reasonable compromise." He ate the piece of salmon roll, then smiled as he continued, "To tell you the truth, I like this city well enough, but it doesn't charge me up, you know. It's okay. I find the people interesting enough, but there's a sameness, if that makes any sense."

"It certainly does," Antonia said with a knowing laugh. "I'm sort of like your wife in that I followed my husband and his career here. It's okay, but it's still better than being in New Orleans."

Clayton looked at her with a kindred smile and said, "Don't get me wrong, it's not that I don't like New Orleans. It's just that there's so much I left back there without fully understanding, and to go back would end up driving me insane."

"I know exactly what you mean. It's a wonderful place, but the layers of life and all those ghosts would just pile up on me down there."

"Exactly. The layers of life," Clayton said in a small voice and seemingly to himself. Then he looked off past Antonia, as if in deep contemplation, before reconnecting with her. "Ma'am, would you like to join me? It feels kind of strange to talk across tables like this."

"Well, thank you," Antonia said, not once considering she decline politely for decorum's sake. She sat in the chair next to his, then placed her pretzel—of which she had not taken one bite—on the table.

Clayton gawked at the mountain of snowy sugar Antonia had put on her pretzel.

"That's funny," she said as she settled herself and rested her purse on the table. "My son would look at my pretzel the exact same way you are. He doesn't even like to see me sweeten iced tea, if you can imagine that."

"I sure can. Just the sight of too much sugar can make my jaw lock up," he said with a good-natured chuckle. "So how old is your son, Mrs.—? I'm sorry, I'm at a disadvantage. You know my name, but I don't know yours."

"Oh, I'm Antonia Jackson, and my son's thirty-seven," she said, extending her hand to him. And when he took it and then smiled, her heart leapt with every passion in it that knew Emeril. She looked into his eyes, and in that moment of connection, hand in hand, eye to eye, deep within Antonia was reborn the part of her soul that died on a Mississippi road forty-five years before.

"Are you okay?" Clayton asked her. "You look stricken."

"Stricken," Antonia quietly repeated. And when she came back to the present, she looked at him and saw him for himself, saying, "I'm sorry for staring. You put me in mind of someone I knew back in New Orleans. It's a powerful resemblance."

"Is that so?" Clayton said laughing, as he dipped a piece of salmon roll into the tiny container of soy sauce. "Maybe you knew my father. I mean, we didn't look alike at all to me. But you never know what people can see."

Antonia's heart nearly stopped. How did he know? But he couldn't know, she immediately reasoned. He couldn't know because Agnes would never allow him to know. Unless, she thought again, he had found out the truth from a place where Agnes could not see. But what place would that be? So she said to him softly, "I'm sorry, your father?"

"Yes. My father, Douglas Cannon. Did you know him? He was a mortician down in New Orleans. Cannon Funeral Homes. There were three around the city."

"Ah yes, Douglas Cannon," Antonia said, feeling a strange relief. "Well, I certainly knew of the business, but I did not know your father." Suddenly this had become far too much for her to take. She felt intrusive, and bothersome, and voyeuristic. Something had brought her there, she thought. But she couldn't let it take her any farther than that moment. And she was afraid of what she just might say next. So she wrapped her pretzel lightly and stood. She extended her hand to Clayton and said, "My goodness, I just remembered that I'm late for an appointment. It's been a pleasure, and I do hope to see you again. But if not, I want you to keep playing as brilliantly as you've always played."

"Yes ma'am I will. And I'm sure we'll run into each other again. New Orleans doesn't keep her children apart for too long."

Antonia had no response to that. She only smiled and walked with a clip toward the stairs.

CHAPTER

4

•

The very next morning, dawn's virginal light slid slyly through the window and crawled on the floor, quietly announcing the new day. Across the room, where the creeping sun was headed, Clayton Cannon stood in front of the mirror, legs apart, arms raised, comb in hand, poised to do battle with the brown in the shade, just shy of red in the sun, curly, disobedient hair that had driven him to distraction all his life. It was the kind of hair that looked downright woolly on humid days, less so on dry ones. A crimp away from having the same tight kink as pure Negro hair, his hair had always intrigued him, since neither his mother nor father had hair like his.

He combed through with one stroke, paused, then watched as it sprang back into unbridled corkscrews. So he combed through again, but this time, just that fast, his attention had been dragged downward to the trash can right beneath the mirror. Not so much the trash can itself, but it was what was inside, sitting all alone with no other refuse to keep it company: a letter ripped in six pieces and scattered carelessly. On one large piece, he was able to see that it was addressed to his mother at her home in Louisiana. And from another piece of the envelope was a zip code. A Baltimore zip code and half of an address that he couldn't seem to make out without actually going into the can and picking it up, which he simply would not do. But whoever wrote this letter, he thought, had handwriting so flourished they were either someone who lived life just on the edge of drama, or simply lived life longing for flourish. He couldn't have cared less about that, though. It was all in the whereto and what-for. Why had his mother torn it up? And what would his mother know of anyone else in Baltimore, other than him? Because if she knew someone else in Baltimore, he reasoned, certainly he would know.

Just as he was about to go at his hair again, there was a knock at the door, and in his Louisiana drawl he responded. Clayton, the master of his piano, erudite in the music of the aristocracy, had come straight out of the bayou with a lazy twang and a family that was anything but blue blood. Way deep in his mind, he knew that much of his music brethren considered him and his family to be of the possum-eating, tooth-picking, trailer-park variety of southerners. Still, with all the irony that can only be found in America, it was this down-homey, trailer, everyman humility, an anomaly in the classical music world, that managed somehow to command enough respect to pack music halls to the rafters.

Agnes Cannon poked her head into the room. She closed the door softly behind her then went up behind him and slid her arms around his waist. "I'm so proud of you, cher. And I can tell you, all of New Orleans is just a big ole party, waitin' for you to come on back down there and play. I always knew you were born to do great things." As she let her hands fall from his waist, she looked around the room at all the unpacked boxes of his life, all labeled MUSIC BOOKS or ORCHESTRAL SCORES or ALBUMS/CDS. "When in the world are you gonna go through all this stuff, honey? This is the only room in the house that's not unpacked after the move from New York."

"I'll unpack, Momma. I'll unpack when I find a place for it all in here," Clayton said as he continued to work on his hair. "I've gotta get some new shelving units, but they have to have the right temperament to take on the mood of every note I play, so I've got to take my time as I shop for them. And I didn't want to get them until the new piano arrives."

"That's right," she said brightly. "Susan says you're getting a new concert grand and that this piano in here is going back into the living room the way you had it in New York. I thought you'd just keep this piano in here to practice on and leave your touring piano at the Meyerhoff. I never knew why you had two pianos in the house, anyway."

Clayton sighed at the burden of having to explain it once more to her, then went on with it while he kept at his hair. "Momma, I've told you before, I have two pianos because one is the living room piano for entertaining and for the boys' lessons, and the one I practice on has to be a concert grand." He stopped to work on a spot in his hair that looked as if it just might behave itself. But it was just an illusion, so he continued, "People come over, see a piano, and want to bang all over it trying to impress me with the few pieces they learned in high school when they took piano lessons from the lady down the street or some neighborhood music school. They can touch that thing over there, because I don't practice on it, and I don't tour with it. But no one will ever be allowed in here to touch my practice piano. Especially this practice piano that's coming. It's a Bursendorfer. The best piano in the world. What it would feel like for me to have someone touch my personal piano is the same as what you would feel like if somebody came into your house and tried on all your underwear."

"Oh, Clayton, it can't be like that," Agnes said with a blush in her voice.

"Momma, I'm telling you, it's exactly like that, and so to avoid the awkwardness of having to tell people to get the hell off my piano, I'd just rather have two pianos in the house."

"So if this piano that's coming is the best in the world, then why not tour with that one?"

"I probably will—maybe, at some point. But I have to personalize it first. Get comfortable with it before I can commit to taking it on the road with me. And that takes some time."

"I see" was all his mother said. Then Agnes stepped back and frowned as she watched him fret with his hair. "Leave your hair alone," she said as she pulled his hands away from his head. "Why can't you just get one of those hair straightenin' processes like I been tellin' you. It would be fine and nobody would know a thing. I know a Jewish gal who gets her hair straightened 'cause it's so darned kinky."

But her words fell on his deaf ears. Clayton went back to raking and tugging through his hair, thinking that miraculously, perhaps, this would be the day when his hair would obey the comb. Giving up, he went to the piano, sidestepping around three boxes of music books to get there, and opened the piano stool to put the comb inside, where it lived. "It's amazing to be doin' this, Momma," he said, lowering himself onto the leather stool. "I've always had immortal longings, but this is far more than I'd ever hoped for. And you wanna know something, Momma? I've played in the finest concert halls on this continent and on the other side of the ocean, but this concert down in New Orleans is really gonna mean something to me, for some reason."

Then he was hit with the memory of his lunch the day before with the woman from New Orleans. Yes, for some reason it was really going to mean something to him, but living back there— now that was something altogether different. Moving back there, he thought, would make him feel as if he were tossing away the tuxedo slacks of his manhood to force himself into his boyhood trousers. And they would never fit.

"For some reason? Of course it's gonna mean something to you, cher. New Orleans is the place where the music was first put into your bones. I just wish Douglas had lived to see this."

Clayton looked distractedly past his mother and said quietly, "Yeah."

"That's all you have to say about your father, cher?" Agnes was beside herself.

"Momma, I don't know what you'd have me say."

Agnes looked at her son as if in intense thought for a few seconds before saying, "I would have you talk about your father's pride in you. Your father knew you had greatness written all over you, and now look at you." Agnes sat on the other side of the desk, shaking her head in frustration. Then she said with a low-boiling agitation, "You just make me so angry, cher, when you sit there and act like that about your father. He was a good man. And he was good to you."

Clayton's eyes grew wide as he asked, "Act like what, Momma? And besides, there has never been any question about whether my father was a good man or whether he was good to me. I may have been only twelve when he died, but I do remember him for the man he was."

"Act like what? Why, you act like you're ashamed, or somethin'. You get all sullen, your eyes go dark. I can't say what it is exactly, but I don't like it, not one bit. And if you do know what a good man Douglas Cannon was, then I don't have to tell you that when I see you actin' like that at the mere mention of his name it gets a fire goin' in my belly, do I?"

Clayton lowered his head and closed his eyes to suppress a rage that could have put her out, then said softly, "No."

"Now if this is about your father not living long enough to feel his pride, then we've been through this before, cher. I've told you before and I'll tell you until you get it that you have to know that you are ennobling your father's memory and he feels his pride where he is, honey, only he feels it bigger now because everything in the kingdom of God is bigger than life."

Clayton, always articulate, always knowing what to say and when, could not answer his mother. There was simply no literal translation for what was in his heart. He could play it for her, perhaps. Maybe it could be told if he played it to her in Chopin's Nocturne in C Minor. That had enough forthrightness to accurately reflect the divinity born into his spirit, but every note was also filled with the earthly angst that comes with trying to balance forthrightness on the end of a memory that could have been a dream, but was nonetheless impossible for a child's mind to understand or even accept. Still it was clear enough to leave a trail of doubt for a grown man's soul to follow. And he wanted no part of the devilment of his doubt; not now, because this being the first decade of the twenty-first century, nobody, not even his mother, would live a lie as a means to an end. But he also knew that if she were, it had certainly gone on for so long there was no turning it around or making it right. If she had set his life on a path of duplicity in which he'd never had a say, then there'd be no way for her to tell the truth without him, through the cruelty of martyred consequences, breaking the faith and trust of those who so graciously and blindly led him to these white keys divided by blackness—and all those who followed him in spirit from the most backward, backwater state in the Union.

In his mind, that was heaped and steeped with nothing but southernness, if that feeling, that hid deep down in places that he couldn't find, were real then there'd be no allowing for the truth without ending up like Louisiana roadkill—dead enough, but not good enough to trust as supper. He'd be crucified, and maligned, and remembered for nothing other than being the lying, sneaky bastard who made white American and even European musical esthetes believe he was one of them. And as he sat there looking deeply into the yawning smile of black and white that could reveal his countenance with but the stroking of a few chords, he could see himself in music's history. The man who could play from a soul of which he possibly never completely knew.

He turned from the window to look over at his mother who could never know the roiling of his thoughts and feelings. Clayton knew that she would never understand and perhaps never even forgive him if the doubts he had of his own conception were unfounded, but also she would never accept his discontent if it were founded. She would never know, he believed, how such a lie would force him to live outside of himself, that's why he had to beat down his qualms and know—not think—that his mother would never have manipulated his life in such a dastardly way. It was all a dream. A childish dream that could just as easily have been of flying dragons. So instead of letting his mind continue to hurtle down a never-ending, unforgiving winding road, he said, "Momma, I have to practice now, if you don't mind."

"I'm leaving, cher. I've got a car waiting for me outside," Agnes said without the merest hint that would tell where she was headed. "Now, I'll be back before I leave to go to New Orleans tonight, so I'll see you for dinner."

Clayton said nothing as his mother left and he regarded the envelope peeking from her purse. Another one. Another letter postmarked from Baltimore, this much he could see because of the zip code—the handwriting, just like the ripped-up letter in the garbage, had far too many flourishes for him to make out a name or even an address. Still he wondered if his mother had contacted this person. He wondered why she hadn't spoken of knowing someone in the town, but mostly he wondered why in the trash can right there in his studio, another letter, clearly from the same person, sat ripped to shreds as if so doing could make the words of whoever had sent it absent from the universe.

Who was this person? he wondered, and did that person have the secrets of his dream? The dream of his grandmother's imprudent whisper all those years ago. Could this writer of the ripped-up letter from Baltimore be an aunt, or an uncle, or a cousin, or even his third grandmother or grandfather simply wanting to know kin. And sometimes, in this particular moment when he couldn't take the mockery of his uncertainty a second longer, he wanted the letter writer to be the one who would just say it; he wanted to give the responsibility of his life and righting his mother's wrong completely up to that man or woman. Or maybe, he thought in one sedate second, the letter writer is just someone from New Orleans who had hoped to bury a childhood hatchet with his mother in the letter. Someone from New Orleans who happens to be living in Baltimore now—just like the woman from yesterday, he thought. Maybe they weren't kin, after all.

So he would try to get his calm back before his first practice of the day, yet what bore and ate away and destroyed his peace like so many maggots on flesh was the ghostly haunting of his grandmother's whisper, actual or dreamt, after his father's funeral, while *"Little Clayton"* slept in the back of the limousine: *"Are you ever gonna tell that child that his father was that colored boy Emeril Racine?"* And so with his memory, whether the whole thing was real or imagined, and with the silence inside that car when his mother would not answer her mother, Clayton was coming to the end of the tether on which he'd hung, from that day, on the belief that if it had not been imagined, they were talking about some other boy he didn't know, and if it had all been a dream, well then, it was all simply a dream.

He played the first thunderous chord of the Beethoven "Sonata Pathétique" that he'd take to New Orleans; doing what he had done all his life—burying those thoughts of what may or may not have been the other half of himself deeper behind the music in his mind. That half of himself that may or may not be present every time he touches his hair, or looks in the mirror at his eyes that have so much to say if only he could speak their language, or sees a half-breed in Baltimore passing for white.

So Clayton closed his eyes and let himself dissolve into the minor chords that empathized with every part of him that could not find peace in that moment. And as he played through into the second theme of the sonata headed for the third, he felt a comfort, a kinship with the multiple personalities that came together, nonetheless, to create one body.

Clayton leaned into the notes with the hope and intention of letting his angst slip between the fine cracks separating the white and the black. And it did, as he played this commanding sonata with the brilliance of a man who could scarcely be topped in his world. The whole thing positively put him in awe of himself, because if his mother was indeed guilty of the subterfuge of hiding his true race from him and the world, what a wunderkind he'd really be. And how was it, he wondered with all earnestness and disconsolation, that no one ever found him out? Someone would have seen it in him, right? Especially blacks, and particularly blacks in New Orleans. It was always so easy for him to spot passers. No matter how fair the skin, or straight the hair, or fine the features, Clayton could tell when someone was passing—in fact, there was an opera singer with the Berlin Opera, who was originally from Mississippi but spoke as if she were straight out of the queen's court. Marion Bright he believed her name was, and she, without his doubt, was passing. But Clayton knew from where he'd come. He came from a part of the country where octoroons, and quadroons, and all other combinations were a fact of life. Someone, somewhere along the way, he thought, would have questioned his bloodline if it weren't pure.

And then he smiled, not with the beauty of what he formed beneath his fingers, but with the thought of the day he met André Watts, a man who lived quite knowingly with the duality of his selves—black and white. Clayton remembered the way he fawned with a certain awe at the way the man slid into the room with his walk as smooth as butter; a walk Clayton envied each time he remembered it for its confidence and power. The walk of a man who surely knew himself beyond merely his name. Clayton's smile faded slowly, its metamorphosis almost undetectable.

Once he finished the first movement, he barely let the final chord dissolve to its conclusion before he leaned forward and snatched up the phone that sat on the edge of the piano. He dialed. "Momma," he said once she answered. "Where are you going? You didn't tell me before you left." And he listened as she told him she was headed to the shopping mall to buy something for his New Orleans concert—an explanation he found most dubious. So then he asked, "Momma, I also saw a letter that seemed to have been addressed to you, torn up in the trash here in my studio. I was wondering if you tore it up, or if maybe one of the boys did it in their mischief." And when she confirmed that she had indeed ripped up the letter, he asked, "Why did you tear it up?"

And after she gave him a sufficient enough lie, he simply replied quietly, "Okay, bye." Then Clayton sat slouched on the stool to ponder exactly why it was so easy to believe his mother even when he knew she was lying.

Agnes turned off her phone and slid it back into her bag, and she wondered what had happened in the few brief minutes since she'd left her son that brought him to question her torn-up letter. How in the world could she have forgotten that she'd hastily slipped the letter into her purse as she was leaving New Orleans? She should have just thrown it out back home. But no, she had to drag it all the way to Baltimore, only to find it by surprise, rip it up, and throw it away right in front of Clayton. And who in the world, other than Clayton, would even care about a discarded letter? But then again, it didn't fall on her as such a surprise when she really gave it some thought. She believed her son just may still have every single letter ever sent to him since his first summer at sleep-away camp.

Agnes loved her son and even admired his often melancholy nature, but she believed that it was this sentimentality that would only serve to undo all she'd done to bring him to center stage. Especially if he were to know how much of her soul she'd had to sacrifice since the day his father, Emeril, died. And she thought about how he never really had her full attention, considering how the distraction of his life always kept her an inch away from him in every way—at least it seemed to her now. Agnes shuddered, then shifted as if to distance herself from the thought. Pulling her fur coat tighter around her bosom and shoulders, she snuggled into it and sank down into the seat, looking like some despondent aged starlet. Her head fell back on the seat as she looked out at the tall row houses that did not stand with nearly as much splendor as they could, or as they possibly had on a long-ago day, with their three marble steps out front along this shambled stretch of street. Thank God they were passing by too fast to really see. And she thought about what she was doing, and where she was going, and why. And what would she say, she wondered. Because she hadn't laid eyes on Antonia Jackson in close to forty-five years, yet somehow from the thumping of her heart, Agnes knew that she was more afraid of Antonia than she was of the devil.

Before Agnes knew it, they were at a crossroads, it seemed. She looked up at the street sign to see that it read NORTH AVENUE. It must have been the same street they were on just miles back, but out of the window the cityscape had changed to reveal somewhat better houses, even a lovely church with steeple and a funeral home right across from it that was white and bright enough to make death seem like nothing to be feared. "Driver, are we here?"

"Well, this is West Baltimore, the part of town where she lives. We're gonna be there in a few minutes; her house is on this road up here that we're gonna turn onto," he said as he sat waiting for the light to change.

As they moved forward, Agnes suddenly felt forty-five years younger, cowering with the same insecurities that put her in the arms of Emeril, the only boy, besides Douglas Cannon, who ever bothered to look beyond the base words that had swirled around New Orleans about her. And what would she say to Antonia who, she knew, was certain to still see her as the Agnes of un-Godly ways? When she looked up at the passing street sign, it said Garrison Boulevard, and underneath the sign was the bawdiest prostitute she'd ever seen outside of Bourbon Street. Agnes's heart quickened as the woman sized up the limousine. She could just see the headlines: DRIVER OF PIANIST'S MOM PROPOSITIONED BY STREETWALKER. Holy cow, she thought, this is all I need. But she breathed lighter again when the woman was distracted by a more likely payoff, and she walked to a car stopped at the traffic light, then opened her coat to display her bare nakedness. This is the street? she thought. This couldn't be the street, and she wrung her hands. And when the limousine pulled to a stop beside the curb, she couldn't move.

"This is it, ma'am."

"Thank you," she said as she waited for him to come around and open her door. As she stepped from the car, she said, "I may be a little while. I'm not sure."

"That's fine, ma'am. I'll be here."

Agnes climbed the three stairs that led her to a long path that emptied at the foot of a wide set of porch steps. So she walked the path like a woman in no hurry. This place, this walk, these trees standing tall on each side of the walk to announce this grand house took her back to New Orleans; and it was like New Orleans in every way, with this splendor of a home tucked away from a boulevard where bare-butt prostitutes, covered up with just a coat, romped up and down. She couldn't be away from New Orleans for a day without something reminding her of it. She was a daughter of the Big Easy with every drop of blood in her body, and the smells, sounds, the *laissez les bon temps rouler* spirit of the city brought about a melancholic fear-of-distance-from-it that wouldn't be shaken until she was back there. Who knew Baltimore was this colorful, she thought, as she recalled that even in the days when Clayton lived here when he was in school at the Peabody Conservatory, she'd never traveled outside of the general downtown area when she came for visits. And she knew that it must have been this taste of back home that had brought Antonia to this place.

She rang the doorbell twice before she heard Antonia shuffling through the hall to answer it. And when the door opened, Agnes stood with her fur slung dramatically around her shoulders saying, "Antonia, do you remember me? I'm—"

"I know who you are. Why did it take you so long?"

"I've been a little busy."

Antonia took Agnes in with every sense she had, then said, her tone laden with bitter sarcasm, "Well, I'm glad that whatever it took you to finish is finally done after forty years."

"May I come in, cher?" Agnes inquired, holding herself so uncomfortably she felt positively tortured.

"Yes, I think you should. And don't give me that cher nonsense. This is not New Orleans."

Agnes stepped into the front hall and looked around at its grandeur. And Antonia had it fixed up so nice, she thought, with a Louis XIV knock-off fainting couch in just the right place underneath the staircase. "This is lovely," she said as Antonia guided her into the living room where she went over and sat on the sofa. Antonia, though, sat in the chair on the other side of the coffee table, facing Agnes.

"So Antonia Racine . . . well, Jackson now," Agnes said, as if their relationship had ever been such that this type of small-talk was appropriate. "So you went and married Jackson, huh?"

"Yes I did, Agnes, in spite of the fact that his mother was actually simple-minded enough to name him Jackson Jackson," Antonia said without warmth.

"She gave him some kind of funny middle name, too, didn't she?"

"Jackson Junior Jackson."

"Yeah," Agnes said, laughing. "That mother-in-law of yours sure was eccentric, and that's puttin' it mighty kindly."

Antonia looked at her and slid her mouth sideways before saying, "Agnes, she's only considered eccentric in New Orleans. Any other part of the world they'd call her what she was—touched. But then again, who's to say. After all, nearly everybody down there called me fou-fou Antonia since I can remember just because I carried my cat around in a basket all the time. And there are some who still think I'm fou-fou. Well, we'll just see how fou-fou I really am." Antonia was deadpan in a way that made it difficult to tell if this were a part of some sort of latent dry humor, or if it were simply some mean-spirited statement of fact-according-to-Antonia.

"So how is Jackson, Antonia?"

"Not as alive as he once was, but not as dead as he could be." There was nothing that could be heard in her flatness that would indicate whether her sarcasm was meant to shock in jest or wound with a jab.

"I see," Agnes said nervously.

"Listen, Agnes, I know you didn't come here to talk about my husband's ridiculous name or about what a character his mother was. What do you want? Have you finally decided to respond to my letters?"

"Antonia, I want to ask you what you think you know."

Before she answered, she got up and said, "I'll be right back, Agnes," and she left the room, seemingly for some urgent matter. When she came back in less than a half minute, there was a lump in her pocket that wasn't there when she left. She entered talking. "I don't *think* I know anything!" she said defensively. "I *know* that your son is my brother's boy and I told you in the letters why I know it's so. And for the first time since the day you brought him into this world, I'm going to make you accountable for the decisions you've made since that day to cover up his race and deny my brother. I have told you in my letters over all these years that I know that the timing was never right.

"That baby was born a full month and a half earlier than it would have been if he had been Douglas's. I told you, I was watching you and I know the exact day you and Douglas had sex for the first time. You brought him to the same place where you lay with my brother down in the Garden District when you were baby-sitting for that little boy and girl, and I know 'cause I saw you take him in there and then I stood underneath the window while you two went at it." Antonia hung her head as if embarrassed by such voyeurism, then said, "Anyway, I saw you. And I'm telling you, it does not add up. And the only thing more amazing than you thinking you could get away with it, Agnes Cannon, was Douglas actually believing that that baby was his, which could easily make him the stupidest man ever to be born in the state of Louisiana—and that takes some doing."

Antonia shifted where she sat to reposition the lump in her pocket. "Agnes, I'm not stupid. I knew about you and Emeril when you two thought you were being so careful. I tried to stop my brother. You're just not the kind of woman who's worth a man risking his life for. Do you remember that day when you met Emeril at the Dupreses' house for a romp and somebody rang on the doorbell like crazy?" Antonia paused as if she was going to give Agnes a chance to answer, but she didn't as she continued, "Well, I was hiding underneath the willow tree when you came up, and that was me who rang the bell that day, but you know that." Antonia stood up to pace. It wasn't working, because it was clear as she held herself in a clench that went from her jaw on down that her annoyance was beginning to peak into anger when she said, "But when I saw that child once he started making a name for himself as a concert pianist, I paid real close attention because he started looking more and more like his father. And I'll tell you, he looks as white as any white man I've ever seen, but I still know he's black. I still know he's kin."

Agnes was left with nothing to say, and as she looked off to the side, she wasn't sure if she was gathering thoughts or tears, or both. And then her mind wandered back to New Orleans, and the oppressively hot summer days when the air was as thick as Louisiana swamp water. She thought of the front porch of Antonia's and Emeril's house where Antonia would sit in the summer afternoons, drinking lemonade and patching clothes with one eye and watching her suspiciously with the other, as she passed by from any one of her rendezvous with Emeril. The most bizarre and out-of-the-blue thought she had, though, was of the little half-wit from next door to the Dupreses' who, on his daily journeys from yard to yard to eat spoonfuls of dirt, almost caught her many times sneaking behind the house.

"But he's not your kin, Antonia," Agnes finally said, nervously, but strongly, as if her lapse into silence hadn't happened. And even though she was just barely able to look Antonia in the eye as she said it, she had to look away when she continued, "I would have loved to have been left with a part of Emeril when he died and I would love nothing more than for Clayton to be Emeril's boy, but he's not, Antonia."

"Agnes," Antonia replied while she wrung her hands furiously, "don't you think I know that you have every reason in the world to lie to me. Look, Agnes, I don't want to make trouble. I just want you two to do right by my brother's name and memory. Now, something drew Clayton back here to Baltimore. I never did anything in the way of trying to contact him when he was in school down at Peabody, mostly because he would have considered my words to be the ranting of a lunatic after everything you've filled his mind with. He wouldn't have believed me, and honestly, I just might have made him more resistant to the truth when it did come. But let me tell you, hardly a day went by when I didn't want to just get in my car and go down there and tell him straight out what I thought. So now, if you don't do something to set this right, Agnes, I'll have to, because right is right, and blood is blood. Now, I guess you figured you lucked out when my brother died. You were able to have your little walk on the wild side, then settle into a well-to-do life with your own kind who was none the wiser that you had laid with a black man. Well, that's fine, but your lies have caught up to you, Agnes. You've got to come clean."

Agnes sputtered incredulously. "Don't you dare make it seem like that, Antonia Racine! I loved your brother. Still do. I went to our special place behind the Dupreses' house for days, just waitin' for him to come, but he never came. When I found out he was dead, it was like to kill me. And you could have told me, Antonia. You saw me the day after he died and you never said a word. The worst part of it all is that I couldn't even grieve right for the only man I ever loved."

"You got over him fast enough. A month and a half later you were marrying Douglas Cannon."

"A man I didn't love, but the times were what they were, Antonia, and livin' the way I was livin' a girl like me wouldn't have stood a chance to get married. I thought Douglas was gonna be the best I could ever hope to do after Emeril died. And you know, I never remarried after Douglas died. Antonia, why are you doin' this? And what if what you're saying is right, that Clayton is Emeril's son and therefore a black man? Can't you see that he has done more than Emeril could have ever hoped for himself? So what if the world was unaware that he was black? He would know it. I would know it. *You* would know it. Even Emeril himself would tell you that bein' a black man never got him anywhere. Bein' a black man is why the ambulance took so long and why he died. I only came here to ask that you stop this and stop doing more harm to your brother's name by saying these things about Clayton being his son, because it's just not true."

"I'm sorry, but I won't leave this alone until you admit the truth. Emeril was the only brother I had. For God's sake, he was my twin! We shared a womb together and a life together until the rules of bigotry took him from me. It was just the two of us and now he's gone. I want the world to know the kind of man that Emeril Racine produced."

Agnes sat for a moment before saying, "Antonia." Hesitating for a few seconds, she wrestled with the decision whether or not to speak her thoughts, then she continued. "Antonia, is it money you want? Because if it is, I can try to help you out."

Antonia's face fell so far in what seemed to be a concoction of disbelief and pure fury that she looked as if she could have exhaled fire. Slowly and regally, as was her way, she leaned forward in her chair in a gesture that was so menacing and unpredictable that it made Agnes draw in what could have been her last breath. Shaking with angry tremors, Antonia said, "If I were less than the lady my mother raised me to be, I would drop-kick your wrinkled white-cracker butt back to New Orleans this very instant. This is not about money. Never has been. I have money, probably more than you. This is about love and pride for my brother, something it seems you never had. Now, I would like you to leave my home."

"Antonia, please. I didn't mean to insult you, cher. I'm so truly sorry. It's just that this is very hard for me, these accusations you've been writing me with. I just don't know how else to handle this."

Antonia said not one word. She went to the door, opened it, and stood. Stiffly she stood, not blinking, not moving.

With a humiliated shuffle, her head lowered, Agnes submitted to Antonia's demand and left. And when Antonia closed the door determinedly, Agnes was left with nothing else to do but descend the porch steps and walk the long path made longer in her mind with the heartbreaking feeling that she was losing Emeril all over again.

CHAPTER

5

•

After Agnes left, Antonia spent most of the evening and the better balance of the next day dissecting every word, facial expression, and eye movement of Agnes's visit. Antonia was more convinced than ever that she finally had proof to take to Aaron that would convince him. And as she took her sink-bath in the middle of the afternoon preparing to take him the evidence of things he could not see and therefore not believe, she remembered that he had always been a doubter. Aaron was the child who always needed proof that anything was real. Even his belief in Santa Claus, Antonia recalled with a faint smile as she lifted her arm and smeared on deodorant, lasted only until he was six. Yet for three years after he'd let Santa go for lack of proof, Aaron let her hang on to the miracle that he still believed. It amazed her that he could even believe in God, she thought as she slipped on her trousers and zipped herself into them. Or was he biding his time, she wondered, before telling her that the missing physical proof could not stretch his belief to a place like heaven? And that was fine, she thought, because she remembered those months after Emeril died when heaven, that place where life is lived after death, was an abstraction that was no soothing balm for her heartache; and so she couldn't believe. She couldn't believe until Emeril's son was born, and so she could again look beyond the physical world to the place that would always ease her sick soul. The birth of one man's son had fanned that which had been diminished by death to a mere flicker of faith, into a burning bush. So now she was dressed and going out the door, hell-bound for the television station, ready to save her son from his cynicism.

Antonia was walking through the doors of Channel Eleven by 4:15. She went to the young lady behind the desk and smiled until the woman ended her call. Ordinarily, Antonia knew her name well enough, but with everything swirling in her head the way it was, she simply said, "Hello, young lady, do you remember me?"

"I certainly do, Mrs. Jackson. How've you been?"

"I've been just wonderful, and getting better by the minute," Antonia said with the slyest grin. "But right now I'm here to see my son. Is he around?"

"He sure is. Does he know you're coming? Because he usually tells me when he's expecting someone, and he didn't tell me you were coming."

"Oh no, he doesn't. This is a surprise."

"Well, how nice. Just have a seat and I'll get him. He's around the newsroom somewhere, I'm sure."

Antonia went to the comfortable-looking chair that had been deceptive in its appearance, which she discovered once she sat. Firm and bouncy. No comfort in that. She shifted this way and that, slouchy then straight-backed, trying to settle into some semblance of ease, but it was not to be, not in this chair. So she sat upright and crossed her right leg over her left, then dangled her board-flat shoe on her toes. She glanced over at the receptionist, for no particular reason, unintentionally prompting the woman to give Antonia an update.

"He'll be right out, Mrs. Jackson."

"Oh, thank you. It's really no rush at all." And just as Antonia said that, her attention was snatched away from the woman by the opening of a door.

Aaron let the door drift closed behind him as he moved toward Antonia with all the verve of a doomed man. When he got to where she sat, all he could do was stare blankly at her, seemingly unable to breathe or blink or move hurriedly. Quietly, with his rightful perturbation and a barely perceptible low-grade fear amazingly under control, he said, "Ma, why are you here?"

Antonia stood so as to be as close to eye to eye with her son as she could. She clutched the bottom of her bag in her hand as if it had some heft to it, then said, "I finally got it, baby. I finally got the proof you've been telling me I don't have."

Aaron looked suspiciously around before whispering, "Ma, come on. How could you come to my job with this? This is where I work, Ma, please." His voice cracked with desperation.

"How could I come here?" Antonia said incredulously. "I came here to help you. You have a chance to break a story in which you are directly involved. I came here to give you the opportunity of your career. You could put this on the five o'clock news tonight!"

Aaron said nothing as he took her by the arm and directed her through the door and into the newsroom. They went down a long narrow walkway that meandered past a number of cubicles and in every single one sat a woman, except for two with men, who all talked on the phone with the urgency of news. And when Antonia and Aaron came to the end of the line of all those pseudo-offices, Aaron led her into a room with a long table and chairs twisted haphazardly around them, as if the last people in the room had had to evacuate in haste. As he closed the door, he said, "Ma, sit down, please."

Antonia went to the head of the table and sat. Only when Aaron closed the door and came to sit beside her did she say, "I'm going to show you exactly what I have and shut your doubts up once and for all." She dug in her purse and pulled out the small rectangular box. "Just wait till you hear what I have here."

Aaron looked questioningly at the thing, then at her and asked, "Ma, is that a tape recorder?"

"Well, it sure isn't a Victrola," she said as she looked to make certain the tape was cued up.

"Ma, where did you get that?"

"I bought it, and that is, as the young kids say, *so* not the point," she said with a mockingly arrogant throw of her head. "The point is what I have on this tape recorder."

"Ma," Aaron shrieked, twisting where he sat in agitation. "I don't want to hear this! I can't imagine what it is you think you have here, but I swear I don't want to be party to this!"

Antonia turned on the tape recorder and Agnes Cannon's voice, nasally and drawling nearly every word, floated from it in its one dimension. And Antonia watched with an intense smile as her son stared intently at the recorder as if he were looking directly into Agnes Cannon's mouth, waiting for the moment when she'd say it. "Just wait, it's coming," Antonia whispered to him. She sat in anticipation herself, until the electronic version of Agnes said all that Antonia would ever need to confirm that she'd been right all these years. "You hear! Did you hear that? She's admitting it in her sly old way," she said excitedly.

Aaron looked at her with squinted eyes, then said, "No, Ma. I didn't hear anything. I heard her talking about the supposition of Clayton Cannon being your brother's son. But—"

"Here, let me rewind it. And this time really listen," she said as the high-pitch squeak of Agnes's voice going fast and in reverse took over.

But Aaron spoke up urgently. "No, Ma, I don't want to hear it again." He stood up and walked to the other end of the table, rubbing the back of his neck like a man filled to his capacity with frustration before continuing, "Look, Ma, about the only thing I'm willing to believe right now is that, okay, you knew Agnes Cannon down in New Orleans where she had a love affair with your brother, and yes, okay, I do believe that somehow you got the woman over to your house. But there was nothing that she said on this tape that even comes close to her admitting what you're saying about Clayton Cannon being Uncle Emeril's son. Now I want you to be reasonable, Ma, and tell me what you really hear that woman saying on that tape, because I swear to God, I don't see how you hear anything she said as an admission of anything other than the fact that she loved Uncle Emeril."

Antonia, her face fallen to the floor, put the recorder back into her purse. She blew out a long defeated breath and said in the smallest voice she'd ever known, "You had to have seen her eyes. Her eyes said it all, and just her whole spirit told me." She slumped back in the oversized, boss's chair, knowing that she couldn't begin to conquer the heft of Aaron's skepticism. Then she continued in a deflated tone, "I'm not making this up, Aaron, and I'm not crazy enough to be imagining this, either."

Aaron's demeanor softened as he went back to where his mother was and sat beside her again, saying, "All right, Ma, I agree with you. Half of what is truth is visual. But you've got to admit that she didn't say anything on this tape about Clayton

Cannon being Uncle Emeril's son. I mean, what am I supposed to think? What am I supposed to believe? Nothing in what she said there on that tape incriminated her in the way you're suggesting it did. I'm sorry, Ma, but it just didn't." He drew in a considerable breath that brought with it the nerve to say, "Yeah, Ma, it's clear that she and Uncle Emeril were gettin' it on, but from where I sit, she came there to see you because of all those letters you sent her harassing her to death."

"Harassing her!" Antonia said, pumped up with angry breath.

Just then, the door opened with an immediacy that, along with the thin face of a man with a shock of white hair streaking toward the back of his head, was enough to startle Antonia into a small quiver and shake of her head. She regarded the man's creamy brown face for a few seconds, trying to decide if he was bona fide handsome or if he was one of those rare, unfortunate few people born with such exotic beauty that he had actually gone the next step, becoming positively odd-looking. So, since she'd always known that staring was ill-mannered, she said, "Hello."

"Hello," the man said. "Aaron, I thought I saw you come in here. Listen, we've got a story breaking out in Randallstown. A hostage situation and shootout with the police. All the information is pretty sketchy at this point, but the word is that it's a domestic thing. I just sent Keith out there to set up for a live feed. Anyway, I need you in the studio at the desk, ready to roll with it if we need to break into *Oprah* before five. Maggie's already in there waiting for you, so I really need you to move your—" He regarded Antonia with a half, insincere smile, as if he were holding back the salt at the tip of his tongue for the benefit of this elder woman. Then he continued with no less urgency, "I need you to hustle."

And hustle he did. Aaron jumped up, leaving the chair haphazardly twisted from the table. "I'm there, Mark," he said. Then he turned to his mother quickly and said, "Come on, Ma."

"Oh, this is your mother?" Mark asked.

"Oh, yeah," Aaron said. He paused before doing what would be natural under most circumstances, as if too hurried for an introduction, or possibly too doubtful about it. Then he continued, "Ma, this is our new news director here, Mark Allen. Mark, this is my mother, Antonia Jackson."

"Mrs. Jackson, it's a pleasure to meet you," Mark said.

Antonia passed by Aaron and quickly studied the chair he'd just let fly willy-nilly, thinking that this must be the way chairs end up in newsrooms, with breaking stories and all. Then she got to Mark and took the hand he offered her and said with enough smiling charm to warm a newsman's guarded heart, "The pleasure's all mine."

As Aaron brushed past the two, he was stopped when he heard Mark say, "Mrs. Jackson, would you like to sit inside the studio and watch Aaron do the show?"

"Oh, I'd love that!" Antonia chirped giddily. "All these years he's been working here and he's never, ever asked me to come in and watch him work live. I would just love to."

Well, even with a story breaking and Baltimore's need to know about it, Aaron could not move from where he'd stopped in mid-stride. He looked absolutely stricken with his eyes shocked into a widened stare and his mouth open. And at first, what came out were unintelligible words that seemed to be garbled by some kind of dense filter just inside his mouth that would not let his thoughts free. Then as if he'd just spit the filter out like a man with the sheer desperation to save his own life, he said, "Oh no, Mark, I don't think that's such a good idea. I don't like having anyone in the studio other than the people who have to be there. Besides, I'm not sure if it's such a good idea with that story breaking and everything."

"Oh, come on, Aaron," Mark said, slapping Aaron on his back and leading the way toward the studio. "What could happen? Let's just get on in there. I need you on that desk ready to go right now, and there's no time to debate something this trivial. Your mother's a sensible lady. She's not going to interrupt the newscast in any way. You won't, will you, Mrs. Jackson?"

"No, of course I won't," Antonia said, staring daggers into the side of Aaron's face, trying to get him to look at her and take them directly like a man.

"Okay then, it's all settled. Your mother will sit in and you'll give her the thrill of her life—to watch her son do what he does best."

Aaron picked up his pace as if he were trying to lose his mother in the newsroom. He said over his shoulder, "Besides, Ma, don't you need to get home and feed Tippy the Fourth?"

"Since when have you been so concerned about Tippy the Fourth? You hardly know she's alive," Antonia said in a whisper to hide the snippiness of her agitation from Mark. Then, she said a little louder, but no less acerbically, "Tippy the Fourth will be just fine till I get home, and you know that."

So, with that resolved, Mark said to a large rugged man in dungarees and a faded well-worn shirt who looked more like he'd be ready to fell a tree than work in a news studio, "That's Aaron's mom. She's going to sit in the studio and watch the newscast. Can you get her settled in there?"

"Sure can, boss," the man said, smiling at Antonia who was just past Aaron's shoulder.

"Terrific," Mark said in the way men accustomed to always having their commands obeyed speak. "Josh here's the floor director, Mrs. Jackson. He'll take care of you. Enjoy the show, Mrs. Jackson." And then he walked away with a swagger that wreaked of his authority.

Josh led Antonia into the studio as she watched Aaron, out of the corner of her eye, go through another door for his makeup. Once inside the studio where it seemed as if the space above her head went on forever in infinite darkness, she looked all around, amazed by everything, and knowing what absolutely nothing was called. And she never would have imagined that one side of the studio would be so brightly lit in such striking comparison to the other half, which was in stark darkness. So as she marveled at it all like a tourist dumbfounded by newness, she was suddenly aware of more than the presence of just herself and Josh.

"So, Maggie, I didn't get a chance to say welcome back from vacation. How was your New Year's Eve?" Josh said.

And without looking up from the pages she studied, Maggie Poole said, "Oh, Josh, you know how it is. New Year's Eve is like bad sex. It's nothing but weeks and days and hours and then seemingly unending minutes of basically uninteresting foreplay leading up to one anticlimactic second you'd rather forget anyway."

And at Maggie's analogy, Antonia let out the bashful twitter that seemed to have been channeled from a virginal youngster. She wasn't quite sure which embarrassed her more—hearing her son's lover say such things, or knowing that none of it would ever have been said for her to hear had Maggie been aware of her presence.

The worst part, though, was that Antonia felt like an accidental voyeur, particularly since it was possible that she was being given a glimpse into her son's sex life, which was somehow dysfunctional by the sound of Maggie's lackluster account. So the only thing Antonia could think to say that would possibly make an itchy nightmare of a situation less so was "That was very funny."

"Mrs. Jackson!" Maggie said, her voice crumbling with the same fear it just might have had if she'd unintentionally said what she'd said into an open microphone for all of Baltimore to hear.

"Maggie, how are you sweetie?" Antonia said as she stepped gingerly over wires and maneuvered around things to get to where Maggie sat on the set.

"I'm fine, Mrs. Jackson. It's just so good to see you." Then Maggie hung her head and looked past Antonia's eyes to say, "About what I was saying to Josh. You know, we . . . Well, I was just—"

Antonia stopped Maggie's fumbling and stumbling for words by grabbing her up. She hugged her close, and when she was through, she took one step back and said, "Why haven't you two been around lately? You are still seeing one another, aren't you? You know Aaron wouldn't tell me if you weren't because he knows I'd give him the devil for it."

Maggie laughed, smiling broadly before saying, "Oh yes, Mrs. Jackson. We're stuck in love with each other and not going anywhere. It's just that I've moved my aunt in with me and she's nearly blind, so I've had to make a lot of adjustments to my schedule to accommodate her and all."

Antonia didn't speak right away, being under the momentary spell of Maggie's smile, which always made her think of the sweetness of children. Then she said, slapping her flattened palm to her thigh, remembering, "Oh, that's right. Aaron did tell me that you'd taken in your widowed aunt. And he did say that that's why you're not doing the eleven o'clock news anymore. You are such a good woman. I guess that's why I love you so much," and Antonia took Maggie into a hug once more.

"Well, I guess it's like they say, I'll get my rewards in heaven," she said as she patted Antonia's back in a way that seemed instinctive.

"You'll get them there, and you'll get them right here on earth too. You'd better believe it, because I know it's true." Antonia slackened her hold on Maggie and whispered, "And part of your reward will be my son. I can't wait until the day you're my daughter-in-law, although I don't know what my son could have done to deserve a peach like you, but you didn't hear that from me," and she laughed heartily, giving Maggie one last squeeze before she stepped back, having heard footsteps that she assumed were Aaron's.

Maggie let out a nervous burst of laughter, then said, "Oh my, well that's some praise you sing of me, Mrs. Jackson."

"Okay, okay," Aaron said good-naturedly. "Let's knock this off. We've got a show to do." He sat in his chair, just to the right of Maggie's and looked at his mother impatiently, then let his eyes drift down to study the news copy in his hands.

"All right, I'm going. Josh, where do I sit?"

"Right over here, ma'am."

"I'm not going to be on camera, am I?" she said as again she navigated her way over cables and around things.

"Oh no ma'am. You're way out of shot of any of these cameras."

"Where are the cameras, anyway?" she asked as she settled herself into the chair in which Josh directed her to sit, which sat among two other chairs and a small table that looked good for absolutely nothing. The whole little area, which was hidden in darkness, looked to her like an abandoned living room corner.

"See those three big structures right there? Well, they're the cameras."

Antonia looked skeptically at them, studying them with her head turned first this way and then that, and said, "Well, now, I didn't expect them to look like that. To be that big. I always thought they'd look like regular movie cameras. You know, like the ones you see those guys out on the street carrying for those reporters."

"Well, these are the studio cameras" was all that Josh said distractedly. His tone and actions made it clear that something was about to happen and he was about to turn his attention from her. He looked over to Aaron and Maggie, who had already slipped into their five o'clock news personas, ready for the camera. He said, "Cue to Aaron. We're ready to go in five, four, three . . ."

And that's when Aaron said, "Good afternoon. We're interrupting regular programming to take you to Randallstown where a hostage situation is underway. Six people are being held hostage in a home on Allenswood Road, including a three-year-old girl. The shooting between the hostage taker and the police has prompted the police to block off Brenbrook Road from Liberty Heights to McDonough, and all the side streets surrounding Allenswood. People in this area are being warned to stay in their homes. Right now, we're going live to Keith Pettiford who's at the scene. Keith, what's the latest?"

Antonia could hear the reporter's voice coming from somewhere to the right of where she sat, and judging from Aaron's and Maggie's gazes, the screen Maggie watched must have been smack between cameras two and three, and the one Aaron watched must have been smack between cameras one and two. As badly as she also wanted to be taken live to the scene of the crime in progress, she couldn't go. No matter how hard she strained and craned her neck, her just-barely side view of the monitor was blocked by the bulk of camera three. Camera three. She suddenly thought about camera three, and then two, and then one. There wasn't a soul behind even one of the cameras, yet these things moved back and forth, from Aaron to Maggie as if someone were pushing and pulling them. They had to be computerized, she thought, and operated by someone up there in that dimly lit room with the board full of buttons and knobs and sliding doo-dads, whatever that place was called. She'd only been in there once, and then only briefly. Still, that couldn't help her to reason why the age of computers had come to this place to take three good jobs from three men who just may not be competent to do anything else but push and pull a camera around.

While she'd sat pondering the fate of the displaced cameramen, the news had gone into its regular hour and Maggie was talking about something completely unrelated to the shooting out in Randallstown. Whatever it was that was hot enough to be news had eluded Antonia in that moment, because all she could wonder about now was why Aaron was burning a stare into her. She couldn't imagine what she could have done while simply sitting there quietly that would warrant such a look from him. So she stared back at him, with questioning eyes and an unsure smile. They locked onto one another in this way until the commercial break, and even though there was no possible way her voice could have been heard throughout Baltimore, Antonia still whispered to Aaron, "What?"

And Aaron answered, "I'm trying to figure out why you have that look on your face."

"I'm not the one with the look on my face," Antonia said, not in a whisper, but still not in her full voice. "You're the one who's looking at me as if I've just done something wrong."

"I was looking at you because of the way you were looking," Aaron said defensively.

"Oh my goodness," Maggie said, turning to Aaron. "This is ridiculous. What's wrong with you? Your mother's here watching the show, watching what we do for the first time and you're picking on her over the look on her face. Maybe she was thinking about something."

Aaron looked at Maggie, then at his mother, then lowered his head and said, so deeply beneath his breath it was as if he'd swallowed the words, "That's what I'm afraid of."

"What?" Maggie asked.

"Nothing." And Aaron went on studying his copy.

So Maggie looked over at Antonia and said, "Are you enjoying the show, Mrs. Jackson?"

"Oh, it's just fine. So exciting. But what happened to the men who're supposed to be running these cameras?"

But there was no time for her to learn of the cameramen's fate. The floor director was bringing them back, and this time it was Aaron's chance to tell Baltimore the newest news. And Antonia watched as her son did his best to beat back the disquiet that she was certain only she could see through the affected evenness. It was in his eyes, which wanted to do something else, look someplace else but had to stay trained. It was then, only then, that Antonia asked herself: *Am I really vexing him so?* She watched him from home every evening, and sitting there now only feet away from him, she couldn't recall Aaron ever being this agitated. But within the context of the news colliding with his personal life, it all made painful sense to her. Still, the unnerving sound of Aaron stumbling through the news about a man that his mind, lacking hard evidence, could not accept as his cousin crept up her backbone like a thief headed for the place where it would steal her repose.

". . . and Baltimore's newest resident, barely in the city for three weeks, is off to do his first consent—excuse me, *concert*, not here in Baltimore, the town that loves to claim him, but in his true home-town of New Orleans tomorrow night where he's expected to, uh," and Aaron stopped after the blunder, as if uncertain of what he should say next, as if it weren't all written out for him. Then he looked squarely into the camera and continued, ". . . where he is *expected* to, uh, play to a sold-out house for both nights of the engagement. He's explect—I'm sorry, *expected* to add some jazz standards to the end of his program of Brahms, Chopin, and Bartok. We'll go now to Clint Hargrove who's live downtown with the president of the Meyerhoff Hall with more on Mr. Cannon's concert to be played there next month."

By now, Antonia was sitting on the edge of the chair, ready to get out of that studio once the getting was good. She looked into the lap of her skirt, where she found the truth—she shouldn't have been there, shouldn't have even come. And when she looked up to catch Aaron in the eye, she wanted to disappear, because she knew his angst. What kind of mother would cause a son so much vexation? She had to get out of there, and there was nothing that could stir up a tempest in her heart more than being stuck like a fly in molasses in a place she needed to leave. So when Maggie was through with what she had to say, and the place could relax for the next two minutes or so while they were out for another commercial, Antonia gathered her bag to her side and stood.

But before she could tell Aaron what she was about to do, he said, "Ma, I think it would be best if you waited up in the news-room for me. Is that okay? I mean, you can see all the stuff that goes on up there that helps us put the show together." Then he looked as if he were holding his breath in anticipation for some sort of explosion. And he bore guilt in his eyes.

"Yeah, that's just fine," Antonia said, stepping across the wires and cables to make her hasty exit. She wasn't exactly sure what she was feeling, but it came somewhere close to shame. Whatever it was, it kept her from looking at her son when she said, "That's exactly what I was thinking. In fact, I just may go on home."

"No, Ma, don't go home. I'd like you to wait for me until the show is over. Just go on up to the newsroom. You can go back to the room where we were sitting, or you can go to my office. It'll be in the opposite corner from where you'll be once you enter the newsroom. Don't leave, though." And he sounded as if he meant it from his depths.

That's when she turned to see him and said, "Okay, if you really don't want me to leave, I won't. I'll just wait for you," and she faded from the studio.

When she reached the newsroom she stopped to get her bearings, then spotted Aaron's office, exactly where he said it would be. If she could have walked in a straight path, it was across the newsroom in the corner diagonal from where she stood. So she started off through a narrow opening between cubicles and found herself in a larger space and just to her right was a stool that sat in front of what looked to her to be a smaller version of those robot cameras in the studio. She jumped a step back, at first, thinking she was on camera until common sense prevailed and she realized that there'd be no cause to have that camera filming the empty space of the stool. Then she turned to see the wall the camera faced, then looked back to stare at that camera with pride because she, all on her own, figured out that this was where Aaron and sometimes Maggie sat when they had to give the highlights of the news before *Oprah* was over. And that wall, she thought with a faint, sideways smile, as she looked again to the wall in the back of the newsroom, is what's behind them. Her attention was snatched away from the wall when she heard someone addressing her.

"Don't worry, Mrs. Jackson," Mark said. "That camera's not on."

"Oh yes, I figured as much." She went over to where Mark stood in front of a large glass-enclosed room. "Why is it that not one camera around here is being run by anybody? I mean, when did cameras start thinking for themselves?"

Mark gestured with his head toward the camera and stool and said, "That stationary camera over there is called our flash cam, and because it's stationary we don't need a man behind it to run it. It's actually operated, you know, turned on and off, by the people up in the control room. But I suppose what you're talking about are the cameras in the studio. Well, they're called robotic cameras. And actually, they are operated by someone. Do you recall seeing a fellow sitting by the door when you first went into the studio?"

"Yes, I do remember him. I thought he was just there to keep people from coming in there. Like a guard, you know."

"Well, I suppose he does that too," Mark said with a questionable laugh. "But if you had looked at the desk where he was sitting, you would have noticed that he has three joysticks with which he operates all three cameras. One man doing the work of three."

"Robotic cameras, you say?" she said with a wide grin. "That's exactly what they reminded me of—robots." Then her smile evaporated when she continued, "So, what happened to the other two cameramen?" Antonia asked. She couldn't even answer for herself why she had fixated so on those out-of-work cameramen.

Mark stared blankly at her for a second or two, then said, "I'm not quite sure what you mean, Mrs. Jackson."

"The men who used to work the cameras by hand. What happened to them? Did they find other work?"

"Well, I guess so. I don't really know. The robotic cameras were being used when I joined the station, but if those guys were friends of yours or something, I can find out."

"Oh no," Antonia said in a panic. "I mean, I didn't know them. It's just that for some reason I wondered about them since computers seem to be taking over a lot of people's jobs these days."

"Yes ma'am, I understand," Mark said awkwardly, but with the politeness due to an albeit nonsensical senior woman. Then he switched the subject from the robot cameras. "So what are you doing in here and not in the studio?"

"Oh, well I decided to come out here and wait for Aaron in his office. It's not as exciting in there as I thought after all."

"I see. Well, why don't I take you in to see the real brains of the operation around here." And he turned to head into the glass-enclosed room. He checked over his shoulder as if to make certain she was following, and once inside the room said, "This room is the heart of the news operation, and that guy over there is the one that makes it all beat. This is Bill Watts. He's our assignment editor. He's the one who gets the calls when there's news and he's the one who decides which reporter gets which story. Bill, this is Mrs. Jackson, Aaron's mom."

"It's a pleasure, Mrs. Jackson," the man growled with a throat full of gravel, which was somewhat disconcerting since he was rail thin with spindly hairless arms that swung awkwardly when he moved, and his face was gaunt. All of him came together in a way that would make someone expect a pip-squeak of a voice, not the voice of a man who sounded as if he'd just swallowed broken glass. He cleared his throat, but it didn't much matter as he went on to say, "You can have a seat over here, if you'd like. Things can get pretty crazy at any given moment, but right now things are calm, so I can tell you a little bit about what I do in here."

Bill said, "Now what happens is that when calls come in about a story, I have to decide whether or not it's newsworthy and whether to send someone out to cover it. Most of the time it's news, but sometimes it's not."

"How can you tell which is which?" Antonia asked as she leaned farther back in her chair away from Bill.

"Most of the time I can tell just by asking a few key questions to the person calling. Sometimes, though, I'm not sure, so I send someone out anyway, and if there's nothing there, the reporter will call back here and say that there's really no story. That doesn't happen too often, though."

"Uh-huh," was all Antonia said before she began staring off into her thoughts, trying to pick and choose and piece together the words for the question burning a trail through her mind. And only when it was formed completely, succinctly, did she say, "What happens if a story directly involves a reporter or an anchor?"

Bill looked at her with narrowed eyes and asked, "A reporter covering the story, or just another reporter at the station?"

"Either one."

"Well, a reporter directly involved in the story would not be sent to cover it, I would guess. I mean, it's never happened. It's never happened, at least since I've been here, that any story we've covered directly involved a reporter or anchor at the station." Then he studied her for several intense seconds before asking, "Mrs. Jackson, just out of curiosity, what makes you ask that question?"

Antonia looked past him at nothing particularly fascinating, except she saw the true answer to that question that was dancing and prancing and taunting her off in the distance of her musing.

But she could also imagine the look of complete and utter astonishment it would spawn from Bill. So she let her eyes slide back to his face and said, "It's just something I've often wondered about." Then she clutched her purse to her and stood, pushing the chair toward Bill. "I've got to get going, now. Would you just tell my son that I had to get on home. I'll see him later." And with that she was on her way, and torn. She was quite torn.

Aaron stepped onto his mother's front porch and brushed away the flakes of a newly fallen powdery snow that had collected against the black wool of his coat. The light of day was long gone, and the only brightness that shone on him was the dim glow of the porch lantern. He took out his key and stopped just before opening the storm door to identify the muffled sounds from beyond the windows. There was thumping, and sliding, and then a moan and sigh. So he then moaned and sighed, already wearied by only the thought of the task that lay ahead of him once inside.

Pushing open the door and stepping into the darkened hallway, Aaron slid his key from the lock and shut the door, then stood in the shadows of the faint light of the living room, dreading the command he knew was imminent. He slid into the room through the opening of one of the French doors as he peeled off his coat. "Hi, Ma. What're you doing?"

She looked at him with eyes that were not surprised at all to see him and said, "I'm doing interpretive dance," she said good-naturedly, with a mock high-brow accent as she leaned forward onto the back of the chair she was pushing and stuck one playful leg out behind her. "What do you think I'm doing? I'm moving this furniture back the way your father wants it. He'll be home on Sunday, so I thought I'd get a jump on it. I've got a lot to do, so come on over here and help me."

Aaron undid his tie and slid it off. He dropped it onto his coat, which he'd strewn across the sofa. He went to where his mother struggled with the awkwardness of the table lamp and took it from her. His face strained, revealing doubt, he then chuckled and said, "Geez, we've shuffled this furniture around the room so much, that I honestly forgot where this thing goes."

"Oh, stop it," Antonia said with a self-conscious smile. "We don't move this stuff around that often."

"Every other month counts as a lot to me, Ma."

"All right, all right. Just put it over there in between those two chairs. Then we'll move the sofa back into place. That's going to be the toughest," she said with a round fist on one hip and a troubled face. Then, it seemed, out of nowhere and completely without context, she said, "Are you and Maggie having sexual problems?"

Aaron set the table lamp in place and straightened the chair that had been pushed astray in the move. Scarcely able to believe what he'd just heard, he couldn't think of anything more fitting to do than simply follow through with the only thing in the room that made perfectly good sense to him at that exact moment. There was nothing in his history with his mother that would have prepared him with words to respond to such an unprecedented question. And while he'd become accustomed, through the years, to his mother's non sequiturs, there was no telling how even she could have taken the leap from clandestine furniture moving to his sex life without stopping to breathe. Unless, he suddenly thought, she was trying to avoid what he believed she knew he was ultimately there to discuss, and he couldn't imagine a better way to evade the discomfort of *his* question than suggesting he discuss with his mother his sexual performance with Maggie.

He looked over at the sofa where his mother had stooped to get her grip on it for the haul back to its home just in front of the windows that faced the front porch. And he would have joined her, would have gotten to the other end of the sofa and hoisted it up, doing what he knew his mother thought he was there to do, except he could not find a way to move. So he shifted his weight to his other leg, just to make certain he could, then shoved his hands into his pockets in the manliest way before finding the calm to say, "Ma, I don't know what made you ask me such a question, and believe me, the last thing I want is for you to tell me, but rest assured that I'm not going to answer that even if there were a problem, which there isn't, but I still would not talk about something like that with you."

"Well, that's fine. It's just that Maggie was talking to that fellow Josh, and she didn't know I was there. She said something about New Year's Eve being like bad sex the way you wait and wait for something to happen only to have nothing terribly special happen. I thought she was talking about you, that's all."

Aaron nervously scratched his neck and looked up at the ceiling, where he pondered just what advice his mother might have given him in a universe where he would take her into his confidence over such a thing. Then he decided that the mere thought of that kind of talk with her crossed too far over the line of reason, so he said, "Yeah, well that's just Maggie talking her talk. Maggie might say anything. She's a lot like you in that way." Then Aaron turned and sat in one of the chairs beside the table lamp, knowing he had to say what he'd come there to say. "Ma, can you come over here and sit for a minute? There's something I want to talk to you about."

Antonia let go of the bottom edge of the sofa and stood straight up to look at her son. She smiled distantly at him, then went slowly to the chair on the other side of the table lamp and sat on the edge. Turning to face Aaron, she said, "I know what you're gonna say."

"No, Ma, I don't think you do." Aaron moved to the edge of his chair and leaned closer to his mother. He drew in a slow, deep breath then blew it out, wondering the whole time how a man confronts his mother about her lifelong obsession that had always stood between them, without the boy in him quaking with fear. So he just let it out. "Ma, today I experienced a feeling that I never thought I would have, and that was a fear of you. I was absolutely terrified of what you would do, and I can't live like that. Coming to my job like that with the tape of Agnes Cannon, Ma, was just going too far with this whole thing and it has to stop."

"I know, darling, I know. And believe me, I knew it for sure after I got there. That's why I didn't stay around, because I was really ashamed. I could see that you were afraid that I might say something or do something to disturb the show and have my say about Agnes and Clayton and the whole mess, but please tell me that you know in your heart that I would never do something like that to hurt you."

Aaron shifted and slouched back against the chair. He stared out the window at the falling snowflakes that were illumined by the lamplights lining the walkway as they carelessly made their descent. And there was something in their falling that took him deep inside himself to look for the spot where he might find that kind of faith in his mother; the faith that she would not place that piano-playing interloper of her heart over him in all that she did and all that she thought. He searched, but to no avail, because for the whole of Aaron's life, Clayton had always come first. Aaron realized in that moment what he had always known was true— throughout his life, Clayton Cannon had been like the older brother who had been touched by the divine golden light that would let him do no wrong. The older brother who lettered in every sport and brought home straight As, and always said please and thank you, and yes ma'am and yes sir, and never ever sassed, and always got the girl, and then grew up to become a bright star of the world of classical music; except Clayton Cannon was worse than any older brother could have ever been because he wasn't Aaron's brother. Moreover, he wasn't even real, not in any practical sense. He wasn't a physical presence for Aaron, at least not in any significant way that should matter other than the fact that he was worshiped by the woman who should have been worshiping her only son. And that's exactly why Clayton mattered because in the world that Aaron's mind had created around the thought of Clayton Cannon, it was Clayton's physical absence that made him more of a threat than if he had actually challenged Aaron for the love of Antonia with brawn and free will.

So now, Aaron's mother waited for him to reassure her that his trust in her had not been shaken or weakened by one ill-conceived act. And actually he could assure her that his faith in her had not been compromised by only one misguided trek to the news station. What he couldn't tell her, though, was that his expectations of her had been lowered in random moments from the very first day, thirty-two years before, when he was just five and impressionable and already forming an interminable cognizant memory of Emeril and Clayton that had been ratcheted into his consciousness by Antonia. And since that was something he needed to tuck away for another time, on another day when there wasn't furniture to move and snow falling outside through which he'd have to make his way home soon, he kept as loyal to his belief in truth as he could when he said, "Yes Ma, I know you would never deliberately hurt me, and I'm not even saying that you hurt me today. It's just that today was the very first time I've thought in my gut that you had really gone way too far, over the top of what is acceptable and reasonable with this Clayton Cannon thing. Bringing that tape recording to me at the station . . . I don't know, Ma. I don't know." He wouldn't continue because if he did, he would have been forced to admit what he'd beaten down inside of him from the time he had the mind and heart to reason. Aaron would have to admit that with all things pointing to his mother's sound mind, it could all very well, most probably be true.

He got to his feet and slapped his hands together in one loud clap as if to clap away the thought like some bothersome gnat. And with his mood seemingly altered by the magical smack of his hands, he reached for his mother's hand to get her to her feet and said, "Okay, let's get going. We've got some furniture to move."

So Aaron followed his mother over to the sofa and went to his respective side after watching his mother return to the spot where she was obviously most comfortable. He crouched and got his grip, and just as he was about to count down to the moment when he'd heave, Tippy the Fourth jumped onto the sofa and smack onto Aaron's coat. "Get offa there!" Aaron yelled with all the discontent he'd always had for that cat. "Go on, shoo! Get on, now," and this time he reached over to give the cat a firm swat.

"Don't you hit her!" Antonia scolded. She stood straight and nearly arched her back in catlike defense of her feline love. "She's not hurting a thing," she said as she gently picked up Tippy the Fourth and set her down in the hallway just outside the French doors.

"I just don't want all that yellow cat hair all over my good coat," Aaron said, sulking as he picked up his coat to brush off yellow hairs he couldn't see but was certain were there.

"She is not gonna hurt your coat" was all Antonia said as she closed the doors between the living room and front hall.

Then Aaron mumbled beneath his breath, "Stupid cat," knowing his mother wouldn't hear as she went back to her couch-hauling squat.

"All right, are we going to do this or not?"

"Okay, all right, just let me get back in place," Aaron said, laying his coat gingerly across the rocking chair that had come up from New Orleans with his mother.

So once more, Aaron went to his side of the sofa, and actually got his end in midair. Antonia managed to lift her end a few inches off the ground, just high enough to move it several feet. In fact, they got Antonia's end just past the edge of where the chairs sat before the phone rang.

"Just let it ring, Ma. We need to get this done."

"I can't leave a phone ringing. I just can't," she said, pleading with her son with her eyes. "I'm gonna set my side down now, all right?"

"Okay," Aaron said as he blew out a breath of annoyance. "Just tell whoever it is that you can't talk long because I've got to get on home, Ma."

"Just keep your calm. I won't be long," she said before she picked up the phone.

Aaron watched his mother's face shift as she listened to the voice on the other end of the phone. And as if it were as reflexive as a blink, his eyes narrowed with curiosity when he heard Antonia say after a series of *uh-huh*'s, "So why're you calling now to ask me? I've been here. You've known where I've been for forty years because that's how long I've been writing to you."

And that's when Aaron knew. So he stood erect from where he'd crouched, stepped in front of the sofa, and plopped himself down for what he knew would be the duration. But then, to his surprise, his mother was reeling it in.

"Okay. All right," she said with a curious grin. "Okay. Okay, I'll be there. I'll see you then. Bye, now." She put down the phone and joined Aaron on the sofa, only she sat at the complete opposite end.

"So who was that?" Aaron asked.

She smiled distantly then slowly took him in, announcing, "It was my past, my present, and my future. I'm going to lunch with Agnes, darling. At Clayton's!" Then she looked over at her brother's picture sitting on the sofa table and spoke to it, "In just five days, I'm going to finally meet your boy."

Aaron took her in for several long seconds before closing his eyes. He had to get away, just remove himself emotionally, because in those moments, after he actually heard what he never thought he would, Aaron couldn't decide if this was the beginning, or the end. Letting out a long, deep sigh, as his head slumped onto the pedestal his hands and forearms had formed, he could only manage to say, "Well, this is just fine."

CHAPTER
6
·

Ellen chopped garlic with slow precision, and with the memory of her mother's fingertips. She remembered with fondness the way she used to take her mother's hand, then breathe in a nose full of her mother's fingers that filled up her every sense with the perfume of garlic. They made her think of a woman who cared enough about her family that she didn't mind that her fingers carried a pungent smell. All that mattered to a mother like this, Ellen always believed, was that her family was well fed with the food that only she could prepare for them.

When she looked down, Ellen noticed that the tips of her fingers were wet with a thin film of garlic juice. So she laid her knife softly on the chopping board, then tore off a paper towel. She dabbed her fingers dry on the paper towel and pressed them lightly on the side of her belly, where she thought the baby's face might be. "This is what mommy's fingers are going to smell like when they're not smelling like hospital antiseptic," she said quietly with a thin smile she knew her baby couldn't see but believed it could feel.

And she was so caught in that moment with her baby that she didn't even hear Rick when he walked into the kitchen.

Rick took her in with puzzled eyes for a few seconds before asking, "What are you doing?"

"I'm letting the baby smell my fingertips. I want to let this baby feel comforted by the fact that his mother's always going to cook good food. This garlic smell will make that clear, I think."

"Well, I don't think that baby's going to appreciate the smell of garlic any more than an adult can, to tell you the truth."

"I like the smell of garlic. I think it smells like perfume."

Rick said nothing to that as he put a tablecloth and matching napkins onto the counter. "Okay, I found the tablecloth and napkins. Do they need to be ironed?"

Ellen regarded him with a certain disturbance, then took her fingers off of her belly. As she picked up the knife and went back to chopping garlic, she said with the barest edge, "What do you think, Rick? Do they need to be ironed?"

Rick looked at them, then blew out a breath of exasperation and said, "Yeah, I guess they do. I'll go and iron them." As he scooped them back into his arms and went to go into the laundry room, he turned to Ellen and asked, "Tell me again why we're all of a sudden doing this?"

"Because, Rick, we've never had any traditions in my family. We never had Sunday dinner, or anything like that. Today is Sunday, and what better day to have a tradition than on a Sunday?" She chopped some more, and then as she felt Rick about to walk away, she continued, "Even Thanksgivings and Christmases weren't celebrated in any traditional way. It was just Ma and Poppa, me and Aaron. We didn't have any cousins, or anything, who would come over for dinner because they all lived down in New Orleans. One year, I remember, Grandmommy Jackson came up from Louisiana, and that was nice enough. That felt like tradition, except that was the only year she came up. I don't want that for this baby. I want this baby to feel and live with a tradition that only family can give."

Rick walked toward the laundry room, and just as he went in, yelled back, "Well, I have to tell you. I still find it odd that your family never did this on Sunday. I mean, in a way that's as dispassionate as a white family."

Ellen's eyes widened with the prick of aggravation. She turned toward the laundry room, and asked, "What in the hell do you mean by that, Rick?"

"I just mean that my family never did anything like the bonding through Sunday dinner, and neither did any of the other white families I knew when I was growing up in Brooklyn. But black families did. It shows a kind of emotional detachment not to, that's all."

Ellen stretched a difficult smile onto her face, then walked to the aperture of the laundry room and said, "Rick, honey, I know you don't mean to, but what you just said sounds racist."

"Racist?" Rick said with amazement. "How in the world do you get racism from what I just said? I was saying that white families have no passion to bond through something like that, and I was just making the same comparison with your family. That's all."

"Rick, the tradition of a Sunday dinner is not cut along racial lines. I know many, many white families who get together every Sunday for dinner come hell or high water. It's not even a tradition, it's a command. Maybe that your family didn't or the other white families that you knew didn't either says more about your family's values and those of all the families you knew in Brooklyn."

"Well, all I'm saying is that it's been my experience that white families who have that tradition are anomalies. White families just don't seem to do that."

"That's what you say. I don't agree."

"And I don't agree with you. So I guess we just disagree on this."

Ellen watched him as he tested the iron to see if it was truly hot enough by putting an old-fashioned licked finger to the metal plate to hear the sizzle. All he had to do, she thought with a certain annoyance, was check the ready light. But anyway, that wasn't even half of what bothered her as she stood there waiting for something else. How dare he, she screamed in her head, stand there so sure in his correctness. She had thought to walk away, simply go back to chopping her garlic and not pick at something so insignificant. Except that it wasn't so terribly insignificant in the grand picture. If he thought she came from a dispassionate family, then that shouted out loud exactly what he thought of her level of passion. So she went closer to where he stood ironing and prodded, "Rick, how can you say that we don't have any passion for one another in my family?"

Rick ironed with a stiffness that said he wouldn't answer. But then, he looked up at Ellen and replied, "Because, Ellen, your family is so uptight about how you really feel about things."

"How can you say that, Rick?"

"Because it's true. You and your brother go around talking about how your mother has lost her mind thinking that Clayton

Cannon is her nephew, but not one of you has ever admitted the truth about that whole thing."

"The truth," Ellen said flatly. "And the truth as you see it is what, Rick?"

"Neither one of you has ever admitted that you hate your mother for showering him with the attention that should have been yours and Aaron's. And you two have never admitted that you hate Clayton Cannon even more for just existing."

"I don't hate my mother, Rick," Ellen said with eyes that had glazed over into steel.

"Well, okay Ellen. I'll give you that. Maybe you don't hate your mother. But you certainly don't love her without questioning her love for you. And you all have just never dealt with that. All I'm saying is that Sunday dinner would have brought that out a long time ago, and I don't think any of you want that. So Sunday dinner could never have been a tradition for your family."

Ellen stood for a few seconds contemplating whether she should give him a dose of angry passion, but she was sure it was clear in her bearing without actually bringing up his shortcomings. But then, as if it had a will of its own, her ire simply slipped from mind to sound when she said, "Well Rick, I wasn't so uptight about my feelings when you cheated on me. I told you exactly how betrayed I felt and how hard it was for me to forgive you. But most importantly, I told Aaron all about it too. He was my rock through that whole time, and I don't know what I would have done if I hadn't confided in him. You call that lacking passion with one another?"

Rick put his head down as if to focus on one stubborn spot of wrinkles as he moved the iron back and forth and in circles over one corner of the napkin. Then, looking only partially at her, said with the faintness of residual shame, "That's different, Ellie."

"How is it different, Rick?"

And then, looking fully at her, he firmly answered, "It's different because I'm not a part of this whole thing, Ellie. I never have been. Everything going on between you and your mother was here long before I came into the picture. I'm sort of like filling. The backdrop. I'm like some pawn in this thing, except I'm a pawn without a clearly defined purpose. That's what I am. I've always been a pawn who's had no idea how or why I'm being used, but the one thing I know for sure is that I'm most definitely being used."

"Rick, where is this all coming from?" Ellen said with an amazed stare directly into his eye.

"Well, Ellie, I'd say it started the day you took me home to meet your family. Surely you must remember that, because you didn't give your family a clue that I was white. Do you remember that?"

"Yes," Ellen said softly, staring at nothing in the far-off corner of her mind.

"Yeah, well I'll never forget it. I'll never forget that it felt like someone was peeling the enamel from my teeth when your mother followed your father into the dining room and, before she could even get out of earshot, said, 'All I have to say is that I have nothing to say.' She was in shock, Ellie. In shock because here was this white boy sitting in her living room loving her daughter, and he was not what she expected her daughter to bring home as a suitor."

Ellen went to the corner of the room and sat in the chair that was pushed between the wall and the dryer. She leaned her head against the dryer disconsolately. "Rick, we've been over this again, and again. I don't know how many ways I can tell you that I didn't think you being white would bother my mother so much."

Rick went to her and knelt in front of where she sat. He took her hand gently and said, "And see, Ellie, I can't believe you could have thought such a thing. Because to just say that you didn't think she would have had a problem with me being white doesn't explain it completely enough for me. Why didn't you think it would bother her, Ellie? And really tell me why this time."

Ellen let tears that had come to her from some surprising place fall freely as she gazed into her lap. Then she said in precisely measured words, "Because, Rick, she had wanted this white man to be her nephew for as long as I can remember. It never even crossed my mind that she wouldn't except a white son-in-law as lovingly. I'm always dealing with my patients' subconscious actions regarding their impending motherhood, but I guess if I were to look at my subconscious feelings about my mother, I'd have to admit that in a way, I thought I might be gaining her favor by marrying you."

Rick's face shifted further into shock with each word Ellen spoke. His lips moved in unintelligible shapes, as if his words were about to be dubbed seconds out of sync like a bad foreign movie, before he said, "Ellen, you just don't get it, do you? Antonia has never seen Clayton Cannon as a white man. To her, he's as black as she is, and you are, and Aaron and Junior. In your mother's eyes, the only thing white about Clayton Cannon is his skin. In her soul, in *his* soul, she sees him as black."

"I know that now," she said. And then she leaned into Rick and let him fold her in his arms. She let her head fall softly on his shoulder, and she simply stayed there. Safe. Impassioned.

It seemed to be some sort of miracle to Ellen the way her mother and father, and Aaron, arrived on her doorstep at the exact same time to ring the doorbell as a group. Ellen was all the way in the kitchen, so she drew in a deep breath and started on her way down the hallway, straightening a knickknack here, a candlestick there. When she finally reached the door, she swung it open with the excitement she'd built on top of layers of emotions in varying degrees of genuine joy, and not a little woe. And so there they were, ready and willing, she could only presume, to try something new. So why did all their faces look so dubious?

"Well, come on in," she ordered them. "Don't just stand out there. Come on in for Sunday dinner."

They walked into the front hall, each one with steps more halting than the other's. But it was Aaron who guided the whole group into the living room. He took the three steps down and crossed the room to sit on the couch against the wall. But when he saw his mother and father just standing there at the top of the steps as if waiting for something more formal to bring them to sit, he prompted, "Well come on down and sit. Don't just stand there."

"Yeah, don't just stand there, Ma, Poppa," Ellen said, descending the steps herself. "You don't need to be invited to sit down."

Junior sat down next to Aaron, looking with expectancy at Antonia. And by his example, it seemed, Antonia slid past Aaron to sit next to her husband.

Ellen crossed the room and sat in the chair on the side of the coffee table. She slid off her little ballet slipper house shoe and rubbed her foot intensely, back and forth, on the carpet for a good scratch. "What is it you say, Ma, about when your foot itches?"

"It means you're going on strange land," Antonia answered.

"I think it means you need to wash your feet," Aaron said as he plucked and dipped a piece of broccoli from the platter Rick was placing in the middle of the coffee table.

Rick laughed as he stood up.

Reacting to the encouragement, Aaron said, "It is funny, isn't it? And true, too."

And by now, the rest of the room was having itself a healthy chuckle at Aaron's humor when Ellen, with her laughing tears welling in the corners of her eyes, said, "Aaron, you are so nuts. It does not mean my feet need washing."

"Well, that's what it sounds like to me," Aaron said, taking her in with eyes he'd forced to become sober, humorless, as a part of his gag.

Ellen laughed her way down to a comforting simmer, then reached over and took her brother's hand. "See, this is what I'm talking about. Us getting together every Sunday and doing just this."

"Just what?" Junior asked.

"You know, having fun with the laughs and the jokes. This is fun!"

"Ellie, we've laughed and had fun before. What is it you think we do, get together and discuss all the troubles of the world?" Aaron said, looking with a wrinkled forehead at his sister. "Besides, if we haven't had fun before, we'd be one miserable group of people calling itself a family."

"I know we have, Aaron. We've just never done it on any traditional day like today. Like Sunday dinner."

"So, is that what this is about?" Antonia asked once she finished crunching a baby carrot. This is about starting a family tradition?"

"Yes, Ma, it is. We've never had a family tradition."

"Sure we have," Antonia replied. "What about Thanksgiving? What about Christmas?"

"Only twice a year, Ma? Two days when we're *supposed* to, almost by law, get together? They certainly don't count. Anyway, I'm talking about a once a week where we can talk to each other about what happened in our lives the week before and what we hope will happen in the week to come."

"And that day can only be on Sunday?" Junior asked earnestly.

"Yes, Poppa. Sunday is holy, and the most sincere day of the week."

"I see" was all Junior said sagely.

"Well, Ellen, I'm hurt that you don't think we have tradition in this family," Antonia said with a certain mother's sadness that seemed to come from someplace very deep and lined with guilt. "I mean, I've always tried to make Thanksgiving and Christmas dinners as nice as I could possibly make them."

"Thanksgiving always is, but Rick and I are in New York every Christmas with his family, so that doesn't count for me. But then there's New Year's Eve. You and Poppa don't even come over on New Year's, but Aaron does." Then she paused and remembered New Year's just past and continued, "Except this past year when he took Maggie to Paris."

Aaron looked at his sister at first, then let his eyes drop to the floor saying, "Umh, yeah."

"What?" Ellen asked, wanting to understand the emotion behind his near-grunting response.

"Nothing," he said as his face seemed to have smoothed over the recollection of an unwanted memory.

"Anyway, this is what this family needs. Some kind of tradition."

"All black families do this Sunday dinner thing, you know," Rick said, as if it were a solid fact, as he dipped a piece of broccoli and ate it.

Aaron took Rick in with narrowed eyes that clearly had far more behind them than their focused bafflement. "How do you figure all black families have Sunday dinner? I think we can deduce from just what's been said here that at least one black family doesn't, and we're not alone."

"Well, most black families do it," Rick said as he sat on the arm of Ellen's chair. "I'm telling you that's why I loved that movie *Soul Food* so much. Something as simple as taking the time to get together with all of your family at one place once a week can keep a family strong. That's where family values are. Maybe the lack of Sunday dinner is the breakdown of the moral fiber of America."

Antonia's face was set with the exactness of a woman about to defend her singed honor. "I think the moral fiber of this family has done just fine without dinner every Sunday," she said. "You don't turn out two children like Aaron and Ellen without a strong moral fiber."

"Oh, Ma, I wasn't talking about this family at all when I said that," Rick said, with more contrition than any man could offer up, finding himself having just insulted a mother. "I'm just saying that there are families out here that are weak and end up going astray, and maybe if they had some kind of tradition to cling to like Sunday dinner, then it could make them stronger. My family would certainly have been stronger with a tradition like that." He reached over and took a handful of vegetables, munched a cauliflower floret, then continued, "I mean, my family's done all right, and we're strong enough, just like this family, but it could be better. That's all Ellen's trying to do with this new tradition of having dinner every Sunday. She's trying to bring this baby into an even stronger family."

Antonia looked at Junior, who was staring at nothing, then she looked at Aaron whose raised eyebrows seemed to share her sentiment when she said, "I don't know, Ellen, this is a sweet idea, and all, but how long will it last?"

"What do you mean? It'll last forever. We'll do it forever. That's what a tradition is all about, Ma."

"I know, but what I'm saying is that, it seems to me, you're trying to turn this family into something it's not. Something it's never been. I've never been the kind of stand-all-day-in-the-kitchen-cooking-on-Sunday kind of mother, and I'm never going to be." Then she looked with the impatience of a fed-up mother at Rick, let out a long breath, then continued, "Now, for all these years, we have been a strong family, in our way. That's how every family exists, Ellie, in their way. And in our way we have had our traditions. They may not have happened every Sunday, but don't you and Aaron remember how I taught both of you how to do the Second Line? And don't you remember how we listened to my zydeco records and I taught the two of you all about it? That's our tradition that we brought up from New Orleans, and I've given it to you two. So don't sit over there and tell me that we don't have tradition in this family, because we do, and we always have."

"Well, of course I remember that," Aaron said. "I just don't know why it stopped."

"It didn't stop. You two just weren't interested anymore," Antonia replied. "There was just no time."

Faster than she thought a woman with a lap full of child could get to her feet, Ellen was standing, looking squarely at her mother and nearly yelling, not with anger but with definite passion, "Exactly! No time!" She reeled in her voice and softened her eyes on her mother when she continued, holding an imaginary umbrella over her head, "I remember the Second Line." Then she dipped and did a few steps to the perfection of her mother's training. And when she came back from her second dip, she stood where she stopped and said, "But there was never any time. Sunday dinner would have given us that time." She turned and shuffled from the room, uncertain of the future of her Sunday-dinner tradition. Wondering if tradition could indeed be found in its own way in every family. Mostly, though, she found a certain prickly discomfort in the conjecture of exactly what her son would one day think of his family.

CHAPTER

7

•

Aaron walked into Ruth's Chris Steak House, where his mother told him to meet her, and took off his sunglasses so that his eyes would adjust to the shock of the murky light in the room. As he looked around for her in the shadows of the restaurant, he wondered what she could possibly want now.

Then he spotted what seemed to be the back of her head in a booth. He had started toward her when the hostess approached him, but before she could offer her assistance, he said, "Thanks, but I see who I'm here to meet."

The woman smiled coyly the way she might have blushed in the presence of a rock star, then said, "Okay, that's fine."

When he got to his mother, she was pouring four packets of sugar, two in each hand, into a tall glass of iced tea. She looked up at him to find his disapproving face. "Don't give me that look. In the summertime, you can drink this stuff with only a drop of sugar, because all you want it to do is cool yourself. In the winter-time, though, it's a completely different thing. In the wintertime you know this stuff needs lots and lots of sugar."

"Whatever you say, Ma," Aaron said as he slid into the booth to sit across from his mother. "I'm just amazed that all that sugar doesn't lock your jaws shut."

Antonia only smiled as she crumpled the empty packets of sugar and set them aside. Then she took a sip of her tea, and said, "Well, ever since you were a little boy, you couldn't stand sugar.

You were the only child I ever knew who couldn't even be bribed by a sweet treat."

"And nothing has changed. Sugar leaves a sour taste in my mouth," Aaron said plainly as he picked up the menu and opened it. He let his eyes slide over it for a second or two, then looked at his mother and said, "You know I don't have a lot of time. I've got to get to work. I told them that I'd be in late, but I can't make it too late."

"Oh, I know. I'm not going to keep you. I just wanted to talk to you about what's going to happen after I have lunch with Agnes."

Aaron looked at his mother questionably as he wondered what had happened between the night of the call from Agnes when he'd left her home and this day that made her think her lunch with Agnes would be more than lunch. So he took her in and smiled faintly, then said, "And what's going to happen after you have lunch with Agnes?"

"Well, Aaron, don't be so naïve. The only reason this woman could possibly want to have lunch with me is to settle this whole thing. She's ready to tell me that Clayton is Emeril's son."

Or, Aaron thought behind his wry smile, Agnes is luring her to lunch for the purpose of having a restraining order placed against her, but instead he asked, "What makes you think so, Ma?"

"Aaron, what else could it be?"

The possibilities, as he thought of them, were endless, but the one his mind kept looping around to had to do with Agnes telling his mother to stop harassing her, or else. And the or else was too daunting to ponder, so he said, "I don't know, Ma."

"Well, anyway, I wanted to talk to you to find out how you're going to feel about our lives changing the way they're going to. I mean with Ellen, there's never any question for me with how she feels because she never misses an opportunity to tell me. But you," she said as she stretched her hand across the table to touch his, "you have always been a quiet thinker. You don't say much at all, but I know you think about so much, though you've never told me about it. But I know you must have been thinking something as far as all of this is concerned."

"Not really, Ma," he said, fully aware that he was lying to his mother by virtue of never telling her for all these years how much he hated the very name of Clayton Cannon. He'd lied to her in the vaguest way possible—by omission.

"Well, how are you going to feel about our family changing? I mean, it's always just been me and Junior and you and Ellen. Now we're going to be adding Clayton, his two boys and his wife. For the first time in our lives we're going to have extended family right here in Baltimore, and on top of that, he's famous. You mean to tell me that you've never thought about any of that?"

"No, I haven't, Ma" was all he said as he looked off to notice a group of four women who had come in and were smiling— actually, more like giggling—and whispering while pointing at him from their booth just across the room. So he smiled and nodded to acknowledge them and their adoration. And just as he'd always done in such a situation, he couldn't help but let the thought trot across his mind to wonder if these white women would have even noticed him, much less bothered to speak in such an obsequious way, if he were just any old Aaron Jackson and not on television every day. He came to the same conclusion each time—of course they wouldn't. He only remembered what he and his mother had been talking about when he heard her continuing with the matter at hand.

"Well, I just thought you might be jealous, thinking that Clayton might come into my life and replace you, or something."

Aaron was suddenly completely present, those women be damned, as he took his mother in with eyes that were severely focused. It could not be possible, he thought, that she is only now thinking of the possibility of a jealousy he might have for Clayton. How did she think his ten-year-old self had regarded Clayton? How did she think the fifteen-year-old Aaron managed to maneuver through the cruelty of high school and the torture of a mother distracted by Clayton Cannon without a silent and internal rage exploding in him at the mere mention of the name Clayton, or even the simple word *cannon* in any context? And so now he didn't know—could she really have been that checked-out for his entire life, or was that dark place where he'd always kept his torments really undetectable by the ordinary eye? But hers should have been a mother's eye that could see what didn't appear to be there.

So he softened his eyes on her, smiled thinly and said, "Come on, Ma. Feeling replaced? That's the feeling a little boy would have, not a grown man."

"Okay, well I was just making sure." Antonia sipped her iced tea, then noticed the table of women who were still staring at Aaron. She looked back at Aaron and said, "You see those women over there making goo-goo eyes at you?"

"Yeah, I saw them," Aaron said quietly.

"I'll tell you, it's just like having lunch with Billy Dee Williams the way women go wild over you."

"Ma, nobody's going wild over anybody," he said with a somewhat embarrassed chuckle. "You know, it happens. People recognize me."

"Yes, they do, and that's because you're such a good anchorman."

Just then, Aaron's eyes came in contact with those of a man walking toward him, smiling with his hand stuck out, as if it were guiding him straight to Aaron.

When he got to the table, he said, "Hey, man. You're Aaron Jackson from the news. How you doin', brother?"

Aaron gave the man his hand for a shake, then replied, "I'm doing just fine, man. How's it going?"

"Yeah, it's going real good, brother, real good. I watch you all the time, because you're one of the few brothers on the news who's not frontin', you know, actin' like you're some black version of some white boy, or somethin'. You keep it real, brother, and that's what we need out here—some positive brothers like yourself doing positive things, and still keepin' it real."

Aaron smiled and said, "Thanks, man. I appreciate it."

"No problem, brother. Check it out, my name's Roscoe, Roscoe Massey."

"It's nice to meet you, Roscoe. And this is my mother, Antonia Jackson," Aaron said, pointing his hand at his mother.

"Aw, man, this is sweet. This is real sweet," Roscoe said as he beamed with some sort of pride and held his hand out for Antonia's. "How you doin', ma'am?"

"I'm doing just fine, young man," Antonia said as she shook Roscoe's hand.

"I know you must be proud, 'cause this is a good brother you've raised up here."

"Yes, he's a good man. And it makes me even prouder to see people like you come up and treat him like royalty. I will never, ever get enough of that."

And Aaron knew she wouldn't, so for as much as he wanted to get on with his day so that he could get in to work, he wanted Roscoe to stay there for just another minute and then another, to extend for as long as he could the star his mother saw in him through the sycophancy of strangers. Then, as if through telepathy, two of the four women made their way over to the table and stood behind Roscoe patiently. How did they know, he wondered, that I need the adulation to continue? How did they know that his mother should be made never to forget that her son was as outstanding, in his own way, as Clayton Cannon? So when Aaron craned his neck to look around Roscoe, he greeted the women.

"Hi," one of them giggled.

"We were wondering if we could get your autograph," the other one said.

And that's when he realized that they were young, really young, perhaps nineteen, maybe twenty. So he said, "Certainly."

They handed him a napkin that had the restaurant's name emblazoned in the middle of it, and he took his pen from inside the pocket of his jacket and, with an illegible flourish, signed his name. He handed the napkin back to the first woman with a smile and took another napkin from the other woman and signed it. Handing it back to her, he said in a way in which he acknowledged that he owned the moment, "Thanks. You all have a good day, now."

"Thank you, Mr. Jackson," they both said as they walked away.

Roscoe, smiling and nodding, finally said, "Boy, I guess the honeys just come out of the woodwork. I guess you don't even have to look for a date."

But before Aaron could say anything, his mother said, "He sure doesn't. He's going with Maggie Poole, and she's all his eyes can see."

Aaron said nothing as he looked at her with certain incredulity. She wasn't trying to convince herself, he knew, because she was as sure of him and Maggie as she was of Clayton. What he didn't know was whether she knew just how much he needed convincing. So he slid his eyes into Roscoe's face and said, "Yeah, Maggie Poole and I are dating."

"Maggie Poole?" he questioned. "The woman who anchors with you?"

"Yes," Aaron said.

"Huh," he said questioningly, as if he had such authority. "Well, what do you know. I don't know, though. I just don't see that, but I guess you never know." Then he stood staring off at the lights overhead as if contemplating whether Maggie and Aaron should stay together. "Okay, well it was good seeing you, man. I'm gonna bounce and let you good people get on with your lunch. But you stay positive, brother. And you take care, ma'am."

"Thank you. You take it easy," Aaron said.

"That's right," Antonia said. "Bye, now."

"So anyway," Antonia said as she buttered a roll, "I think that once Clayton knows that we're his family, we should all establish some sort of tradition so that we don't lose the connection. Tradition, Aaron. Like meeting once or twice a month on a Saturday night at a restaurant downtown for dinner. That is if he's in town.

At first Aaron didn't know why what she'd just said gripped him so viscerally that her words twisted and turned in his gut until they simply plain out irked him. As his narrowed eyes took her in, he repeated *tradition, tradition,* in his mind, trying to imagine starting such a tradition. Trying to imagine having to interrupt his only day off to fight Saturday-night traffic all the way downtown by dinnertime just so that Clayton could live like black folks once a month or so to keep true to the flip side of his life. And anyhow, he thought, how in hell does Clayton's presence suddenly get to start a tradition when Ellen had just attempted to do that? "Where did you get that?" he finally asked.

"Get what?"

"That whole thing about meeting downtown for dinner. You hate to go downtown to eat. You've always said there're too many people down there. Why can't he just come to Thanksgiving and Christmas dinner and be done with it."

"Well, I just thought it would be nice. That's all. Is something wrong with it?"

"Well, I just think it's odd that tradition is suddenly important to you now that Clayton might be coming around. I mean, what's wrong with the telephone for not losing the connection."

"Well, it was just a suggestion, Aaron. We don't have to do it."

"It doesn't matter to me, Ma. If that's what you want, then you should start it."

The waitress came over to take their order. Aaron hadn't even looked at the menu, but knew what he wanted. "Prime rib," he said. "What veggies come with that?"

"It comes with a house salad of baby greens, a baked potato, and your choice of broccoli or squash," the waitress said with an overstretched smile.

"Squash, please."

"And I'll have the sirloin tips," Antonia said.

The waitress wrote down Antonia's order, then said, "Okay, so that's it? Can I get you something to drink, sir?"

"No, I'm all set here with the water," Aaron said. And as he watched the waitress walk from the table, he was captivated by what he saw just beyond her. It was her, he was certain. But as magical as it was to see her, this fortuity was anything but that with his mother sitting there, with everything but a pompom set to sing a cheer for Maggie.

So now he could see that she saw him, and she smiled, just as sweetly as he remembered. When the hostess collected her and her lunch companion—thank God a woman, Aaron thought—they headed directly toward him. And he with his mouth open with not a word to say.

When they were only steps from the table, she slowed as if she would most certainly stop, which she did. "Aaron, it's really good to see you again," and she bent to kiss him softly on his cheek.

Her lunch companion stopped along with her, then grabbed her arm and seemed to try her best to whisper, "That's Aaron Jackson! I didn't know you knew Aaron Jackson!"

Tawna smiled awkwardly at Aaron, then at the woman and said, "Yes, I do. But you go on to the table and I'll be right there."

Once the woman left, Aaron said, "It's really good to see you too, Tawna. What are you doing out here, of all places?"

"Oh, I suppose I'm doing what you're doing—having lunch," she said, then laughed with a lightness that infected him. "You know I work around here, right up on Painters Mill Road."

"Oh, sure. T. Rowe Price, right?"

"That's right."

And then he felt his mother's heat on him, so he said, "Tawna, this is my mother, Antonia Jackson. Ma, this is Tawna Stokes. Tawna is new to Baltimore."

"It's nice to meet you, Tawna," Antonia said, shaking Tawna's hand. "How are you liking Baltimore, so far?"

"It's real nice, ma'am. I moved up here from Winston-Salem. It's very different here. Bigger, you know."

"Yes, I'm sure. I've only been to Winston-Salem once. It's a very sweet town. So what brings you here?"

"My job, and the need for a change of pace."

"Oh, well I guess we all need those every once in a while," Antonia said, boring a focused eye into Aaron that said she'd have plenty more to say once Tawna was gone.

And Aaron saw, but only Tawna was on his mind in that moment, and there was only one thing he could think as he heard Tawna's voice in a hazy distance talking to his mother about something he really couldn't hear: *God, she's so lovely.* Just as that night when he remembered sitting across the table from her at a dinner party, he was now equally as mesmerized by everything that came together to be her. Her laugh that was certainly more blithe than any spirit he'd ever known within himself. And when she talked, it was with an effortlessness that said she was intimate with every part of herself. But more than that, there was this southern thing to her, not necessarily a belle quality, but just an easy southern way that seemed to make her more womanly than any woman he'd ever known, and he was certain that it was something maybe only she could carry off to such heights of perfection. When he became aware that Tawna and his mother were finished chatting, he asked, "Tawna, do you have a card so that I can reach you? I'd like to have lunch with you one day because I'd like to talk to you about doing some investing with T. Rowe Price."

Tawna looked at Aaron with definite surprise, then she smiled and, digging into her purse, said, "Oh sure. It'll be my pleasure, Aaron." And she handed him her card.

"Okay great," he said eagerly, slipping the card into his jacket pocket. "I'll call you soon, Tawna. It was really good to see you again." Aaron took the hand she offered him as she bent to kiss him good-bye, and when he kissed her on her tawny cheek, it was closer to her lips than he had intended, but certainly not as close as he wanted.

"I'll look to hear from you," was all she said to Aaron as she went to leave. "And Mrs. Jackson, it was very nice to meet you."

"Same here, dear," Antonia said as she watched Tawna leave. Then she slid her eyes into Aaron's and said, "All right, what was that all about?"

"What was what all about?"

"That whole thing with that girl over there. You're sweet on her, and don't you sit here and try to deny it, because I could see that you didn't know what to do with yourself. You fidgeted in a way you haven't done since you were in the seventh grade and discovering a girl's womanness for the first time."

"Ma, I don't know what you're talking about. All I'm interested in is finding out about the financial services T. Rowe Price might offer."

Antonia looked skeptically at him, then twisted her mouth into a wry smile and said, "Okay, if that's what you want me to believe, but keep in mind that I know that you work with a fancy New York stockbroker on Wall Street." Then she took away her smile and grew stern when she said, "I just don't like this one bit, Aaron. You know how much I love Maggie, and now you just sat right here in my face and made a date with another woman. And I don't care what you want to call it, you were making a date with a woman you're sweet on. I would just die if you broke things off with Maggie to be with that woman, Aaron."

Aaron picked up his ice water and took a large swig from it. As he put it back down on the table, he thought, You might get pretty doggone sick, but let's hope you won't die. But he actually said, "It's just lunch, Ma."

CHAPTER
8
•

Junior's suits were flung formless across the bed as Antonia went meticulously through each pocket for miscellaneous remnants of his trip to New Orleans. This man's pockets, she thought as she pulled receipts and stray pieces of paper from the folds of his gray slacks, are just like her purse. The major difference being that she would never, except maybe under the circumstance of death over which she'd have no control, allow Junior to clean out her purse. There was no telling what he'd find that she wouldn't want him to see. The thought of it sent a spasm through her that shook her shoulders. Why, he'd be likely, she thought, to find out exactly what she paid for things, like the amethyst earrings she told him she got at a half-price sale in Hecht's but actually paid nearly a king's ransom for them at Bailey, Banks and Biddle. That's why now, sitting going through her husband's pockets with his full knowledge, she knew he had nothing to hide. And before he left to go out to Aaron's, he said what he always said when he saw her going through his pockets—"*If you find a million dollars, it's mine.*"

Before Antonia got to the last suit in the pile, she gathered up all the others and put them in a sack. The pickup man from the dry cleaners would be coming any minute, and she wanted to have everything collected and in the sack for him when the doorbell rang. When she went through the pants of the last suit she found only a spent tissue and a dime. But when she picked up the jacket, something metal tinkled. She shook it again, just to make certain, then stuck her hand into one pocket. Nothing. When she went to the other pocket she felt it. So she pulled it out and studied it—two gold pieces of what seemed to be a broken locket. She studied the first piece; it was well worn, but definitely pure gold. Antonia would have held on to the immediate thought she had of the broken locket, that it was obviously an antique piece Junior had picked up in New Orleans as a surprise for her once he'd gotten it fixed, until she picked up the other piece and looked at the inside of the locket that held the picture of a boy. But it wasn't until she turned it over that she saw the sight that could have stopped her heart had it been weaker, and completely let pass the thought of it being a gift for her—*To Cora, with love from JJJ* is what the inscription read.

Suddenly, the yellow glow of the lamp on the nightstand had cast a dimness in the room for her. And nothing within these walls was as it had been just seconds before. Everything had taken on another nature—Junior's chair that sat in the corner was merely a chair, Junior's chest of drawers was nothing but a bulky mystifying place of compartments that only kept secrets, and Junior's side of the bed was just a space. What had this room been to him, where they had created two lives from the intimacy in which they pleasured in the private moments of their own life?

Antonia made certain there was nothing in any of the other pockets, then slid the jacket hastily into the sack. She got up and paced around to the other side of the bed and back, wondering just how she'd let him know that he's a cheating low-life bayou rogue fool. However she'd do it, though, she knew this much— she'd take that broken locket and throw it right in his face before she'd say one word to him. But what was the standard after forty-two years of marriage? This is what she didn't know. After all those years put into one man, she wondered, would it be reasonable to tell him to pack all that he called his own and go back to Cora, whoever the hell Cora might be? And then, as if it were a physical entity with breath and spirit, the truth tapped her on the shoulder. "Cora Calliup," she said softly. That crazy Cora Calliup from next door down in New Orleans who grew up to have a different daddy for each child and named each one of those four children after herbs. Sage, Basil, Rosemary, and Thyme; and oh God, she screamed in her mind while putting her hand to her forehead like a fainting belle as she looked at that picture once more. If this boy, one of those herb children, belonged to Junior, it would be enough to make her curl up and die, she believed. What could Junior want with her? she wondered. One thing she knew for certain, that locket told her that it was definitely something. She and Cora had gone their separate ways years ago, but would Cora's loyalty have gone with it? There should be no statute of limitations on friendship, particularly when it comes to laying with another friend's husband. "What kind of trash have you become, Cora?" Antonia said into the locket that had become the inorganic incarnation of a long-ago friend.

Thank God for the ringing doorbell, she thought as the chiming reached her all the way up in the bedroom, otherwise her runaway mind would conjure images of Cora and Junior, which she'd be stuck with forever. Antonia grabbed up the bag of Junior's suits, then went into her closet, took down the three dresses, stuffed them into the bag, cinched it up, and went quickly into the hallway and down the stairs.

By the time she got to the door and opened it, the man looked as if he had just about had his fill of standing there in the cold. "I'm sorry it took me so long, Mickey," she said.

"That's quite all right, Mrs. Jackson," Mickey said, holding out his hand for the sack. "How many do you have here today?"

"Five of Junior's suits, and three dresses."

"All right, Mrs. Jackson. When do you need them?"

"Oh, I guess by Friday."

"Friday it is," he said as he handed her the slip onto which he had just scribbled something. Then he turned to leave with the sack. "You have a good evening, Mrs. Jackson."

"You too. And thanks for the late pickup."

"No problem."

Closing the door on him and the cold, she paced the hallway, clutching tighter to the locket she knew was digging its impression into her palm. So when she opened her hand to look on it, that's when she knew what she had to do. Antonia grabbed up her furry coat from where it lay across the settee, took her purse and keys from the side table and headed to the door. She closed it behind her and crossed the porch. Still clutching that locket, she went down the path that was covered with a thin layer of ice, and she was so mad she didn't even care that she marched like fury going off to war, nor did she care that her feet could slide out from under her with any one of those steps she took to bring her crashing down with a broken something or other. How could any of that matter when she had to get to Aaron's to make a scene? It was only when she descended the three steps at the end of the path that she was aware that that locket she clutched with such a vengeance was actually hurting her hand, but she would not release her grip. Poor Antonia was so beside herself with her anger at Junior, then at Cora, then at Junior and Cora, that she couldn't remember where she'd parked. As she searched first up the street then down, she heard Jackie call to her.

"Oh, hello, Jackie, honey," Antonia said, distractedly. She watched Jackie tip across the ice to her, doing her best, it seemed, to balance on heels too high and too thin.

"Miss Antonia, I must have called your name three times. You all right?"

"No, Jackie dear, I am anything but all right. Look at this," and she opened her hand for Jackie to see the broken locket.

Jackie looked quizzically at it, then asked, "You broke your locket, Miss Antonia?"

"This is not my locket, honey. This is the broken up locket of Junior's mistress. That's right. Junior's having an affair, and I'm going out to Aaron's where he is and send him right back to Jesus, the only one who could ever love him with what he's done."

"Now, Miss Antonia, I just can't believe this. Are you sure? Sometimes things aren't always the way they seem. Sometimes we can jump to all kinds of conclusions that don't have nothin' to do with what's real, you know."

"I know that this locket says 'To Cora, from JJJ with love.' I think that makes things pretty doggone real."

Jackie glanced quickly at the locket, then said, "Well all I'm saying is that you just never know, and you don't wanna go accusin' him of somethin' he may not be guilty of."

Antonia blew out a breath that she seemed to be holding since she first took that locket into her sight. "Jackie, so what are you saying I should do?"

"I'm saying that you should calm yourself down before you go out there throwin' that locket in his face."

Antonia let out a small chuckle, then asked, "How did you know I was going to throw this in his face?"

" 'Cause that's sure enough what I would do," and she laughed with Antonia.

So while the anger was still with her, Antonia had just been gently shaken from the red-hot intensity of its core. She looked down at the locket, then back into the compassion in Jackie's eyes and asked, "So what am I supposed to do now?"

"I guess you're supposed to work on how to approach him with this, and then work on forgiving him."

Antonia let out a laugh, its undertone steeped in sadness. "Well now," she said, "forgiveness. That's something altogether different. That's going to take some time, if it ever happens at all."

"Naw, Miss Antonia, it's gonna happen. I don't have no doubt about that. I see the way Dr. Jackson looks at you, and I know he loves you bigger than anything he's ever felt or done in his life." Jackie looked off across the street, and when she turned back, it was as if she had collected a bit of sorrow in her glance away. "And I'll tell you something else, Miss Antonia. I'm out here because I know I'm never gonna have somebody love me that big, or look at me with that kind of love. So just don't throw it away. Please."

Antonia took Jackie's hand and smiled thankfully. With the other hand, Antonia put the locket into her coat pocket. She looked around the street where passing cars were getting scarcer by the minute, with the falling ice that only now began to irk her. Then she turned to look deeply into Jackie's eyes and said, "There's nothing happening out here for you, girl. Why don't you come on inside and have some tea with me. Besides, you don't want anybody who'd come by here tonight because they'd have to be unbalanced to be out here on a night like this looking for sex."

Jackie laughed heartily, then said, "I guess you're right, Miss Antonia." And she followed Antonia up the steps and down the path. When she got to the end, she hesitated. "Are you sure it's okay? I mean, I see the way Dr. Jackson looks at us out here, and the way he hurries you on when you stop to talk to us."

"Oh, who cares," Antonia said sharply. "I'm not okay with him sleeping with Cora Calliup, but he's doing it, so to hell with him. Besides, this is my house too."

When they stepped into the front hall, Antonia noticed how

Jackie shuddered, then rubbed her hands and arms now that she was inside the warmth of the house. Antonia smiled, took Jackie's jacket, and laid it with her own across the settee, then led her into the kitchen. As she went to the stove to get the teakettle, she saw Jackie take a seat at the kitchen table—in Junior's seat. Antonia poured out the water that had been standing in the kettle and put more in. When she set it on the stove, then turned on the burner, she said, "Don't look so tentative."

Antonia walked toward the table, picking up a container on the counter as she went. Once she sat, she opened the container and said, "Do you want a brownie? They're fresh-baked, and not Duncan Hines either. Fresh-baked from scratch."

"Thanks," Jackie said as she reached over and took one out. "You know, Miss Antonia, I don't know what it is I said that changed your mind, but I sure am glad that you didn't go and get in Dr. Jackson's face before you really know what's going on."

Antonia plucked a napkin from the holder in the middle of the table, took a brownie from the container, then broke off a piece. She held it in midair and said, "You know, I'm not altogether sure what it was you said, either, except that your words made me think of what I've always said, which is that I would never leave a man for cheating on me because cheating is just a symptom and not the problem. As long as you're willing to get to what the problem is, then you can make the symptom go away. That's what I've always believed, but I guess it's a lot easier to believe that when your husband isn't cheating on you. Once your husband cheats on you, the rules change and the dynamic shifts." She ate the morsel of brownie and continued, "Anyway, what you were saying about things being different than they appear made me think of that, and I'm only going to know that by getting to what the problem might be."

"There you go," Jackie said excitedly. Then her expression grew curious as she finished her brownie. "So what do you mean by the problem?"

"Well, what I mean is, what's going wrong in the marriage, maybe, or in his life, or our life together that made him use cheating as the solution."

"I see," she said as she chewed another bite of brownie. "So I guess maybe it's the same thing that makes men come to me, huh?"

Antonia looked at her suddenly with that bolt from the blue and replied, "Well, I suppose you're absolutely right." Then she got up and went to answer the whistling kettle. She set two mugs from the cupboard down on the counter and took two chamomile teabags from the Mason jar where she kept them, put them in the cups, and poured water in each. And as she took the cups of tea to the table she saw Jackie looking at the CD on the top of the stack that sat on the edge of the table, pushed against the wall.

" 'Babyface—MTV Unplugged NYC 1997,' " Jackie read aloud. "Is this yours, Miss Antonia?" Jackie said with joyful surprise in her voice.

"Yes it is. Do you want to hear it?"

"You listen to Babyface?"

"I do," Antonia said, getting some pleasure from this young woman's reaction. "What is it, you think I'm too old for Babyface?"

Nodding her head as if pleased by the discovery of this side of Antonia, Jackie remarked, "I don't know, Miss Antonia. I mean, I knew you was cool, and everything, but I had no idea just how cool you really are."

"Just because I like Babyface's music?" Antonia laughed, quite enchanted by the closing of the generational abyss between herself and Jackie through music. Then she said, "Well, I don't want to burst your bubble or anything, but I do happen to think that Babyface is a perfectly silly name for a grown man to call himself."

"Yeah, you're right," she said with a giggle as if she were a pubescent girl talking about rock stars with one of her peers. Then she continued, "Except that I think he goes by his real name these days, but I don't remember what that is."

"Well, it doesn't matter. He's talented, and that's all that counts, so it doesn't much matter what he calls himself."

"That's the truth. Like Louis Armstrong. What kind of name is Satchmo? Sounds too close to sambo, but he sure could play that horn."

And now it was Antonia's turn to look at her with a stunned glee. "You know Louis Armstrong's music? That's hardly the music of *your* generation, any more than Babyface's is the music of mine."

"Well, I played trumpet in a band when I was at Lemmel Middle. So they had one of those assembly programs at the school where this Dixieland band came and entertained us, and they played some Louis Armstrong music. That just did it for me. I fell in love with the way he played that horn, and I would try to imitate him. I've always said that one day I would go to New Orleans and see where it all began and listen to that music."

Antonia smiled at her own little slice of heaven. There had always been something drawing her to Jackie, but she never knew what to name it, how to see it, or the best way to hear it. Now she knew. "Jackie, do you know that I'm from New Orleans?"

"No way!" she said with as much excitement as if she were sitting there talking to Satchmo himself. "I never knew that. Oh my God, why don't you still live there? Why'd you come to tired old Baltimore?"

Antonia considered the best answer for a few seconds, then said, "To tell you the truth, I'm not altogether sure why or how I ended up in Baltimore, except that it mostly had to do with Junior's career. He wanted more than anything to be over at Hopkins, so here we are. I suppose if I had had things my way, I'd still be in New Orleans."

"Oh man, I can't imagine what it was like growing up there with all the good music and the good food." Then she stopped, looked down at her tea, and back up at Antonia with a certain shame in her eyes. Nonetheless, she continued, "And women like me add color to the place, not shame."

Antonia stared into her tea as she put dollops of honey into it. She thought of shame and its nature, and she thought of how a shameful life was not in what one did, but in how one did it. Whether in Baltimore or New Orleans, what Jackie did with her body and soul was not shameful because she did it honestly. She hid from no one—except, perhaps, she thought, from the occasional cop, but that was a legal matter. Mostly, though, she did not hide from herself. But for Junior and Cora, whether in Baltimore or New Orleans, what they were doing was full of nothing but shame, because they lived in deceit; and they hid, from their own souls, from each other, from her. Shame, shame, shame on the both of them.

When she realized she'd dropped more honey than she'd wanted into her tea, she hurriedly put the honey dipper back into the jar, saying, "You're a good girl, Jackie. Don't ever let anyone make you believe that you're not."

Aaron stacked five plates on the edge of the counter then put five mismatched napkins on top of the stack. He carried them into the dining room, where Maggie was busy unfolding the tablecloth. He still placed the pile of plates and napkins on the table, so distracted was he by wishing he'd not gotten on the phone within a minute after leaving his mother's house two days ago to tell Ellie about their mother's luncheon at Clayton Cannon's. Despite that he doubted his mother's story, Ellie was compelled to call this impromptu family dinner-summit sans their mother the night before Antonia was due downtown. And so here he was, heading back into the kitchen and plucking five forks and five knives from the drawer, then examining each one for spots and encrusted bits of food which his dishwasher was known to leave behind every now and again. And as he scraped with one thumbnail, he wondered if he'd actually heard right when he heard Ellie say something about taking their mother for a psychiatric workover. He may have even heard her say something about their mother needing to go to a home. Aaron really couldn't be certain since the mere mention of the words *Ma* and *psychiatrist* spoken by Ellie in the same sentence and with such certainty sent a puff of fog into his mind that clogged his ability to perceive anything as real.

So at the moment all he had to hold on to was his knives and forks. And when each was inspected to his approval, Aaron gathered them up in two clinking, clanking bundles and went back into the dining room. When he found Maggie standing there on the other side of the table with the tablecloth still in her hands, but nowhere close to the table, he regarded her with narrowed, questioning eyes. "Maggie, I thought you were going to set the table. Why haven't you at least put the tablecloth on?"

But all Maggie did at first was point, with her head, to the stack of plates and napkins on the edge of the table. Then she said, "It's a little difficult to spread the tablecloth when the plates are on the table."

Aaron looked at the plates then blew out a troubled breath and snapped sarcastically, "It wouldn't have killed you to move them."

"Well, it won't kill you to move them, either," she said with a reactionary sharpness in her tone.

So Aaron simply picked them up without another word, and placed them on the chair at the head of the table.

Maggie snapped the tablecloth out over the table then let it float down, as if it were being lowered on the wings of small birds, to cover the table. She smoothed out the puckers and then made certain it hung evenly on every side. And after she'd picked up the plates to place one at each end, then two on one side and one on the other, she stood back and twisted her mouth, saying quietly and mostly to herself, "It's uneven. There should be another person coming."

And as he put the knives and forks on either side of the plates, Aaron replied, even though it was clear to him that she wasn't speaking for the sake of a response, "Well, it's not like we could invite my mother since she's going to be the topic of discussion."

"Is that what's bothering you?"

"What do you mean?"

"Come on, Aaron. It's all over your face and in everything you say. You're bothered by something. Is it this talk that Ellie wants to have about your mother that's getting to you?"

He sat down in the chair at the far end of the table and took in every crease in Maggie's forehead. Even though its incarnation was, he believed, a mere shadow of her murky judgment, maybe of him, maybe of the whole situation, in that look of hers, in the constancy of her judgment, he found an oddly begotten solace. So he nonetheless answered, "Well, yeah, I guess it is. Do you remember how bothered you were when Colette was sixteen and went around telling everybody that she was born in Canada?"

Maggie chuckled quietly with the memory of her daughter, then said, "Yeah, of course I remember that. I'll never forget that, because even when I confronted her, she stuck to her story, 'Mommy, I'm Canadian,' she'd tell me. But that was a nightmare because it didn't have any basis in reality and I had some genuine reason to worry about her sanity. There's nothing your mother's saying that's that far outside the realm of possibility, Aaron."

He looked at Maggie with stern and steely eyes for several prickly seconds, then said, "Except that Clayton Cannon is not her nephew."

"All right, Aaron. That's what you say, and quite honestly, I don't believe he is either. But you and Ellie can't slap a crazy sign on her back just because she believes it. She's got circumstantial evidence, and peoples' lives have been broken *and* redeemed with circumstantial evidence."

"Maybe," he said as he rose from the chair, pushed it into the table, and then continued, "But her circumstantial evidence is weak, Maggie."

She took him in with hard eyes that seemed to be filled with some lesson she had to tell. "Maybe this isn't about circumstantial evidence at all, Aaron. Maybe what this is about is a scared little boy who wants to keep his mommy all to himself. I'm telling you now, you need to get over it, because if that man is your uncle's son, it's going to happen, it's going to come out no matter how much you deny it."

And though Aaron knew there was as much truth in the light of what she'd just said as there was in the rising and setting of the sun, it was either in the way she said it, or the way sarcasm had claimed her expression when she said it, but Aaron could only submit to the flash of anger that wanted to claim him. What struck him most in that moment was how she knew no tact when it came to her opinion. "Maggie," he said, "you don't have any idea what you're talking about. My mother is my mother and Clayton Cannon will never change that fact."

The doorbell rang, which set Maggie off on a rush to put the napkins underneath all the forks. "You go get the door," she commanded Aaron. "I'll unwrap the food and put it out."

When Aaron opened the door, he saw his sister's belly before it was clear to him that she was attached to it. And her coat couldn't come anywhere close to fastening around it. That gut of hers could have just as easily been the big beer and sausages paunch of a turned-around trucker trying to find his way. He blinked furiously, then shook his head playfully and said, "Good God, Ellie, you haven't had that baby yet? It looks like you've grown just since the other day."

Ellie stepped through the door, humorless in that way expectant mothers can get when the subject of their form is broached. She moved past Aaron and said, "Oh that's real original, Aaron. Do you have any more of your incredible witticisms?"

Aaron let Ellie and her sardonic challenge pass, extending his hand to greet her husband. "Rick, how's it going?"

"I'm hanging in there, Aaron. Just playing the waiting game for this baby," Rick said with a tension that seemed, with his sheet-white pallor, to speak to the edginess of his eminent fatherhood.

"Yeah, well, I guess we all are" was all Aaron said as he took Ellie's and Rick's coats and laid them across a chair in the living room on his way back to Maggie.

"Hi, Maggie," Ellie yelled.

"Hi, Ellie. Hi, Rick," she responded through the door that was opened when Aaron walked into the kitchen. She took the last container of food from the bag, then looked sideways at it and asked, "What is all this stuff, by the way?"

"It's fried catfish. Ellie loves it, and so does my dad."

"I thought you said you were going to Boston Market. Where did you get all this, the fish, the cornbread, the red beans and rice, the fried chicken, and the collard greens?"

Aaron looked over the food, wondering why she had to ask. They had gotten takeout from that place at least a half-dozen times on their way home from the station, so where else could she possibly think he would have gotten it? "Doesn't it all look familiar to you?"

Maggie studied it for a couple of seconds, then with the elation of a child discovering a speck of the world on her own, said, "Micah's! Oh, wow! This is a treat!"

"And string beans. Shouldn't there be a container of string beans in there too?"

"Yeah, they're right here."

Ellie walked into the kitchen, hand-in-hand with Rick, saying, "Boy, it smells good in here. What's for dinner?" Then she stopped short and regarded the takeout containers with an ironic, skeptical smile. "When you said you'd have dinner for us, baby brother, I thought that meant you were going to be cooking it—you know, homemade food. And Maggie, as good a cook as you are, how could you possibly be a part of this store-bought food caper of his?"

"Ellie, on Friday when I called you after I left Ma's and you said you wanted this meeting, I offered to have dinner because I thought it would make things easier, but I never said I would cook it myself," Aaron said with his voice dancing on the edge of defensiveness.

And Maggie, with an unyielding conviction, only said, "Besides, girl, once you've tasted this food you'll be glad that neither one of us cooked."

"Maggie's right," Aaron said with the low-level stirring from the innate pressure he'd always imposed on himself to please his sister since somewhere around the time of his arrival into her life. "I wouldn't just give you all any old carryout. I got it from that place down on Reisterstown Road called Micah's."

Ellie looked at him with her face twisted in confusion, then asked, "On Reisterstown Road?" She continued without waiting for an answer, "I thought that was a church. I treated a woman at the hospital a few months ago who said she went there, and some of her church people came in one day and prayed over her."

"Well, it's the same place. It's a church *and* a restaurant," Aaron said.

Through stunned and nearly mocking laughter, Maggie said, "What in the world do you mean, Aaron?"

"I mean that on Sundays they have church there."

"You're lying," Maggie said as if without a doubt, and her laughter yielded to straight-faced incredulity. "He's lying. Whoever heard of such a thing?"

"No, I don't think he is," Ellie said determinedly, yet in a manner that said she understood the absurdity of it all. "I told you, I had a patient who went to that church."

"So what do they do, sit at the tables and have church, or do they take the tables out of there and roll in an altar?" Maggie asked with an urgency that said she truly needed to know.

"I don't know, Maggie, I've never been there to worship," Aaron said impatiently, hoping to put an end to her questions about something he'd pondered long ago and many times only to find his musings pointless and meandering. "I'm just telling you, Maggie, that it is a church *and* a restaurant. Besides, I thought you knew. This seems like one of those quirky things you'd definitely know about since you know about every other one of Baltimore's oddities."

"Well, I've got to tell you, this one I missed." Then a low rumble of a laugh boiled up again from her belly, when she said, "But our people sure can combine stuff, can't we? I mean a place to feed your soul in every way, I guess is what they were thinking. Next thing you know we'll be finding all kinds of combinations of things with places like MR. JIMMY'S CHICKEN AND WAFFLES SHACK AND LAW OFFICES, or something like that. Go in and get your divorce and a little chicken and waffles with some collard greens on the side."

Rick stood stiffly by Ellie as she and Maggie and Aaron exploded in laughter throughout the kitchen. And though the humor seemed to elude him, he still said with a bookish weightiness that sucked the room dry of its former lightness, "Well, sociologically speaking, I think there's a connection to food and spiritual worship with African-Americans. It may even go back to the days of slavery the way African-Americans make food a part of the Sunday ritual. Going to church, and then having Sunday supper right after church was like an extension of that fellowship, breaking bread with relatives as well as fellow worshipers. In most parts of the South it's as natural a phenomenon as breathing."

And now that the laughter had stopped, and there was nothing left in his kitchen but Rick's intellectual account of things, Aaron somehow felt dissected. Mostly, though, as he recalled his mother's new tradition of family dinner with Clayton, he felt ganged-up on. When did my mother and Rick become of like mind? he wondered. But he had to take them on one at a time, and right now, all that annoyed Aaron about Rick was hanging right there like stagnant air.

Dissected. There was no better way to define how Rick had just made him feel. As if Aaron, by virtue of being *African-American* were some sort of antediluvian subject to be studied the way an archaeologist might study the bones of prehistoric apes to know their social patterns. The worst part, Aaron believed, was that Rick's white maleness would put up a deflectable wall, built out of all the ways he would deny, deny, deny, that would never allow him to see clearly; that's why Aaron vowed that it was scarcely worth ever trying to tell him. It would be like spitting up in the air—it would just end up falling right back in his face.

And so it continued to echo through Aaron's mind, the way Rick said *"African-Americans"* with such affectation, as if it made him somehow evolved, enlightened and correctly liberal. And this irked Aaron even more. He recalled the times he had argued up a purple storm his reason for disavowing that term, *African-American*. Yet Rick continued to use it in his presence with what Aaron could only deem as sheer disrespect of his view that it was an insubstantial description. Africans from Morocco and Tunisia living in America with green cards, he remembered telling Rick, were as white as Rick, yet these Africans were more entitled to that hyphenated status than those who were once simply known as black and born and raised in America, as were their parents and their parents' parents. Yet a Moroccan or a Tunisian would certainly not be what people, particularly sociologically exact and *up-to-date* white people such as Rick, have in mind when saying African-American. He could still hear himself shrieking this at Rick in their last go-around over the label as he pounded his fist. And so even with what he knew he would be up against this time as well, it would have been like stopping the order of nature as it flows in a river if Aaron had kept himself from saying, "I've told you before, Rick, I've never lived in Africa, nor have my parents nor their parents. And that would be the case for nearly every black person in America."

"Aaron" was all Ellie said crisply, as if her brother should know that she'd had quite enough of his proclamations in the name of his people.

But he continued as if Ellie had said nothing. "As for Micah's following some sort of anthropological tradition possibly brought over from Africa with Sunday supper, I can't say for sure because quite honestly, man, I've never thought enough about it to study it. But I doubt it. It sounds to me more like myth you should be exploring in one of your novels. And if I were a betting man, I would say that there're probably more black families who go to church and then come home every Sunday without feeling the need to do the whole Soul Food thing."

There was a full and hearty silence in the kitchen, ripe for echoes of enmity. And Rick seemed to have wallowed in it all before he finally responded. "You know, Aaron, when I told you that that movie was my favorite movie about African-American family life, I didn't tell you about it to be mocked now for it. And as far as *African-American* is concerned, I have every right to use a term that I consider a respectful way to honor the past, present, and future of an entire race of people that white America never wanted and never accepted in spite of a legacy that they set in motion. Maybe that's not important to you, but it certainly is to me."

With a smile too private to be seen by anyone but himself, Aaron relaxed. And sitting right on the edge of his mind, ready to explode through voice and words was Aaron's question, *"And you don't see this as stinking of your white liberal guilt?"* But instead of saying what would drive his sister to have a fit powerful enough to bring that baby right out onto his kitchen floor, he only said, as carefree as if it were all far behind them, "All right, let's eat."

He put several dishes in Maggie's hands, then gathered up all he could carry of the food and went to head out of the kitchen. And it was only when he turned to see what was keeping Rick and Ellie from following him that he saw Rick's wounded face, the same face of some nameless boy in his memory from the playground of his childhood who could never seem to fit in. Aaron, being who he is, simply could not leave Rick there to flounder in his awkwardness, waiting for contrition that would never come, so he said, "Come on, man. It's cool. It's over. We have a difference of opinion about this and we probably always will. It's no big deal. I say what I feel, you say what you feel. That's just how it goes. That's just family stuff."

"Yeah, all right," Rick said as he looked at Ellie for some sort of affirmation.

She smiled softly, then turned with hardness to Aaron and said, "I get whiplash craning my neck to look at you up on your soapbox, baby brother."

"Whatever, Ellie. Let's just eat."

"Well, where's Poppa?" Ellie asked. "I called him and told him to be here at eight-thirty. He said he'd be here."

"It's only eight-thirty-five, Ellie. I'm sure he'll be here. And he just got off the plane from New Orleans this afternoon, so give him a minute," Aaron said, smiling with the thought of Ellie and Antonia being essentially the same person when it came to their lack of patience. Yet, were he to tell her so, he knew with every bit of instinctual self-preservation that she'd throw a wild fit of temper, so he simply said, "Just relax, he'll be here soon. Besides, you know Ma has probably asked him a million questions about why he's coming out here. That could take time."

"Well, you're the one trying to rush us to sit down for dinner."

"There's no rule that says we have to wait for him if everybody's hungry and wants to eat now. All I'm saying is put the food out to give everybody the option."

"Well, I want to wait for Poppa."

"Do what you want, Ellie," Aaron said firmly, as his fraying patience with her contrariness inched toward full.

Maggie walked past Aaron with her arms full, and just before she went through the door to the dining room, she said in a tone that seemed to consign shame, "Sometimes when I listen to the two of you it makes me glad that I'm an only child. I swear, it's always something with you two. You find the craziest things to fuss over."

Aaron said nothing as he followed Maggie into the dining room. Before he had emptied his hands of the food, the doorbell rang. "That must be Poppa," he said, setting the last dish of food he carried on the edge of the table. He went off to the door with quickness, swung it open, and stepped outside. "Hey, Poppa," he said as he took his father close in his arms and, in spite of the icy wetness from a frozen rain that had been falling all day and was now coating Junior's overcoat, shared a father-son hug that included the standard back-pats required to make it manly.

"How are you, son?" Junior said as he stepped back to hear the answer.

"I'm doing okay, Poppa. Come on in and eat. We just put dinner on the table."

"Have y'all started eating yet?" Junior seemed to ask with some worry as he peeled off his coat.

"Naw, not at all. Ellie made sure of that. She would have chewed off our hands if we had looked as if we were going to as much as take a crumb off the crust of a piece of chicken," Aaron said as he closed the door and took his father's coat.

And from behind him, Aaron heard Rick say, "How are you, Dr. Jackson?"

"Just fine, son," Junior said, handing his coat to Aaron.

But Ellie had a point to make that had to come before greeting her father. "I heard that," she snapped at her brother from the aperture separating the living room and dining room.

"Good, because I meant for you to hear it," he said with humor as he followed his father toward the dining room, laying the coat across the back of a chair in the living room. When he reached his sister, he playfully chucked her on the chin and said, "But that's why you're the family's sweetheart. This family wouldn't be nearly as colorful without all those neurotic ways of yours and Ma's we've come to love."

"I am *nothing* like Ma," she said with a firmness that seemed more intent on convincing herself than the rest.

"You're exactly like your mother," Junior said as he took a seat at the head of his son's dinner table. Then he chuckled and added, "But you only inherited the best parts of her neuroses. The ones that are easy to find charming. That's the only reason why I drove on ice-covered roads to be here tonight, because you made it sound as if it were a matter of life and death when you called me down in New Orleans yesterday." He took his napkin from underneath his silverware and spread it across his lap, then drew in a deep breath. After letting it out, he smiled at Ellie, and said; "Yet, something tells me it's not, but I showed up anyway. It's one of your more charming neuroses—making something out of very little."

"Smooth save, Dr. Jackson. Very smooth," Maggie whispered as she put a kiss on his cheek. She moved around his chair and sat, right across from Aaron, and Ellie sat down next to her. So she said to Ellie, "There are worse people in the world to be like other than your mother."

Ellie took a piece of fish from the platter, then scooped up a spoonful of collards and replied, "That's easy for you to say, Maggie, because she's not your mother. When Antonia Jackson is your mother you're dealing with a whole other ball of wax."

"I suppose so" was all Maggie said before digging into the food herself.

"And besides," Ellie continued as if someone had asked her to, "there is no way I'd do something quite so irrational and neurotic and downright insane as believe some white man is my nephew and then harass his mother until she had no choice but to invite me to lunch. Did you know about that, Poppa?"

"Yeah, that was the first thing she told me today when I got back," he said directly.

Ellie looked incredulously at her father, then said, "You know? And you think this is okay? You're not at all ready to lock her up and keep her from going anywhere near that woman?"

"Look, Ellen, your mother's got a lot of air to clear with Agnes. She's waited a long time to do it, and I think that meeting that gal face-to-face after all these years just might do your mother some good."

Aaron stared for several long seconds at his sister, taken with but not terribly amazed at how swiftly she worked when her will had a particular ambition. And for one mere second he let his mind wander and imagine that she'd already had a room with brown-speckled linoleum floors to camouflage food thrown in fits of rage and walls the mind-sickening color of mint green reserved for their mother. He plucked a piece of chicken from the pile, then said, "Well there's nothing like getting right down to it, hey Ellie?"

"Why waste time, Aaron? That's why we're here, isn't it? To talk about Ma and the way this obsession with Clayton Cannon is making her mind take a turn south. If that's not why we're here then I should leave right now, because I think she needs some serious, serious psychiatric help. That's just my professional opinion."

"What about your opinion as a daughter?" Aaron asked pointedly. "Are you really ready to brand Ma as insane? Because I'll be the first to admit that I've had quite enough of Clayton Cannon, but honestly speaking she's no more obsessed now, Ellie, than she was when we were growing up." He paused briefly to gather his thoughts, which were actually not terribly far from Ellie's, but certainly closer to the fence. He dropped his hands helplessly into his lap, then said, "So okay, maybe she does need to see a therapist of some kind, but you're acting like she's psychotic, Ellie, and needs to be locked away and heavily medicated to protect society at large, or something."

"I think she is psychotic!" She paused, then softened her tone. "Okay, so maybe she's not psychotic, but at the very least she seems close to some sort of dementia. Not in any way where I think she's a danger to others or herself, but certainly in a way where this obsession, which by the way has absolutely no foothold in reality, could make her act out some pretty bizarre fantasies that could have unfortunate circumstances. Don't you think so, Poppa?"

Junior had taken a bite out of his catfish, and without fully swallowing said, "About the only thing I'd be willing to agree with is that she has held on to this Clayton Cannon thing like a hound with a jackrabbit, but the one thing your mother is not is crazy." He looked first at Maggie, then across the table to the other end at Rick. And then as if there was a need to set things right with them, said, "Now, Antonia has always been a little bit different. A little bit eccentric. Why, she did things as a young girl that nobody could understand, especially when it came to that old yellow cat of hers, the first Tippy," and then he laughed, mostly to himself, with what seemed to be memories too numerous to tell. And then he grew serious again, saying, "But now, you two just have to understand all the circumstances that led her to believe what she believes."

"We know it all, Poppa," Aaron said with weariness, wanting to hear anything other than the Emeril and Agnes story once more. He knew it hadn't been told to him every day of his life, but surely, he thought, if the number of times he'd played it in his head counted at all, then without a doubt he had indeed heard it every day of his life. "We've heard all about how Agnes and Emeril had this wild forbidden love affair and then Agnes turned up with a baby after Emeril died."

"Yes, those are the bare facts, son, but it's the timing of the whole thing. I'm not saying your mother's right, but I have to tell you, there's something mighty fishy in the way that gal married Douglas Cannon before Emeril was even cold in the ground, and then nine months to the day after Emeril died Agnes has this baby." He took a bite of his fish, then a forkful of greens, chewed thoughtfully and swallowed. "I guess the clincher for your mother is that on the morning of the day Emeril died, she'd caught the two of them, Agnes and Emeril, having relations. Anyway, my point is that the math never lies, son. It's the only absolute in life. Now, maybe that baby was early and he really is Douglas's son and the date is nothing but a big old coincidence, which personally I think is closer to the truth because hardly any babies are born to that kind of exactness. Then again, maybe that baby came right on time. Either way you look at it, though, that boy came into this world right on time for Agnes, literally and figuratively. So all I'm saying is that your mother has held tight to her belief that that boy's her nephew because the math gave her every reason to."

Many seconds passed without word and very little sound. Aaron lowered, then raised his head as if there were something to add. But there was nothing, because he had never, ever given any thought to the math of it all. Math sure didn't lie, and if what his father says is true, he thought, he and Ellie would be forced to reshape all that mattered. So all he could say quietly was, "I never knew all that about catching Agnes and Emeril on the day he died. Did you, Ellie?"

Ellie never responded, but her silence told Aaron that she had not known.

But then, as if he had given the words to her through an odd telepathic communication transmitted through moving forks, Maggie said, "So Emeril died on—"

"July the twenty-third, nineteen fifty-six," Jackson said like a man who would take the memory of that day into eternity.

"And Clayton Cannon was born April twenty-third nineteen fifty-seven," Aaron said, answering Maggie's next expected question before she would ask. It was a date that had been stamped in his mind as cleanly as his own birthday, and Ellie's, and his mother's and father's—with no fuzzy edges whatsoever around it. And so now that he had the memory, he was left to sit and ponder just what his mother had done with all those birthday cards she'd bought every April 23, the ones emblazoned with some such message as *Happy Birthday To My Nephew* or *From Your Loving Aunt*. And she'd signed every single one, he knew. But he also clearly knew that she hadn't mailed them, so all he could imagine was a strongbox with a combination lock tucked away somewhere—maybe under her bed, or in the bottom of her closet—holding forty some-odd years of birthday cards she had most likely tied with a ribbon of some pale color, and God only knew what else.

Ellie laid her fork on the side of her plate, then looked squarely at Aaron and said, sternly, "So what are you saying, Aaron? You really think that what Ma's been saying all this time is true? Because I just can't talk to you if that's where this is headed. Besides, do you know how few babies are born exactly nine months later to the day of conception? As an obstetrician, I can tell you that very, very few are." And she had the determination of someone ready to walk out.

"No, Ellie, I'm not saying I believe her. What I am saying, though, is that before you slap a CRAZY WOMAN, KEEP YOUR DIS-TANCE sign on her back, we should have a little more patience with her point of view, especially in light of what Poppa just said. I've already set her straight about not coming to my job anymore with this stuff, and she understands that she crossed a line when she did that."

Ellie, with her fork in midair, gave Aaron a stunned stare, as if she had misheard, or he had misspoken. Then, with a tone too calm to be real, she said, "What? Are you telling me that she came to the station ready to go on the air with this nonsense? You didn't tell me about this."

"Well, no Ellie, I didn't tell you about it. I guess her coming to the station was trumped by Agnes calling to invite her to lunch, and when I called you, that was the only thing I had on my mind. Besides, she didn't come there ready to put anything on the air. It wasn't like that at all. She just came there to let me hear a tape recording she had made of Agnes Cannon's visit. For some reason Ma thought that in the conversation Agnes had all but outright admitted that Clayton Cannon was Emeril's son. In actuality, though, she never admitted anything of the sort. Never even came close. But she just wanted me to hear the tape, that's all." Then Aaron looked to his father for help of any kind, a look of empathy, or even as little as a half-smile of encouragement. All he got in return, though, was his father's even eyes that were filled with the resolve of a man, Aaron knew, who had long ago made his peace with having spent the better part of his years loving Antonia while the ghosts of Clayton and Agnes, but most of all Emeril, hovered always right alongside them.

"Well, this is just unbelievable!" Ellie said, her ire clearly visible. "Do you see what I mean now? Do you see what I mean about her actions creating situations that could have ugly consequences?" Then she turned to her father, nearly sticking her head full in Maggie's face, and said, "Poppa, did you know about this?"

"Yes, Ellen, honey, I did know. It wasn't a big deal. No harm was done and I don't think it requires you to overreact about it" was all Junior would say.

"Well, I just don't know what to say. I don't know when any of you will start listening to me," and up she jumped from the table in an explosion of tears, squeezing her belly past her father and running into the kitchen.

Rick got up to follow her, but Aaron stopped him when he stood. "Just let me handle this, Rick. Just give me a few minutes with her."

"But she's so upset," Rick said sharply.

"It's mostly the hormones," Maggie said flatly, as she continued to eat. "She'll be okay as soon as she cries out whatever it is she's crying about, and believe me, she may not even know."

Aaron went into the kitchen unsure of which form Ellie's temper had taken. He'd heard Maggie's account of hormones, which gave his mind a reason for the tears that rarely flowed from his sister's stubbornly dry eyes. Still, her ire could have been in his kitchen blasting every felt emotion like so much spewing hot-spring water, or simply sitting there trapped inside her anger like torpid pond water that's given up on any hope of trying to move from nature's unmovable binds; there was no telling, even if she had been in her ordinary condition because when it came down to their mother—and only when it came to their mother—Ellie's emotions were red-raw and volatile. So it was only when he walked nearer to her that he saw she was shaking as if the room had become a deep freeze. He put his arm around her for warmth and comfort, then asked with a calm that went beyond calm, "Why are you in such a state about this, Ellie?"

She sucked in a generous breath, then deflated herself and said, "Because I'm tired, Aaron. I'm just so tired of trying to make that man not matter."

And Aaron thought about his own futile attempts to do the same before saying, "Yeah, I know. But the fact is, Ellie, he does matter. So now what? What are you afraid of? Because being tired of trying to make him matter would not make you shake with this kind of terror."

She looked up at him with surprised eyes, then looked off, as if in shame. "I'm scared, Aaron, because in four weeks I'm supposed to give birth to this little boy—"

"A boy, Ellie?" Aaron said louder than he immediately knew he should have. Then he brought himself down a level or two before continuing, "You didn't tell me it was a boy."

"We didn't tell anybody. But I especially didn't tell Ma, because I'm so afraid, Aaron, that when this baby is born, she'll have a grandson she can't fully love because that damned man is taking up too much of her mind space and heart space. And I won't know how to explain that to him as he grows."

Aaron hugged his sister a little closer then said with a softness filled with shared and unspoken memories, "I don't think it works like that. I think a mother always finds room in her heart for her children and her grandchildren. At least that's what I want to believe." And the possibility of the truth being vastly different, the same thought he'd always danced on and off with, sent a momentary fear through him that he desperately needed to beat back, so he repeated, "No, it just doesn't work like that."

"Doesn't it, Aaron? I mean think about it. Did you really feel, when we were growing up, that you had Ma's full and undistracted attention?"

Aaron's face grew smooth as he thought about the question of his mother's distractedness, and he knew his answer would take far longer than either he or Ellie would have ever anticipated. It would veer him off down paths that would wind and twist and gnarl into more questions too hefty for his slight sister, particularly in her state and condition, to take on. So he took his arm back because he needed it for his own succor, then rubbed the back of his neck and said, "I don't know, Ellie. It just seems to me that none of that matters now. It's in the past. I mean, do we really want to drag all of that up as if it could possibly change anything now? Growing up was growing. Now is now."

"And now, we need to settle this once and for all," Ellie said as she clutched Aaron's forearm desperately. "If we take her and have her evaluated and the doctor says that she's perfectly fine, which I doubt he will, then I'll drop this whole thing, Aaron. I swear I will. I just need to know if she's got some kind of imbalance going on that would explain all these years of my life."

"What do you mean, Ellie? Something like an obsessive-compulsive disorder?"

"Yes, exactly. Something just like that."

"I don't know, Ellie," Aaron said, wrestling with every part of his mind that gripped the dilemma.

"And you know what? It may even be chemical!" she said with

an enthusiasm that seemed to have the purpose of giving her plan validity and acceptability.

And finally, a good enough reason, Aaron thought. It may be chemical. "Well, I guess you're right about that. Let me go talk to Poppa." Aaron left his sister's side and walked with slowness to the door. He turned to see her once more just before he went through, still with doubt, because there was that part of his memory that will never let go of the time when he was four and Ellie was nine and she told him that his socks walked around by themselves at night when he went to sleep. She told him then with the same passion she was now using to convince him of something far more sobering. Back then, the only fallout from her exaggeration was a solid month of him not being able to sleep at the babysitter's, since he stayed up practically all night to catch his socks in their frolicking act. That went on until one night, tired and barely able to keep his face out of his dinner plate, Aaron was remembering, he finally asked his mother about the walking socks and learned that Ellie had lied. She got a sharp and immediate punishment for the lie. This time, though, if Ellie was exaggerating and leading him down a path behind a band of walking socks, she would leave behind a messy trail of ill will, the likes of which he knew she has never known from their mother. But right now, her look—that was less of a nudge than a two-armed shove with all her might—sent him the rest of the way into the dining room. And all he needed to do was enter the room to command everyone's eyes on him. So he went back to his chair and sat, saying, "Poppa, I need to talk to you about what Ellie and I were discussing in there."

"All right, son. I'm listening."

"Well, Ellie brought up what I think is an excellent point, and that is that maybe Ma could have some sort of chemical imbalance that makes her do so many odd things."

Junior ate the last morsel of food from his plate, leaving it looking nearly clean enough to put back on the cupboard without a washing, then said, "Aaron, I don't know how you and your sister are seeing things, but I don't think what your mother does would really qualify as 'so many odd things.' I mean, yeah, she goes on and on about it, but you don't have as many years with it as I do, so you don't know how to become numb to it. Now, I hear your mother talking and going on and on, because God knows she talks all the time, but I don't start listening until she gets to a point. That goes for this and for everything, because everything with her is something. I just thought you kids had done the same thing. But if it bothers you that much, then I'll go along with whatever you two want to do."

Aaron put a forkful of collard greens in his mouth, then labored to chew them, shocked by their coldness. He took a sip of cola that was but a thin film of water on the top from the melting ice. Then, resting his fork on his plate, he looked firmly at his father and said, "Poppa, Ma would kill me if she knew that I was telling you this—"

"Then don't tell me."

"No, I have to tell you, just so that you can see the odd behavior we're talking about that just might be caused by a chemical imbalance." He cinched his forehead, thinking for only the briefest second about the trust he was about to breach, then said, "Whenever you go down to Tulane to your board meetings, Ma moves all the furniture around in the house. And she's been doing this for years. I know because I help her do it."

Junior gave Aaron a sideways stare with a twisted smile, then let loose a burst of a guffaw. "You think I don't know what she does when I leave town after forty-two years of being married to that woman, and then knowing her forever before that?"

"You know?"

"Of course I know. I also know that she's been feeding those prostitutes out on the boulevard for the last two years, too. But I've known about the furniture for years." He pointed a playful finger of shame at his son and said, "But I didn't know you were helping her. I'm not quite sure how I figured she did all that moving, or for that matter exactly what she moved, but I had no idea you were her partner in crime."

Aaron let his hands drop into his lap as his shoulders slumped south. Cocking his head sideways, he turned to his father and said, "How in the world did you know?"

"Oh, just in little things. Like the way she never really moves everything back to where it's supposed to be. Some things will be a little askew, and some things are in an altogether different place. The funny thing is, I'll put them back in their right place and she doesn't even notice. After a couple dozen times of coming home and finding things out of place only to have to fix them, I started to put it all together."

"Why didn't you ever tell her that you know? I mean, if you told her that you know, then maybe she wouldn't have to do it all the time and then she could rearrange the furniture just the way she wants it."

"Well now, why would I do that? I like my furniture just the way it is. The way things are now works just fine. She gets what she wants when I'm away, and when I come back, my house is just the way I want it."

Aaron smiled sardonically, letting his eyes fall into his lap. He almost told his father his true thoughts on such lunacy, but he thought better of it when he remembered that it had very little to do with the matter at hand. So he looked head-on at his father and said, "Well, are you for it, Poppa? Do you agree with Ellie and me—but mostly Ellie—that Ma needs to see a professional about this thing with Clayton Cannon?"

Junior rose slowly from where he sat, then stepped to one side and slid his chair to the table. He put his hand on Aaron's shoulder, then squeezed with what seemed to be the warmth of a father feeling the pain of his son. "I don't see where it could hurt things. I do love your mother, but I am a medical man too, so I do take into consideration that there could be a chemical imbalance that would explain so many things about her that I could never make heads nor tails of about her except simply to say that it was just her way. The problem might be getting her there, though. But you kids go ahead and do what you think you need to do." He let go of Aaron's shoulder and gave him a soft pat on his back. And as he walked past Rick he did the same. Then he went to the chair that sat in the living room, just beyond the indiscernible demarcation where the dining room becomes the living room, and picked up his coat. As he snaked his arms into the sleeves he gave his son a fair enough warning. "I've got to get on home now, but I just want you to remember one thing, son. I know your mother, and the one thing you can count on is that she's going to kick and holler and resist this; and even through all of that, if you do manage to get her to a doctor, she will carry a grudge against you and your sister as if it had handles. So, if you two are prepared to deal with that, then go through with this and I will be right there with all of you. Just do me a favor. Go in there and ask Ellie who she's planning to take her to see, because if it's somebody over at the hospital chances are good that your mother and I will know him, and that wouldn't be a comfortable situation for your mother at all."

Aaron rose and went swiftly into the kitchen. And when he walked through the door, he didn't immediately find his sister. So he called for her, and when he heard her whimpering answer and then saw her bent over the counter, clutching her stomach, he went completely cold. Every instinct he had to scream was taken over by his inability to accept that there was something wrong. "Ellie, what is it?" he asked quickly.

"It's the baby, Aaron. Tell Rick that I'm in labor."

Aaron said nothing as he turned on his heels and left the kitchen as steady as flowing brook-water. But when he got back into the dining room, all evenness was lost when he bellowed at Rick, as if Rick should have sensed that his baby was on its way, "Come on, man, get in there! Ellie's in labor, and she cannot have that baby in the kitchen! It's not due for a week and being born on a kitchen floor is just not going to be a good thing for it." Aaron sat down at the table before his pounding heart would steal away every ounce of strength that kept his knees from completely buckling beneath him. He slumped back in the chair and watched as everyone hustled, and listened as the whirl of wind in the room became more indefinable and muffled. And all the commotion to call the doctor and get her to the hospital made him angry— angry that Ellie had to bring her mulish self out on a night like this, angry that his mother had preordained this night so many years before. But mostly, he was seething with a newly steeped hatred at the fate that brought his stark nemesis, who was the only living creature standing between him and his mother, right there to Baltimore again, only fifteen minutes away and almost near enough to touch.

CHAPTER
9
•

Antonia took jerky, skittish steps, as she approached the bench in front of the Science Center where she'd sat just a few weeks before, watching the door of the Harbor Court Towers for a glimpse of Clayton. She was at least twenty minutes early, and it was the middle of January, for goodness sakes, far too cold to sit on the bench as if it were a lazy, balmy day just right for watching strollers. And so it was no wonder that she caught more than a few stares of passersby. But she couldn't feel the cold. Her mind had ducked inside and taken the elevator up to the penthouse—he had to live in the penthouse because that's what tortured musical geniuses do—and into Clayton's musical retreat.

She had fashioned him as tortured since she'd tried to imagine him as a young man studying piano at Peabody. Tormented in his world of notes, sharps and flats, majors and minors—mostly minors—with no one truly able to understand what drove his soul. Tortured in the way in which he, himself, couldn't fully understand his genius—all he knew, as she imagined him, was that he had to play, and if he didn't, he'd die. Mostly, though, angst-ridden because there was a cavernous gap in the soul that he tried desperately to fill with music, written from the beleaguered souls of others. To be in that world in which he lived, of formal music written, at least initially, for patrician ears, would require a meticulous high-brow mystique foreign to the average bayou man. And inside his music den, which must have been darkened, lit only by sparkling crystal chandeliers, were old paintings of famous composers and furniture no one could ever picture fitting with ease into their own home; and busts—only one of himself—of some such stone or bronze carved with immortality in mind, she was sure. A place that was decorated as if no one from recent centuries had been inside it, except for the table, set for some sort of imminent formal meal—because in her mind, that's how he took his meals. Alone. Solitary. And his repast was heavy with the aura of the long-ago communality of souls once he filled it with their music.

And so there she sat, her mind back outside with the rest of her in the cold on a bench, clutching her purse like a lifeline. Then she heard the voice of a woman descending the steps of the Science Center speaking, possibly, to her.

"Ma'am, are you lost?" a black-coated woman said. She had a striking, fine-featured, yet no-nonsense and unsmiling face, which made Antonia wonder why she even cared.

"I'm fine, thank you," Antonia said, offering the woman a smile, thinking she'd get one in return, which she did. "You have a nice day, now."

"You do the same," the woman said with a smile as she walked on her way. "And go on in out of the cold, now."

The woman walked off, leaving Antonia alone again, the cold exacerbating the fact. She watched the woman disappear down by the Rusty Scupper. Without being conscious of it, her fingers drummed nervously against her purse. And why would a pretty girl be eating alone? Antonia assumed, since the woman was walking alone, and went into the restaurant alone.

Well, they grow women differently these days than they did when my mother was raising me, she thought, and she smiled. Especially when she thought about raising Ellen, who nearly brought her first grandchild into the world the night before. Either through the water or the air, Antonia thought with a shadowy smile as intangible as memory itself, Ellen got something into her as she was being raised up that made her just want to grab for everything—first being the smartest doctor Antonia had ever seen, except for maybe Junior, and then being pregnant at forty-one for the first time, for goodness' sake. Then she let that thought dissolve into the harbor as she began to paw through her purse trying to scrounge up a mint, but mostly to quiet her pounding fingers, asking herself aloud, "Why are you so nervous? Just calm yourself. He can bring a crowd to its feet with his piano playing, but before he could do all that, he was your nephew, for crying out loud."

So Antonia checked her watch once more and saw that in her daydreams of the man Clayton must now be, she had let fifteen minutes pass by. She rose from the bench, and walked toward the crosswalk. A strong gust of wind kicked up while she waited for the light to take the long trek across Light Street. Once the light had changed, she stepped lively across the street and studied the towers of Harbor Court—up and down she looked, then side to side, and by the time she had reached the median smack in the middle of the street, she was certain that this place was where the old McCormick Spice Company once sat.

She reached the front door where she stood, first looking one way, then the other until she finally had to concede to her made-up mind that it was possible that McCormick had not been in this spot at all, but perhaps just across the street on the other corner. And then she smiled, comforted by the memories of those smells that were so strong it seemed as if they still lingered in the leafless trees or perhaps in a stationary cloud somewhere up above. She went back to a summer day, not one in particular, but any summer day along the harbor with the perfume of cinnamon wafting through the air like an exotic seductress, making her long for something more to sate every sense. It didn't much matter which spice they were preparing for market—cumin, turmeric, allspice—it all made her miss New Orleans, with its bouquet of the food unique only to the Crescent City. Food—that's what it meant to her to miss New Orleans. And to miss Emeril and Creole spices.

By the time she finally got herself into the lobby of the Harbor Court Towers, there she was, walking across the lobby at a clip.

"Antonia, honey, there you are," Agnes said.

Antonia went to her as if she just might oblige Agnes's want to embrace and said, "Where are they?" She had waited long enough, and she wanted to meet her nephew and his family. So she looked behind Agnes to the elevator through which she assumed Agnes had just come, then around the lobby, as if perhaps they had appeared during the few seconds her eyes were on Agnes.

Agnes, with her eyes squinted, looked at Antonia, then behind her, following Antonia's gaze. "Where are who, honey?"

"Where are Clayton and his family? That's why I'm here, isn't it?" she said in a tone that would make it clear that there was no point to her staying if they weren't going to be around.

"Honey, I'm sorry, but Clayton's in New York about to catch a plane to Milan," she said, her twang bringing it out of her mouth sounding like *M'Laan.* Then she shrugged and said, "And Susan and the boys wouldn't be here. Susan's over at the house, and the boys are in school. I told you to come and meet me down here because I thought you might like it, and because it seems to me that our conversation wasn't finished from the other day."

Antonia took a step back, and when she tightened her face she stared at Agnes as if through a tunnel and said, "Don't give me that, Agnes. I'm not stupid, and I know you're more conniving than that. You planned it this way because there's no way you were going to have me down here while he was here. Isn't that true?"

"Antonia, that is simply not true."

"Don't lie to me, Agnes. We've got too much history, and you know I know you."

Agnes pushed out an exasperated breath, as if it were meant to blow Antonia right out of there. Then she started toward a door on the other end of the lobby and turned to Antonia, saying, "Well, are you coming or not?"

So Antonia followed her through the door and up an escalator and into a restaurant. And when they entered the dining room, the tables, every single one, sparkled like Christmas ornaments from the crystal that caught the low lights that shone through the prisms of even more crystal hung in the chandeliers. Antonia looked around the room and said, "My, this really is lovely. But you still haven't answered my question, Agnes."

"All right, Antonia. You're right," Agnes snapped. "I did know that he wasn't going to be here, but I really do believe that we've got much more to talk about so let's just get to our table so that we can get on with it, okay?"

A man dressed in a business-black suit approached them. He

had the tightened stride of landed gentry, which he could have carried off had he not spoken to let his South Baltimore drawl slide out to reveal his true station. "Do you have a reservation?" he asked as the overpronounced *r* in *reservation* told his tale.

"Agnes Cannon. Reservation for two," Agnes said confidently.

Actually, with more confidence than Antonia ever thought Agnes could have. It's amazing, Antonia thought, what high living off of a famous son can do. But then she imagined, as she followed Agnes and the waiter to the table, that Agnes must feel constantly like a catfish in the ocean. Completely out of her element, and always looking from side to side to make certain she's correct; knowing that she's breathing air, yet feeling as if she's suffocating with every futile breath she attempts to take.

As she sat, Agnes smoothed her dress underneath her with the unnatural movements of a woman unaccustomed to such feminine protocol, then laid her napkin across her lap in an equally pretentious manner. Once the maitre d' had gone away, Agnes said, "All right, Antonia, you're right. I brought you here because I thought you were going to do something rash."

Antonia shifted where she sat and studied the young man busily filling the water glasses. When he finished, she said, "And? . . ."

Antonia could feel in every part of herself that could sense and know that there was more to Agnes's motivation. If she would just say it, just once in her misguided life tell the truth, at least Antonia could believe that staying there wouldn't be in vain. And she stared determinedly at Agnes for her answer, and when it wasn't instantaneously forthcoming, she said, "You tell me the rest of it right now, or so help me God, I'll walk right out of here and the next time we talk it will be with Clayton. I was at the hospital with my daughter till one this morning because we thought she was in labor and I'm working on very little sleep. I'm tired and I'm short on patience and you're about to test me in a way I don't think you should."

"Okay, Antonia," Agnes responded desperately. Then she diverted her eyes out the window and onto the gray harbor and continued softly, "*And* I wanted to bring you here because I hoped that if you were able to come here to the place where Clayton lives, then maybe that would be enough for you, and then maybe you'd leave Clayton alone. Now, can we please just have a nice lunch? The food here is simply the best."

Antonia wouldn't move, as she looked around at all the old splendor in the room. She smiled thinly and said, "Now doesn't that feel good, Agnes? That must have been the first honest thing you've said to me since I've known you. But just to set the record straight, if all I wanted to do was come to the place where Clayton lives and skulk around and eat lunch like some star-struck groupie, I could have done that by myself and a long time ago."

Agnes only smiled, then said, "I suppose you could." Shifting the subject with the gentility of true southernness, she continued, "If you like prawn salad, they make quite a good one here. It's on the prix fixe lunch menu."

"I like it well enough," Antonia said, trying to remember when she'd last had prawn salad. Then she decided it didn't matter, since such dishes hardly have a universal rule of preparation and so would most likely taste different than the last, whatever that tasted like. And it didn't much matter anyway, since she wasn't really there to eat. So, lacking for anything else to say to fill in the silence, she said, "The table looks lovely."

"Yes it does. This is a fine, fine restaurant," Agnes replied with the wonderment that said the elegance of her son's perquisites were still like a dream to her. "Clayton says it's been written up in *Baltimore* magazine, and even *Zagat*, too. And you know, on the prix fixe menu, they have pralines-and-cream for dessert. I remember just how much you love your pralines." Agnes picked up her water glass, and before sipping from it said, "So you say your daughter had false-alarm labor last night?"

"That's right. She was at my son's house with her husband, and Junior was there too," she said, then Antonia picked up her water glass. She sipped and lingered over the distraction of having forgotten to ask what the family were all doing at Aaron's house together in the first place. True enough, she knew Junior was going to Aaron's. But what was Ellen doing there? And if Ellen and Rick were there having a big old family get-together, why wasn't she there too? Somebody had some secrets to tell about whisperings behind her back. Then, setting her water back in its place, she tucked her suspicion away and continued, "It turned out to be indigestion. She'd just eaten too much over at her brother's house."

"Oh yeah, that's common. I remember when Susan was pregnant with the boys. We made no less than three dashes to the hospital only to find out that it wasn't really labor. By the time they really were ready to come, they came so fast the doctors didn't even have time to get her out of her dress. That was some night, I'll tell you."

"Sounds like it," Antonia said, laughing without the burden of the last forty-five years bearing down on her. She held back, as she saw the waiter approaching. But before she let him ask, Antonia spoke up. "I think we'll both have the prix fixe lunch." Then, realizing she'd just spoken for Agnes, she looked at her with widened eyes of contrition and asked, "Is that what you want too?"

"Yes, that's fine. That's just what I was going to order," Agnes said, more to Antonia than to the waiter.

And only when he left did Antonia continue. "So, anyway, I was just beside myself with happiness when Junior called me and said Ellen was in labor. I've had two children and I know what that's like, but I suppose there's nothing like the moment when your first grandchild comes into the world. I'm just so excited, Agnes." And Antonia was positively giddy.

"Oh, I know you are, honey. And you are so right about the moment your grandchildren are born. I will never forget one thing about the day Clayton was born. I still remember the room I was in over there at Oschner Hospital as if I was just in there yesterday. But you have no idea what kind of joy you're in for. I know for me, all the mistakes I made in trying not to spoil Clayton I don't have to worry about with my grandbabies," she said with a hearty laugh. "Yeah, that's right. I just let Clayton and Susan do all the saying no and I just say yes, yes, yes. And you're gonna do the same, too, honey. Just you wait and see."

And what Agnes couldn't see, maybe wouldn't see, was that the light that had been lit, barely long enough for scarce joy to transcend their enmity, had been doused. Antonia's anger rose in one solid wave of sadness at what she'd missed—Clayton's birth. But for Agnes to flaunt, so brazenly, so blithely, that Clayton was born at Oschner—the hospital for whites—just brought all of that woman's subterfuge back into the room to tap Antonia on the shoulder and remind her of the trickery that kept Clayton from being born over at Charity Hospital—the hospital for coloreds. She wondered what to say. Although her ire was burning at her core, it had yet to tell her mind to shift from the enchantment of babies and childbirth to the vulgarity of Agnes's cruel-hearted machination of Clayton's truth to nourish her own insatiable low-down selfishness. Antonia cast her eyes down into her lap and longed for the moments just passed when she had shared a second of likeness with Agnes, so she made the decision, right there, to let the brightness in her life outshine the darkness. "Yeah, well I know what you mean. Momma died before Ellen was born, so she never got to know the kind of joy I'm going to have when my baby has her baby. Last night was scary, though, because Ellen's only just barely nine months pregnant. Of course nowadays they can do a lot for those kinds of preemies, but still, you just want them to stay protected in that womb so that they can be as strong as they can when they have to face this world."

"So she's okay now?" Agnes asked with the sober face of concern.

"Oh yes, she's just fine. Her pride was a little hurt, though, because she was just as sure as anything that she was in premature labor," Antonia said laughing with her memories of the night before. " 'This is what I do all day long, so I should know,' she told them. 'I bring babies into the world every day, even premature ones, and I should know when I'm in premature labor.' That girl with her headstrong self was over there trying to tell everybody what to do. I guess it's true that doctors really do make the worst patients. I remember when Junior had to have his appendix out about twenty years ago. Oh my God, Agnes, those doctors had to put a sign on his door telling people not to go in there because Junior was so crusty and ornery to everybody. It was like I had a third child. Anyway, she's at home taking it easy today and for the rest of the week. In fact, I'm going past to see her when I leave from down here."

The waiter appeared carrying two prawn salads, which he placed gingerly in front of each of them. He offered the pepper-mill without saying a word, as if just showing it should make it clear what he was offering.

"Yes, I'd like pepper," Antonia said.

Then Agnes nodded for the same as well. And when he pep-
pered her salad sufficiently, she simply held her hand up in the
universal sign to halt. When he left them to their food, she picked
up the conversation. "Well, anyway, I know that must have been
something with Junior, 'cause men are a mess like that. But it's
good that your daughter's resting herself. It doesn't matter how
old you get, a girl needs her momma at a time like this. I always
wished I'd had a little girl, but we just didn't have any more children after Clayton," she said, her voice growing weaker as the
sentence went along so that by the end of it, *Clayton* was barely
audible.

But Antonia's mind had breezed by the perfect opportunity to
question Agnes as to why they never had more children, at least
for now. Her thoughts were with Ellen, wondering just how much
she really needed her mother. Ellen was always so complete,
Antonia remembered. There didn't seem to be anything in Ellen's
whole life, since she'd left diapers, that she couldn't manage to do
or get for herself. So Antonia chewed a prawn and, before it was
barely swallowed, said, "Yeah, I suppose that's so for most other
girls. But you don't know my Ellen. She's so self-sufficient.
Doesn't need a thing from anybody, it seems." She grew quiet and
pensive for the barest second, then let out a thin laugh. "By the
time she was ten years old I knew that if she'd had a job, she
would have had her own place."

"Oh, honey, it might seem that way to you, but believe me, she
needs you," Agnes said to Antonia, with sympathetic eyes that
held Antonia tightly. "From the time they get out here they're trying to conquer this world on their own. And I don't mean high
school or college either, honey. I mean from the time they take
those babies from our wombs we are having to learn step-by-step
and stage-by-stage how to let them go, because instinct makes
them want whatever is meant for them in this world."

"Well, then that's my Ellen, wanting everything that's meant
for her in the world." She fell quiet long enough to finish her
prawn salad, which was sparse to begin with, even though the
prawns seemed as big as her hands. Antonia dabbed the corners
of her mouth with a corner of her napkin, then smoothed it back
across her lap. Looking over at Agnes who'd had one last prawn
she seemed to be coveting as if she wanted to take it home with

her, Antonia said, "Tell me something, Agnes. Why is it that you and Douglas never had more children?"

Agnes looked sharply at Antonia, and only when she loosened her tightened lips did she say, "Now listen, Antonia. I know what you're getting at, and you're wrong. Douglas and I tried for a few years, but then we both decided that we were happy just to have our Clayton."

Antonia smiled with just a hint of irony. "Agnes, I simply asked a question that was nothing if not innocent. My question has absolutely no bearing on what I truly believe."

"And what you believe has no validity," Agnes snapped. Then she cut her last prawn and ate half of it. She let loose a chest full of air, put her fork down and said, "Now listen, Antonia, I don't know why all this has to happen between us. Why, just now we were getting on fine, and then just like that we're at each other's throats. I don't want to be that way with you." She skewered the last bit of prawn on her fork and put it in her mouth, chewing it slowly and deliberately as if it would be some sort of sin against the culinary artistry of the chef to swallow, but she did, then said, "The truth is, Antonia, I've always liked you. Not just because you're Emeril's sister, but because you've always had spunk. You were so sure of yourself with every step you took, and even though everybody else around thought you were crazy, calling you fou-fou Antonia and all, just because you went around with that yellow cat of yours in that basket, I defended you because you knew who you were. None of that fou-fou Antonia stuff ever made you doubt for one second who you were. Even when you were running around behind me and Emeril tryin' to make our lives miserable, I defended you."

"Of course I knew who I was. I was Emeril's twin sister and I was loved. There wasn't anything or anybody that could have ever changed that," Antonia replied defiantly, looking starkly at Agnes. Then, as her lips softened just enough to let one corner of her mouth turn up toward a smile, she said, "Besides, I don't believe you defended me back then."

"I did, though," Agnes said assuredly as she looked briefly at the plate of food that was just put down before her. "Why, do you remember that first summer the three of us met and we all worked over there at the Devereuxs'?"

"Yes I do," Antonia said sprightly with the memory of a time long forgotten. "You were their nanny, and I worked in the kitchen with Cora Calliup's mother, who got me and Emeril jobs working over there."

"That's right. And Emeril was their yard boy." She waited for the waiters to clear their salad plates and get completely behind them before continuing, "Okay, so one day, Mrs. Devereux nearly tossed you outta there when she found the bones from the ribs they'd had for dinner the night before tucked away in your sweater pocket. She couldn't believe that you had dug those things outta the garbage and was savin' them to take home with ya. She thought you were some kind of dangerous nut for doin' that. And honestly, honey, I couldn't think of a darn good reason myself, but I still told her, I said, 'Mrs. Devereux, Antonia ain't crazy. She's just gifted is all. She's one of those seers, and them bones is what she uses to help her see what us regular ungifted folks can't see.' Anyway, I knew you weren't no seer, honey, but she believed it, and she didn't fire you. Why did you take those bones, anyway?"

"I took them because I thought if I strung them on some pretty gold string, they'd make a pretty necklace. Turned out I was wrong." Then with an emotion that boiled up from way down deep, from a place that had been constructed so long ago and then abandoned, Antonia shared a laugh with Agnes that gave her a freedom that had eluded her for so long, it was all at once unnerving and the most ebullient life could ever offer. And it lasted, because as with anything that can make a body tingle from its soul, Antonia was in no hurry to let it leave. But then as it drew to an end, she said, "Well, anyway, it's a good thing I didn't get fired, because if I had I wouldn't have been able to get another job that whole summer. And most of the money I made at the Devereuxs', Momma and Daddy made me put in the bank, and I couldn't touch it till I got to college. It's a good thing they did too, because that money plus the money Momma and Daddy would add to it from time to time helped me when I went to Spelman. So I guess I ought to thank you."

"I guess you ought to," Agnes said with a lilt of jest in her voice that somehow seemed to restore her whole face, dancing eyes and all, back to her former girl-self.

Antonia sliced off a piece of what she could only identify as some sort of fish with her fork, then scooped it up and put it in her mouth to discover it was catfish. She thought to tell Agnes of how she'd never, ever thought to fix catfish any other way but fried, but that what they were eating now was quite a tasty way of fixing it, but she chose instead to say, "Agnes, I wish I could understand why it's so hard for you to just admit to me that Clayton is Emeril's son. I mean, I know I've said all of that stuff about how the world should know what kind of man my brother was and what kind of man he fathered, but that was just a lot of other stuff in me talking. Really, it would only have to be between the three of us, me and you and Clayton. I don't want anything else from you, Agnes, except to know my brother's child. I don't think that's asking for the world."

Agnes only chewed, staring straight ahead at Antonia. Her face had fallen flat, coming back to her present woman-self. And as if waiting for minutes to be added to the day, she sipped from her water glass, set it back on the table, then replied, "Antonia, there is absolutely nothing I can say to you that I haven't said a million times before. You're going to believe what you're going to believe, and all I can do is tell you that what you believe isn't so. I've always known, Antonia, that we wouldn't even be going through this if I was black."

"You're right. We wouldn't be going through any of this if you were black, because there'd be no reason for you to hide his color, now would there be?"

"That's so unfair, Antonia," Agnes said, diverting her eyes from Antonia's as if a force larger than she had snatched them away.

"It may be difficult for you to hear, but there's no way it could be unfair because it's true."

Agnes went to pound her fist down on the table until she seemed to remember where she was, and then she simply slapped the tips of her fingers on the edge of the table. Though it was nowhere near the same explosion as her fist, the tenacity was quite clear when she said, "What in the hell do you want from me, Antonia? I have tried to be reasonable with you. I have come to your home. I have invited you here to have a beautiful lunch, and all you can do is continue to needle me and take me round and round in your circles about something that cannot possibly be true."

So Antonia stared back and said with an even firmness, "Well if as you say it's impossible to be true, can you tell me why it is that Emeril died on July twenty-third nineteen fifty-six, and Clayton was born on April twenty-third nineteen fifty-seven? And just in case you're bad with math, that's exactly nine months to the day after Emeril died."

Agnes twittered with nervous laughter, then said, "Antonia, what are you saying? Okay, so he was born nine months to the day after Emeril died, not nine months to the day after the first time Emeril and I made love."

And Antonia laughed, as well, only with slyness, and said, "But Agnes, do I need to remind you that on the morning of the day he died, I caught the two of you doing it right there in the living room of the house where you looked after those children down in the Garden District? Now I am married to a doctor and I do know that most babies are not born exactly nine months to the day after conception, but I do also know that it *can* happen."

Agnes, flustered, flushed and, stammering all over herself, seemed to be pecking in the air right before her in search of what to say. And when she looked into every corner of the room and back, it seemed as if she needed to search in another part of the dining hall's atmosphere for words that only Antonia would understand. "So—So—So, how in the world do you know that about him? How is it that you know when his birthday is, Antonia? Have you been stalking him or something?"

"Agnes, are you serious?" Antonia said with an incredulous, stammering laugh. "Clayton Cannon is a concert pianist. A public figure. Do you have any idea just how easy it is to find out that information? Sometimes it's as easy as just looking in the paper."

And Agnes, unaware that someone was heading toward her, completely oblivious to her daughter-in-law and grandchildren walking across the dining room, whipped herself around and pointed an accusing finger at Antonia and screamed in a whisper, "Stalker! You are a stalker, that's what you are!"

"I'm no stalker, Agnes, but if I were, it wouldn't matter, because the Bible says 'Be thy brother's keeper, and keep his children from deception,'" Antonia said with all the confidence of what she believed.

"The Bible may say that, Antonia, but you don't have no right to stalk my son. You're a stalker. Stalker! Stalker!"

But Antonia's attention was not on Agnes's ranting that was wrapped tightly, Antonia presumed, in fear. She was awed by the miracle of what stood before her. "Hello," was all she could say to the woman and two children.

"Mother Cannon?" Susan Cannon said. "Is everything all right?" She looked suspiciously at Antonia, then at Agnes, then back at Antonia who was regarding the twins with an exacting interest, and this made Susan cinch her forehead even tighter.

Agnes collected all the parts of herself that she had splattered all over the room when she exploded and said, "Oh yes, honey. Everything's just fine. I'm just having lunch here with an old friend of mine from New Orleans, Antonia Jackson. Antonia, this is my daughter-in-law, Susan, and my grandsons, Noah and Luke."

"It's a pleasure to meet you all," Antonia said meekly. The weakness in her fluttering heart, the sense of scarcely being able to believe she was near enough to touch Emeril's grandsons, had taken her voice nearly completely from her. There he was, Emeril times two as a boy. Everything was duplicated, even the one dimple in the right cheek—that dimple told her that fate simply wouldn't create such an uncanny coincidence. But even with the uniqueness of the dimple, it was the eyes that told her all she'd ever need to know. Those boys had Emeril's eyes, which meant they had her eyes too. And she wondered if they could see it; if they could look into her eyes and see that they were the same as their own. And so she blinked slowly, half involuntarily and half as a beacon to bring home lost souls in the dark night of secrets.

"The pleasure's all mine, I'm sure," Susan finally said once she'd finished staring at Antonia, who was still staring at the boys. "Boys, did you say hello to Mrs. Jackson?"

"Hello, ma'am," the boys said in unison.

"Hello, darlings," Antonia said softly.

Then Susan went closer to her mother-in-law, took hold of her hand and said, "Mother Cannon, why would you have lunch down here? I mean, it's lovely and all, but why didn't you just have your friend over to the house? I would have fixed you all a lovely lunch."

"Well, I wanted some atmosphere. You understand, don't you?"

"I guess. Well, anyway, the doorman is the one who told me

where you were, otherwise I'd likely to never find you. You didn't leave a note, or anything."

"So why were you looking for me?" Agnes asked with her voice just barely on the edge of impatience.

"I wanted to see if you might be available this evening to stay with the boys. Clayton and I were invited to a dinner party tonight at the home of the president of Peabody, but since Clayton's in Milan I didn't think I would have to go without him. Turns out he wants me to go anyway. Says it'll be good to get to know the president of Peabody just in case his career goes south and he needs a teaching job. Can you imagine? The man's at the top of his career and he's trying to line up a safety net."

"I think that's pretty smart," Antonia said, adding her unsolicited opinion.

Susan regarded her with questioning eyes and said, "I suppose it is." Then she turned to her mother-in-law and asked, "So anyway, can you stay with them?"

"Oh, of course I can. Even if I had plans I'd cancel them for these two sugars," she said as she went to the boys and squeezed them to either side of herself.

"All right then, we'll see you upstairs. I suppose you won't be long, will you?" and she looked at Antonia as if she'd find the answer with her. "I need to run to a store and pick up some pantyhose."

"No, we're almost through here, aren't we, Antonia?"

"Yes, we are," Antonia said without a trace of the disquiet she was certain she'd feel at the end of a luncheon with Agnes Cannon. Instead, she felt fortified, lifted up in integrity with the fact of life that would inextricably tether her to Agnes forever. And the only twinge of sadness she felt was that Susan had no idea that those boys' great-aunt was sitting right there, willing and ready to watch them at any hour. So she let that thought go, and said to Susan, "You have beautiful boys. Love them well."

"Oh I do," she said with the pride of a mother. "They're beautiful in every way. Such blessings. Say good-bye, Noah and Luke."

"Good-bye, ma'am," they both said.

Then Noah said, "It was nice meeting you." And he watched Antonia with a half-smile and studying eyes that couldn't seem to let her loose as his mother gently shooed him and his brother along.

"I'll see you later, Mother Cannon," Susan said.

"Bye Grandmama," the boys said together as they moved farther across the dining room.

"Bye babies," Agnes said. Then she turned her attention back to her plate, taking large bites of food as if they were a day and a half from Armageddon and all earthly pleasures had to be consumed. She looked up only to say, "We should finish up since I have to get to the boys."

And so Antonia ate toward the finish without any thought of those pralines in cream waiting for her in spite of their devilish temptation. She just needed to be gone from Agnes and downtown altogether, even though she'd only gotten a mere sliver of what she'd come to get. That little bit was enough, though, and even if nobody else believes it, Antonia knew in her heart that she had just laid eyes on Emeril's grandsons. Agnes can call me foufou, she can call me evil, she can call me angry, Antonia thought with a sly smile that let the edge of her lips barely curl. None of it mattered, because she knew that her tenacity, in the name of Emeril's honor, is what was putting the fear of the devil into Agnes, the one living in the morass of mendacity.

CHAPTER

10

•

Ellen was stretched out on the sofa, staring at her musings as they pranced across the ceiling. She wanted so badly to close her eyes and drift off into the pillowy part of her mind where nothing could reach and torment her. But after the dash to the hospital with the fear of losing her baby pumping every ounce of blood through her body, the threat of doom would simply not leave. Her eyes had been stretched wide since three in the morning, and she looked at the clock to find that it had been a solid twelve hours now. Every time it seemed that some curtain of rest was about to descend and take over, the tape of mischief that had been playing all day long in her mind would loop around to its three A.M. beginning and play all over again.

So before it could start again, she reached over to the coffee table and grabbed the *Parents* magazine she had picked up at the hospital newsstand days ago when she was feeling particularly warm with daydreams of motherhood. But lo and behold, there it was, right there on the cover of the magazine. It was as bold as day and something she hadn't noticed till now: PROTECTING YOUR CHILD FROM DANGER. And so it started her up again, thinking about those two killer men who'd escaped from jail as they were being transferred to Lewisburg. She could barely think about anything else after she heard her brother first report it on the news nearly a week before. Yes, she thought about them during the day, and as chilling as the thought of two maniac convicts on the loose was to think about in the crisp light of an afternoon, there was something about the three A.M. hour that opened her eyes from a stone sleep, making her certain they had shimmied up the side of her house and were climbing through the bathroom window as she lay there stilled with fear. And she couldn't let go of the possibility now any more than she could at three in the morning that maybe they'd scalp her and Rick just as they'd scalped their other victims, leaving their bloodied pads of hair at the front door, a gruesome calling card for which they'd become known.

Not even Rick lying next to her offered up any solace for her disturbed heart, she remembered, because watching him lie there with the peace of sleep in every part of his form, she thought about dying, as she thought about it now on the flip side of night—and so there'd be no hope for their forever. Ellen sat up and looked across the room at the picture of her and Rick as an hours-old married couple, she beaming with joy unparalleled and he looking at his new bride with the warmest love that even now, some eight years later, still made her misty. Mostly because she thought about her vows that were supposed to be forever, but it seemed to her now, as she thought about forever, that it could only be realized if they were both to die together. If she died first, maybe in childbirth, or some freakish accident, or suddenly in her sleep the way death can sometimes flash, she'd only be promising him her forever. He'd have to live the rest of his forever alone. Alone with a baby and a mortgage, collecting a writer's fickle wages. What if his books stop selling? What if he finds himself at the bottom of the bestseller list, or worse, off the list altogether? What in the world will he do?

But before she had a chance to come up with solutions to her imagined scenario, the doorbell rang. So she got to her feet and went as slowly as she could stand to go—since she was supposed to be taking things easy—to the door. Once she got up the three steps that sank the living room into a grand valley, she went through the double-wide portal into the hallway, and just before she opened the door, she looked through one of the narrow panes of glass framing the doorway to find her mother. That's right, she thought as she swung the door open, she did say she'd stop by.

"Ma, come on in. I almost forgot you said you were coming by."

"Hello, my baby," Antonia said as she pushed the door closed with one arm and put the other around Ellen's vanished waist. They walked together back to the living room where she helped Ellen down the three steps and back to the sofa. "Are those steps too much for you, baby?"

"No, Ma. There're only three of them."

"I guess that's true," Antonia said as she took off her coat, tossed it to the other end of the sofa, then settled herself down next to Ellen. "Honey, are you sleeping? Did you get any sleep when you got home from the hospital last night—or should I say this morning?"

"Ma, I may have slept about an hour, that's all. I know I must look like hell."

"You look beautiful. Any woman with a baby in her belly can't help but look beautiful."

"I agree, Mrs. Jackson," Rick said as he stood in the doorway that led down the hall to his office. "Did you get any sleep, honey?" he asked as he descended the stairs and started across the room, only to be diverted by the blazeless fireplace. "Let me build you a fire."

"I'm not sure if I slept," Ellen said as she watched Rick build a fire. And something simmered warmly in a very visceral part of her that sent tears to well, first, it seemed, in her heart, then in her eyes. A gesture so small, yet so overblown with his love, she thought, and she was so touched that all she could say was, "Thank you, honey."

Antonia took her daughter's hand and gave it a squeeze. "Why are you crying, Ellen?"

Should I tell her? Ellen wondered. Certainly, as a woman who'd carried two children, she would understand gratuitous weepiness because, after all, it was one of those enigmatic sacrifices of pregnancy. So she said, "I've just been weepy a lot. I guess it's from not getting any sleep."

"Oh, well most likely you did sleep," Antonia said. "Maybe it was shallow, but it was sleep, nonetheless, and that's better than no sleep at all."

Ellen glanced over at Rick who had not gotten the fire going yet. So she pressed her eyes into him as if the pressure would make him get it started faster. Just barely minutes after sentimental tears fell for the gesture, she now questioned just why this fire was so all-important, especially since she was anxious to talk to her mother about matters that her husband did not need to hear. "Rick, honey, can you leave the fire alone for a minute and get me something to eat?"

He looked over his shoulder and said, "I've just about got it going now, Ellen. Can I get it in a minute?"

"I'd really like it now, Rick," she said plainly with just a hint of contrition for sending him from the room on a wild-food chase.

So he stood from where he stooped, swiped his hands together, then said, "All right, sweetie. So what do you want?"

"Maybe some pasta with olive oil and a little grated cheese."

"Okay. Antonia, can I get you anything?"

"Oh, nothing to eat, thank you. I just came from a big lunch so I'm not hungry. You can bring me something warm to drink, though, like some tea."

"Tea," he said pointing two fingers at Antonia. "And pasta with olive oil and cheese. I'll be right back."

Ellen waited until she knew for certain Rick was in the kitchen before she turned to her mother and said, "Thanks for asking for the tea. That'll keep him in there for a while."

"Well, I had the feeling that's what you wanted. What's going on? Why'd you want him out of the room?"

Ellen slumped against the high arm of the sofa and softly wept. Then, wiping her tears with the hem of her bathrobe said, "Ma, I've been having some awful thoughts lately. Scary thoughts. Thoughts about death and murderers and just plain horrible things that no one about to have a baby should be thinking about. And I worry if I'm going to be able to keep this baby safe from all those awful things that I can't stop thinking about." She sat up and wiped the rest of her tears with the back of her hand. Then, with as much composure as she could muster for the moment, she turned to her mother and added, "And I keep thinking about those men who escaped from jail last week. You know, those men who broke into those people's houses, then robbed them, killed them, and scalped them?"

"Oh, my stars, Ellen. Why in the world do you want to think about those animals?"

"I don't want to think about them, Ma. I just can't help myself."

"Well, you've got to now. You don't want to be thinking about anything so terrible," Antonia said as her face screwed itself up into a scowl. Then, as if she'd figured out the right thing that would put Ellen at ease, she brightened her face with a near smile and continued, "But to tell you the truth, you've always been this way. When you were young, like about the fifth or sixth grade, it got to where your father and I had to stop watching the news altogether because if somebody was murdered, you were certain the killer was on their way to North Avenue in search of you. I don't know where you got that stuff."

Ellen stared straight across the room in front of her as a chill tingled its way through her. At that moment, with her mother taking her all the way back to the beginning of her fears, she knew that she had never felt safe. From somewhere in clear air this came to her, the memory of always feeling like a small piece of thread that could irreparably be unraveled to an obliterated, unidentifiable bit of nothingness with the wrong word, or the wrong act, or the will of one man, and then she'd be gone forever. Dispensable. And before she could even begin the struggle within of whether or not to tell her mother, she'd already begun to blurt out, albeit with a quiet flatness, "I've never felt safe."

Antonia looked at her from the corners of her eyes, and asked, "What do you mean, you've never felt safe?"

"I mean what I said, Ma. I've never felt safe because I've always thought that someone could come and take me away. Or make me go away. That somehow death would come to me by the will of someone else, not by God, not even by my own choice to take my life. But it would be evil and ugly and torturous in every conceivable way. I can't remember when I wasn't afraid of this, Ma, and now I have to figure out a way to make this baby know that he—" Then she turned to face her mother and matter-of-factly noted, "Oh, by the way, the baby's a boy." And without letting her mother emote in any way, she continued, "I've got to figure out how to make him feel safe in a world in which I've never felt safe myself. No easy task, Ma."

Antonia's face had fallen as she stared at Ellen for several long seconds before taking her in her arms and saying, "I just don't know what to say, Ellen. You've always been so together, and so fearless. It never seemed to me that you were afraid of anything. I mean, just look at you. You're incredible. You're my incredible, marvelous daughter who can do anything. Why, I was just thinking earlier today about how you just went after everything you ever wanted. Do you know how fearless you have to be to do that?"

And if Ellen could have made that moment solid matter, and tucked it away for whenever she needed reminding, she would have. She would take it out whenever she needed to remember that her mother could have, in times like this, moments of complete and total lucidity; and be the soft place she needed to cushion her fall. But then it would only be counterbalanced, she thought, by the likes of that yellow cat, Tippy the Fourth, which had absolutely no bloodline back to the first Tippy, except in her mother's abstracted mind. Then there were all the other oddities, like the way she actually seemed to believe in the authenticity of her bogus Bible quotes, and the way she moved furniture around in secrecy. But now here my mother sits, Ellen thought with a sideways smile, the paragon of a mother's solidness as if her wacky ways were the figment of everyone else's active imagination given to exaggeration. So she smiled softly, just for the warmth of her mother's faith in her, and said, "Well, that's nice, Ma, but they're just accomplishments. Anybody can accomplish anything. You just have to want it badly enough. It doesn't take any particular bravery to become a doctor."

"Yes, that's true. You do have to want it badly enough, but first you have to be fearless enough to want. Cowards don't want, Ellen. They sit back and make excuses as to why they can't get what they want. Not you. You just went after it. You just *go* after it. And that makes you brave in my book."

Ellen sighed, and shook her head with the frustration of being unable to really make things clear—to her mother and to herself. It didn't seem to make much sense to her to continue down a road not even she could navigate. A road that had only been brought into her consciousness by the rush of hormones. So she knew she had to put it all away for another day's pondering when she asked her mother, "Ma, when Uncle Emeril died, what was it like for grandma? How did she take it?"

"Oh, honey, why in the world do you want to talk about that now? You don't need to think about a mother mourning her child when you yourself are about to have a baby."

"Okay, fine," Ellen said dismissively. She didn't need her mother's protection as much as she needed to hear of the primitiveness of a mother's grief; because it would have to be raw, like a blistering, festering sore that all the salves on earth or balms in Gilead could never seem to heal. "It's just that you've never talked about how grandma took his death. It was always pretty clear to me how it hurt you, but what about her? I never knew her, I know, but I still want to know."

Antonia twisted her mouth into a tiny feline-like bow of a smile, as if she were trying to keep herself silent. And as if edginess couldn't keep her still, she shifted where she sat then recounted, "Well, she never got over it. It was as if she cracked in half the day Emeril died and nothing could put her back together again. She was like that till the day she died. And we couldn't ever say his name in the house. It was just like Emeril never even lived. Sometimes, I would think I was going out of my mind, having my heart break every minute of the day when I was remembering and grieving with everything in me for somebody who seemed to have never been born, so I would have to look at that picture of us as babies to remind myself that he had lived and had been born right along with me. So that's why when Daddy died and she acted like it didn't even matter to her, there was nothing else I could do but marry your father, or else I would have had to stay up in that house and go the rest of the way crazy with Momma. When she died, she hadn't been in her right mind for years, not remembering anything and forgetting people. Everybody said she was senile, but Momma was too young to have been senile. I think she just died from her grief."

Ellen looked into her mother's eyes with an empathy for her pain that had, till now, been elusive. She understood the connection, and as naturally, as basic as air, Uncle Emeril was still the foundation of it all. "I think that's what's going to happen to you. You're going to die from your grief over Uncle Emeril's death."

Antonia's mouth hung open in a way that seemed as if it would be forever void of what to say to Ellen. Then with a laugh that sat on the edge of something that was anything but humorous, she said, "Ellen, what would make you say something like that?"

"Because nothing in the world is going to make you get over his death. That's why—" She stopped before telling her mother of the plan, because given the state of things—the baby that could come early, those murderers on the loose that won't let her sleep—she couldn't possibly be sure of the prudence of anything said or done.

"That's why what, Ellen? What is it you want to say?"

"Ma, I just don't think you've ever gotten over the death of Uncle Emeril, and as a result, maybe your grief has digressed over the years since he's died into some sort of obsession with him that makes you also obsess on the outlandish possibility that Clayton Cannon is his son. That's why Aaron and Poppa agreed with me last night when I suggested that maybe you need to see someone about it all, because it's gotten so out of hand now. Ma, I want this baby to grow up knowing his grandmother, but more than that, I want his grandmother to know him. I don't want you to lose your mind and end up dying from grief."

Antonia got up and went to the window where she stood look-ing out at the gray and white day. She folded her arms together as if trying to keep herself bound together tightly, then turned to face Ellen with dull and hurt-filled eyes and said, "Ellen, you've said things like this before, but I always thought it was just talk. I never in a million years really thought you were serious. So that's what you all were doing last night over at Aaron's?"

"Yes. We talked about it, and we agreed that we'd all like some answers so that what you've done all these years with the whole Clayton Cannon thing can make sense to us." Ellen got herself up, with some effort, and went to her mother because she knew she had to get to her mother and touch her, and let her feel the warmth of a daughter's heart that missed the part of her mother that had been buried with Emeril. So Ellen wedged her arm into the tight fold of her mother's arms, and when her mother loos-ened to let her completely in, she held on to Antonia like a child afraid of imagined bogeys in the dark. And when her mother held her in return, it was all complete. "Ma, I don't want to live with this fear anymore. Can you please do this for me? I just need to know if there's an explanation for why you can't live your life without imposing that man Clayton Cannon where he doesn't belong."

Antonia squeezed Ellen tighter to her, without showing Ellen her bemused eyes and tightened jaws that implied she possibly had something altogether different on her mind to say other than what she did. "I'll see whomever you want me to see, Ellen. If it will make you happy or take your fears away and give you peace, I'll do it. And believe me, I will tell this doctor everything that he needs to know. There's nothing I wouldn't do for the happiness of my children, and that's something you'll learn when you have that baby. But there's something you need to consider that I don't think you've given any thought to. What if I see this doctor, and he finds me in perfect psychological form? What if your fears aren't abated after this?"

"What are you asking me, Ma? Are you asking me if I'll believe that Clayton Cannon is Uncle Emeril's son if the doctor says you don't have an unhealthy obsession with him?"

"I suppose that is what I want to know."

Ellen slid from her mother's embrace and went slowly back toward her spot on the sofa, hoping that slowness would give her enough time to think about the gorilla sitting arrogantly in the middle of the room to which she'd never paid attention. What would she do? Would the only alternative, she asked herself, be acceptance of her mother's obsession, which in fact would no longer be an obsession but rather her mother's truth, possibly? She laughed ironically as she sat, wondering why she hadn't seen it coming, then said, "I don't know, Ma."

"You don't know because you've never thought of any possibility other than me being troubled? Or is it that you don't know because there's something that's keeping you from knowing?"

Ellen lowered her head feeling the full throttle of shame only a mother can impose with nothing more than a disappointed stare. And as she picked nervously at her thumbnail she couldn't look at the discontent she knew was in her mother's eyes when she responded sullenly, "I just don't know, Ma."

Just as the whistle of the teakettle made its way into the room, the doorbell decided to keep it company. Ellen went to get up, but when her mother started to the door, she settled herself back down and said, "I wonder who that could be?"

"Most likely it's your father. I asked him to pick me up from here because I took a cab downtown. Some of these roads are still icy and slippery and I didn't want to drive," Antonia said as she disappeared into the hallway to open the door.

Ellen heard her father's voice faintly, then heard the affection of her parents exchanging lip-kisses. And she wondered when it would go away, that prickly chill that would crawl all over the back of her ears and the base of her neck that said, somehow, her parents were doing something so very anti-parent. Just as long as she didn't have to see it, she thought, the urge to giggle and blush and hide her face would be forever kept at bay. "Hi, Poppa," she yelled hoping it would end her discomfort by breaking up the affection.

"Hello, sweetheart," Junior said, walking into the living room behind Antonia, who was carrying his coat. "How're you doing today?"

"I'm okay, Poppa. I'm just tired as a dog."

"That's because she hasn't gotten any sleep," Antonia said with a soft compassion as she stood at Junior's side with her arms crossed, both of them looking down at Ellen from the top of the steps as she sat in the valley of the living room.

"Yeah, my mind just keeps going around and around with all kinds of craziness."

"Well, from what I can remember with your mother, that's pretty common at the end of the pregnancy. She just couldn't seem to turn her mind off, thinking about the baby and what she needed to do to get ready. Why, I remember one night, when she was expecting you, she woke me up at three in the morning because she didn't know anything about the kindergarten teachers down there at Gwynns Falls Elementary school." He laughed heartily, then turned to Antonia as he descended the steps and asked with the tenderness of his memories, "Do you remember that?"

"Yes, I do, Junior," Antonia said with an edginess that seemed offended by the effrontery. She followed him down the steps and added, "But you have to think about those things. There are people who do far crazier things when they're expecting children, particularly when it comes to naming them."

Junior looked questioningly at Antonia. "Who said anything about naming children?"

"I'm just saying," she said evenly.

"Well, all I'm saying is that Ellen hadn't even been born yet, and you were worried about something she wasn't even going to do for another five years."

"That's right," Antonia said with a definite defiance. "I stood by it then, and I stand by it now."

Ellen laughed with an absolute abandon of everything that had troubled her. After all these years, she thought with wonderment, after raising two children only to have them pack their worldly possessions and go off all too soon to discover the world on their own, her mother and father were still strong in the fully experienced knowledge of their past, and the propinquity of their present, and the expectation of their future. What they had, she thought as she couldn't stop herself from grinning at them, was set inside diamond—rock solid, but forever changing with the natural shimmer from the light of life. And when it occurred to her that she was staring, she pulled herself from them and said, "Poppa, come on and sit down. Rick is making me something to eat and getting some tea for Ma. Do you want anything?"

Just as she asked, Rick appeared with a tray carrying the pasta and tea. He looked with surprise at his father-in-law, as if Junior was the last person he'd expected to see. "How are you, Dr. Jackson?" he said as he set the tray down in front of Ellen, then stood to shake Junior's hand.

"How are you, son? How're you holding up under the pressure?" Junior said as he eased into the chair by the window after helping Antonia ease into its twin on the other side of a small table.

"Oh well, it's nerve wracking, that's for sure. The anxiety of knowing that this baby is really coming is enough to make me shake in my shoes. Last night I slept in my clothes, and most likely I'm going to do the same thing tonight."

"Oh yeah, Poppa, he's a mess," Ellen said twirling the skinny pasta onto her fork, as she split her mind between what she was saying and how the pasta really did have the downy texture of what angels' hairs must feel like on the tongue. And while she twirled away, it struck her that Rick wasn't moving fast enough to get her father whatever he wanted, so quick as lightning her humor shifted when she completed, "Rick, get something for my father. I'm sure he wants something."

"Ellen, honey, I was just about to ask him," Rick said as if trying to keep tight hold of his patience. Then he turned to Junior and asked, "Dr. Jackson, can I get you anything?"

"Well I'll take a cola if you have one."

"We sure do. Can I get you something to snack on, like some cheese and crackers?"

"That might be nice," Junior said.

"Come to think of it, Rick, I wouldn't mind a few myself," Antonia said.

"No problem," Rick said as he turned to leave. "I'll just bring a tray." Then he looked at Ellen, as if he knew he'd be expected to ask, "Honey, are you all set? Can I get you something else?"

"I guess some water, please" was all she said before sliding another forkful in her mouth. And before she took another bite, she said, "So you two don't have to rush back home, do you? Why don't you stay for dinner?"

"Dinner?" Antonia asked, surprised. "I would think that pasta might be your dinner."

"Well, Ma, dinner's not for another three or four hours. I'm sure I'll be ready to eat a little something for dinner. The point is not what or whether I'll eat, it's that you two don't have to worry about dinner when you get home, *and* I'll get to spend some time with you."

"Before you send me to the crazy house," Antonia said jokingly.

Ellen's face fell so suddenly that tears seemed immediate, and then she realized the levity her mother had found in it all. She looked at Antonia then cocked her head one way and the other. There was so much about this child of New Orleans that Ellen would never understand, much in the same way she could never quite get her mind to process that place in the bayou that had a box for every shade in the race of black folks. And it was in this moment that she knew her mother was like the jazz whose roots also grew up out of the Big Easy—never the same way twice, and much more complex than the simplicity of a mere melody. And because of her mother's ability to laugh off something quite so hurtful as her family wanting her to have her mind checked for cobwebs and cracks, Ellen said, "Ma, are you really okay about this? I mean you're joking about it now, but does it hurt you?"

"You told her?" Junior said, regarding Ellen with the shock of his widened eyes.

"Yeah, Poppa, and she said she'd do it."

Junior sat forward in his seat and turned his whole body

toward Antonia and said, "Antonia, you're really going to do this? I thought you'd kick like a mule."

"Junior, please. How long have you known me?" And she hesitated as if she'd let him answer, but before he could, she continued, "For as long as I can remember everybody thought I was crazy. Fou-fou. I knew a long time ago that I wasn't crazy. That's always been enough for me. Because whether you're crazy or whether you're sane, somebody, at some point, is always going to think they have cause to question your sanity. Remember that. Both of you." Then she leaned toward where Ellen sat on the sofa and lowered her voice as if she was attempting to whisper—but not really—and said, "And remember, honey, down south, you don't ask people *if* they have crazy people in their family, you ask which side they're on. It's just your bad luck that they're on both, because this one isn't playing with a completely full deck either," she said, raising her eyebrows drolly and pointing playfully at Junior. But not so playfully. "Anyway, it's like the Bible says, ye who has the truth lives without fear."

Ellen let out a child's giggle knowing she was the only one who saw her father shake his head from a years-old vexation and frustration with her mother—his wife—and all those biblical nonquotes. Then, as her laugh faded, she smiled distantly and to no one else, and thought about her baby boy and just what he might think of her, his mother, forty-one years hence. Yet it was a thought too daunting to ponder thoroughly, placing herself across the room in her mother's shoes, sitting with her son and his wife—oh, heaven forbid his wife!—with their talk of having her mind checked for the same cobwebs and cracks that she thinks are in her own mother's mind. And so she looked despondently at her mother and thought about jazz.

Aaron sat at his computer fighting against the momentum of his heavy, nodding head that could have slammed his face down onto the keyboard in a solid sleep. After the night he'd just had with Ellen—and until she gets that baby out of her, he thought, any time with her was more than one man should have to bear—and having gotten only an hour of sleep after that, he couldn't imagine how he would get through the newscast. He'd hit a wall hours ago, and now all that was keeping him awake was sheer will.

It seemed to him that his mind was taking hold of information several seconds behind real time, which would turn him into quite the fool on the air so he reread the script that one of the writers had put into the system for him, because it didn't completely register the first time. It read well enough, close enough, he thought to his own speaking style. He went on to the next one. This time around, though, he read it aloud, but plainly—without his newsman's voice. "Today, as Clayton Cannon comes to the last leg of his European tour, back here at home he got a rather special delivery. Cannon will return to Baltimore to a new concert grand piano that was delivered to his condominium at Harbor Court. But the piano was too large for normal delivery, so it had to be lifted by crane way up to the twentieth floor. The piano is reported to be a Bursendorfer, a German-made piano that is said to be the best made today, better, even than the renowned Steinway. Nothing but the best for the best. He will store the Steinway concert grand he's now touring with at the Meyerhoff, making it easier to take on the road with him." He paused to read *cut away to interview of president of Meyerhoff*, then *cue back to Aaron*. Then he continued to read aloud, "Apparently, his new residence high up on the twentieth floor makes taking the Steinway piano in and out for tours a bigger production than a staging of *Aida*. He will not tour with the Bursendorfer because many concert halls are not willing to pay the costs of insuring it."

Aaron stared blankly at the screen while he felt his ire rise—rise higher and hotter until he could no longer sit there and abide it another second. He leapt from where he sat as he brought his fist lightly down on the edge of his desk. Before he knew it, he found himself in the newsroom, not really in a rage, but furious despite his natural evenness. "I need to see the writer who wrote the script on Clayton Cannon."

"I think it was Bobby," someone said.

"Where's Bobby?" Clayton demanded. "I want to see him right now."

A young face turned from across the room with surprised eyes. "Yeah, Aaron, here I am. Is something wrong?"

"Yeah, something's wrong. The script you wrote for me on Clayton Cannon. What kind of crap was that?" Aaron said walking over to Bobby with his hands on his hips in a challenging manner.

"What do you mean?" Bobby said.

"What I mean is that I wouldn't say anything so absolutely cornball as 'Apparently, his new residence high up on the twentieth floor makes taking the piano in and out for tours a bigger production than a staging of *Aida*.' Who in the hell is going to get that, man? Not everybody in this city is an opera fan and most don't know *Aida* from their Aunt Ada. It's just a stupid reference, that's all."

Bobby opened his mouth to defend his script when Mark sauntered from his office to stand in the middle of the newsroom, directly between the two. "What's this about?"

"It's about this script, man," Aaron said, throwing up his hands in frustration. "He wrote this script about Clayton Cannon having a new piano delivered to him, then he writes this corny-ass reference to a staging of *Aida*. I mean, Mark, do I need to point out to you what's wrong with that? How many people are going to get that, man? How many people are going to, first of all, know that *Aida* is a reference to an opera, and then understand that it's a damned difficult opera to stage? I'll tell you how many—about two." He was visibly disturbed, but on his face, in his posture, in the way he paced in a circle, he revealed emotions he wished he weren't putting on exhibition. Aaron simply couldn't help himself.

Mark stared at Aaron for several seconds, then turned to Bobby and chuckled when he said, "Well, Bobby, I'm going to have to agree with Aaron on this one. It's too obscure a reference." And then he turned back to Aaron, regarding him with sternness, and continued, "But, Aaron, where's all this anger coming from, man? I mean, you don't like it, fine, then change it. That's all that needed to happen here. You didn't need to get in Bobby's face like that."

"I'm not in his face. Does it look like I'm in his face? I'm all the way over here. If I was in his face, I'd be all the way over there." He turned to walk back into his office, when he thought of another thing. "And I'll tell you where the anger's coming from, if you need to know. I don't know how this is news, anyway. Who the hell gives two good damns whether Clayton Cannon gets a new piano."

Mark reared back his head, then lowered it to peer at Aaron over the top of his reading glasses and said, "Well, first of all, it's news because I say it's news. But second of all, it's news because everybody in this town, whether they can tell Bach from Beethoven, is proud to have him choose their humble town to make his home. Concert pianists of his stature are generally not living in places like Baltimore. They're living in New York or London or Paris. So do you know what it does to the psyche of the people in this town to have him living here? In their small way, it's just as impressive as having Madonna move in down there at Harbor Court. Celebrity is celebrity, no matter how esoteric the field, Aaron. When a guy like this moves to New York, it's no big deal. Just another celebrity in the crowd. But when he moves to Baltimore, they claim him. And when the people of this city feel that he's a celebrity that they can embrace and claim, that's what makes this story news. You got it now?"

"I've got it," Aaron mumbled as he walked into his office, slamming the door behind him. He sat in his chair and leaned back. Suddenly, with only an hour before he had to go on the air as a steady, unflappable newsman, he couldn't have cared less about reading scripts, or writing them, or even correcting them. All that mattered to him now was wondering what part of his life Clayton Cannon would invade next.

Before he could become too ensconced in his thoughts of all the ways and whys for which he detested Clayton, he was distracted by Tilly, his producer, who had come in and settled herself in the chair in front of his desk. It was clear she was there for some undetermined duration, so Aaron simply stared at her questionably without saying one word.

"Well, I guess I'm approaching you at my own risk after what just happened in there a few minutes ago, but I'll take my chances," Tilly said superciliously, with a grin of equal scope. It was just her way.

Aaron stayed steady in his glare for several seconds, then replied, "Okay, I guess I'll bite. So what is it you're taking your chances with, Tilly?"

"It's a special I'm thinking about and I want you to be the host of it."

"What kind of special?" Aaron asked with a curiosity that had nothing to do with actual interest.

"Okay, well, what I'm thinking about is doing a one-hour show

with four of Baltimore's famous children. I'm thinking of Barry
Levinson, and Jada Pinkett-Smith, and Cal Ripken, and Clayton
Cannon." Tilly stopped as if to give Aaron his moment of erup-
tion. But when none came in five or so seconds, she continued, "I
figured, two who live here, and two who don't."

Although Aaron still held Tilly in his gaze, she wasn't in his
focus. He stared through her to see Clayton sitting before him, no
longer the phantom of his boyhood and manhood imaginings,
but a man in full. Flesh and feeling. And would that feeling tell
that man's flesh of the bad blood boiling in Aaron for him? The
interview. Aaron wondered what he would possibly ask him,
because his most reasonable question, the only one in which he
had interest was somewhere in the neighborhood of outright
impudence—"Why in hell did you drag your sorry ass back here to
Baltimore, anyway?" Of course he'd have to word it a little better.
Mostly, though, the one question Aaron would have is the one
that had hovered beside him for as long as he'd had memory, and
it was one to which Clayton would never have the answer—"Why
did you steal my mother from me?"

Finally, Tilly broke through the silence when she said, "Well,
don't just sit there and stare at me. Tell me what you think."

When Aaron brought Tilly back into focus, he said, "First of all,
Cal Ripken doesn't live in Baltimore. He lives in Timonium."

And Tilly snapped, "Oh please, Aaron. Do not pick that nit
with me. If you take somebody who lives in Timonium across the
country and ask them where they're from, they're not going to
say I'm from Timonium. They're going to say I'm from Baltimore.
Pikesville, Randallstown, Towson, Timonium, who cares. It's all
Baltimore. He's from Baltimore."

"All I'm saying is that, technically, it's not. Furthermore, technically Clayton Cannon is not a child of Baltimore, since he
wasn't born and raised here."

It started in her eyes, then Tilly's sarcasm became fully known
when she said, "Okay, well let's just say for now that Timonium is
Baltimore and Clayton Cannon has been given honorary child of
Baltimore status by me, and leave it at that. Now, what do you
think you see for a show like this in terms of the interviews?"

"So I wouldn't just be the host doing an intro and closing. I'd
have to do the interviews too?"

"Yes, of course. It would be your show. You'd have them take you to their favorite places around the city, tell you what they love about the city, what makes it special to them. That kind of thing. Any ideas?"

"Why me? Why not Maggie? Nobody loves Baltimore more than Maggie. She even knows the Banfield sisters—the mother and the aunts—pretty well, so she'd be the best one to interview Jada. Anyway, Maggie would love this kind of stuff."

"Are you telling me you don't want to do it?"

"I'm telling you I don't want to do it," Aaron said flatly. And he was flat in every way.

Aaron watched Tilly rise up and leave without closing his door, and he wondered about her thoughts of him. And in those moments as he watched her back decrease and then disappear into Maggie's office, he had to wonder what he thought of himself. But only mere seconds later, Tilly was out of Maggie's office, with Maggie following. And here they come, he thought. So he braced himself for what came next.

When his door opened, he looked at the two of them and said, "Tilly, what is it, now?"

"What this is, Aaron, is that you should be the one doing this story," Maggie said.

"I don't want to do it."

Maggie turned to Tilly and, with her hand on the door asked, "Tilly, can you give us a moment alone, please?"

Tilly left without a word, pulling the door closed behind her.

Then Maggie turned to Aaron and said, "Is this about Clayton Cannon? Because you know a piece like this can't be done without including him. It would be like doing a documentary about the Chesapeake Bay without talking about crabbing. But you need to do more pieces like this. Maybe it's time you confront your demon."

Aaron lowered his head and then looked off to the side of his desk where he'd hoped to find calm, but didn't. He looked back up at Maggie and said, "Maggie, you're about to make me mad. I have said that I don't want to do it, that I'm not going to do it, and I don't need you coming in here telling me about the bay, or my demon, or what I need for my career, because you're my co-anchor and the woman I date. You're not my agent or my psychiatrist."

Maggie took him in with a stunned gawking and said, "I'm the woman you date?"

But Aaron didn't understand the question, because if she wasn't that, if he had misspoken or insulted her in some way, he didn't know how he'd managed to do it with what he'd said. So with the previous second's anger forgotten, he replied earnestly, "You're the woman I date. Is there something wrong with saying that?"

"It sounds meaningless," she said flatly. "After four years together, it never occurred to me that it was still that meaningless to you."

"Maggie, I think you're blowing this all out of proportion. We're not married, we're not engaged. I'm too old to be the boyfriend to a girlfriend. What else am I supposed to say?"

"You could say something that makes me feel like I'm more than somebody you occasionally go out and have a burger and a beer with, Aaron," Maggie said in a whisper.

Aaron set his jaw, then rubbed his head with the frustration of too much, too many on his back in one moment. "Maggie, I'm not going to discuss this right now."

"You mean you're not going to discuss it ever," she said scornfully.

"Look Maggie, when we first started this relationship, the major ground rule was that we were never going to drag any part of our personal affair into this office, and now what are you doing? You're dragging our personal stuff right in here for us to discuss, and I'm telling you I'm not going to do it."

Maggie looked to the floor with widened eyes that seemed to have nothing else to do, nothing else to see in their angst. So she said nervously, "Okay, Aaron, you're right. I'll stop." Then she looked to him imploringly, as if something quite critical depended solely on him in that moment. "It's just that you've been so different lately, and I don't know if it's Clayton Cannon, or if it's about me."

Aaron smiled benignly at her and said, "Everything's cool, Maggie." And that was all he could say, because to tell her that it was actually both would have taken far more words than he knew just then.

Antonia settled herself on the sofa next to where Junior sat. She had waited the whole way home in the car from Ellen's and

Rick's, she waited as they took the long walk down the path from the street to their house, she even waited as they peeled off their coats and hung them in the closet, while Junior talked about everything under the sun but never asked about her lunch with Agnes. Then again, she talked about everything under the sun with him and never mentioned Cora's locket that she carried with her everywhere and swore she'd throw in his face when the time was right; and there was no way Cora Calliup was going to eclipse the news that Antonia was one step closer to Clayton. After all, he was there with her now, and not with Cora. And right now, they had something truly pressing before them that could change the face of their family.

How could anyone be so uninterested in what would be most curious to anyone else? How could he just not want to know? And as she looked at him, sitting there reading his medical journal as if there were even one thing in there that could possibly be more fascinating than what had happened to her that day, she grew bothered. Sure, she could just tell him, and though she knew she would eventually, simply telling him without so much as a slight inquiry from him would somehow suck all of the energy from the heft of the story.

So she drew in a chest-full of breath then blew it out in an overblown sigh, because maybe, she thought, he was in such deep thought about whatever medical matter he was reading about that he wasn't even aware that she was sitting right there next to him. Evidently he was aware of her, and she realized this as he continued to read without a word as she respired next to him on the sofa with all the subtlety of an air pump—for nothing. That's when she decided to shift restlessly. That would surely get his attention, because who couldn't take notice of such itchy movement so close to them. And then she knew who couldn't—a husband ignoring his wife with all his might. So finally she snapped, "Junior! Aren't you going to ask me about today?"

And without looking up from his medical magazine, Junior said flatly, "Antonia, do you want to tell me about today?"

"Well, what do you think? With all your lack of curiosity, for all you know, I could have met Clayton and resolved this thing once and for all."

"Well, I know that didn't happen, Antonia," Junior said as dispassionately as before.

"And you can be so sure because of what?"

"Because, Antonia, you wouldn't have been able to hold on to that for this long. You would have told us all over at Ellen's." Junior put the magazine on the coffee table, turned toward Antonia, regarded her from over his reading glasses and continued, "Now, if you want to tell me about it, Antonia, then tell me, but don't sit there and go on and on about why I didn't ask you."

And, oh, how she wanted to go on and on, but Junior had snapped at her reins and stopped her in mid-gallop, just as he'd always known how to do since they were one another's puppy-loves. Junior could always cut, she thought, with the precision of his sharp mind and clear vision, clean through to expose the pulsing heart of anything. Most of the time, she remembered that it was this quality of his that endeared him most to her. But then there were other times, like now, where she believed that the very part of his being that made her love him was the very thing that could one day scrape her nerves to such a red pulp that she'd have no choice but to send him packing back to where he began. And nowadays, she thought, with this Cora business, which she wanted to know about as badly as she didn't, sending him back to where he began just might be the ruin of whatever it was they still had. So she resolved that the point wasn't worth the fight, then looked at him squarely and said, "She's just as stubborn as she can be. She's still refusing to tell the truth. But I got to her, Junior. That girl nearly jumped out of her skin when I told her that I knew that Clayton was born nine months to the day after Emeril died."

Junior perked up at that bit of news, and as his eyes widened and fixed on Antonia he said, "You mean you'd never told her about that in any of those letters you wrote to her?"

"No. I wanted to save that until I had her face-to-face. I needed to see the look on her face."

"So what'd she say?" an excited Junior asked.

"Well, she flew off the handle, Junior. She called me a stalker and accused me of stalking Clayton just because I knew his birthday. But I'll tell you something, when she did that, that's when I knew it was true." Antonia fell silent with the most contented smile on her lips as she gazed past Junior's face at nothing on the wall. And she savored the thought of that exact moment when she knew, and the fear of truth shone in Agnes's eyes, like a delectable of which she'd been deprived for far too long. "And you know what else? I met Clayton's twin boys, Noah and Luke, and I'm telling you, Junior, they are the spitting image of Emeril. You remember that one little dimple Emeril had on his right cheek?"

"Yeah, I sure do remember that. That thing drove the girls wild."

"Well, those boys have that same dimple in their right cheek. And their eyes. Those are Emeril's eyes just as sure as I'm sitting here. I've seen Emeril's grandchildren. What a miracle."

Junior's smile faded like day into dusk, as if some dour notion had come back to him and settled itself in the place where the lightness of fancy had just sat. He reached over and took Antonia's hand lightly in his, then said, "So what are you going to do, Antonia? Because it's nice that you went and saw Agnes, and you got to see those boys too, and I know you don't want to hear this, but I've got to say it. Even if he is Emeril's boy, and I'm not saying he is, but even if he is, he will never admit it. He's got way too much to lose, being in that uppity white man's world of classical music that he's in. We may be living in the twenty-first century, but we may as well be in the nineteenth, because there's no way that this kind of thing coming out isn't going to stir up a lot of talk that his career just doesn't need. I'm not saying somebody would kill him, or anything like that, but there're a lot of people, especially in some of those places in Europe, I'll bet, that sure would make him wish he was dead. The world's not as liberal as people think it is, Antonia."

Antonia slid her hand from Junior's and stood. She smoothed out imaginary wrinkles in the skirt of her dress, then said, "Well, I don't know what I'm going to do now. But I do know that somehow I feel a satisfaction that I have never, ever felt about this whole thing. Just seeing Emeril's face in those boys has given me half the peace I'd been looking for. I almost feel as if I don't need anything else because any doubt I had—and there was very little to begin with—was removed by the physical proof of those boys." She walked toward the door to leave, thinking about the clothes she'd lay out for herself for the next day, when she was stopped by Junior.

"So, those boys looked just like Emeril, you say?"

"The spitting image," Antonia said over her shoulder at Junior. Then she turned full around to face him and added, "I know that most of the time I see what I want to see and hear what I want to hear. I will admit that that's been true sometimes in the past, but this time, Junior, I know that what I saw is real. Now, I just have to figure out if knowing that what God and I know is the truth is enough for me, or if nothing will ever be complete for Emeril until Clayton knows too." Then she went on her way through the doors of the living room. Crossing the front hallway, she thought about her canary yellow suit that everyone at church always says makes her look like sunshine itself. Or maybe, she thought, the navy skirt and white blouse with the bow would give her a more sober, milk-toast appeal. Then there was the crimson pantsuit that was neither bright nor bland, but gave her a certain verve that made her more confident. She couldn't decide, but as she climbed the stairs, Antonia wondered just what a woman should wear to her own sanity judgment.

CHAPTER

11

•

Aaron slid the chair from the table clutching its high back with both hands—because his chivalry had to evenly balance the perfection of her womanliness—and Tawna sat. But she didn't just sit. She smoothed her dress beneath her like a lady from another age and lowered herself into the chair with her unhurried southernness, and the lightness of down. Everything about her every move fascinated Aaron, and even if other women had smoothed their dresses and lowered themselves with as much femininity in his presence at any time, it simply went disregarded by him. There was something in her way that healed him from that which he didn't even know he ailed—and still, there was no naming it.

And as he took his seat next to her, there was absolutely no understanding why he thought of himself sick with Tawna by his side. Not sick with anything that could pluck him from the planet, but sick for a mere few days—the kind of sick that required the cooking of chicken soup and aspirin and side sitting. He imagined Tawna bringing the soup, but taking his temperature before he sipped the soup because she'd care enough to want an accurate read. And when his temperature wasn't acceptably low enough, she'd ply him full of the soup she'd made and the juice she'd squeezed. Then she'd read to him from the *Sun* papers until he fell asleep. But then, he thought, when he'd get better. Oh, when he'd get better. Just then, before his mind would let him explore the many possibilities of the tenderness of making love to her after having been sick, Tawna shook him from his fantasy.

"This place is really nice," she said in her songlike drawl. "I've always seen it from over at Harbor Place, and was always curious about it. Thank you for bringing me here."

"Oh, you're welcome. When you mentioned it I thought it was a really good idea that I don't think I would have necessarily come up with."

"You don't like it here?" she said with a surprise that seemed to have underneath it a genuine unease.

"Oh, of course I like it," Aaron said with an unwavering forthrightness in his tone he hoped would allay her concern. "That's not what I meant at all. What I meant was that for some reason, I hardly ever think about this place. Then again, I'm hardly ever downtown." He laughed, first low and then it grew, so he let her in on his thought. "But every time I'm down here and I see this place, Mo's, I can't help but think that the owner's some French guy named Maurice who's calling himself Mo to fit in better here in Baltimore."

Tawna let out a very girly laugh. She took a sip of the water that had just been poured into her glass, then looked at Aaron and asked, "How's your mother?"

"She's fine" was all he would say.

Then Tawna looked off past Aaron, smiling awkwardly, as if nervous to say what she did next. "And so how's Maggie, your girlfriend?"

Aaron shifted where he sat, with the slap of that question still stinging his face. Yet he knew exactly why she asked. So without looking at her he responded, "She's okay."

"You know that I needed to ask that, right?"

"Yes, I know," Aaron said, now looking into her deep brown eyes, because that was the only way to pay respect to her raw honesty. "So, I suppose you're wondering why I asked you here."

"Yes, I am wondering that, because I think you're aware that I know you didn't ask me out to dinner to talk about the financial services at T. Rowe Price."

Aaron breathed deeply, and was about to answer when he saw the waiter headed for them. "I think they're about to take our order."

"Hello, I'm your waiter, Sidney. How're you this evening?" the waiter said with as much cheer as he seemed able to muster.

"We're fine," Aaron answered.

"Are you ready to order?" he asked with a peculiar smile.

Tawna hurriedly grabbed the menu and said, "Uh, yes, in just one second."

"I can come back."

"No, that's not necessary," Aaron said. "We can find something."

"Well, would you like to hear our specials this evening?"

So when Aaron and Tawna agreed, the waiter recited a memorized list of dishes, and Aaron forgot each one as soon as the next was told. By the time Sidney had finished, all Aaron knew was that there had been four, and there was halibut prepared some sort of way, so he inquired, "How was the halibut prepared?"

"Grilled, with portabello mushrooms."

"That sounds real good to me," Aaron said, but actually he didn't much care what he ate. "I'll take the grilled halibut."

"And I'll take the pan-seared salmon," Tawna said.

"Would you like wine with your dinner?" Aaron asked her as the waiter hung around for her answer.

"Yes, that would be nice. I'll have a glass of chardonnay."

"I'll take the same," Aaron said.

The waiter finished scribbling their orders down, and when he was done, said, "Thank you."

"Well, he was a laugh a minute, wasn't he?" Aaron said.

"Now, that's a man who clearly does not love his job," Tawna said. Her eyes grew distant and her countenance pensive.

But Aaron knew what was whispering in her head, and he had to answer it, clear things up before the evening was through and she was certain she would never want to see him again. "Tawna, I'm not a playboy."

"I never called you that," she said with a kind smile.

"No, you didn't, but I know what it must look like, me being involved with Maggie and asking you to dinner."

And as if continuing the thought for him, Tawna said shyly, "Under false pretenses." Then she laughed.

Aaron laughed as well, hanging his head with embarrassment, and said, "Yeah, under false pretenses." Then he looked up at

Tawna. "It's just that sometimes, I'm kind of sitting around reading, or at work writing scripts, or in a production meeting and
suddenly I think about you. I just needed to find out why."

"So what do you think?"

"I think there are a lot of women who don't make apologies for
who they are. But who they are often offends and rubs against
most people's grain. They believe they're excused from the fallout
because they're only being who they are." He paused, because
though he never mentioned Maggie's name, he was certain Tawna
would think him a brute for speaking so ill of a woman he loved.
When reality told him that Tawna could not possibly know, he
continued, "You don't make any apologies for who you are, and
who you are, what you seem to be more than anything else, is this
bright light. You don't even have to smile for it to shine. It's almost
blinding and too much for someone like me to take sometimes.
And believe me, Tawna, I wouldn't be telling you any of this if I
didn't know that if I don't say it now, I most likely never will, and
then I just might lose my chance forever. But I just can't imagine
anyone meeting you, whether it's a man or a woman, and not
falling in love with you." It was then that he realized just how
contagious honesty could be, because the truth in which she
seemed to him to live gave him no choice but to try his best to live
up to it, and then honor the virtue. But the contagion of truth
brought him to suddenly know exactly how much integrity was in
what he just said when it was clear to him that whether he'd love
her completely as a man can love a woman, or if he'd simply love
her as plainly as she compelled anyone to love her, he would
always know that something special had happened the night she
appeared in his life.

Tawna watched him silently through eyes that had become liq-
uid. She lowered her head bashfully, then said softly, "That was
so nice. I don't think anyone's ever said anything quite that nice
to me."

"I doubt that's true," Aaron said, finding himself struck by
shyness.

Tawna slowly looked up at Aaron and said, "Well, maybe it's
who's saying it to me that makes it special."

"Well, it's how I feel."

And then, through nothing that was forced, a tender silence

landed between them. Aaron tapped one nervous finger on the table to the beat of some tune in his head that had never been real outside of himself. He watched Tawna, who seemed to be formulating something to say. So he said, "Were you going to say something?"

"Well, I was just going to say that you don't have to apologize to me if your relationship with Maggie is dying a natural death."

Aaron's head reared back with a certain surprise before he said, "Who said anything about my relationship dying a natural death?"

Tawna laughed with a certain confidence when she replied, "Aaron, you're not a cad. I didn't need you to tell me that you're not a playboy to know that you weren't one of those. So what else is there to explain why you've asked me out?"

Aaron chuckled nervously like a man who'd just been caught. "Well then, I guess you know people, huh?"

"I don't know if I know people, but I feel as if I know you. And I'll tell you another thing, I know what it looks like when a relationship has lived as long as it was ever destined to live. I left one of those back in Virginia."

"Really? Well, what happened, if I'm not overstepping?"

"It just went as far as it was going to go, and we . . . or at least I, knew from the beginning that it would come to an end eventually."

"Did you love him, or were you guys just hanging out—you know, having fun?"

Tawna took Aaron in with a face that seemed just shy of offended, but she continued, "Of course I loved him. I wouldn't have been with him for four years if I didn't. It's just that there was an issue between us that was never going to change. He was white, and while that never, ever got in the way of our love, it certainly got in the way of our future. He wanted to get married, and I swear, I definitely think we would have had a wonderful marriage, but he also wanted children, and, well—"

"You don't have to tell me if it makes you uncomfortable to talk about something so personal," Aaron said as he shifted nervously, thinking she was going to tell him that she couldn't have children. And while that wouldn't have mattered one wit to him, it just seemed to him to be too much to tell him on a first date.

"No, it's okay. The truth is, I have dated white men and black men, but when it comes to the idea of interracial children, I know that for that reason I couldn't marry a white man. I think a child has enough pain and heartache to navigate from childhood through puberty and into adulthood, and to add the whole issue of dual races to it. I don't know, it just seems like it's unfair for two people to make that kind of decision, play God in that way with another life."

"So, how do you date someone without the idea that one day you two will get married?"

Tawna looked at him with a Cheshire grin and asked, "How do *you* date someone without the idea that you two will get married?"

Aaron only nodded and smiled with a thin smile of nonplussed awkwardness. Then he said quietly, as if he didn't want her to hear, "I just thought it was different for women."

"Different how?"

"Just different in the way women want to get married."

"Aaron, I mean this in all loving kindness, but when the glacier melted down, you just stepped right on out, didn't you?" and then she laughed with complete abandon, and seeming comfort. "I'm not sure I'd feel right about saying *all* women want to get married, but this woman wants to get married. I'm not on such a mission to get there, though, that I can't welcome and appreciate a sound and profound relationship with someone for whom I care deeply for however long it lasts, even if going into it I know it's not going to end in marriage. Hopefully along the journey I've learned enough about myself and life to make me that much more prepared for when I do get married. But that's just how I see it."

Aaron thought that what she was saying sounded quite progressive for a southern woman, but thought better of saying it out loud because then she'd truly think he was the missing link. So he said instead, "I guess I've just never thought it all through before about interracial children."

"It's an issue, at least to me it is because this is a world that will love them or hate them for all the wrong reasons."

"Love them for the wrong reasons?" Aaron questioned, because it didn't make much sense in any way he looked at it.

"Now, you know there are some black people who're going to love an interracial child just because of their exotically colored light skin. To those people, it's not going to much matter what the child really looks like or how smart the child is, as long as one parent is white, those people will think that child is pure perfection in every way."

"That's a pretty sad statement of things, if that's how they really are."

"Yeah," Tawna said pausing to let the waiter put her salad in front of her and Aaron's salad in front of him. When he was gone, she continued, "It's sad, and it's cruel too, because it gives them a false sense of reality that'll do nothing to prepare them for the hatred that'll come from some whites and blacks alike just because they're not one thing or another."

Aaron put a heavy-handed sprinkling of pepper on his salad, then looked at Tawna with a serious stare and said, "So you've given this quite a bit of thought, it seems."

"From the first time I was blown away by finding myself attracted to a white man," she said before putting a forkful of lettuce into her mouth and chewing rigorously so that she could swallow. Then she quickly said, "Look, I've thought about it because when I do have children, I want to be able to give them the best of myself in order to make them the best they can be. I can't do that if I can't get a complete understanding of how to raise a child who has to find a way to bring two halves together in a way that society tells them they can't and shouldn't and still try to make them somehow whole. I mean, how do you introduce the concept of color the way it's understood here in America to a child? I think even if that child were, through some miracle, to somehow make it all the way to adulthood before knowing that they're two races, I think from the very moment they found out, it would change forever their concept of themselves, from who they knew they were to who they might be now."

Aaron only stared blankly into the flickering candle at the center of the table while he finished his salad. What if, he wondered, someone managed to make it all the way to adulthood without knowing—like Clayton. So Aaron fought with everything in him to keep quiet a sliver of sentimentality that wanted to creep up for Clayton, if it all was true. But it wasn't, so the pity wasn't needed, and he would put it away for some other man who'd grow up to find out that the one true thing, in which he would always know himself, was painted, half of it, another color. When his salad was done, he looked up at Tawna, who was still eating hers in small bites and said with a fresh, sideways smile, "Well, at least I can take comfort in knowing that you wouldn't turn down a marriage proposal from me because of my color."

Tawna laughed heartily, filling their little space in the room, then replied, "You never know, Aaron. The one thing we know about this world is that nothing is as it seems, and no one is as they seem." Then she did laugh, staring at him through her squinty, amused eyes as if to make it clear that she knew there was far more to him than what he seemed right there in front of her.

And though he laughed, laughed with every ounce of true mirth he could find in himself in that moment, it wasn't funny to him. It wasn't funny at all.

When the laughter faded, Tawna was left with a faint smile that would not leave when she said, "You think far more than you speak, don't you?"

Aaron looked into the flickering candle again, then up into Tawna's eyes. There was no telling why he should let her in, he only knew he had to. So he said, "Yeah, Tawna. I think a lot more than I speak. But the circumstances of my life have made that necessary."

"To protect yourself, or something? Or is it not quite that simple?"

"It's not quite that simple."

Tawna sipped her water, then put it down quickly when the waiter arrived with their meals. She leaned back to make way for the waiter's arm, then smiled graciously at him. Once Aaron's plate was placed in front of him and the waiter was on his way, she picked up her fork and speared a portion, then said, "So, do you ever speak of what torments you?"

Aaron stared blankly at her as he chewed for several long seconds. He shifted where he sat. Then he shifted again the other way. He took out his glasses and slid them onto his face. Then he took them off, folded them up and placed them on the table next to his plate. How dare she reveal him. "How do you know something torments me?"

"It's in every part of your way, Aaron. But mostly I know because the only reason anyone thinks more than they speak is because they're afraid of what would happen if they give voice to their torments."

"And you think I'm afraid."

Tawna chewed a bite of potato, then looked plainly at Aaron and said, "I think you're afraid." She ate a few more bites of food in the quiet that had slid between them, and then she snapped toward him and said, as if with a desperation to explain, "But that's not to say that you have to tell me what torments you."

Aaron laughed with a low chuckle, aware of and quite sobered by her truth. Then he looked at her and let his laughter fade to a smile for her that was churning with everything in him that not even he understood, and said, "I will, though. One day soon, I will tell you."

Aaron had just gotten back into his car after leaving Tawna at her doorstep. He did what any man raised by a woman whose sensibility was screaming in his ear *don't you dare go in there*. As badly as he wanted to go in, and with the way she invited him out of her southern politeness, he knew it was no place for him to be. Not on their first date. So as he turned the ignition, put his car into gear, and pulled away from her apartment, he was struck smack in the face with the memory of his first date with Maggie. It had left him warm, he remembered. Warm with a comfort that made him feel as if he had just slipped into an old and familiar sweater. And he remembered how they'd laughed and talked as they danced on the surface of everything that didn't have the least bit of a chance to chafe.

So as he drove toward home, he found the juxtaposition between that long-ago first date with Maggie and the still-present first date with Tawna far too troubling. Tawna had made him itchy in a way that left him not knowing what to do with himself.

He drove along mindlessly with Tawna in full focus. And as he did, he missed by mere inches the puffy coattail of a jaywalker who stared him down with the impudence of a streetwise toreador.

Then his thoughts went back to the comfort and acuity he had gained from the years with Maggie, knowing how to balance so elegantly on one heel atop a bed of eggshells. And though at first the stance was discomfiting in every way, it became part of everything he knew. But now there came another comfort. The comfort of serenity. And even though he had never seen it, never thought about it, never knew it existed, when he watched serenity approach him in Tawna, Aaron knew he could finally put his feet down— those shells be damned and crushed to crumbs.

So definitely, he thought, Tawna was the gift of serenity he'd give to his life, but mostly, she'd be the gift he'd bring to his family. And just as serenity approaches, hers will come and cover so softly and so gradually that nothing will ever be the same and only he will know why.

And this made him wonder what his mother would think if she were to understand, as gradually as a sunrise, that nothing ever comes down to this or that, right or wrong. And what his sister would think if the palette of life's logic had more colors than black and white. Neither would know the sieve of reasoning through which their sensibilities had gently been squeezed and shaped and made lithe. But he would know. And so he smiled as he pulled into his driveway with the thought of Tawna. Then he couldn't help himself when an out-loud laugh just jumped from him as he got out of the car and made his way toward his front door, because the funny thing was that he'd never heard of such a thing and most likely neither had anyone else—one woman's salvation for one man's life.

Antonia was in the kitchen peeling potatoes when she heard Junior step into the front hall from the cold and close it out behind him. There was a time, she thought, when only the sound of him could send her to a placid place inside herself. Just knowing he had come in from the cold to her had always given her a belief in the constancy that her love was safe with him and his with her. When Junior came home in days past, it was because there was no other place he wanted to be, no other place he could be. Now, there was another place, and perhaps he'd never go, or perhaps it was only a question of time. No matter what his decision might be, there was no more peace she could find in his opening the door to close out every element of the world.

When he reached the kitchen, he went to her and offered her a kiss on the cheek that became awkward due to her stiffness.

Antonia glared at him with everything she knew. Then, after several long seconds, when it was clear to her that he was not aware that she was staring him down, she went back to peeling her potato. While she peeled, she couldn't imagine how he'd come to believe that he lets her do anything, as if he ruled her and everything in her. And with his mistress down in New Orleans, she thought, he ought to know that he no longer had the same intensity of power in their home. Then again, she thought, even days after finding that locket and shooting the venom of her hatred at him with her eyes, Junior still had no idea she knew about Cora. If, she had to remind herself, there was even anything to know. But there had to be, because that locket and its inscription made it quite something to know.

And when Junior made no attempt at conversation, Antonia noticed there was something about the way he sat in the comfort of one of his worlds. Did he sit like that at Cora's, she wondered. So that's why that unknowable demon in her compelled her to disturb his peace. "When is your next board business down in Tulane?"

"I have to go down next month to discuss hiring this doctor from out of Atlanta. Why do you ask?"

"Oh, just because I thought I might come along," and without lifting her head, she looked over at Junior to see his immediate reaction. There was no measuring her silent ire when she saw that it was nothing. He didn't even seem to as much as blink, from what she could see from where she stood. So she pressed, "Is that okay?"

"I guess, Antonia," Junior replied with a slight edge. "Although, I don't know why you want to go back down there after all these years. You haven't been down to New Orleans in nearly twenty-five years, and then we didn't even stay in New Orleans that long since we were on our way to Plaquemine to visit Momma. You don't know anybody down there anymore, anyway."

She gave him a sly smile, then said, "That's not true. My cousin Vera Sue lives there, and her three children. Well, two of them live in Baton Rouge, but that's close enough. And then there's Cora Calliup." She waited to see what he would do, how his face just might change. But nothing. He was even in every way. Then she continued, "I haven't seen her nearly since I left

New Orleans to come live here. I know she has all those children named after herbs. Do you ever run into her down there, Junior?"

He didn't answer her. He just slid the newspaper that sat on the other side of the table toward him and proceeded to read it.

But she knew he was only pretending that he either hadn't heard her or wasn't paying attention. So this time, she said it quite loud enough for the deaf to hear. "I said, do you ever run into Cora Calliup when you're down there?"

Junior looked at her firmly for several tense seconds. Seconds that seemed as if at the end of them, Junior just might unburden his soul. Instead, he stood from the table, newspaper in hand, and said crisply, "No." And with that, Junior floated from the room like an amorphous vapor that was headed for anywhere it could twist and turn and eventually vanish.

Antonia only stared after him, part of her wanting to follow him, but most of her simply wondering if Junior's reality had been able to be split in two—life in Baltimore, and life in New Orleans. And she supposed that when a man had polarized his life with two disparate women like herself and Cora, reality could only be so—in halves. So she put her attention back on her potatoes, and could not fathom just how it might come to pass that she would be able to throw that locket in Junior's face and simply say, *I know.*

CHAPTER

12

•

Clayton sat in the master's throne at the dining room table waiting for his dinner, wearied from a weeklong European tour, not to mention the oddity of Europeans that never failed to amaze him. There was nothing specifically anomalous about them other than their unrivaled arrogance in believing they could lay claim to him simply because it was from European stages that he had been catapulted to the heights of his renown. And as he noticed the old wooden clock that made itself the center of attention atop the buffet, his mind was forced back to his first night on the continent in Milan. It was at a reception in his honor where he found himself in the company of a woman trying to do the same thing as that clock—make herself the center of attention. The only thing was, as offensive as that clock was to him, she was nowhere near as charming. She was an Englishwoman, the wife of some bloated-belly Englishman who moved and spoke with the superciliousness of a man who, under less cultured circumstances, might try to pass himself off as aristocracy. Clayton could barely abide what the English accent did to his ears to begin with, but he could still hear the woman's nasally accent as she spoke with rather proficient haughtiness at the way America was only capable of producing the lowest levels of talent, among the likes of which were Madonna and Britney Spears. *"And whether a performer can play the kazoo or sing like a badly wounded animal, Americans don't care because they're merely seduced by the celebrity,"* he heard her shrill voice echoing in his head. And Clayton actually laughed out loud when he remembered that in less than two minutes of berating Americans' seduction by celebrity, she was inviting him to take summer holiday with her, her husband, and his belly at their villa in Lake Como. *"Everyone would just die of envy if they knew you were taking holiday with us."* Was someone as narcissistic as this woman capable of seeing the irony in which she was swathed?

Susan came into the dining room carrying a casserole, and before she could set it down in the middle of the table, Clayton said, "I've been thinking that we should find something else to put on that buffet. What do you think?"

"What's wrong with my grandmother's clock?" she asked with a guarded tone.

"Well, Susan, I've never bitten my tongue about the fact that I think it's a terrible-looking thing. I'm just saying, now that we're here in Baltimore and considering we've been dragging that thing up and down the road since we've been married, maybe we should rethink the clock and all this stuff that we've had since we first moved up to New York from New Orleans. You know, get a more updated look in our home."

Susan stood straight and settled her hands on her hips. "You know I don't like that modern stuff, Clayton. Half of it looks like it belongs in the waiting lounge for a shuttle to outer space. All that glass and chrome, and chairs that look like they're not meant to hold a bottom for longer than five minutes. Why you'd think that they'd never even heard of wood."

"I'm not saying it has to be modern, just more updated."

"I like our antiques. That clock is an antique, Clayton."

"And there is no law that says every antique is a beautiful one, Susan. That thing is just plain old ugly. All I'm saying is that maybe we can update the look of our home without going too far in the modern direction. I love antiques just as much as you, but I like attractive antiques. I just want us to get some attractive antiques in here."

"Well fine, Clayton," she said as she turned to go back into the kitchen. "Let me get the rest of dinner on, now."

Once she left, Agnes came through the swinging door so quickly Clayton wondered how it could have happened without them crashing headlong into one another. He followed his mother's movements intently as she placed another dish in the middle of the table, then asked, "So what's that?"

"It's kale. I made it," Agnes said, as if to assure her son of something.

"Oh" was all Clayton said at first. Then he continued, "Did you make it the way Susan makes hers? Because I like the way Susan makes it. She sautés her kale with onions and garlic and pepper sauce instead of boiling it with meat."

Agnes took her son in with seeming incredulity, then replied, "I made it the way *I* make kale. You ate it when you were a boy; now all of a sudden my kale's not good enough for you?"

Clayton only laughed, nearly under his breath, then said, "Momma, in case you haven't noticed, I haven't been a boy for some time now, and I've had a lot of years eating Susan's kale, that's all."

"Ummf," was all Agnes said before she went back into the kitchen. And when she walked right back in behind Susan, with the twins trailing behind her, she went to her seat for dinner, settled herself, and said to Susan before her daughter-in-law could get into her chair, "All of a sudden, my kale isn't good enough for him now. He wants *your* kale."

"Oh, Mother Cannon, I'm sure Clayton still loves your kale, don't you Clayton?"

"Of course I do, Momma. I never said I didn't love your kale." And he thought to say that he simply had his mouth set on tasting Susan's kale, but he couldn't see how that would make anything better, so he simply left things as they were. He reached past Noah for his mother's kale, then scooped a good helping of the soupy limp greens—that had been cooked to their certain death and hardly resembled their former form—onto his plate. He gave the dish to Noah, and before he had anything else on his plate, before they had even blessed the food, Clayton took a forkful of greens and ate them eagerly. "Wow, Momma! This sure does bring back memories, come to think of it. They sure are good."

Agnes gave her son a smile that said she had been duly placated. "Thank you, baby."

"So, Momma," Clayton said as he proceeded to dish more food onto his plate, "how come you didn't go back to New Orleans once I left for Europe?"

"Oh, well honey, I just wanted to spend more time with my beautiful boys here," she said in a way that said that was all she would say.

But Clayton was clearly expecting more. He looked at his mother with questioning eyes, then at Susan who was watching Agnes in much the same way. So he shifted his gaze back to his mother and said, "Well, what did you all do?"

Agnes put the spoon back in the bowl of kale, then placed her hands in her lap like an uncertain child being taken to task for her actions. "We just spent time together, Clayton. Susan went to dinner and the boys and I stayed here and played cards and popped popcorn. There aren't many other details to tell you."

Then Susan, as she plucked boiled potatoes from a dish, said, "Speaking of that dinner, Momma, I got the distinct impression that there was some tension between you and that woman you were having lunch with that day. I've been meaning to ask you about that. What in the world were the two of you talking about? Because you sure were agitated enough."

"We were just having a disagreement about something that happened in the past, darling, that's all. She saw things one way, and I saw them another." She looked at Clayton, and then to the opposite end of the table at Susan and defended herself. "That does happen, you know?"

"Oh, of course it does, Mother Cannon," Susan said as if to assure her mother-in-law that she wasn't accusing her of anything. "I was just wondering, is all. I wanted to make sure everything was okay."

"Well, everything was just fine. Who's going to say grace?"

"I'll say it, Grandma," Noah said.

"Isn't that just like my good boys," she said, giving them a grandmother's fawning smile, as if Noah and Luke were one, no matter what, just by virtue of having been born together.

Glancing around the table, Noah began, "Dear Lord, make us truly thankful for the food we're about to receive for the nourishment of our bodies. Amen."

"Wasn't that just wonderful?" Agnes said, her voice filled with inflated pride.

"That was quite nice, son," Clayton said as he cut into his meat. Then he turned to his mother, still with her contentious visit with her friend on his mind, and went to inquire but was cut off by Susan.

"What was your friend's name, anyway, Mother Cannon? I forgot it."

But since Agnes didn't rush to answer, it gave Noah plenty of opportunity to blurt out, "Antonia. Her name was Antonia. Right, Grandma?"

"Yes, that's right, honey."

"She has a nice face," Noah said. "I think she liked us."

"Of course she liked you," Agnes said, smiling at the boys. "What's not to like about you two sweeties?"

Clayton was barely aware that he was staring dead ahead into the meat in the center of the table when his gaze was disrupted by the intensity of Susan's attention on him. But she would have to wait. All that mattered to him in that particular moment was the Antonia he had met. And how could it be happenstance, he wondered, that two women from New Orleans—one knowing his mother, the other drifting into him at Harbor Place—could be two separate women. Chance simply wasn't that profound. When his eyes did make their way to Susan's and slid into them, he could see that she wanted to know what was the matter; what had sent him off to a most distant place. But Antonia had now become another name, like Emeril, that had come to epitomize a mystery that had long ago perched itself over his life; like the raven, nevermore. And all he knew about this mystery, the only thing possible for him to know, was that it had roots that were planted deep. And it was the very nature of the mystery that always made him question his state of consciousness in the back of that funeral car so many years before. Perhaps, he thought—particularly now with a completely formed woman named Antonia haunting and overtaking his every thought—he was indeed asleep that day when he thought he'd heard his grandmother suggest that his father was someone different than the man they'd just put into the ground.

So he snapped out of the stupor and sliced off a bite of meat from his plate, but before he would eat it, he asked his mother, "So what did you and this friend Antonia talk about that caused so much tension between you two?"

Agnes set her fork down in what seemed to be certain frustration. And when she'd finally swallowed the bite she had been

chewing, she answered, "Clayton, there are far, far more interesting things for us to discuss than some boring old lunch I had with
an old friend. Why don't you tell us about your concert tour? How
was it? Did you get standing ovations at every performance?"

"Momma, it was no different than any other tour I do over
there. Self-important, self-believing aristocracy are the worst
sycophants on earth. That is, of course, until I leave and then they
can talk about what an unsophisticated, boorish American I am
with my southern drawl and simple clothes."

"That's what makes you so much better than them," Agnes
said. "You're brilliant, and yet you still have the elegance to be
humble. Not like those wine-swilling pigs."

"Brilliance and elegance are subjective ideals, Momma," Clayton pointed out with a certain unease in his voice that slid into his
countenance. This was what had bothered him most about his
mother through the years. She had the most irksome way of
showing her devotion to him with praise while vilifying anyone
she could on the periphery, whether she had just cause or not.
And there were times when it made her praise of him lack sincerity. But he didn't want to think about that, so he simply continued,
"Even as hard as it is for me to admit it, I think we have to assume
that every European is not arrogant Euro-trash."

"I'm not saying they're all like that, Clayton. I'm just saying
that so many of them think that all they have to be is European to
be elegant."

"And you know this based on what, Momma?" Clayton asked
firmly.

"Just based on the way they seem," she said, sounding a bit
wounded. And then she lashed back, "I'm giving you a compliment and somehow I end up being attacked and accused of I don't
know what."

"Oh, Mother Cannon," Susan interrupted. "Nobody's attacking you or accusing you of anything. Are you Clayton?" and she
gave Clayton a hard-eyed mother's glare for misbehavior.

"Of course I'm not accusing her or attacking her. I just don't
want her going around saying something like that to the wrong
people. It only takes one misspoken word to be the lead story
on the news with this town being so absolutely, unexplainably

captivated with me moving here. I'll tell you, I don't get it. I'm like the Cal Ripken of classical music, or something in this town."

"Well, I'm not stupid, Clayton. I would never say something like that outside of this room with just you and Susan and the boys. What do you think I'm going to do, go across the street and shout it from the steps of the Science Center?"

"Now you're being ridiculous, Momma."

And just the way a child knows how to bring the spotlight of their family's attention directly onto themselves, Luke interrupted with what would seem to most others as incongruous kid-talk when he said, "Today at school, the teacher asked me and Noah to tell the class about New Orleans since Daddy is from there and going down there to play a concert."

"Did she, now," Susan said interestedly, as if she were relieved to be drawn into anything other than the nitpicking of Clayton and his mother. "So what did you tell them?"

"We told them about Mardi Gras, and we told them about the music that's special only to New Orleans."

"That's right," Luke said. "And we also told them about funerals, right Noah?"

"Yeah, we sure did. We told them about how some people have parades and Dixieland bands to take them to the graveyard. And they laughed and thought we weren't even telling the truth, Daddy." And the boys giggled until everyone else joined them.

But then Luke sobered up and asked his father earnestly, "But, Daddy, they wanted to know why they carried on like that for somebody who's died, like they're happy the person died, or something? Why do they do that?"

"Well, we're not happy when people die," Agnes told her grandsons. "What we're doing is giving the people a good send-off to heaven. That's what it's all about. We want to make sure they go off to heaven with their spirits high."

"That's real nice," Noah said, seeming to grasp wholly its profundity. "Did you all do that for Grandpa Cannon's funeral, Grandma?"

"Well, no. Grandpa wanted a traditional funeral with limousines and regular church music. He was a very Catholic man, and

way too conservative to be a child of New Orleans," Agnes said
with a hearty laugh that seemed to come directly from her memories. She smiled at Clayton, then at the boys and continued, "Anyway, he didn't go for all that—as he called it—'hoopin' and
hollerin' and carryin' on.'"

"Grandpa sounds funny," Luke said with a little boy's giggle.

"He was funny in his own way," Agnes said fondly.

Clayton said nothing as he ate determinedly while his mind,
in spite of his efforts to halt it, harked back to his father, and
with everything in him that he could remember, he couldn't
recall one time in which he would have considered his father
possessed of any kind of humor—not even *in his own way*. He
remembered a man, quiet and retiring and quite innocuous, but
a man who nonetheless had a very strong marriage to his beliefs,
and issues in which he did not believe, as Clayton had come to
think of it, were simply wrong in Douglas Cannon's eyes. That
was the thing that always made the man's condemnations so
confusing for Clayton as a boy living in Douglas's presence and
as a man living with him as memory. His father was never very
fired-up in the telling of where he stood regarding anything, but
it was oh so clear that what he said came from some simmering
heat at his core.

For some reason he could never seem to understand this one
moment out of all the others, and that Clayton couldn't forget. It
contrasted the strength of his father's convictions with the meek-
ness of his spirit. During the family news-watching hour, his
father stared with plain, impenetrably cold eyes at the bleak faces
of Mexican migrant workers, some of them as young as new
money, some as old as the legacy of bigotry, who were a rag-
tag clan dressed in tatters of clothes that only had a vague resemblance of their former lives. Clayton watched his father as
nothing—not the old, not even the young—seemed to stir any
emotion regarding the sentimentality of humanism. And all of it
was made to look even more abysmal rendered in grainy black-
and-white sixties' television news. *"America is for Americans."*
Clayton could still hear his father's determined, yet impassive
judgment about the Mexicans as it floated softly amidst the thin
light of the television in the darkened living room, while father

and son reclined in the contented stupor of their well-fed bellies. Could he see the disparity of fortune? Clayton now wondered about things he, himself, only understood clearly from the turret of his manhood. Still, he heard his father's voice, judging and piti-less, but always docile in its tone: *"If things are so bad here, they should go on back where they came from."* Yes, Clayton thought with a weakened smile as he pondered the humorless man, Douglas Cannon was one of those—the kind who might not be impas-sioned enough to actually lynch a man, yet he would never do anything to stop it.

So Clayton finished his meal without saying a word against what his mother most likely *had* to believe about his father. And he supposed, as he cleaned the last morsel of food from his plate with his fork and ate the last piece of his dinner roll, that the only thing left once a man is dead, the only thing that matters after the fact, are the pictures in the hearts and minds of those who loved him. If his mother's perception was of a man who had even an ounce of funny in him, then who was he, as the son, to negate that opinion?

And with the swiftness of a shifting wind, Clayton went back to what was important. "So tell me about this Antonia woman, Momma. What's her last name?"

"It's Jackson, if that's important at all."

As hard as Clayton tried, all he could remember about the woman's name was Antonia. But that was enough. These two women had to be the same. So he continued, "Well, it's important because I met a woman named Antonia. Maybe it's the same one."

Agnes turned slowly to see Clayton, then stared at him as if she were looking at him from another realm. "Where did you meet a woman named Antonia?"

"Over at Harbor Place. We had lunch together. She told me that she had followed my career since the beginning. She's from New Orleans too. It must be the same woman. She's about five-foot-five, she's a black woman with sort of a light brown complexion and she's got a short haircut. Is that her?"

"That sounds like what she looked like," Noah said.

"Well so, Momma. Was that her? I mean, if it was, then why didn't she tell me that she knew you?"

Agnes answered nervously. "Well, Clayton, what are the

chances that it was the same woman? I mean, for goodness sakes, there must be a million Antonias running around the world as we speak."

"I don't know," Clayton said skeptically. "It just seems like too much of a coincidence to me for it to really be one."

"Well, that's all it can be," Agnes said sternly as she studied her plate while she ate. "It's not the same woman."

And so Clayton understood that this would be the last word on the matter. To press it would make it all become futilely frustrating, and there was not much point he could see to going through that much angst with his mother only for it to end up being exactly what she said—a coincidence. So Clayton pushed away from the table, and just as he stood, said, "Well, I'm going to excuse myself now, if you all don't mind. I want to take a drive around the city to get to know it again."

"You want more to eat?" Susan asked.

Clayton smiled at the southern womanliness that compelled her to ask him the same thing after every meal, as if he didn't have the sense God gave a goose to know when he wanted more to eat, much less how to ask for it. But he nonetheless responded as he went over and kissed the boys on the tops of their heads. "No, thank you, honey. I'm all set. I expect to be back before you turn in, but if I'm not, don't wait up for me." When he reached Susan, he bent and gave her a kiss that lasted just long enough to be decent viewing for other eyes. Then he stood straight and blew a kiss to his mother. "I'll see you in the morning, Momma."

Clayton went to the living room and called down to the garage for his car. He left, giving one last good-bye to them all. He closed the door softly behind him and stepped across the hall to ring for the elevator. When the doors slid open there was only one man in it, and Clayton stepped to the back wall. From where he stood, he had a peripheral view of the man. It didn't take Clayton long to realize that the man was who he thought he was, except he couldn't remember his name. All he knew was that he was a Baltimore Oriole and quite a player. This he knew from the times the birds would fly into town—or at least his former town, New York—to take on the Yankees and this was the only other player, aside from Ripken the golden boy, who always had a New York press microphone stuck in his face. And isn't it a shame, Clayton reflected, that even all the way in New York, that Ripken name was trapped in his consciousness for no other reason than the legacy. He looked up at the floor indicator and saw that they were closing in on the lobby, so Clayton quickly said, "Say, aren't you one of the Orioles?"

The man turned awkwardly to see Clayton over one thick broad shoulder and said in the simplest, most monotonous tone of the disinterested, "Yeah, I am."

"Clayton Cannon," Clayton said, sticking out his hand for a shake with the overexcitement of a little leaguer, hoping for the majors one day. "I've seen you play in New York. I just moved from there," Clayton noted as the elevator doors opened to the lobby.

The man stepped out, and turned halfway to face Clayton and said with only a modicum of sincerity, "Good to see you."

"You too," Clayton said as he stepped into the lobby. "Take it easy," and he watched as the man, more the height of a basketball player than a baseball slugger, went on his way without thanking Clayton for the good wishes. Then he remembered that he had one more level down to go to get to the garage and his car, so he turned swiftly, certain the elevator had taken another trip to collect others. But it was there, the door wide open. He got back on with one fleet step and rode it down.

When he stepped off the elevator, he ran headlong into the garage attendant, all pink acne, crooked teeth and bubble gum, who was just standing there with the biggest Cheshire grin on his face that put a start of fear for the briefest second into Clayton. It was as if this young man had just seen whatever object of his fascination that someone his age, just barely sprung from high school, might worship. But Clayton knew it couldn't be him that this young man held in adulation, so he decided the young man was touched in the same divine way as simpletons and only smiled thinly, saying, "Good evening, young fellow. Thank you so much," and Clayton slipped a five-dollar bill into the attendant's hand, then went to step around him to get to his car that sat idling off to the side.

"Yes sir. Thank you, sir. But I also wanted to tell ya that I'm from Louisiana, too. I've been a fan of yours since forever."

"Really?" Clayton said, scarcely able to stop looking at the young man's overgrown teeth that went this way and that, but mostly stunned by this unlikely fan.

"I sure have been. My ma and daddy, too."

"Well, how do you like that?" Clayton said through a stupefied laugh.

"Oh, yes sir. Matter of fact, I've been up here for two years tryin' to get into the Peabody. I audition every year, and every year I get turned away. But I ain't gonna give up. I want to do just what you did. I only got two heroes—you and Harry Connick, Jr. What y'all do to the piano, I'll tell you, that's what I wanna do," the young man said as he stood there shaking his head in his own private reflection. Then he perked up. "Say, do you know him? Harry Connick, Jr.?"

"Sorry, never met him," Clayton said, trying not to let his utter sadness for this young man's life be heard in his voice. But then again, he thought, who's to say? Who's to say that rejections from a conservatory of music has necessarily written the epitaph on this young man's dreams? Far stranger things have happened in the world of music.

"I guess you two travel in different circles, huh?"

"Something like that" was all Clayton said with a thin smile.

"Well, I ain't gonna be crazy about this, you know. I'm gonna audition two more times, and if I still don't make it, I'm goin' back to New Orleans 'cause I ain't tryin' to make Baltimore my home, you know what I mean. I mean, it's nice here and all, but I ain't gonna give up my citizenship down in Louisiana. I just needed to give it a shot."

"Well, you should go for it, that's what I say. And it's good that you've got a job."

"Oh yeah! That's the first thing I did when I got here. It don't pay much, you know, but in this building I sure as heck do get to meet a lot of good and important people. Like you! And you know, some Orioles and Ravens live here too?"

Clayton only smiled at the sheer irony that he could be celebrated in the same light as an Oriole and a Raven in the mind of this pimply-faced car-parker who, at first glance, looked to Clayton as if his only other talent just might be picking beans in a ripe field. So he chuckled, partly from the thought, but mostly with the young man's characterization of Louisiana as an entirely different country to which one had to claim or denounce citizenship. "By the way, son," he said, "though I'm sure sometimes it doesn't seem that way down there, Louisiana is still a part of the United States, so you don't have to worry about giving up your citizenship just by moving up here."

"Ah, yes sir. I know that," the young man said through shy laughter. "By the way, my name is DeWitt. DeWitt Dilly. Anything you ever need, sir, you just come right on down here and ask DeWitt Dilly. I'm at your service."

"Well, that's good to know, DeWitt," Clayton said, extending his hand to shake DeWitt's. "And I want you to call me Clayton. It's kind of good to know that I have such a big fan working right downstairs. I'll see you later, DeWitt." Clayton went to his car and opened the door, and just before getting in, he turned to take DeWitt in one more time, smiling at how simple life can truly be with young dreams.

"Bye now, Clayton," DeWitt said with a proud smile.

Clayton slid behind the steering wheel of his car and closed himself in, then pulled out of the garage wondering if, in the spaces between words, DeWitt could hear the speciousness that contradicted his encouragement. And it got him thinking about just what he might have done if he had camped out in a town auditioning for only one school of music, only to be turned down time after time. He believed, with everything in him, that he'd go back to New Orleans and play honky-tonk in saloons. It was respectable enough and came with its own adulation, he supposed, in its way. Yet whatever it was he said, it made DeWitt Dilly feel that he was right on with fighting his good fight; and what's the matter with that? he thought. So whether it was sincere or fraught with doubt, it didn't come from an altogether bad place.

So he drove along Light Street until he reached the light at Pratt. It was amazing to him how much he remembered and how much he'd forgotten in the twenty-three years he'd been away. But what crept up on him from some abandoned corner of his memory was the thought of the *News American* newspaper that had been gone from Baltimore for at least twenty years, but he remembered it; and remembered that the building had been right over there where Stouffers and the Galleria now stood.

By the time Clayton had gotten to Mount Vernon Place, it

occurred to him that he didn't have a clear destination in mind—until he had reached the Peabody Conservatory.

He parked in front of one of the prewar buildings along the square, and it only served to make him reflective over this little quaint gem of the city, with its cobblestone streets, that Gothic-style church, and the red-brick apartment buildings that somehow blended in an esoteric enough way with the gray-stoned buildings of an olden era, and the Washington Monument—the original one with a statue of the man himself right on top. Nothing like the giant inverted writing utensil that Clayton had never seen as a fitting monument to the nation's first president. To that degree, that gray pencil with its point to the sky over in Washington fell upon his sensibility in the same way as did modern art—he simply didn't understand such a contemporary tribute to an early man any more than he could regard paint dripped, flung, and splattered on a canvas as art.

So now he was out of his car and walking, gawking, remembering, wishing he had thought to move back to this place that suckled him when he was fresh out of Louisiana. There was something about the cobblestones or the old-world ornamentation adorning the buildings ringing the monument that somehow made him feel as if he hadn't left New Orleans at all. Maybe, he thought, it was the charm of another more genteel time that did it.

When he got to the door, he paused before grasping the handle that he had opened every day at one point in his life. But he resisted the urge to stand and meditate on the sentimentality of a door handle—which he couldn't help but notice had not changed in all these years. Once he stepped inside, he faced a guard who sat at a desk just on the other side of the vestibule, his features illuminated by fluorescent light.

"May I help you, sir?" the man asked.

Clayton smiled, thinking it would illicit the same, and said, "Oh, hello sir. I used to be a student here. I just thought I'd come by and take a look around. Maybe go down to one of the practice rooms."

"Well, most of these practice rooms are reserved. You can't just pop into any one," the man said, as if he took his responsibility quite seriously.

"Oh, yes sir, I know that," Clayton said contritely. "I remember the policy very well. What I was wondering was if there might be one that hasn't been reserved tonight. Any one will do, because I had practiced in them all." But what he didn't go on to say, for fear the man would consider him a kook, was that each practice room held some sort of specific memory for him.

The guard flipped through pages until he stopped at one, and once he finished studying it, offered, "Okay, well tonight, you can have practice-room five. But first, you have to show me an alumni card, or something."

"Certainly," Clayton said as he went immediately into his wallet to pull out the card that he couldn't even begin to understand why he carried around with him. "Here you are, sir. You see there? I was in the class of seventy-nine."

"So I see," he said, as he scribbled something onto a pass. Then, handing it to Clayton with the alumni card and a pen, he said, "Just sign in right here in the book, and you can have two hours down there. If you need more time, you can come up and ask for it, but just keep in mind that the building closes at eleven."

"Thank you, kind sir," Clayton said as he handed the man back his pen. And as he started on his way, he noticed a question in the man's eyes. So he asked, "Is there a problem, sir?"

"Well, naw, except that I was wondering where your books are. You don't have any music books with you."

Clayton smiled, touched his fingers to his temple and replied, "It's all up here."

Heading down the hall and down the stairs, Clayton found his way to the practice rooms. There were the sounds of muffled pianos, four, five, maybe ten all going at once. So now, just as then, it made him think of Liszt, frenetic, with an energetic insanity that he really had to listen carefully to, and become one with, before it could become sane and coherent in a theoretical way that could prophesy life. In fact, he thought he just might play Liszt once he sat down at this piano of his youth. But when he finally got to practice-room five and opened the door, and saw that baby grand standing alone in the room, he could think of only one thing to play.

So he closed the door behind him, peeled off his coat, and dropped it on a chair next to the door. He sat at the piano and played the first chord, and before he knew it, he'd launched into

"Baby Grand." He hummed as he played, and he made it more bluesy than its original, feeling the power of his connection as deeply as those words. Then, right there in his head, was Ray Charles and his voice of a life lived in the lyrics of songs. Minor keys, Clayton thought as he played and rocked with an uncanny likeness to Ray Charles when the words and notes mingled in his soul and became electric; songs in minor keys like this one could always cause a rumbling in a man's foundation. The keys of the blues. Beethoven, Rachmaninoff, Berlioz, even Bach; all those guys, he mused, wrote the blues before its time.

When he'd tinkled the last keys of the song, he stopped and considered the music. Maybe it was the soundproofing that created a particular acoustic to the room, or maybe it was a fluke of the moment, but without one doubt he believed that he'd played just like Ray Charles.

As his fingers crawled across the keys, playing nothing in particular but beginnings of this and phrases of that, he felt as if he were being watched. Not as if there were some kind of spy camera trained on him, but watched by actual eyes in faces that he'd be able to meet. So as he continued to play, he looked up to the most likely place they'd be—the square window set into the door. And there they were, two pair of gawking smiling eyes. How in the world did they know I was here? he thought, trailing his mind back along the path he took without finding a soul, other than the guard, who would have known him. And even the guard didn't know him from the man who empties the garbage pails.

So he got up and crossed the room to open the door. When he got it open, to his astonishment, there were no less than ten others standing there waiting their turn to view him. "Hello, how are you all?" he said with the distracted smile he'd become accustomed to slipping on whenever adoring fans occupied his privacy.

"Hey, man!" yelped an excited long-hair who looked to have just crossed the bridge into adulthood. "What're you doing here practicing?"

And just as Clayton was about to answer, he looked up to find, in the very back of the pack, Larson Fletcher, the man who had taken the fear of God out of him and made him, as much as taught him, how to soar. So as if he were seeing him in a dream, Clayton said softly and with the awe he thought the man was due, "Professor Fletcher!"

"Clayton," Professor Fletcher said, returning the reverence. "I can't believe how much of your boyhood looks you've actually maintained." He made his way through the small crowd of fans, and when he reached Clayton, he turned to the crowd and said in an unyielding professor's voice, "Go back to your practice rooms. Some of you are playing for me in the morning and I expect brilliance."

And Clayton smiled as he watched them, with only that one command and the unspoken threat of the consequences for playing without brilliance. He remembered that unspoken threat, knowing he wouldn't get throttled, or even berated, but would receive the lecture. If he was the same Professor Fletcher, which he seemed to be, then those students would do all that was within their physical ability, and then count on anything divine, to play brilliantly and avoid the lecture. And the lectures were never the same twice.

So Clayton backed up as Professor Fletcher moved into the room and closed the door. Clayton embraced him with all his fond memories, then said, "I can't tell you how good it is to see you, Professor Fletcher."

"Well, I was giving you enough time to settle in before calling on you. It was my surprise when I heard a few of the kids upstairs whispering like the groupies of a rock star that Clayton Cannon had signed in to practice-room five."

"Ah," Clayton said, nodding his head with the mystery solved. "So that's how they knew I was here. Because the guard didn't have the foggiest idea who I was, which is just fine by me."

Professor Fletcher took Clayton's coat from the chair and laid it on top of the piano. He pulled the chair closer to the piano, sat and crossed his legs, then said with a broad grin, "So, how's life, Clayton?"

"Well, it's impossible to complain about anything, Professor Fletcher. I mean, I've got a wonderful wife, two beautiful sons, a career that's inaccessible to most people with equal talent. How do I complain about that?"

Professor Fletcher uncrossed his legs, then with a flourish crossed them the opposite way, threw his hands in the air to bring them to rest in a clasp on his knee, and said, "Well, there are two things here. First, when does one of the best pianists in the world stop calling me Professor Fletcher and begin calling me Lars? I mean, I do appreciate the deference from someone of your stature, but I no longer hold your fate, in any small way, in my hands. The other thing is, the trappings of a good life do not grant anyone an exemption from being able to complain."

Clayton chuckled lightly at the way in which this man, who had unknowingly been his greatest influence in his life, still experienced every aspect of life fully without exception or explanation. So it was no wonder that he knew Professor Fletcher would consider him harshly if he were to realize that Clayton still bore the mass of his deepest consternation. As his smile dissolved like water into vapor, he looked at Professor Fletcher directly and knew that in spite of how this man might view him, this was the best place to lay it all bare. "Well, there's still the matter of that dream," and he knew he needn't say another word.

Professor Fletcher glared at Clayton. "The dream from when you were twelve?"

"Yes, that's the one," Clayton said, hanging his head ashamedly.

Professor Fletcher stood and walked to the far edge of the piano, shaking his head as he walked. Then, he finally said, "Clayton, you must know that there isn't a time that I don't think of you when that dream you told me about doesn't cross my mind right along with you. But I was certain you had addressed it and worked it all out by now, either with your mother or in therapy. Something."

"I haven't even mentioned it to my wife, and I've known her since I was nearly twelve, you remember."

"Clayton, when I met you, you were that far removed from twelve. You were eighteen years old and as unsure about who you were as you must be now."

"I've learned to live with it."

"Live with what? Half of yourself." Professor Fletcher went closer to where Clayton sat at the piano, then leaned in closer to him and said, "Clayton, don't you see? If this dream is still with you after all these years, then there's something to it. Maybe it's not a dream. A dream would have long since faded, don't you think?"

"I guess it would depend on the power of the dream." Clayton let his fingers mindlessly crawl up and down an arpeggio as he pondered over whether to say what he was thinking. And when he realized that he simply had to put it in the safest place he knew, he said, "Besides, since the dream, there've been little things that add up to nothing but more mystery."

"Like?"

"Well, like a few weeks ago, I found a torn-up letter that had been addressed to my mother from someone here in Baltimore, only whoever sent it, sent it to her in New Orleans. Yet my mother brought it all the way here to Baltimore, then ripped it up and threw it out. Who is this person, and why is she writing to my mother, and how does she even know my mother?" He launched into the energetic staccato rhythm of Liszt's *Mephisto Waltz*, then turned to Professor Fletcher and out of nowhere said, "I'm thinking I'll close with this one when I play here in Baltimore. I don't really know why, except that it just makes me think of a jaunty dance with the devil, and that's what I feel like I did in some of my most melancholy moments in that dream when I was here in Baltimore another lifetime ago." And as he lavished his attention on the melodic, rhapsodic midsection, he let his head drop back, and moaned, "And now the seduction. The devil's seduction."

Professor Fletcher asked quietly, "And how did the devil seduce you?"

"He brought me back here, didn't he? And I don't know why, but I think my answers are back here." But what he didn't go further to say, and what he'd never even said in his earlier years of taking Professor Fletcher into his confidence, were the calls from his mother, every day, wanting to know if he'd met anyone today, or if he'd heard from anyone today. Those calls made no more sense now than they did then, and to admit them out loud would probably make them sound even more absurd and devoid of context. "Something drew me here, Professor Fletcher . . . Lars. Why did I choose Peabody over Juilliard or the Curtis? I got into all those schools, but why did I come here?"

"You always said it was because of André Watts. You said, and I remember, 'I always wanted to study in the place where he honed his brilliance.'"

"Maybe," he said as he brought the *Mephisto Waltz* down to its dramatic end. Then he looked up at Professor Fletcher and smiled ironically. "And so why André Watts, when there were a plethora of giant footsteps to follow at the other schools?"

"I can't answer that for you, Clayton. And I don't know if you noticed it or not, but that dance with the devil you just played, ended with a somewhat dissonant crash of a chord."

Clayton laughed out loud and with an intensity that came from a place that had never before sent forth laughter. He looked squarely at Professor Fletcher so that there would be no mistaking his words, and said, "And maybe that's how this whole torment will end for me. In one loud, dissonant, resounding crash." And the drollness of the previous seconds was wiped clean from his face by the sobering thought of possibly learning in Baltimore that he should have left sleeping dogs lying in the blissful ignorance of their slumber.

When Clayton pulled into the garage, DeWitt Dilly waited eagerly as if his only assignment for the evening was parking Clayton's car. Clayton didn't look directly at him, trying to stave off for as long as possible the moment when insincere grinning would have to begin. He took his time inching the car to a complete stop, then putting it into Park, and then putting on the emergency brake. What did this young man want from him? A kind word, a smile maybe, he presumed, but there were some times, like now, when that was simply asking too much from him. He recalled his life in New York when he wouldn't leave his apartment for days at a time because his mood wasn't conducive to cordial greetings with neighbors on the seemingly interminable slide down in the elevator from the thirty-eighth floor. And now in Baltimore, the elevator ride isn't as long as in New York, but no less interminable in his mind when he didn't want to be the charming legendary pianist who had come to be known for a steadfast good nature, and who would never even consider telling someone to step completely out of his space. Only now, he thought as he could see nothing but DeWitt Dilly's crooked teeth, it was much worse, because the image that had been glued to him by some random article or television profile had gone beyond making him well-respected by those with a certain authority of music and musical dilettantes alike, but it had made him revered, and reverence, as he'd come to know it, was a difficult zenith on which to stay balanced on a daily basis. Particularly now, he thought, as he slowly opened the door to get out of the car.

"Evenin' Clayton," DeWitt said, saying Clayton's name with a certain pride for the privilege.

"Hi, DeWitt" was all Clayton said as he shoved his hand in his pocket for a tip. When he pulled out a five-dollar bill, he handed it to DeWitt, saying, "Thanks a lot."

"Oh, thank you, sir," and he gladly put the money in his shirt pocket. "Say, you're kind of late tonight. Did you have some big to-do somewhere, or somethin'?"

"No, not tonight. Well, good night, DeWitt." And that was the most gracious way he could think of to leave.

"Good night, now. But tell me, before you go, how do you like Baltimore, so far?"

Clayton turned to find DeWitt leaning against the door of his car, arms folded, settled in for a long talk. He simply couldn't do it, so he said, "Well, DeWitt, you know I lived here before."

"Yeah, I know that. But has anything changed? Do you still like it?"

Clayton collected himself, resigned that he practically had no choice but to stay, short of out-and-out rudeness, so he said, "I guess I find it colorful in a one-dimensional way. You know how it is in New Orleans and even up in New York where it's colorful in every way you can imagine. Well, it's not like that here. There're only about two or three colors here, but those colors are just deep enough to make this place interesting."

"I guess you ain't talkin' about people, huh?"

Clayton chuckled in a reserved, nearly condescending way. "No, DeWitt, I'm not talking about people."

"I didn't think you was, because this place is filled with nothin' but people of color. I'm tellin' you, I ain't never seen so many black people livin' in one city as I seen here. You know, somebody told me that this city is somethin' like seventy percent black. Did you know that?"

And Clayton tried to imagine under what circumstances he could possibly have come to know such a statistic during the course of his lifetime. Still, he only answered, "No, I didn't know."

"Yeah, so I'm wonderin', you know, if that's true, is it gonna be hard for me to find a nice white girl to marry up here? I mean, does it make the pickin's slimmer for a white guy to get a girl, with this city havin' more black people than white?"

Clayton looked at DeWitt through tired, impatient eyes, then smiled as if he meant it and said in a way that would have made anyone believe he was really pulling for such a love match, "I don't think you'll have to worry. I think you'll do just fine finding the white girl you're looking for. You'll find each other." Then he turned and pulled the door open. He looked back at DeWitt over his shoulder and continued, "Well, with that said, I've got to get going now, DeWitt. I want to see my boys before they're in bed."

"Oh, all right," DeWitt said as he turned and opened the car door. "Good night, Clayton."

"Good night," Clayton said as he went through the door.

When he got to the lobby, he found that smack in the center was a group of people either coming or going, he couldn't tell. And he couldn't determine whether it might be a crowd who'd swarm him for his autograph, a photo maybe, and then benign chitchat, or a gathering of souls who didn't know him from the next man who'd cross the lobby. He wouldn't take a chance on a night when he had no tolerance for his fame, so he lowered his head and crossed the lobby at a clip. That's when the doorman beckoned to him, possibly blowing the whole thing, anyway.

"Mr. Cannon," the man said.

Clayton looked up and smiled, then said, "Yes, Maurice?"

"Everything's all set for the delivery of your piano. I've arranged for the crane to be here to lift it up to your apartment."

"Thank you so much, Maurice." And he thought that would be that until he heard someone recognize him, and then felt the throng of eyes on him.

"Aren't you Clayton Cannon?" a woman said, while tapping his shoulder simultaneously.

"Yes, ma'am, I am," he said, turning to find the woman standing next to another woman and two men. The rest of the pack stood back in the distance with puzzled faces. Clayton smiled and tried to bring as much of his true self to these people as he could.

"I thought so. We just love you. And we doubly love that you're living right here in Baltimore," the woman said.

And then the other woman said, "Yeah, even when you were living in New York, we still claimed you just because you went to school down here."

Then every one of them laughed, and Clayton could do nothing but join them out of courtesy.

"Then again," said one of the men, "this one here, my wife, claims anybody who even passed through Baltimore down at Penn Station. She claims Oprah Winfrey, and we were in New York a few summers ago on vacation sitting in the hotel room watching the news one afternoon and she sees Sue Simmons, you know, the anchorwoman up there, and so now she's claiming her just because Sue Simmons stopped through here to work on her way to fame in New York. So don't mind her." And then the man laughed heartily.

"Do you folks live here?" Clayton asked.

"Oh, no we don't," the man's wife said. "We live out in Hunt Valley, but we've always been curious about what the inside of this place looked like, so we were having dinner over at Harbor Place and decided to come in here and take a look around. It's real posh."

"Yes it is," Clayton agreed for lack of anything else to say. "You would think I'd be tired of apartment living after being in New York, but we've found that it suits us. Particularly this building and where it's located."

Then the man who had not yet spoken, who Clayton presumed must have been married to the other non-speaking woman, put out his arms as if to bring the encounter to an end and round everyone up all at once. He smiled kindly at Clayton and said, "Well, we just wanted to come over and say hello and tell you how much we enjoy your playing. This is my wife here, and we have two of your recordings, one of your Beethoven Piano Concerto Number Three, and the other where you're playing Brahms."

Then, the talkative woman who initiated their encounter said, "We have a recording of you playing Bach's Goldberg Variations. It's really wonderful, but I enjoy listening to you most play the big classical and romantic pieces, you know, Hayden, Chopin, Beethoven, Liszt. To me, that's where you really shine."

"Well, thank you," Clayton said, and there was only the slightest twinge of something indescribable he felt at the center of himself with the understanding that someone, maybe only this one person, felt that he didn't shine in every single period of music, every single composer he played. Then he smiled graciously and began shaking each of their hands, saying, "Well, I need to get going now. I want to see my boys before they're in bed."

"Oh, of course," the motormouth woman said. "We've got little ones to get home to, too. But it sure was nice meeting you. I'm Julie Pratt and this is my husband Brad. This is Brad's brother Mike and his wife Patsy."

"It's a pleasure to meet all of you."

As the four of them began to turn and walk away, Brad said, "And we're going to be at your concert here in Baltimore. We're really looking forward to it."

"Good. Come backstage to see me afterward," Clayton said only to wonder immediately afterward why on earth he'd extended such an invitation that was now impossible to retract.

"Oh my God!" Julie said. "Do you mean that?"

"Yes," Clayton said as forcefully as he needed to say it to keep his truth from being known. "Yes, I do mean it. Just come to the stage door and I'll leave your names with the guard there."

"Oh, thank you so much, Mr. Cannon," Julie said.

"Okay, good night." And with that, Clayton was at the doorman's desk writing their names down on a slip of paper. If he was going to honor a commitment he shouldn't have made in the first place, he was going to have to do his best to at least remember their names. When he finished, he shoved the paper into his pocket, and when he turned back, they were all, the whole lot of them, nearly completely out the door. He went to the elevator, and by the time the doors slid open and he stepped on, he had resigned himself to what he had done in the throes of a haze that had taken him out and up to the Peabody Conservatory in search of an unknown something.

When he walked through the door and closed it behind him, the silence of the apartment at first made him think that everything had been rolled up for the night and everyone was down for their slumber. But as he walked through the vestibule and into the living room to put his keys on the coffee table, he could hear the low-tone voices of Susan and the boys coming from the bedroom. Good, he thought, because he made his way home early from his tour of reminiscence for this peaceful time with his family. He went immediately down the hallway toward the bedroom. Underneath the guest room door where his mother stayed, he saw the yellow glow of her bedside lamp and the muffled voices from her television, but he kept going. He'd see her in the morning.

He got to his bedroom and stopped to listen to what they were talking about, but when he simply couldn't get the substance from just the snatch he'd walked up on, Clayton opened the door slowly. All three of their startled faces turned to see him standing there, so he said, as he closed the door, "Why the surprised looks? I live here, you know."

They all laughed, then Noah said, "Dad, we've been talking to Mommy about something we've been studying in school. We're talking about the Civil Rights movement and how black people had to go on marches and everything just to be treated equal to white people."

"That's true, Noah," Clayton said as he emptied his pockets onto the top of the dresser. He took off his jacket, threw it across the chair, then said, "It was mainly down in the South. And in fact, blacks couldn't do things like go into department stores and shop, they couldn't eat in certain restaurants, and even when they could, they had to eat in the back. And they had to ride in the backs of buses."

"Yeah, that's what the teacher said," Luke added. "She told us about Rosa Parks and how she got arrested because she wouldn't move to the back of the bus one day when she was tired."

Clayton went to the bed and sat next to Susan and, after kissing her hello, said, "And boys, that's only one of many, many, many stories about all the injustices done to black people by whites."

"How come the president didn't make it stop?" Noah asked.

"The president, or *presidents* did what they could, but you see, in the South, blacks lived in fear for years after slavery, and after a while it just became a part of life. In those days if you were black, you didn't go to the white part of town because you knew you'd come back dead. Black men didn't do something as simple as say hello to a white woman because they'd end up being hung from a tree." Clayton thought for a moment about music, because everything in life can be attached to music. Then he continued, "Tomorrow after school, I want you guys to come into my studio and I'm going to play a song for you by a woman who's from right here in Baltimore. Her name's Billie Holiday, and she sang a song called 'Strange Fruit.' It says an awful lot about most of the years of the twentieth century in the South, when black men were killed mostly just for being black. And in a way, all the presidents of this country did was to look away while all of this happened, trying to stay true to a legacy that men like George Washington and Thomas Jefferson put into place with slavery. Of course all the presidents since the end of slavery would have denied that, but it's the only thing that makes sense to me since they could have put an end to all the bad things whites were doing to blacks long before it finally stopped." Then he happened to look into Susan's eyes that were peering into the side of his face with fire. But he only smiled, then asked the boys, "Don't you think?"

"They sure could have stopped it," Luke said. "They were presidents."

Susan finally spoke up. "I don't think that's an altogether accurate account of things, Clay, honey. I mean, if things were as bad as the way you tell it, then there'd be absolutely no black people left down South whatsoever."

"That's true, Daddy," Noah said.

"Susan, don't confuse the boys," he argued sharply, turning a stern face to Susan. To the boys, he said, "I'm not saying that this is something that happened to every single black person in the South, but I am saying that it happened to far too many people at a time when it shouldn't have been happening, not that there's ever a good time for that kind of inhumanity. And I'll tell you something else. It happened so often that there probably wasn't a black person who wasn't related to or knew someone who ended up being a victim of white violence."

But Susan countered with, "What I'm saying to you, boys, is that there are two sides to everything, and you can't fault people for being scared. A lot of bad things happen in this world because people are scared, and all I'm saying is that some of the white people in the South in those days were scared and so they did those bad things out of fear of black people. I'm not saying it's right, I'm just saying that's why those things happened."

"Why were they scared of them?"

And before he would give Susan the opportunity to give some indulgent answer that wouldn't come anywhere close to the heart of the question, Clayton answered with swiftness, "Because they had been conditioned by their fathers, who had been conditioned by their fathers who had been conditioned by their fathers to consider black people less than human because they didn't have white skin. And so all the bloodshed and hangings in the South can be blamed on white ignorance." And he had no idea why he blamed the brainwashing on fathers, except that as he spoke, Susan's father was coming clearer into his mind, as if the evil thoughts had summoned the man's image.

Noah and Luke hung their heads pensively, as if to observe a moment of silence for passed-on souls. Then Luke said, "In a way, it makes me feel ashamed to be white. I mean, if George Washington who was the father of our country made black people be slaves, then how come he's so special?"

"No!" Susan snapped furiously. "I don't want you to ever say that. Now, what happened, happened. It was an unfortunate part of history, but the important thing is that it's over. Why, there're black people in this country who have way more money than we do. They can be educated at whatever college they want, eat at the finest restaurants, and they can even drive the bus now—forget sitting in the back of it. I want you to feel just as proud to be white as black people have a right to feel proud to be black. And as far as George Washington is concerned, well, you should still consider him special because he fought for this country's independence from British Colonial rule. You boys know that. Sometimes people who do good things also do bad things, and it's important that the bad things they do don't cancel out the good things they do."

Clayton gave his wife a sideways glare, knowing that the only reasonable thing for him to say in answer to what she'd just told their children was that she needed to acknowledge how easy it was to feel pride at being white. The white that had never had to fight to be equal in any way. White owned the world. Where was the humility in that? But what he said was, "All right boys, it's getting late now. So is homework all done?"

"Yes, Daddy," Noah said. "What we were doing here was trying to decide what we were going to write our reports about the Civil Rights movement on, and I think I'm going to do mine on how the presidents should have stopped the mistreatment of blacks before it got to the point where blacks couldn't take it anymore and had to riot and march to be treated equal to whites."

"And I'm going to do mine on black people who lived through the Civil Rights movement and grew up to do special things," Luke said.

"I think those are both really good ideas," Susan said, almost distractedly. "Now, why don't you two go on and take your showers and get ready for bed. We'll be in when you're done to say good night."

The boys gathered up their books and papers that had been strewn over the bed. One by one they kissed and hugged their mother, then kissed and hugged their father and left. And it was clear by the stagnant energy still in the room that once the door was closed, things had to be said.

So as if to give the boys some time to be out of earshot from the other side of the closed door, Susan waited before she said, "Clay, what on earth is the matter with you?"

"Me? There's nothing wrong with me, Susan. I'm just trying to teach the boys something about history that's not all that distant."

"You're teaching them that white people are evildoers. You heard what Luke said. It makes him ashamed to be white."

"No, Susan," Clayton said getting to his feet with angry passion. "What I'm teaching those boys is about man's inhumanity to man. It's an intangible notion on many levels for them, but there is no greater lesson on the matter than what I told them. And there are people alive now, parents and grandparents of kids in their class, who can tell them firsthand what it was like."

"Well, as it is, you already told them too much."

"I told them enough to keep their thinking right."

Susan got up and went to the window. She looked out at what was going on way down on Light Street and the few people milling around over at the harbor, then turned to Clayton and heatedly said, "Clay, I don't want them going through life feeling as if they have to answer for the sins of—"

"Your father?" Clayton said, without letting her finish, and peering at her from a place within that had hardened him with an unexpected suddenness.

Susan glared back at him, set her jaw firmly as if to hold back some out-of-control response waiting to break free, then said, "I was going to say white people. But you brought up my father, so I guess there's something you need to say."

"I don't need to say anything, Susan. You know who your father is and what he's done. What I'm saying is that I don't want some hell-bent horde coming along with the same views as your father and leading them to an inhuman place where they see black skin as something less than their white skin."

"My father's inhuman to you?" she said as if it just might be a direct disparagement of her.

"His views are certainly inhuman, and I don't think you can disagree with me on that." Clayton went to the door and put his hand on the knob. But before he turned it, he said, "You know, when this country was in the midst of slavery, Thomas Jefferson wrote something like this to John Quincy Adams: *If there is a God, we will have to answer for this*. He knew then what everybody knows now. Except maybe your father as he sits in prison in answer to his sins from those days." And he turned the handle and went through the door.

CHAPTER
13

•

This time, it was Clayton lying in wait for Antonia. He had watched and waited for her every now and then since their chance meeting. And the part of his unconscious mind that did not want to see her again is what compelled him to seek her out. It was like an unrelenting tap on his shoulders, first one, then the other, where no matter how hard or fast he turned to either side, he couldn't find the finger tapping him, and something in him said it was Antonia—there was nothing chance about this woman's presence, he believed. And so if he were to see Antonia now with her deceptive lunch tray, he knew he would still have no choice but to acknowledge a more substantial connection between his mother and Antonia than his mother had claimed. An association that would place him directly at the center, and this is what his extra sense—the one that had grown suddenly in him for no reason other than the appearance in his life of a mysterious woman who may or may not have just been passing through for lunch—made him believe.

So he ate his salmon roll and looked one way, then another. Then, just when he was about to get the first twinge of impatient jitters for her arrival—in spite of New Orleans never keeping her children apart for too long—he looked up from where he sat just as she turned the corner carrying a tray of something, he couldn't see what, and couldn't have cared even less. It was her. She knew he'd be there and she'd come to see him. And at first, he could have believed that she did not see him, expected anyone but him to be there, as she looked everywhere around her but at him, who was the most obvious person in her sight, since he was the only one there. There was an inexplicable twinge of hurt when he felt that her darting eyes, that would not dart on him, were trying to avoid him altogether. But when the passing of time within vacant space seemed to give her no choice but to acknowledge him, it was her face that gave his restlessness pause, as it was at first tightened with what looked to him to be dreaded expectation before she finally offered him a softened smile full with teeth as she headed straight for him.

"Miss Antonia," he said, standing and tipping his head with a southern man's charm and courtliness. "This is a surprise, running into you again down here."

"Yes, it is a surprise," she said through a wide grin.

"Please join me."

"Why, thank you," she said, as she smoothed her furry coat beneath her and sat. She unhooked the top of her jacket and said, "I must say, I'm surprised and flattered that you remembered me."

"Well, it's not exactly easy to forget you, being that you're from New Orleans, and all," he said with a soft grin.

"Yes, well of course. But you must meet people from down there all the time with the way you travel. Do you remember them all?"

Once he'd swallowed his bite of salmon roll, he smiled at Antonia and said, "Only the memorable ones." Then a silence fell between them; they weren't exactly seated smack in the middle of an itchy awkwardness, but it was certainly a fearsome quiet that left Clayton, and seemingly Antonia, without the nerve to follow the thought to its conclusion. But Clayton knew it had to be resolved, so he continued, "So, I guess now you know that you're memorable."

"I guess I do know that," Antonia said with a bashful laugh that seemed to hint at her southern girlhood. "What I don't know is what makes me so memorable to you."

Clayton put down his chopsticks and moved himself slightly away from the table. "Miss Antonia, what makes you memorable to me is that I found out that you know my mother. At least I really believe you know my mother. You had lunch with her. My boys remembered your name—Antonia. There can't be too many Antonias from New Orleans runnin' round here in Baltimore."

Antonia's eyes rounded with surprise as she took him in. "I do know your mother. At least I did know her in New Orleans."

"Why didn't you tell me you knew her when we met the last time?" Clayton asked simply.

She looked, first curiously at him, then honestly when she answered, "Because I had no real reason to tell you. We ran into one another by chance, something that didn't have anything to do with her. If I had mentioned that I knew your mother—I don't know, maybe you would have thought that I was angling to get some free tickets to your concert or something. Maybe you would have thought that I had ulterior motives."

"But don't we all, Miss Antonia, have ulterior motives at one time or another?"

"I'm sorry, I don't understand," Antonia said as she studied him with eyes that seemed to question his intent. "There was nothing underhanded about the way we met here the last time."

"No, I didn't say underhanded, Miss Antonia. And please don't be insulted. What I'm saying is that of all the places, empty places, vacant tables, you could have sat at that day, you sat right over there next to my table. You don't think that speaks of an ulterior motive of you wanting to introduce yourself to me? Get to know me?"

And with an impulsive passion that seemed laced with bashfulness and the disappointment of being caught that showed itself in her lowered eyes, Antonia said, "Well, it just didn't seem possible that there you were, right in front of me having lunch."

"And I'm sorry, Miss Antonia," he said swiftly. "I made an assumption, that didn't necessarily have to do with anything at all but a coincidence, but the theory remains the same, whether it's real or not."

Antonia put her eyes in her lap and smiled thinly, then looked up at him and said, "I love your music and have always been proud of you being from New Orleans and all, but that's it. I'm not trying to weasel my way into your life, or anything like that." And then she seemed to close down, fold into herself and away from him, moving with haste toward the finish of her lunch.

Clayton lowered his head like a scolded little boy and said,

"I'm sorry, Miss Antonia. I know it sounded as if I'm accusing you of something, and I'm really not. It's just that the coincidence was way too striking. In my world where I can anticipate every chord progression, every key change measures away, sudden happenstance from out of the blue fascinates me."

"So, do you know that I wrote to her about a long-ago matter that she and I needed to settle?"

"Well, I saw a couple of envelopes addressed to her from you, but I don't know what was in them. I really didn't think that much about them, till now," he said as he absentmindedly moved his food around with his chopsticks. "So is that why my wife said you two were in the middle of some sort of heated argument when she and my boys walked in? Is that when you two were trying to settle this thing?"

"Yes, exactly," and Antonia laughed, seeming to put as little care into it as she could manage to fake. "I'm going to tell you something, Clayton. No matter how old you get, you can still find yourself going all the way back to your teenage years to settle things that don't matter to anybody anymore because your feelings were hurt and you can't forget."

"My mother hurt your feelings when you two were kids?"

Antonia looked at Clayton, then swiftly away from him, with something in her every movement resembling unyielding guilt. "Well, yes, but it was so long ago, and there's no way I'm going to talk about it with you. She and I talked about it, though, and that's all I wanted to do. Talk about it with her."

Clayton chewed and swallowed his last piece of salmon roll, then smiled at her with a grin that wore all his charm and said, "So, Miss Antonia, you're definitely not going to tell me what it is that was between you and my mother. What it is she did to hurt your feelings?"

Antonia fastened the top hook on her furry before she stood. She picked up her tray, looked down at Clayton, and simply said, "That, you would have to ask your mother. But she may not discuss it either, and she may not want to remember it all." Then she touched two fingers softly to Clayton's cheek and smiled as if he were her own. "It was wonderful seeing you. You take care of yourself and keep playing that piano with the fingers of angels that were given to you when you were born."

As he watched her turn and walk from him, the memory of himself as a sleeping or maybe awakened little boy pulled him up by his lapels and took him to her before she could get too far, and away perhaps forever. He took two steps, touched her arm firmly until she turned around, then asked, "Miss Antonia, did you know someone down in New Orleans named Emeril?"

There was nothing in the straight line of her mouth, or the controlled stare she gave him, or even the stillness of her arm he held that could have told him, or anyone, anything. Yet her eyes, whose passion, as they drank him down in a guttural slurp he believed he could hear if he stayed still enough, shifted something sharply within him. And it made him want to crawl into and stay in those eyes that, for the first time, he knew possessed him now and would most likely do so forever. And so to Clayton, through all of what seemed in every way to be her holding on to some semblance of tranquility, she said plainly, "I had a brother named Emeril. But just like there're a lot of Antonias, there're a lot of Emerils too."

And that was all she said as he watched her walk away, leaving him as unsure as he had been sure that Antonia, with a brother named Emeril, had simply not made some cursory visit into his life for the sake of chatting with a concert pianist.

So he went back to the table and slid into the comfort of the quirkiness of it all as easily as he slid into his seat. If he believed at all in his mother, he had to believe in the happenstance of this most uncommon situation of same names and places. And if this were indeed the coincidental, he could let it do nothing but continue to twist and freefall into his life until it fell directly into his lap with everything configured neatly and explained thoroughly for him. That's what flukes do, and for that he would wait. And even though he knew the origin would be no different by fluke or force, by waiting for chance—if it would ever come—he could still love his mother with fullness.

CHAPTER

14

•

Aaron was reading through pages of background information for the live interview he had to do for the next day's newscast. Then he picked up the questions the producer had come up with for the interview, but they just weren't complete enough for him relative to the pages he was reading. Just as he was about to add his own questions to the bottom of the page, someone rang his doorbell, which snapped his head to attention with surprise. He wasn't expecting anyone, and so he had to be careful as he remembered with a particular annoyance the time some star-struck woman had found out where he lived through Baltimore's notorious grapevine that ran through the home of every black person in the city. She rang his doorbell at an hour only reasonable for those intimately connected to him, and then she stood there with hair that rested just so in its perfection on her shoulders, a face that could have been chiseled to the exquisiteness of some man's vision of beauty, and an oddly beguiling, yet nonetheless disturbing smile. He couldn't imagine the day when he wouldn't remember her crestfallen eyes when he told her, politely but without a sliver of doubt, that she shouldn't have come to his home; as if, he recalled, she were expecting him to welcome her into the most intimate part of his life simply because of every part of her that, under other circumstances, would have had his eye slightly more than interested.

So he stood, slid into his slippers, and went to see who it might be. When he got to the door, he looked through his peephole to

find Maggie's face distorted by the hole's magnification. He collected himself from the immediate uneasiness he felt at seeing
her. This wasn't the time. She just couldn't give him more time. So
he unlocked the door and opened it.

"Hi," she said cheerily, stepping across the threshold.

"Hey," he said quietly. "What're you doing here?"

"I can't come by and see my fella for a quiet unexpected inter-
lude?" In her eyes that were afraid, she seemed to know the
answer.

"Of course you can. It's just that I'm working on that interview
I have for tomorrow, and I wasn't expecting you."

"Well, there'll be plenty of time for that," she said as she took
off her coat to reveal a dress that seemed meant only for the rise of
her bosom, and the dip of her waist, and the curve of her hips; and
clearly meant only for his eyes.

And it did get his attention. So he said, "Well, I was just wrapping things up with this. I'm working up in the bedroom." And
he locked the door, then placed her coat across the chair and went
toward the staircase. As he ascended, feeling with each step the
heat of her desperation, he knew that she realized he was slipping
away. The regret of what he knew they would inevitably do was
fully upon him.

Maggie reached the bedroom before Aaron, who lagged farther
and farther behind until he might just as well have stayed downstairs. When he finally got there, he found her already organizing
his papers into piles, as if she had decided his work was done. So
he stood back, astonished at first, and then perturbed at second
glance and asked, "Maggie, what are you doing with my things?
I've got work to do."

"You've got work to do that can easily be done tomorrow. For
now, it's our time," and she went to him, unwrapping herself
from the dress she wore that held itself together with a tether
round her waist. She stopped suddenly when she looked at
Aaron's tentative face.

"What are you doing?" he asked.

Maggie's face fell to what seemed to be a most uncertain place.
She looked at him with eyes that could only be as secure as his
assuring answer, then asked in a small voice that fought against
itself to show bravado, "Aaron, should I not be here?"

"Maggie, no! I-I mean—" Aaron stammered badly over himself trying to determine what to say. "Of course you should be here. It's just that I've told you what I need to do." But he saw her eyes that could not be cast off, and he knew that if he ever loved her, he had to love her right then, otherwise nothing would ever matter again. So he went to her and said, "Okay, let's just forget the work. I'm tired anyway."

Maggie's bearing softened with his touch. "I didn't come here to sleep, Aaron," and she smiled in the way he knew.

And so he wondered how he'd do it, as he brought her to him from his shame. He put his warm breath to her neck and felt her dissolve in his arms. Following, as she pulled him to his bed, Aaron unbuttoned his shirt with the same reflex he did anything else in the course of his day that required no thinking, and very little passion. And because she had to guide him like a lost soul, he found himself, scarcely without knowing, connected. He loved her by rote only to the place where history and devotion converged, and then no more.

When truth settled itself back down in the room, he lay next to her, not nearly as breathless as love had once made him. He prayed she wouldn't see him, wouldn't look his way, yet she was; staring right into the side of his face, looking for something—something he did not know how to give her. So he closed his eyes and took his arm from around her to lay across his forehead. And so if she would never say anything, not one word, they could drift off to sleep and the bright light of the new day would eventually make its way into the room to steal from them the memory of the last few minutes.

But it wouldn't be that way. Maggie said, "Aaron, I can't keep pretending nothing's wrong. I'm just wondering how long you can pretend."

Aaron blew out a sigh of frustration he'd been waiting to release, then said mostly to himself, "Here we go again." He sat straight up on the bed, turned halfway to Maggie so that he'd see her enough, but not fully, and she wouldn't see him, and continued, "Maggie, I don't know what you're talking about. Pretend what?"

"First of all, pretend that you were into what just happened, because I'm not going to bastardize lovemaking by calling it that."

Aaron picked up his boxers and snaked his legs into them. He stood to pull them up and completely cover himself. He sat back down on the side of the bed, then said over his shoulder, "Okay, Maggie, so it wasn't lovemaking. Now what?"

"Now what, Aaron, depends on you. Are you sleeping with someone? Are you cheating on me?"

And so that she'd know he meant it, Aaron turned to look squarely at her and said, "No, I am not."

"All right, then, why the disconnect? I could feel it in the way you made love to me, Aaron, that you weren't connected to me in the way that we've always been when we make love. You were there with me, but you really didn't want to be."

"Maggie, I had been working. I had been working and concentrating really hard when you came in here ready for . . . well, just ready, and you expected me to switch modes, just like that."

"Look, Aaron, I've seen you distracted before, and I know what that's like. I've seen you able to switch modes and make love to me like nothing was haunting you. I've also had an ex-husband distracted by the guilt of cheating on me, so I know what that feels like, and that's what this just felt like, so tell me what it's all about."

Aaron turned his whole body to face Maggie, and everything about him was deflated. He took in a breath for courage, then said, "Maggie, twice I have been asked if you and I are headed for marriage." He paused because he was certain that she would ask what he'd said, but when she didn't, he continued, "And I said 'Aren't we all headed toward marriage?' "

"What does that mean?" Maggie said softly, with a fear all over her like he had never seen.

"I'm not sure what it means, and that's what bothers me most."

Maggie seemed to shrink into herself when she pulled the sheet up to cover her nakedness, then said, "So what do you think it means?"

Aaron thought very deliberately about what he would say, because there was no way of answering her without taking her to a place where she'd be stumbling around in darkness in search of her pride. If a guy were about to say this to his sister, he thought, he'd kick him square in his manhood. "I think it might mean that I'm with you because it's easy for me to be with you, but I also think it means that marriage is not a part of my plan."

She asked, but only tentatively, "Part of your plan, period, or part of your plan with me?"

Aaron sat with his trepidation and savored the few seconds left that he would still be tethered in every earthly way to Maggie, because he knew that once he answered her, that would be it. There was a way to answer around it by saying that it wasn't a part of his general plan for now, but it would mean about as much as saying aren't we all headed toward marriage. And as he thought in the scarce seconds he had left before the end of his life with her, he wondered why Maggie couldn't have been the one. He wondered why one woman he'd only seen twice, maybe three times, inspired him to think of his forever-after in a way that Maggie never had. So now that it was clear to him, he owed it to her to say in a small and craven voice, "Part of my plan with you."

It's not so much that he saw, or even heard, but he knew that Maggie had gotten herself up and slipped back into her under things. And without even knowing for certain, he was sure she was wrapping herself back up in her dress as if she'd never been unwrapped and touched. But he did see her when she went to the door and stepped into the shoes that she had stepped out of in the middle of her highest passion when she reached his room. Then she was gone. Just that quickly. It would have made all the sense in the world, he knew, in that gallant, knight in white tights and sparkling armor way if he had gone after her, but that seemed to him to make as much sense as banging a gong that made no sound. So he sat on the side of his bed, and wondered about the next day—first facing his mother in a cold psychiatrist's office, and then facing Maggie in a place that had sparse memory of them as anything but lovers.

CHAPTER

15

•

Antonia had decided that she would wear her canary yellow suit. It simply made the most sense. Why not spread joy in a place where none could ever be found? No joy, she thought, except inside the delusions of those deemed insane. They had plenty of joy if only all these dour-faced, white-coated medical people would just leave them to their world. But then she thought of that world and how it just might not make too much sense to leave them to their delusions after all.

Of course there were also the harmlessly insane who most likely wouldn't be in there to begin with; people like Cora Calliup. Imagine, the woman naming all those children after herbs— and now carrying on with Junior after she's been all used up. Maybe he was harmlessly insane too, for bothering with used goods. But those children with herb names—that's really what gave Cora's craziness away. Everybody would have been just fine with Sage, Basil, and Rosemary, Antonia thought, because nobody would have ever known what she was doing. But when Cora went ahead and named that last boy Thyme, that's when everybody knew that she was naming those kids after herbs. She must have gotten some kind of joy from it, Antonia surmised with a curious half-smile of certain arrogance; some kind of harmlessly insane joy, because she just kept going with those names. Thank God she stopped at four children, Antonia thought, because that kind of absurd compulsion could have made her move on to spices. A girl named Coriander—Cori for short, for goodness' sake. Or a boy named Turmeric or Cumin. It was all too much, and the possibility far too mad to be pondering in the office of a doctor ready to probe through her mind, anyway, searching for loose screws and missing bolts. The one he needed to be checking, Antonia knew as she drew her lips into a tight scowl, was that Cora Calliup for having so little loyalty and class that she'd sleep with a childhood friend's husband.

Then, just that quickly, her anger with Cora swelled large enough to irritate all over again, and so she shifted and folded her arms and pouted, as she looked over at Junior whom she could have beat down with everything in her. So she had to think of something else, and think of it quickly. And so she went back to thinking about odd names. She wondered how in the world she would keep her composure when she'd finally be introduced to this Dr. Lillywhite. That was his name! Dr. Richard Lillywhite. Antonia knew he'd be white, she only prayed that he wouldn't be as white as a lily otherwise she'd have a hard time keeping the laughter suppressed.

"Momma, do you want something to drink?" Ellen asked kindly.

"No, thank you, honey. I'm just fine. But can you tell me exactly what this Dr. Richard Lillywhite is going to be doing to me in there?" And Antonia simply couldn't hold back the smile that, more than anything, wanted to be a laugh at the mere mention of the man's name.

"Momma, I know you find the man's name funny, but please try not to laugh when you meet him. He's actually quite good at what he does. He just might be the best psychiatrist here at the hospital."

"That's a fact, Antonia," Junior confirmed.

Antonia did not flinch at the sound of his voice, as if she did not see, hear, or sense him at all. Her eyes stayed on Ellen when she said, "Okay, that's fine. So what's he going to do in there?"

"Momma, all he's going to do is run some standard tests on you and then he'll talk to you. The whole thing, I expect, will take a couple of hours."

"A couple of hours out of my life to assure my children that I'm not crazy," she said with a sigh. Then she pointed at Ellen's belly and continued, "You'd better remember this day, because this is what a mother's love will make her do."

Ellen looked away, as if too burdened by the shame just looking at her mother put on her, and changed the subject. "I don't know what could be keeping Aaron."

"He said he'd be here," Antonia said. Then she turned to see Ellen better and said, "So tell me something. Why couldn't I go to my regular doctor for this?"

"Because, Ma, your doctor is not a psychiatrist."

"I see," Antonia said with a roll of her eyes and a nearly comical twist of her mouth.

A woman approached wearing a white coat and carrying a clipboard, and that's when Antonia knew that this was it. The woman walked right up to Antonia as if she had a picture of her on that clipboard.

"Mrs. Jackson, you can come with me now," the woman said. Then she turned to Junior and Ellen and noted, "She's going to be a while with us, so you might want to go and get something to eat at some point. When the doctor's finished, he'll have you both come in so that he can brief you on his findings."

"That's fine," Junior said. He stood and took Antonia's hand and said, "We'll be right here. You just take it easy and don't worry about anything. This will all be over before you know it."

Antonia promptly took her hand back and replied with a salty edge, "I'm not worried about anything." She turned to look at Ellen. "You two just make sure you stay here and wait for Aaron." And then she followed the nurse through the metal, windowless door.

And just as the door closed, another opened and in walked Aaron. He looked to the door with eagerness, because all he saw was the hem of his mother's skirt. So as he went to his sister and father and was about to sit, he said, "So I just missed her, huh?"

"Yeah, they just took her back," Junior replied.

Aaron sat in the seat right between Ellen and Junior, where his mother had sat, and it still held her warmth. He unbuttoned his coat and took in the room with a sweeping glance. Why, he wondered, would anyone paint the walls of the place where people have to come for problems in their head a shade of green that could split the sanest of minds in two. This green, he thought, couldn't even have a name. It wasn't exactly mint, but it wasn't seafoam, either. It reminded him of a circle of oil paint on a palette from his boyhood that he'd mixed so much by the dipping and dripping of other colors that it actually had no color at all. He couldn't keep it to himself a second longer, so he turned to Ellen who had picked up a magazine and was reading it, and said, "This is an awful color, isn't it?"

"What's an awful color?" she replied without looking up from the page.

"These walls. Aren't they ugly?"

"I never noticed," she said as she looked around. "They're okay. I guess they're meant to soothe." Then she went back to the magazine.

"Do they soothe you?" Aaron asked incredulously.

"I don't know, Aaron. I guess they would if I were on the edge."

"Well they don't soothe me. They make me want to jump out a window just to get away from them." He couldn't look at them anymore because they really were beginning to make him feel as if they were closing him in. But then he stared straight ahead and blurted out, "I broke up with Maggie last night."

Ellen closed the magazine and set it down in the chair next to her. Slowly she turned to face her brother. "What?"

"I broke up with Maggie last night," but by now his father, who had closed his eyes as if for a doze, had awakened fully and was staring him square in the side of his face. So he turned to face Junior and continued, "There was nothing left to do. I don't see myself marrying her, and so I had to ask what it was we were doing together if that was the case."

Junior sat up straighter in his chair and cleared his throat. "Well, now that's the most ridiculous thing I've ever heard. You don't have to be headed for marriage to enjoy a good and solid relationship with someone, son. Where'd you get that notion? A relationship isn't all about what's written on a piece of paper, or what the law says you are. Sometimes a relationship is just about what two people mean to each other for however long they're together."

"I'm surprised at you, Poppa," Ellen snapped, "telling Aaron something like that. He *ought* to be thinking about marriage, and he ought to be thinking about marrying Maggie." Then she looked at her brother and gave him a light smack on his thigh and scolded, "And what in the world is the matter with you? They don't come much finer, much more solid than Maggie. Okay, so she can be a little overbearing and opinionated, but that's probably more a result of her work environment than anything. I know what that's like because that's my life too. But I'm surprised at you, being in the same industry and not knowing that and having patience."

"You're all wrong, Ellie. It doesn't have anything to do with that. Not really."

"Then what does it have to do with?"

"Look, Ellie, Maggie and I have been together for four years, and in all that time I should have at least thought about marrying her. Yet when I was presented with the question from two total strangers, I realized that marrying her hadn't even crossed my mind. All I could think to say was 'Aren't we all headed toward marriage?' "

"What does that mean?" Ellen asked, her face wrinkled.

"Exactly. I don't know what it means, but I do know that if I felt that she was who I wanted to marry, I would have said yes, we are headed toward marriage. What's that about?"

"Listen, Aaron, love is not going to fall from the sky like a drop of rain and hit you right between the eyes one day. That's some televised version of love, but it's not real love at all. Love takes time. You have to let it grow. You have to nurture it. But to give up on ever loving her just because you don't right now is foolhardy."

"Who said anything about not loving her, Ellie? Of course I love her, otherwise I'd be a real big fool for being in this relationship for as long as I've been in it. It's just that I don't want to be married to her." Then he paused long enough to think about what she said, which didn't take any time at all, mostly because what she said about love hitting between the eyes made him think of Tawna and the way space and time had a way of disappearing every single time he'd been in her presence. So he questioned, "And why can't love be like that, hitting me right between the eyes, and everything? Maybe that's how love is supposed to happen for me, in order for me to know that it's the woman I'm supposed to marry."

"Now, that is just ridiculous, Aaron, and you know it. You can't just trade love in, as if it had too many miles on it, or something.

You stick with it, especially when you know there's something right about it, and there's obviously something right about you and Maggie that's kept you there for four years."

"Oh, really? Is that how it's always been with you and Rick?" he asked with a bitterness that broadsided him, because he thought he had rid himself of all his anger with Rick years before. "Is that what's gotten the two of you through?"

Ellen stared at her brother with pleading eyes that seemed to be meant to shut him up, then shot a tense look at her father. She smiled nervously at her father who only looked plainly at her as if he was waiting for her answer. But she simply slid her eyes back to Aaron and said, "This isn't about me and Rick. We're married." Then she pulled her purse strap onto her shoulder, got to her feet, and continued, "I guess it's your life, anyway. I need to get something to eat. Are you two coming?" But by now she was at the door and opening it.

Aaron and his father followed Ellen in silence as she walked five paces ahead of them. Considering how far along she was in the pregnancy, Aaron thought, who knew she could move that fast; and he knew what had gotten her moving. What good are intentions if you end up still wounding, he thought. His intention hadn't been to touch her exposed nerve with his curt comment about her and Rick. It's just that, without him being aware all these years, it seemed his umbrage for Rick had made a home right on the surface of his subconscious, close enough to be summoned whenever he knew, or didn't know, he needed to remember. But Rick and Ellen had recovered from the time of their discontent, and she was filled up with his child, for heaven's sake. So he needed to get over it. But that wasn't so easy, since he remembered that night when he drowned in her tears that were filled with the torment and fever of a woman betrayed.

When they reached the cafeteria, Aaron stopped, then looked up at the sign that said BLALOCK BUILDING with an arrow pointing in the opposite direction from which they'd walked. He turned to his father and said, "Poppa, remember when you worked down there in the Blalock Building?"

"Sure," Junior said, looking wistfully down the hall. "Boy, I remember when I did my first surgery. It was on this young guy who had broken both his ankles in a motorcycle accident, and I remember going down to that big white statue of Jesus and rubbing his feet and praying for him to guide my hands through the surgery." Junior held the door for Aaron to walk through, then laughed quietly. "Worked, too. Those ankles were masterpieces. To this day he calls me and tells me how perfect they are and how he has arthritis in nearly every joint in his body except those two ankles."

Aaron smiled, not knowing if he should have believed in the miracle of God answering direct pleas or in the precision of his father's skill. He decided, instead, to chock it up to the luck of that hobbled guy's draw, in whichever way he was graced, and leave it at that. When they got into the cafeteria, Aaron followed his father, who followed Ellen to the stack of trays and picked one. As they approached the food, he looked questioningly at it, chuckled lightly, then said in a near whisper, "Boy, nothing smells good in here."

"Tell me about it," Ellen said with as much quiet. "No matter how hungry I get, this place never makes my mouth water. But it's here, and it's convenient, and so I'll find something I can eat."

Junior strained to see what the dish was that had something swimming in tomato sauce, then looked at Aaron, then Ellen and replied, "The food here's not so bad. Try coming out of a surgery that went on longer than you expected, and you're hungry as a horse. Then see if this food doesn't taste like a gift from heaven."

"I guess you're right," Aaron said. He smiled at the humorless woman on the other side of the counter who had served up eggplant Parmesan for Ellen and his father, and said, "I'll take the eggplant Parmesan too, please." Then he got some broccoli and an apple. And when it came time to pay, his father stepped in front of Ellen. No matter how old he and Ellen got, Aaron thought with a shadow of a smile, his father would always have to take care of things, take care of them.

"I'm paying for all three of us," Junior said to the cashier.

And as Aaron watched his father open his wallet and take care of his children, just as he'd seen him do more times than was feasible to count in the years since he was a boy, he knew what kind of father he wanted to be when the day would come—if the day were ever to come, he thought.

He followed the leader to a table in the middle of the room

where he sat opposite his father; and just like the others, he got right to the business of eating. As he chewed, Aaron glanced over at his father and sensed an immediate contentment that he now recalled he always felt when he remembered his father as the one invariable presence that gave perfect balance to the family. There was no telling what would have become of him and Ellen if all they'd had from the beginning was their mother with Clayton Cannon right in front of her blocking their complete access to her; the wall they'd have had to wear down before they could even get to her. But they didn't have just her, he thought with an internal glow. She was there loving them right up to the heights to which she could love them before her distraction, and then there was their father taking up where she had slacked off.

The attention. It was all in the awareness his father had. Aaron couldn't speak for Ellen and so couldn't know for certain, but it was quite evident that she was a doctor because her father was a doctor. But for Aaron, it was the memory of the day his father read a ten-page report of a paper Aaron wrote for his high-school civics class, then asked him if he had an interest in being a journalist and writing about politics. It was in that seemingly clairvoyant question that Aaron knew without doubt that his father had been aware of him, because only someone so present could know that the thought of bringing the world together in some way through his thoughts and words had struck something deep in him long before. And though he hadn't necessarily named it journalism, his father certainly hit it squarely in the center. His mother, he recalled with a smile that slid only to the right corner of his face, once told him that he talked enough to be a lawyer, and that was all.

Since he knew they were bound to ask, Aaron simply gathered his thoughts and revealed them. "Listen, Poppa, Ellie. I swear, I know this breakup of me and Maggie is a shock, but check it out. No part of my opinion ever mattered with her, which always made me wonder why she even wanted to be with me."

Ellen looked at him with a puzzled head-cock, then replied, "Which makes me wonder why you stayed around as a boyfriend."

"Well, maybe that's another story," Aaron said with a certain embarrassment as he stared distractedly into his eggplant Parmesan. "Anyway, I finally reached a point midway through the relationship where I had to constantly say to myself, 'Do you want to be right, or do you want to be happy? Do you want to be right, or do you want to be happy?' It was finally just worth it to me to be happy, even though God knows I would have loved to have been right once in a while."

Junior looked up from his food and said, "Well now, son, that's just the nature of a relationship. That's certainly not going to change with a new girlfriend, or even a wife. Every man has to accept that he's just not going to be right, and that's that."

Ellen shot her father a perturbed glance before saying, "Well, like what kinds of things didn't matter?"

"I never told you about the time I wanted to surprise her and take her to Hawaii for a week."

"Yeah, you told me. But I thought those plans fell through," Ellen replied.

"Well, they fell through after I did some major maneuvering to see to it that we could be off the same week. I had everything in order."

"So she resented you for manipulating her schedule like that?" Ellen guessed.

"No. No, nothing like that, Ellie. She was mad at me because I was wrong for planning a long trip to Hawaii when we could fly for only three hours to the Caribbean. I wasn't thinking practically, she told me. Said I was being a controlling man for making the decision for her to be in the air all those hours."

"Maybe she's afraid of flying for that long," Junior offered as an excuse.

"Maybe she just had to be right, but mostly I had to be wrong," Aaron said as truth.

"Well, I have to admit, Aaron, even with as much as I like Maggie, that is pretty bitchy," Ellen said. "So, I guess things do make better sense to me now."

"Yeah, well you know something else? It finally dawned on me that it was always like it is with Ma. I have to just be wrong—and happy."

"God, Aaron, Ma wasn't that bad," Ellen replied with her eyes focused on Aaron. Then she softened her stare and asked pleadingly, "Was she?"

Aaron looked plainly over the rim of his water glass as he

sipped, and when he finished and set it down, he said, "From where I've always stood in my wrongness, she was."

"Oh, now come on," Junior finally said. "Stop going at your mother like that. It's not so much that your mother always has to be right. It's just that she's tenacious, and tenacity, in any form, can make anybody appear to be what they're not."

And then, as if the question had come from nowhere, Aaron finally asked, "What if the doctor doesn't find anything wrong with Ma?"

Junior cleared his throat and said, "Well, for certain he's not going to find anything wrong. So what are you going to do, Ellen?"

Ellen laid her fork on the side of her plate and finished chewing. But it was in the way she chewed and glared at her father that told of the ire in what she would say. When her bite was swallowed, she looked sternly at her father and said, "Poppa, if you don't think anything is wrong with her, then why are you here?"

"I'm here, little girl, to support your mother. Do you have any idea what it feels like for her to have her children tell her she's crazy?" He hesitated as if willing to give her the opportunity to contemplate before continuing, "Now, she's been real big about this and hasn't acted hurt, or anything, but I can tell you one thing, the Antonia I know is real hurt by this. But she's a woman who'll tap dance in the bowels of hell for her children. Why else do you think she'd go through with this?"

Ellen's eyes were trained on her father, then she shifted them, as if too full of disgrace to honor his truth. She smiled wryly and let out one loud hiccough of a laugh and said, "I never thought about why she agreed to come. I guess I just thought that maybe somewhere deep inside her she knew she was being a little neurotically obsessive about Clayton Cannon."

"Well, I'm telling you, the only thing she knows is that she's right, or at least has every reason to believe she's right. Whatever the case, she believes what she believes, and I don't think it has anything to do with her having a chemical imbalance or just being plum nuts. When your mother gets hold of something she believes in, she clamps down on it like a pit bull."

"Like the prostitutes," Aaron said softly.

"What?" Ellen asked.

He spoke up clearly and repeated, "Like the prostitutes. I said it's just like Ma and those prostitutes out on the street that she's gotten it fixed in her head she has to feed and take care of. She doesn't like what they do and knows it's wrong, but she believes as strongly as she's ever believed in anything that they have a right to be safe and fed."

"Well, safe and fed is one thing," Junior said as he sat himself a little taller in his chair, like the king of his domain. "But they'd just better not be safe and fed inside my home. She'd better not have them up in my house."

Ellen took her father in with a face that seemed to be filled with compassion for enduring something insufferable, then said, "Well, I don't know if she has, Poppa, but you should prepare yourself for the possibility that she's done that. I mean, if she's moving furniture around when you're away, and all, I think she just might have brought those girls in from the cold or heat from time to time."

"I don't even want to think about it" was all Junior said.

And Aaron didn't want to think about any of it, yet couldn't help himself. Since his sister had put the notion in his head that there could be an explanation, a physiological explanation, a psychiatric explanation for why his mother was the way she was, he had found within himself a place of tolerance where he could put her. Sure, she had only seen him from the periphery of her full frontal vision of Clayton, but there was a reason. There was no doubt that there were times when it seemed to him that Emeril was worth more to her dead than her own children were worth to her alive, but now there was something to explain it all. And no one could ever swear against the fact that she was a mother who loved passionately up to that point where her obsession intersected with that love, and then it simply idled right there at its height. So this Dr. Lillywhite will lay the justification for every single fact of his mother that, up until now, had been unexplainable and he will do it, Aaron thought with the most imperceptible of self-affirming nods, in a clinical way that could not possibly be refuted. Dr. Lillywhite, he thought, will hand over to him his life, put back together and wrapped up in reason. And this man of science will put to sleep with unassailable testimony, once and for all, the faith his mother had placed in that mythical white man being her dead twin brother's long-lost son.

The three had spent the balance of the time they had idling away in Ellen's office, talking some about the more ˋone-dimensional wonders of life, but mostly they sat in silence. Aaron dozed shallowly, while his father read, and Ellen wrote. And so now, as they sat in Dr. Lillywhite's waiting room in silent anticipation, Aaron wondered what Ellen could possibly have been writing so intensely. Maybe, he thought, it was related to the baby, writing down in a journal every speck of nothing or something leading up to the moment the baby is born and then continuing on from there. And so what was this entry she wrote, he wondered. Most likely, he reasoned, it could only have been an account of the day we all took this unborn boy's grandmother in to have her mind checked under the suspicion that it was wearing down.

The door to Dr. Lillywhite's office suddenly opened and a small bespectacled black man stood in its aperture writing and then reading something at the back of flipped-over pages attached to a clipboard; a man who immediately put Aaron in mind of archetypical victim of playground taunting. This was most likely an assistant, yet he whispered to his sister, "Who's that?"

"That's Dr. Lillywhite," she said impatiently. "Who do you think it is?"

"I don't know. I just didn't expect Dr. Lillywhite to be black."

"Why, because his name is Dr. Lillywhite?"

And Aaron turned to face her fully with disbelief in his eyes that she wouldn't find the notion reasonable, then said with certainty, "Yes."

Dr. Lillywhite looked up at the three of them, smiled in a way that seemed to hurt, as if smiling were most uncommon for him, and said, "Dr. Barrett, you and your family can come on in now."

So they went, one following the other, past Dr. Lillywhite who had moved to the side of the doorway, and into the office. Junior made his way with swiftness to the chair next to where Antonia sat, and Ellen sat next to him. Aaron had no choice but to accept the chair that was off to the side of the desk, right by the window.

Dr. Lillywhite closed the door and went to his chair with a stiffened gait and sat. He flipped the pages of his clipboard until they were no longer bent back. He looked up, pushed his glasses farther on his nose, then smiled his seemingly pained smile again and said, "Well, after spending this day with Mrs. Jackson, I've been able to get a better grasp on the situation that has brought her to me." He paused only long enough to give a special, knowing smile to Antonia, then continued, "She is under the impression, rightly or wrongly, that the concert pianist Clayton Cannon is the son of her deceased twin brother." He looked over at Aaron and came to a halt.

And for as much as Aaron wanted him to stop talking, just shut up if he wasn't simply going to say it, he needed him to say it. The anticipation put a bug-eyed stare on his face that looked as if Dr. Lillywhite was sucking the oxygen from the room. And Aaron felt as if he couldn't breathe, or think. He just needed this done.

So when Dr. Lillywhite tore his attention from Antonia's stricken son, he continued, "This is evidently causing you concern, based on what you told me, Dr. Barrett, and what you told me, Dr. Jackson, you are all under the impression that she is obsessed with this man and wrong about him being her nephew. Well, I have run every test called for in this situation of suspected obsessive and/or delusional behavior, and in my findings there is nothing that tells me, or even hints at the possibility that she is suffering from any kind of psychosis or even neurosis. And I most definitely don't see any signs of a chemically or even genetically induced dementia in Mrs. Jackson. Aside from a slight elevation in her blood pressure, she's in excellent physical and psychological condition." Then, after he scanned the three faces of Aaron, then Ellen and then Junior, as if waiting for some aberrant reaction, he continued, "Of course the elevation in her blood pressure may be more directly related to the circumstances of her being here."

Aaron felt the judgment and looked to his sister to see if she felt it too, but found her with a look of sheer amazement on her face. His father and particularly his mother were stony with their immediate lack of expression. What was this? How had she done it? How had she managed to fool a nerdy little man with a medical degree from Yale into thinking that she was not confused in the most severest of clinical ways? After all, this was a man who clearly couldn't have ever had a woman and therefore had nothing better to do in his life than hone his craft to an absolute perfection, so his judgment had to be sound. Aaron simply could not imagine what had gone wrong in the process. He lowered his head, because somewhere, something had to make sense.

And just when the doctor said, "What I would suggest—"

Aaron bounded from the chair, bumping it furiously against the wall and shouted, "No!"

At first Dr. Lillywhite looked confusedly at Aaron, then his face grew arrogant. He said, "I'm sorry, Mr. Jackson. I don't understand what you mean."

"I mean, no, this can't be right. We come to you, asking you what we should do, asking you what needs to happen to get my mother to stop this whole thing about Clayton Cannon being Uncle Emeril's son, and you tell us that there's nothing we can do because she's not crazy. Well, I'm telling you one damned thing for sure, you're full of shit."

"Aaron!" his mother scolded.

"No, now I'm sorry," Aaron continued as he paced the floor. "Something has to be wrong with her, because if there's not, then you're telling me, Dr. Lillywhite, that I deserved to live in the shadow of this man who most of the time seems as mythical to me as he seems real. You're telling me that I didn't deserve to have a mother who gave me all of her attention without me having to go to bed at night wondering if I was the last little boy on her mind before she slept or if Clayton was. Is this what you're telling me, Dr. Lillywhite?"

Dr. Lillywhite looked stone-faced at Aaron. "I'm not saying anything of the sort."

"So what are you saying?" he asked, not necessarily expecting an answer as he turned immediately to face his mother. "Ma, do you have any idea what it was like for me?" He chuckled with a nervousness that did its best to mask anguish. "From the time I was ten, I knew that I would never measure up to this man you worshiped. And I knew you didn't worship me like that. I knew that my accomplishments would never amount to the man who could make miracles at the piano. That's what you said, Ma, one day. I remember, you said that that boy can make miracles at the piano when they showed him on television that time for being the youngest person to ever give a concert at the Lyric. 'He plays with the fingers of angels that were given to him on the day he was born.' That's what you said, Ma. I was always one step behind him, at least that's how you always made me feel. I didn't do anything with the fingers of angels. I couldn't play the piano. I didn't look at notes and see a whole different language."

Antonia looked across the room at her son with tears nearing their descent. She softly asked, "Aaron, didn't you know I loved you more than I loved my own life? I loved both of my children more than I loved my own life?"

"Sure, Ma, I knew you loved me. I guess Ellen knew that too. You weren't a cold and heartless mother. Of course you loved us and did the things a mother should do. But I just don't have a memory of you obsessing over me the way you always did over the little white boy Clayton. And most of the time I wondered, if I went away one day, would you be as consumed with bringing me back to the family the way you always were about bringing Clayton into the family? I just never felt safe. I just never felt the special way a boy's supposed to feel from his mother when he's the only son. Yeah, I knew you loved me, I just never knew what it would take to get you to love me the way you loved Clayton."

Antonia put her hand to her forehead, as if she had been completely overcome by a massive spell of a headache. Quietly, she said, "I don't understand. I just don't understand, because I never knew. I thought everything was fine. Why are you just now telling me this?"

"Because he's back, Ma. Clayton Cannon is back here, and it's like he's not going to stop coming back until he just finally leaves with you for good."

"Aaron, that would never happen. You're my son, Ellen's my daughter, and Junior's my husband. I would never leave my family. In fact—" But she stopped before she would say it, because maybe it would be too much.

"In fact, what, Mrs. Jackson?" Dr. Lillywhite pursued.

Then with barely a voice she seemed to direct to no one but herself, she continued, "In fact, I touched him. I followed him over to Harbor Place and then over to where he sat, and he asked me to join him, and we ate lunch and talked about all kinds of things. And I actually touched him. It happened twice that I followed him over there and the second time I took these two fingers and touched them right against his cheek," and with the two fingers she held with seeming awe in midair, she placed them against Ellen's cheek to demonstrate. And when she seemed to come back from the place where she remembered Clayton, she said soberly, "And see, I could have brought him home, but I didn't."

And by now, her children and Junior could only see her through slackjawed stares, and each one seemed filled with unformed questions.

"How's that?" the doctor asked. "How is it that you could have brought him home but didn't?"

"Well, I could have told him. I could have told him that he was Emeril's son."

"And why didn't you?" the doctor asked. "I mean, you had nothing but time and opportunity to tell him what you seem to have been waiting his entire life to tell him, and then you just let the opportunity slip away. Mrs. Jackson, do you really believe this man is your nephew?"

"Of course I know he is!" she bellowed at Dr. Lillywhite. "But this is his mother's truth to set right. All of this is in Agnes's hands. And can you imagine if I were to try? I'm some strange woman he's only laid eyes on twice, and here I come telling him that my brother is his father. That would make that boy run as far away from me and as fast as he can, thinking I'm some crazy ranting woman speaking nonsense. No, I'm not going to lose him that easily. He has to be told, and he will be told. But it has to be right. I'm determined that it's going to be right."

The doctor absentmindedly beat out a light, incoherent rhythm on his desk, then said, "Mrs. Jackson, are you afraid to find out the truth? Because it could go either way. The truth could be that Clayton Cannon is your nephew, or the truth could be that he is not. Are you afraid to find out that he's not your nephew?"

Antonia's neck stiffened, and her eyes became even more sure and steady. "Dr. Lillywhite," she replied, "the Bible says that there is no fear that can destroy perfect love, and my perfect love in my belief in God and the way he showed me the truth lets me know that there's no need to be afraid here because what's true can't be changed."

Dr. Lillywhite looked at her at first as if there were nothing he could say, but then he turned to the rest of them and said, "All

right, well, I want to ask one question of all of you, and I want you
to go down the line and answer with only one word. Okay, I want
to know what this chase for Clayton Cannon has made you all
feel?"

So Antonia answered first with "Exhilarated."

Junior said, "Typical."

Ellen replied, "Motherless."

And Aaron, who looked up from where he studied his shoes,
went determinedly eye-to-eye with the doctor and said without
tarry, "Useless."

Dr. Lillywhite stood and moved to the opposite side of his desk
and said to Antonia, "Now, Mrs. Jackson, you said exhilarating.
That's pretty strong. Exhilarating in what way?"

"Well, it's like anticipating the coming of a child," Antonia said
as if she were explaining herself completely.

"Yes, but you have two children who said they felt, even, if I
may, still feel, motherless and useless. But you were anticipating
the coming of another child in spite of the angst of your children."

"Well, they didn't tell me this till now, did they?" she said as
she appeared to pick at her fingernails for a distraction.

"Well, what I want to suggest, Mrs. Jackson, is that the exhilaration of the chase of this man has actually been your obsession
rather than actually bringing him into your family, because after
all, you did have the opportunity, even though you say it's his
mother's job to tell the truth. Maybe the exhilaration comes from
the fact that this chase keeps your brother alive, and when you
stop chasing Clayton, you'll let your brother die for good."

With her lips pressed together as if they couldn't move, Antonia said tightly, "My brother's dead; his boy is alive. That's all
there is to it."

So Dr. Lillywhite got himself up from the edge of his desk and
went to sit back in his chair. "Dr. Jackson, you said typical. What
does that mean?"

"It means that what she's doing is typical of what Antonia does
to us. She gets her mind set on something and she takes it as far as
she can take it to get at the truth. That's just who she is. Love it or
hate it."

"Do you love it or hate it?" Dr. Lillywhite asked.

"I stopped loving it or hating it a long time ago, Dr. Lillywhite," Junior said as he looked over at Antonia. "It's just who she is, and I accepted that a long time ago, too."

And then Ellen, who had a gaze fixed quizzically on her mother, finally spoke. "The thing is, Ma, you think Clayton's your family, and we don't. That has been your mission since Uncle Emeril died, to make his supposed son your family. You can't possibly be surprised by Aaron feeling that you just might forsake all of us for Clayton, particularly with what you're telling us now about having lunch with him and touching his cheek and all."

"But I am surprised, because even though, yes I do think Clayton is our family, I would never leave my children. And have you been feeling the same way, Ellen?"

Ellen curled her lips into a tight bow, as if in contemplation of holding something at bay, then smiled a tight smile and said, "Let's just put it this way, Ma. You and I have always had an awkward relationship, but I really don't think you ever noticed." Then she turned to Dr. Lillywhite, because after all he was there to help. "Life with my mother was like the way we dream in metaphor, where things are pretty plain in the way they appear and in what we think they mean, but really they mean so much more. It was just awkward."

But Dr. Lillywhite could say nothing, because Antonia then bellowed, "Awkward relationship?" And by now she was in tears that were coming in torrents. "I don't know what you mean! I don't know what you two want!" And her voice trailed off to fragments of garbled words.

"I've only always wanted you to say that I was okay, Ma," Ellen said glumly. She hung her head so low that it seemed as if it could touch her belly. And into her belly she said, "You know what, Ma. When I brought Rick home, I was certain you, of all people, wouldn't disapprove, because I thought that you would think it was okay if I married a white man. But then, when you carried on the way you did after he left, telling me I didn't know what kind of mess I was about to get myself into, I was completely and totally confused. All my life, for as long as I had memory, you had shown me pictures of this white boy who I watched through pictures grow into a white man, and you swore by God that he was your nephew. You were more proud of him than you were of yourself when you looked at him, and for the life of me, I couldn't figure out why, except that it was because he was white and that was all a part of what made him so special to you if he was Uncle Emeril's son. At least that was how I understood it until I married Rick. Now, I have no idea."

Antonia narrowed her eyes, then studied Ellen as if she had never noticed her before. Her smile was only half of one when she said, "Ellen, I couldn't care less what color Clayton is. Just because he's Emeril's son makes him a black man in my eyes. His whiteness was never an issue, and I don't know what would make you think that's what made him any more special than you or Aaron."

Ellen took her mother's hand with a soft compassion, squeezed it and asked, "Ma, do you remember the day I got into medical school?"

"Of course I remember that day!" Antonia said, wiping her tears with the back of her hand. "I could never forget that day, and how that night your father and I took you and Aaron out to dinner at the Baltimore World Trade Center to celebrate, and we looked out at the harbor and talked about your future and—"

"And talked about Clayton Cannon," Ellen continued for her mother. "That night was the first night Clayton Cannon ever played Carnegie Hall, and even though that was going on hundreds of miles away in New York, the conversation somehow always got back around to that—*Did he sell out the concert hall? Are they going to give him a standing ovation?*" Do you know how that made me feel? You know, to this day, when Rick and I go to New York to visit his family and we're walking down Fifty-seventh Street, I can't even look at Carnegie Hall. I don't want to see it, I don't want to even catch a glimpse of it out of the corner of my eye. I must look really crazy, even to crazy New Yorkers because I nearly walk sideways past the place to keep from seeing it. All because it reminds me of the most special night of my life when I didn't even get to be that special."

"I'm sorry, Ellen, but I really just don't remember that," Antonia said with a pleading voice.

"Well, how could you, Ma? I really don't expect you to remember that, because how can you remember one episode in a string of Clayton Cannon episodes that were rendered as naturally for you as if he lived underneath your left arm, right next to your

heart all the time. But trust me when I tell you that it happened."
Then she turned to her father, then to her brother and asked, "Do
you two remember that night?"

"I sure do," Aaron said in a determined tone that put him
firmly on his sister's side.

Junior only sat staring into the nothingness right before him.
Then he got up, took a stroll over to where Aaron stood by the
window, and as he looked out onto Broadway said, "Yeah, I
remember that, little girl, but I just don't know why you kids are
coming up with this stuff now. I knew when I married that
woman that I would never be anywhere near Emeril in her heart.
That's just the way it is. Emeril and all things about Emeril come
first, then it's you kids, then it's me. I accepted my place a long
time ago. You should be happy that you're right behind Emeril."

That's when Antonia rose from where she sat with the slowness
of a much older woman. She walked in small steps toward Junior,
then stopped, and with one finger in the air pointed directly at
him, Antonia said, "How dare you, Jackson Junior Jackson. Don't
you dare do that. Don't you dare try to stand there and say that I
put you behind everything. There's no hierarchy to my love here.
Never has been. But I guess you need to say that to come up with
some excuse as to why you've been having an affair with that
Cora Calliup."

If Junior had been just a few shades lighter, he would have been
positively colorless, because even in his golden brown skin he
seemed to turn completely to ash. And when he opened his
mouth to speak, it was as if his tongue had been swallowed up
whole in the last gulp of air he took. Then he laughed nervously
and replied, "Antonia, you must have gone and lost your mind.
What the hell are you talking about?"

But sarcastically, Antonia answered, "Well, you see, your argument about me having lost my mind just can't be valid, since
that's why we're here and Dr. Lillywhite has already said that I'm
sane. So I'll tell you what. Instead of you standing there embar-
rassing yourself by denying it, why don't I just give this back to
you." That's when she took the locket from where she'd been
keeping it nowadays, in the pocket just on the inside of her purse.
She hurled it at Junior with such a force and such harsh aim that
he had to put his hands up to block it from smacking him square

in the face. "Do you see what that says? It says, 'To Cora, with love, JJJ.' That's what it says." And she went back to her seat and she sat, as if that would be all.

Junior bent down slowly and picked up the locket from where it landed by his feet. He studied it for more than a few seconds while the silence of the room loomed, then he said with a patronizing timbre that immediately became forthright, and afraid, "Antonia, this is just something, some little thing that when . . ."

But the bleakness in her eyes and the firmness in her jaw said she would not suffer the foolishness of a lie. And it appeared that she would just go on staring him down forever until she finally said, "Well I'm glad, at least, that something has given you the good sense to know that you just can't look me in the eye and lie to me. We've got too much history, Junior, for you to do that to me. I've given you two children, I've made a home for you, and I don't deserve anything here but the truth."

"Antonia, it's complicated," Junior said, looking down at the locket. Then he turned to the doctor and said, "I really don't think we need to deal with this here."

And finally, it was Dr. Lillywhite's chance to say, "Quite the contrary, Dr. Jackson. If I may respectfully say so, I think this is the perfect place to discuss this because in its way it's all connected to why she's here in the first place. Antonia has just confronted you with something that is obviously quite painful for her. I think it needs to be dealt with right now. What is it about this that makes it so complicated?"

Junior looked at his children, first at Ellen, who stared back, as if with the same question in her eyes as Dr. Lillywhite, then at Aaron who looked with a certain nothingness that only fear can put on a face. So he took his attention back to the locket and said, "Cora and I have stayed in contact over the years."

"Contact. Now that's an interesting euphemism if I've ever heard one," Antonia said with a clear bitterness. Then, somewhere between a middling frustration and a full-tilt rage, she yelled, "Tell me what kind of contact, Junior, and you tell me now or else I swear to your creator that I will rip your heart out!"

"Okay, Antonia!" Junior bellowed nervously, looking up at her with eyes that seemed to need something from her. Then he continued, "Okay, look, Cora and I have been close, very close. But I swear to you it hasn't been physical for a very long time, and then it was only that once."

But then Ellen said with a sharp and decisive anger, "Only that once, Poppa? Do you think that makes it okay? Do you think Ma's just supposed to say 'Oh, I understand'?"

Antonia took Ellen's hand and squeezed it. "It's okay, honey. This is between me and your father." Then she said to Junior, "But she's right. Only once most definitely does not make it okay with me. And how long is a very long time? Three weeks? Three months? Three years? What?"

And then, as voice and manner seemed to work in tandem to want to excuse it all, Junior said, "It's been over thirty years, Antonia. I swear."

Antonia got up and went to the other end of the room, completely opposite from where Junior stood by the window, lowered her head, and slumped in contemplation for several seconds. When she looked up, she said, "Let me see if I understand this. You have slept with Cora, but only once and that was over thirty years ago."

"That's right, Antonia."

"And so now, you're still carrying on an affair with her in secret and under cover like two lovesick high-school kids, but you're not having any sex of any kind with her."

"Exactly."

"Junior, do you understand why that makes absolutely no sense to me and I find it nearly impossible to accept?"

"No, honestly I don't, Antonia. Because you said you deserve no less than the truth, and the truth is what I just gave to you."

"I believe you gave me the truth, Junior. It's just that you only gave me part of it. What's the rest?"

"I don't know what you want, Antonia. I swear I don't."

Antonia's face slid down, down, down, until it was utterly formless. She crossed the room slowly. Past her daughter's gaped mouth and stunned eyes, past her son's face of sheer foreboding. And when she got to Junior, she moved as close to him as he would allow as he seemed to try to inch his way out the window. But she faced him with a look that seemed to tell of a most wretched betrayal, and she asked with an eerie quiet, "Junior, is that youngest boy of Cora's your child? Is that whose picture is in that locket?"

The room was laden with their tension, and it was quiet enough in there to hear a mouse creeping across cotton. So Junior looked forlornly at some insignificant place just left of Antonia's eyes and in a small voice confessed. "Yes."

The only movement then was Aaron, who slumped back into his chair with the whump of a sack of something burdened with many things quite substantial. In that moment, right there having just learned what no one could have known, Aaron still couldn't believe himself to be something other than his father's only son. For him, this news was like a skittering bug that he wasn't certain at all if he'd just seen, but whose presence made him quite nervous for the violation of its intrusion; and he wasn't certain at all if he had just heard what was apparently quite real. He had always known that in some allegorical way, he was certainly not his mother's only son. And so now, he wondered, how long would it take for him to reconfigure his mind, his heart to understand that things had never been as they'd seemed, but mostly he'd never been as he'd seemed.

The only thing that brought him out of himself in that moment was the look on his sister's face, which he only now noticed after feeling the heat of her pleading stare. The eyes of a woman suddenly slapped broadside in the face with what he could only imagine was the infinite remembrance of Rick's betrayal. And what made him feel her pain with a particular acuity was the overwhelming heft of being the only other one in the room, most definitely the only other one in her universe besides Rick, who knew and who shared the memory.

Then he thought he'd simply leave. Get up from there, go to work where a whole other distasteful matter of a broken heart awaited him, and put this entire episode aside for another day when it would make much more sense to him. Instead, he raised his head to find his mother just standing there before his father, locked in a gaze with eyes that weren't looking back at her. So he got up, took his mother gently by her arm, and urged her back to her chair, saying, "Come on, Ma, you need to sit down."

"No, I don't," she said, jerking away from her son. "I need him to explain to me how he could find comfort in the arms of a woman, and then father a child with a woman who pulls stink weed by the highway for voodoo rituals when he was married to me, the woman he vowed from the time he was sixteen years old that he'd love till a Dixieland band played his soul into heaven. That's what you told me."

"Come on, Antonia, you know I still love you in the biggest way like that. And besides, Cora doesn't do that anymore. We were kids when she did that."

"It doesn't matter!" Antonia snapped. "We were kids when you told me how long you'd love me. And don't you dare defend her!"

"Well, you brought it up," Junior said, defending himself for defending Cora.

"I just need to know how it all started."

Junior rubbed his head, and shifted awkwardly, looking at the floor. He was a man who seemed to be plagued with the frustration of trying to find words. "Antonia, I don't know. I'm not sure I even remember."

"Try."

"I don't know, I guess it started when I was down there after my father died and I was moving my mother out to Plaquemine. We got to talking, and I don't know, I guess I discovered a part of Cora that I hadn't paid attention to when we were kids. I was always so in love with you," and he looked up at Antonia with truthful eyes.

But they met her ire, as she said, "And just what part of her did you discover, Junior?"

"Well, not that, Antonia. Please," Junior said, seeming offended and discomfited all at once. He continued, "She's kind. She's very kind. And she listened to me when I reminisced about our childhood and my father and all. She watched me cry about the death of my father without a bit of judgment. I took it hard when I lost my father, Antonia. Did you know that?"

Antonia pressed her lips so hard they trembled, and there was no telling just what she might say. When she loosened her lips, she took a step back from Junior, as if to get a better look at him, and said, "Junior, how can you stand there and ask me that? Of course I knew how hard you took his death. And I thought you were talking to me, and only me about the most private parts of your grief. Now I learn that Cora was privy, too."

"Antonia, it's just that so much was going on then. My father died and at the same time you were getting more and more fired up about Clayton being Emeril's son. Do you remember how, after the funeral, everybody went back to Momma's house and nobody could find you? Two hours later you came strolling in there telling me how you went over to Agnes and Douglas Cannon's house and saw Clayton playing in the front yard. 'He's Emeril's son as sure as I'm Emeril's twin.' That's what you said to me. I know you didn't mean to be insensitive, but I didn't want to hear that crap, Antonia. I had just buried by father, my hero, and you come in there telling me some nonsense like that. Ah shucks—" Junior waved his hand dismissively in the air, then moved past Antonia to walk toward the other side of the room. When he got there, he turned back toward her. "You know, I didn't want to think about that anymore. I told myself years ago that it didn't have any busi- ness going into the future with us, but here I am thirty-some years later talking about it."

"Well, obviously Junior, this is something that's been on your mind for all these years, and you needed to say it to me," she said in a deflated voice. She went over to her chair and sat, where Ellen put her arms around her. Then she continued, "So I guess you're telling me that it's my fault you had the affair with Cora. I drove you into her arms, huh?"

"No!" Junior said adamantly. "I'm not saying that at all. I'm a man, and I'm a responsible man. I had a choice that night, and I knew that what I was doing was wrong, and I know that what I did was wrong. I'm just telling you how it happened. You wanted to know, so I told you." Then he went and knelt in front of where Antonia sat. He took her hand softly from Ellen who'd held it and seemed not to want to let it go. But he had it nonetheless, and he held it as if it held his life. He regarded her earnestly, then contin- ued, "Look, Antonia, you may believe this, or you may believe that I'm full of stuff, but I swear to you that I had no intention of carrying on an affair with Cora beyond that one night. But then when she came up pregnant, everything got real complicated real quick."

Something needed to fill all the quiet that quickly flooded the room, so Dr. Lillywhite said, "I'm looking at you, Aaron, and you, Ellen, and I would imagine that this has got to seem pretty unbelievable to you. Would either of you like to tell your father your feelings about this?" And even though the question was for both, he was clearly looking at Aaron, whose emotions seemed to be more raw.

But instead of Aaron, it was Ellen who said, "Well, I know you cheated on Ma, Poppa, but I feel as if you cheated on me. I feel like you cheated on this whole family. I'm questioning everything. I'm even questioning if you're on the board down there at Tulane's medical school or if that's just an excuse you use to get out of town and see your other family. And now that I know that we only had half of your attention too, I'm trying my best to see if your two halves made any kind of a whole for us, because you had me fooled, Poppa. You had me fooled into believing that you were giving us all of yourself."

"And how does that make you feel, Ellen?" Dr. Lillywhite asked.

"How do you think it makes me feel?" she said acerbically. "It makes me feel like nothing about my life was as I thought it had been. At least with my mother, I knew who she was and what she was doing. I now realize that I never even knew this man." And she pointed at her father with an indifferent, most impudent wave of her hand, as if shooing away something bothersome.

"And Aaron, what about you?" the doctor asked.

Aaron didn't answer right away, because at first there didn't seem to be anything to say that would change things. All of this— his mother's distractedness, his father's affair, his father's bastard son—was set into motion long before he had been born and could have a say, on the day Clayton Cannon came into the world. Knowing he should say something, he simply offered, "I guess the way I see it is that if my mother had just listened to the first person who told her that Clayton Cannon was in no way Emeril's son—who was most likely my father—we wouldn't be here today. I wouldn't think you were an ineffective quack, Dr. Lillywhite, no different than a con artist who got his degree from a storefront printer in Guadalajara for declaring that my mother's a rational woman. And I wouldn't be sitting here wishing my childhood away for a different kind of mother who would have made me the center of her world. But mostly, I know I wouldn't be sitting here right now torn between anger and compassion for my father because of his indiscretion. That's what I'm feeling." And just when it seemed that he was done, he added one more thing that he knew some part of him should regret but didn't. "Oh, and I wouldn't be thinking from the coldest, blackest part of my heart that my father's bastard son is just who he is—my father's bastard son, and not a part of this family. He's got a mother, and brothers, and sisters from that mother so he's got his family. Not this one. My father's a part of his family. That's his choice. But I'm not his brother, not in any real way, and Ellen's not his sister. So he's nothing to me."

That was all he said as he sat back in his chair. And as he waited for someone to say something, it immediately occurred to him that there was really nothing his mother or father could say in defense of the life they'd given him as a result of their choices. So he wondered what next. He wondered what would happen to him and his family on the other side of the door where their real life would be waiting to absorb all that had just happened. And just as he was about to question them on the very matter, he saw Ellen. It was the same Ellen from his kitchen just a few weeks ago, only this time her face was far more intensely gripped by something. Pain. This time agonizing. He went to get up and go to her when he heard her speak for herself.

"Okay, my water just broke," was all she said.

CHAPTER
16

•

The restaurant seemed to be a living thing, Clayton thought, as he listened to the music's voice that said more to him than the cacophony of human voices. He exercised the fingers of his right hand to the rhythm of the music, lifting each one only to bring it down on the table. And as if every finger had little minds and wills of their own, and as if he had a grand keyboard stretched out before him, he added the fingers of his left hand to the exercise. They moved across the table as if they were playing along with the music swirling around the room. He looked at his fingers and thought of the many years his fingers had been doing this as they went about their business of an evening workout, plucking out an inaudible tune. And yet here he is, he thought and lightly smiled to himself, as famous as a concert pianist can be and still working out those fingers whenever there was a chance to do so.

"This is quite a nice place," Susan said.

Clayton looked at her with a kind yet apologetic smile, his lips only stretching sideways, showing no teeth, an expression, perhaps, trying to expunge the guilt of how long it had been since they had last been out as a man and woman—not as a mom and dad. So he put his hand on hers and gave it a loving squeeze. "It's very nice," he said. Then taking his hand slowly from hers, he continued, "I'm sorry, babe. We should do this more often. I should take you out more."

Susan regarded him with curious eyes and spoke in a puzzled voice, "Clayton, you don't hear me complaining. I love being at home in the evenings, helping the boys with their homework and spending quiet time with them as I read with them and tuck them in to sleep." Susan stared off with a glint that nearly resembled wanderlust in her eyes and continued, "It's the best in the world. Nothing would be better." Then she looked at her husband and took back his hand whose fingers had already returned to their workout and said, "Nothing at all. I have no complaints about my life because I'm doing exactly what I dreamed of doing since the day I married you."

Just then a couple ambled toward the booth and asked if any- one was sitting in the empty space. When Clayton invited them to sit, Susan merely nodded with a tense smile and slid smack up against Clayton—closer than she needed to be. Every move she made—from the awkward, jerky slide toward her husband to the strain in her countenance—spread her voluminous discomfort plainly enough for Clayton to see. He just prayed the couple couldn't see, or even catch in the air, any part of her uneasiness.

So he said, "I'm Clayton Cannon and this is my wife Susan." Clayton slid from the booth and stood, extending his hand first to the woman, then to the man. "Have a seat. Please."

"Hello," they said in perfect unison. "What a pleasure to meet you," the woman said, taking Clayton's hand and shaking it soundly.

"I'm James Woolsey," the man said, "and this is my wife Sharon."

As James and Sharon settled in, a man in a blue suit—the kind of blue with just enough green in it to make it a questionable blue, depending on the light—swaggered up to the stage, which brought the jazz band to a fading silence. He took a microphone from a stand in the middle of the stage with the confidence of a man who ruled some sort of roost. He commanded the crowd's attention without so much as asking. "For those of you who don't know me, I'm Graham Stevens, and I want to thank you all for coming tonight," he said. Once a thin round of applause died down, he continued, "And I'd like to acknowledge a very special guest of mine, a good friend who supported my dream of open- ing this place. Clayton Cannon." Graham looked over at Clayton who only smiled modestly. Then Graham continued, "Clayton has been a great friend since our days at Peabody. I don't need to tell you what he studied." He gave way to a wave of laughter, then said, "I was studying the violin, and I guess I also don't have to tell you whose music career took off."

The room, again, filled with laughter, but Clayton yelled loudly over the guffawing crowd, "Your career just took a different turn, Graham."

"Now, that's a true friend for you," Graham said. "This man has just found a way to justify my parents' paying out four years of tuition at a conservatory of music for a concert violinist's career that never happened," he said, bringing the crowd to a scattering chuckle. He smoothed his deep black hair that somehow made quite a striking contrast against his skin that seemed far too pale in its whiteness to have ever seen the sun. Then he continued, "Seriously, though, folks, I want to thank you all for coming here tonight and I want you to savor our food, drink our wine, enjoy our music, and think of this place as your place." And with that, he swaggered coolly from the stage, surrounded by a healthy applause.

Clayton, with a lingering smile left over from his tribute, sipped the wine that had just been set in front of him, Susan, James and Sharon without anyone at the table having to ask. It was without any doubt his favorite merlot because, as he fondly remembered, Graham always paid special attention to and never forgot, the likes and dislikes of his friends. As he set his wine on the table, he noticed several friendly smiles and waves from various parts of the room. Maybe there was someone in those grinning faces he knew, but right then, it was all he could do simply to smile and wave back. It made him feel like disingenuous royalty. And much like he assumed disingenuous royalty must feel each time they set foot into the world, he simply wanted the smiling and waving to end.

"This is very good wine," Sharon said. "And I can't believe he gave James and me a complimentary glass, too."

"Yeah, well this wine is my favorite," Clayton told her. "That's just the way Graham is, always looking out for friends—and the friends of his friends. He's true blue that way."

James set his glass of wine down and looked at Clayton and said, "So how serendipitous is it that we'd end up sitting at the same table as Baltimore's most recent claim to fame. You're like the rock star of the classical music world down here."

Clayton lowered his head with a chuckle of humility, then
looked at James. "Yeah, I suppose you're right. But it feels a little
surreal, if you want to know the truth. All these people smiling
and waving at me. As far as this city goes, I'm completely claimed
by the people of Baltimore, and I'm not altogether certain I know
why." He took another sip of his wine before continuing, "I
appreciate it, though. I appreciate it very much."

After that, the table fell silent, focusing on the jazz band that
had struck up again. The saxophone in this languorous piece of
music wailed in a shade of blue that Clayton immediately understood. He felt comforted in a way he wished would never end;
and it showed in his far-off gaze and wistful smile that only
slightly tweaked the corners of his mouth. It seemed as if he
would never come back from the place this instrument took him.

But James brought him back when he said, "So you lived here
before, when you were studying at the Peabody?"

Clayton, who willed himself to be present at the table again,
answered, "Yeah. Four years I spent here."

"Do you like it here?" James asked.

Clayton thought for a few seconds about the question as his
narrowed eyes folded into an ironic smile, then replied, "Baltimore makes me wonder half the time why I live here and then at
other times makes me glad I do." Then he shook his finger in
midair like a sage, pointing at no one in particular and said, "All I
can really say is that there's something in this town that keeps
pulling me back here. But on top of that, it's a nice town. Colorful
in its own way, but hardly able to compete with, say, all of New
Orleans's colors."

Then James said, with just a hint of embarrassment in his
chuckle, "You know, I grew up here in Baltimore and I'm
ashamed to admit that until all this buzz over you moving here, I
didn't know that Peabody gave out a college degree. I thought it
was just a place where rich parents sent their kids to take lessons."

"Actually, at these conservatories of music, they have auditions
that sort out the ones who have the talent from the ones who
don't. I mean, you can't just skate into a conservatory on marginal
talent only to end up getting a degree that means you can teach
music lessons from your parlor or at any elementary school in the
country. And to me, if you don't have what it takes to be a concert

musician, then I say, What's the point?" Clayton ran his finger around the rim of his glass, picking apart in his mind every sentiment behind what he'd just said. Then he looked apologetically at James, and then Sharon and said, "I guess what I just said makes me sound like an overblown snob, huh?"

Susan shook her head firmly from side to side in a definite *no*. It was as if she was about to say something, then she just settled herself back in for the rest of the discussion.

That's when Sharon said, "No, not at all. I agree that there are certain God-given talents and no one is ever going to teach someone into a talent."

"I think that is, for the most part, true," Clayton said, after which he swallowed the last bit of wine in his glass. "I guess what I'm trying to say is that, number one, in my field, I don't see the point in learning how to *play* the music if you're not going to share it. Interpret it for the world. And number two, I'm saying that I could no more be a brain surgeon than a brain surgeon could do what I do, because I don't have the passion to be one and I would think a brain surgeon wouldn't have the passion to be a concert anything."

Sharon then replied, jocularly, "Well, maybe he could do what you do, but he just wouldn't do it as well."

And from that, they all shared a hearty laugh until Clayton added, "So, James, what kind of work do you do?"

"Well, I work not far from here. I'm a metallurgist at Bethlehem Steel," James said before he swallowed the last of his wine.

"Now, you see there!" Clayton said in a tone that was about to wrap his point up in a package that would not need reopening. "I know all of the metals, but if you sat me down behind his desk they'd fire me in ten minutes."

"Well, I listen to music, but they wouldn't let me on the stage at the Meyerhoff." Once again, the table erupted in the bit of hilarity James had just given them.

But Susan, who barely laughed, and just gave up the stingiest of smiles said, "It really is all about passion, you know." Then she sat back and waited for a reaction, as if to dare them to continue to leave her out of the conversation.

Clayton put his hand on her shoulder and slid it gently to the back of her neck to apologize for what he knew he, James, and

Sharon had obviously done. It was situations like this, he knew, where she felt small as a mother and wife with all the other careers at the table. Really, he couldn't know for sure, but Sharon certainly seemed to have the savvy and curiosity of a woman with a career. Clayton didn't even have to hear Susan say it to know that she felt that those careers, his, James's, and Sharon's (whatever hers was), mocked in no other way aside from the fact that they took place away from home. So Clayton said to Susan, even though he'd said it himself just moments before, "You're absolutely right about that. It is all about passion. Everyone should have a passion for what they do."

At that point, James seemed to be pulled from the conversation with the distraction of whatever it was that had gripped him and spread clean across his face. James pulled out a key chain from his pocket that couldn't possibly take another key. Then he complained to Clayton, "These things always dig into my leg."

Sharon looked at the keys, raised one eyebrow, and twisted her mouth to one side, then said, "I hope you're not waiting for me to feel sorry for you. Every time this happens I offer to put the keys in my purse, and you say, 'No, I'll just keep them here on the table.'"

Clayton and Sharon, and even James, got a good tickle at the imitation Sharon did of James. Then, when Clayton looked closely at the key chain and saw M.I.T. emblazoned across the round disk, he asked, "M.I.T, is that your alma mater?"

"Yep, it is, as a matter of fact," James answered.

"Did you and Sharon meet there?" Clayton wanted to know.

"Well, in a way we did," James said.

And Sharon picked up the story from there. "James was doing a semester down at Georgia Tech and I was in college down there in Georgia."

"Really!" Susan said with an astonishment that was, at the least, odd. "You went to Georgia Tech?"

"Oh no," Sharon said, somewhat contritely. "I'm sorry, I should have made that clearer. I was at Spelman College down in Atlanta." Then she asked Susan, "And what about you? Where did you go to school?"

Susan sat up a little taller and smoothed a piece of hair behind her right ear, then answered in a high-born tone that came straight from the South, "Well, I attended a liberal arts catholic university over in D.C. called Georgetown University."

Sharon reared her head back, as if to take Susan from a distance, as if to see if she were at all real. Then she looked at Clayton, who seemed to be apologizing with his eyes while holding his breath for something to come. All she could say with just enough sarcasm was, "Well yes. I've heard of Georgetown. I'm a journalist. We kind of have to know little things like that."

Clayton desperately tried to think of what to throw over the situation to alleviate it, so he said, "So you're a journalist. You guys are the darker side of what I do. I hope you're not going to whip out a microphone and notepad on me tonight."

Sharon laughed tightly, as if most of her encounter with Susan had not even begun to fade, then said, "No, of course not. But I did get this invitation to come here tonight because I'm a reporter at the *Sun*."

"Well, I just did an interview earlier today with some guy over at *Baltimore* magazine," Clayton said as he nodded to the waiter who had just brought the table another round of wine. "He found it odd, or at least surprising—I don't know which—to hear me say that I do listen to other kinds of music other than the music of the serious dead guys I play. That would be like someone being surprised at you, James, for building a house out of brick instead of steel, or some other sort of metal."

"Yeah, I guess it would be like that," James said. "Except that I think people assume that a concert pianist wouldn't find value in anything outside of that classical world. I mean, sometimes I wonder just how many true musicians there are out there, and not just dilettantes like rappers who call themselves musicians or Kenny G and whatever it is he's supposed to be playing."

"There is a lot of junk out here, that's for sure, but there are some really true, talented musicians playing some good stuff, too. And believe it or not, there are a lot of musicians out here who aren't giving way to the crap that becomes part of pop culture and those guys are really suffering, let me tell you."

"That's right," James said, nodding his head in agreement.

A lull fell over the table's conversation. More people had packed into the place since the last time Clayton had paid attention. He looked around the room, smiling at all who smiled, and waving at those who waved—mostly old classmates who were more numerous than he ever thought he'd run into in one place again. This was a virtual reunion, he thought. The only thing missing were the name tags, which he desperately needed. Graham sure kept in touch with everybody, he thought. Then he made eye contact with one woman who smiled, and it was so clear that she was on her way over as soon as she could get herself out of the conversation. A name, Nancy, crawled into his mind from somewhere and attached itself to her image, but just that quickly, doubt slid up beside it with the name Marcy. So, as she finally approached, he just decided to let things happen.

"Clayton!" the woman said as her lips were starting their descent for a landing smack on his cheek.

"How are you?" Clayton said as the woman got her peck over with. He glanced only briefly at Susan, realizing that if he didn't remember the woman, certainly she wouldn't.

Then Susan said, as her arm slid past Clayton to take the woman's hand, "Nancy, how are you, honey? God it's been so long."

"I'm just great, Susan. It's so good to see you."

Clayton looked as perplexed as any man would look who didn't, in the most perfect of worlds, expect his wife to know what he didn't in this particular situation. "You two remember each other?"

"Of course," Susan said. "Don't you remember the summer you and I, and Nancy and her boyfriend Don, who was in one of your classes, worked up on Block Island? Nancy and I were waitresses and you and Don were bus boys at that restaurant."

Clayton threw up his hands, remembering that summer, then said, "Of course I remember that now. How could I have forgotten? We had a great time up there that summer."

"We sure did," Nancy said. Then she looked at Susan and replied, "That boyfriend Don became my husband Don."

And before Susan would let her get anything else out, she exclaimed, "Oh, my! Isn't that nice?"

"Well yeah, except now he's my ex-husband Don."

"Oh, I'm sorry," Susan said, with just a little more pink in her cheeks than usual.

"It was for the best," Nancy said. "Anyway, I just wanted to come over and say hello, and to say welcome back to Baltimore. And Clayton, it's so good to see you after all this time. You're still the same unassuming guy I remember from Peabody." She dug into her pocketbook and pulled out a card and handed it to Susan, then said, "Y'all give me a call sometime. We could meet for lunch or something."

"That would be great," Susan said. "You take care, now, honey."

"Yeah, I'll see you" was all Clayton said.

When Clayton turned his attention back to the table, Sharon and James were talking, and rather intimately, it seemed. So he looked away as if he didn't at all notice their private moment.

So Sharon said, "You know, I was just telling James to look at the backs of all the chairs. They're shaped like eighth notes."

Like the others, Clayton turned his attention to the backs of the chairs and said, "What do you know? They sure are. I didn't even notice that."

Then, turning to Sharon, Susan replied, "Oh, how clever of you! How do you know what eighth notes look like? I mean, the chair backs have such a subtle resemblance, how on earth did you make the connection?"

Whatever semblance of frivolity that had been in Sharon's demeanor in the mere seconds before seemed to be wiped off immediately with the rough rag of Susan's implication. Sharon drew in a breath so deep it seemed like something to be feared, then said, "Well, it seems like the backs of the chairs aren't all that's subtle here tonight. But just so you know how I know what eighth notes look like—and this may come as quite a shock to you—but I took cello lessons for five years. Do you want to know what made a little black girl, from some slum in your imagination, ever find her way to the cello?" And when there was nothing but a gape-mouthed gaze coming from Susan, Sharon quietly said, "I guess not."

And when Sharon gathered up her purse and motioned to James that she wanted to leave, Clayton spoke up, "No, please don't. You two stay and enjoy your evening. We're leaving." When he stood and stepped back to give Susan enough room to get up, he encountered the same slack-jawed amazement that Sharon had just seen. So, not necessarily in the warmest of tones, he said, "Come on, let's go."

CHAPTER
17

•

A determined rain tapped at the window as if it would beat its way through the glass. Ellen lay in her hospital bed watching her merely hours-old boy sleep in the bassinette in a way only babies know how—peacefully and completely oblivious to the messy world into which they're born. But for better or worse, she thought, here he is, shielded by the very nature of being a baby from everything that plagues his mother's mind. Or could babies feel tension through the same sixth sense that makes adults know when stress or even danger is all around them? she wondered. There was no amount of sleep for her, she knew, that could take away everything that sat with all its heft in the middle of her mind.

She heard the click of heels out in the hall, and somehow she knew—maybe through that same sixth sense—that those heels were clicking their way to her door and into her room.

Antonia rounded the corner, saying to Ellen, "Hello, my baby." And as she bent to give Ellen a mother's hug and kiss, Antonia pulled a chair over next to the bassinette and stared at her grandchild with wonder. "My baby's first baby. This is a miracle. It's something every woman prays she'll get to see one day."

Ellen looked at the yellow suit, then into her mother's face with squinty eyes that had never seen her mother wear the same thing two days in a row. So she questioned, "Ma, did you spend the night here at the hospital?"

"Of course I did. This is my first grandchild. I wasn't about to leave you or this baby. One of the nurses let me sleep in the room right next door because they had plenty of rooms available. I guess this is a slow time for having babies."

"So where's Poppa?" Ellen asked, even though there was something in the air that told her that her father was nowhere nearby.

"Oh, I sent him on his way home. It was two o'clock this morning before this baby decided he wanted to come out. Aaron left around eleven last night. In fact, I need to call him to tell him about his nephew."

"So have you talked to Poppa about yesterday at the doctor's office?" Ellen knew she had staggered into icy, itchy territory when her mother simply didn't answer. Ellen thought of asking again, but then she figured that it didn't make much sense to single-handedly guide the conversation down a road that would bring her mother's anger and hurt into the room where innocence slept.

Antonia picked up the baby, gazed into his sleeping face and said, "Look at this family this child has come into. Everything's a mess."

"Which mess are you talking about?" Ellen said in a flat and low tone.

"All of it. You all thinking I'm crazy and all." She stood rocking from side to side, cradling the baby in her arms, then looked guardedly at Ellen and continued, "But mostly this whole thing with your father and that Cora is what has thrown this family into such a mess."

So Ellen sat up in her bed and asked her mother to sit, and when she did, Ellen said, "Ma, I know it was a shock for you to find this out after all these years, especially knowing that the woman he had the affair with was your friend. But, Ma, I really think it's just like Poppa said. I think it was a situation where she was simply meant to be a temporary distraction and then things took a turn for the worst, in terms of you and Poppa, when she got pregnant." She slouched and put her back against the bed before saying, "I do think what he did was an abomination against the entire family, but I think it's forgivable."

"You think cheating is forgivable?" Antonia asked in outrage.

"I think that in most circumstances cheating—that is when you're not talking about a serial cheater—happens because that person needs something from the relationship and either goes looking for it, or waits for fate to drop the temptation into his lap. This Cora woman was a temptation of fate. Poppa wouldn't have gone looking for a woman who had three children, each with a different father. He has more class than that. I think this woman was just in the right place at a time when a weakened man was in that place too."

Antonia put the baby back in the bassinette and sat. She stared off at nothingness, as if she were actually seeing Ellen's words. Then, with an acerbic tone that seemed to be meant for Junior and not for Ellen, she glared at her daughter and replied, "Well, what I'm telling you is that he should have resisted the temptation. He just should have been a strong enough man to say that he had a wife at home who could take care of him. That he had a family he loved. That should have taken precedence over temptation."

Ellen watched her son as he moved his mouth into a tiny pucker and back, she said, "*Could* have taken care of him, Ma, or *would* have. There's a difference, a world of difference between the two."

"I'm certain, Ellen, that I don't know what you mean," Antonia said defensively.

"What I mean, Ma, is of course you *could* take care of him. What I'm saying is that you *wouldn't* because there was something possessing your every thought, almost, over which it seemed no one, not even Poppa and his needs as your husband, could ever take precedence."

Antonia clenched her pocketbook to her chest and slid to the edge of her seat, drawing herself in so that it looked as if she would get up and leave right then and there rather than listen to another word of Ellen's. Then, as her head fell to one shoulder and her face wore a puzzled look, she said, "So you're taking your father's side? I can't believe that as a woman, as my daughter, you would take his side."

"Ma, that's just the thing. I'm taking both of your sides. Yes, what Poppa did was wrong. But does it make it worth throwing away more than forty-five years of a relationship, first as friends, then as husband and wife?" Ellen paused for the scarcest moment, as if she wanted her mother to answer, but instead continued, "I don't think Cora, or this son of hers and Daddy's, is worth throwing all these years away. You can forgive Poppa. You can."

"And so how do you know so much?" Antonia asked in a tone

that said the question was mostly rhetorical, but with eyes that said she needed to know. "Forgiveness is not that simple. You don't just wake up one morning and say, 'Okay, I forgive you.' I don't know when I'll be able to forgive him."

Ellen looked at her mother studiously, thinking she saw the beginning of tears welling and about to fall, and she would not continue until she was certain that they wouldn't, then she said, "Ma, the way I know forgiveness to work in situations like this is that forgiving Poppa won't come from anything he can do. Forgiveness happens when you trust yourself enough to know that if he disappoints you again, it will not be the end of your world." Then she looked down, unsure if she could, or even should trust her mother with the knowledge of the deepest pain she'd ever known. But then she lifted her head and said, more to the wall behind Antonia than into her eyes, "And I know this, Ma, because I had to find my way to forgiveness when Rick had an affair a few years ago."

Antonia was stunned to near silence. But in more than a few passing seconds still managed to ask, "Was she a white woman or a black woman?"

Ellen only looked at her mother then blew out a long sigh and said, "It's just not important, Ma. What I'm saying is that he cheated, just like Poppa. It hurts, it takes you outside of yourself, but it's forgivable."

Antonia gazed at the baby and pressed her lips together until they formed to say something, but no words came forth. And so when the words were ready they sprung from her lips, asking, "So how did you find out? And what happened that made you forgive him?"

"Well, I found out in the way most women never find out. Rick told me. He confessed," she said plainly. "He wanted out of their relationship that he said had sucked him so far in that he didn't see a way out."

"Why not?"

Ellen narrowed her eyes that were trained squarely on her mother. With a confounded shake of her head she said, "I have to say that I'm not completely sure because it wasn't really important to me to know why he didn't see a way out. I think the reason I didn't want to know was because his telling me was his way out.

So I think that most likely the affair, just as nearly all of them do, backed him into one of those blackmail corners—either he leaves me or she tells me. Something like that."

"Which is so stupid," Antonia continued, as if speaking for Ellen. "It's stupid because if she had told you, then nobody wins, especially her." Antonia sat stark still as if in deep contemplation. She got up and went to the rain-splattered window and looked out onto the street with its wet cars and wet people under soaked umbrellas. Slowly, she turned to face Ellen and asked in a sorrow-laden voice, "I guess what I want to know the most from you right now is why is it that I'm just now hearing about this? That had to have been the hardest thing to do—sit there and listen to your husband confess about an affair. You know this pain I'm going through, yet you didn't tell me."

"I didn't tell you, Ma, because I knew that at the end of the day, Rick and I would make it through, and you'd still be harboring the hatred I know you must feel for him now." She thought about what she would say for several long and difficult seconds, because it could certainly make things worse. But she said, anyway, "I did confide in Aaron. He knows all about it and was incredibly supportive. I could tell that he secretly wanted me to ditch Rick and the marriage, but he never suggested such a thing. That's all I'm saying to you, Ma. That boy of theirs is good and grown now, and your marriage to Poppa went happily through all those years. And so to find out something like this that happened so long ago hurts, yes, but after all these years is forgivable."

"So now, all is forgiven? Rick had an affair and you've put it behind you?"

Ellen bucked out her eyes so that her mother would be sure to get it, and said, "So you want to know something, after three years, Ma, I'm still in the process of forgiving him because I'm still in the process of trusting myself enough to open my heart again, and open it wide despite the risk of being hurt again. I'm still in the process of that kind of trust, Ma. I think it takes time, but not as much time as it would take you, after all these years."

The baby began to make its waking-up sounds—a squeak here, then another one there. Ellen got to her feet in one move and picked up her baby boy. Feeding time, she thought. So gingerly, she got back to bed, opened her nightgown and began to nurse him. As her mother stood at the window watching the two with the kind of mother's eyes that could weep uncontrollably at any second, Ellen said, "You know, Ma, I discovered something this morning when Rick and I were trying to come up with a name for the baby."

"What did you discover, honey?" Antonia asked softly and with a proud sweetness.

"Well, I realized that since uncle Emeril died you have been so consumed with him that you had given me and Aaron the same initials as you and Emeril—A and E."

Antonia put her gaze on the street below, then turned to Ellen again, saying, "I don't want to talk about Emeril or Clayton or any of it while I'm looking into the face of my first grandchild."

"All I'm saying, Ma, is that it's more than a coincidence. It's subliminal."

Antonia went back to the chair and sat with firmness. She leaned forward toward Ellen and said, "Okay, if you insist then just let me say this: Look at this baby right here, Ellen. If you weren't holding him in your arms, cuddling him and loving him and staking your place as his mother, not a soul would know he's got any black in him at all. Can't you look at this baby of yours, Ellen, and see why things were the way they were for me regarding Clayton, and especially Agnes?"

Ellen turned her attention from her mother in that moment that she knew had never been truer and watched her son suckle her breast. Clayton and her baby had no similarities, none whatsoever, her mind told her. Not a soul, she told herself, could look at her baby boy and think he was white. No one, because she knew that they would have to see him as she saw him—as her sweet child whose sweetness superceded any attachment of color. But as she stared at her baby, really saw him as he was lying in her arms, she had to admit, but only to herself in that moment, that her mother was right. And so with what served as a pathetic segue, she said to her mother, "I think I'll have a naming ceremony for the baby so that the family that will nurture him can help name him. Now that's a tradition, isn't it?"

CHAPTER
18

•

Aaron was at the computer in the newsroom writing his scripts when the news came that Ellen's son had just passed from womb to world. Hopping up from his chair, Aaron bounded toward his office.

"It's your mother calling," his assistant reported. "The baby weighed eight pounds, twelve ounces. The baby and your sister are doing just fine."

"Ah man, that's great," he said excitedly. "Thanks." He went into his office and snatched up the phone before he'd even sat. "So what does it feel like to be a grandmother?" he asked his mother. He listened intently as he watched Maggie come in and sit. He could see her eagerness to know something, so to further his mother along the path of her every-single-detail story of the birth of the baby, he asked, "So, what did she name him? And please don't tell me she named him Richard, Junior, because Richard is just not something you call a baby."

Maggie whispered, but mostly mouthed, "What'd she name him?"

Then he replied into the phone, "I know all Richards have started out as babies. I'm just saying, it feels weird to look at a baby and call it a name that's better suited for a man." He paused as he listened to his mother explain something that wrinkled his forehead. Then what she said contorted his face and prompted him to say, "What do you mean she's not naming him now? What kind of nonsense is that—a baby-naming ceremony? That's just strange." He listened some more, shaking his head with a certain exasperation as he did so, shrugging his shoulders, motioning to Maggie to suggest that nothing he was hearing made sense. Then he said, "Well, okay, Ma. Tell Ellie I'll be by after I leave here to see her and the baby with no name. Bye."

"So what's this about a baby-naming ceremony?" Maggie asked.

"Can you believe this? She's actually going to do this thing."

"I've been to a baby-naming ceremony before, and it's actually quite special. It makes you feel as if you're part of a village."

"So what will we do, write names on scraps of paper and throw them into a hat for Ellie and Rick to choose?"

"No, it's not like that," Maggie said with crooked, pouting lips that showed her exasperation. "You look at the baby, interact with the baby, then based on the sense you get of the baby's personality and all, everybody gives a name, and then the parents decide."

Aaron took her in with eyes filled with doubt. "And you say that it was special? It sounds like the craziest thing I've ever heard in my life."

"Well, I suggest you refrain from telling Ellie that, because she'll most likely ban you from coming," Maggie said.

Aaron scribbled something onto a pad as he said, "That would actually be fine by me, but I won't say anything about how nuts this is because it's special to Ellie. I'll just show up and keep my mouth shut." When he finished writing, he tore off the piece of paper, then called, "Sara, can you come here for a second, please."

"Don't you mean Sari, Aaron?" Maggie whispered. "Your new assistant's name is Sari."

"Aw man, that's right. Why can't I remember that?" he said, embarrassed.

"I guess because it's so close to Sara, your old assistant," Maggie reasoned.

"I suppose," he said as he watched Sari approach. He smiled humbly, then said to her as she came into his office: "I'm sorry, Sari. I called you Sara."

"I understand," Sari said in a way which said she most likely did not. "You need something?"

"Yes, if you don't mind, could you send my sister some flowers? I've written down what I'd like the card to say. And I've written my credit-card number here on the bottom," he said as he handed her the slip of paper.

"Okay, sure," she said. As she turned to leave, she looked back and said, "Is there any particular arrangement you'd like? Any particular flower?"

Aaron looked to Maggie for help, then said, "Oh, I don't know. I guess roses."

"Roses are good," Maggie said.

"Roses," he said more to himself than to Sari. And as he watched Sari leave, he leaned back in his chair, then looked at Maggie and said, "I should have said on the card 'Congratulations on the birth of baby-no-name.' A baby-naming ceremony," he murmured with a shake of his head. Then he laughed, bringing Maggie right along with him. It was as if all at once, they both seemed to recognize that right there, in that space and time, was where they were always good with one another. Yet Aaron knew that there was no explaining how and why this was where it ended. And when their laughter faded naturally, Aaron took Maggie in with soft eyes, whose longing not even he understood.

But it was Maggie who put words to their shared gaze of longing. "You know, this is nice, what we have right here. But there's still a sadness because it feels like something has died."

"I don't think it's so much that something has died," Aaron said, rubbing his temples to try and soothe the pain of the talk. The talk. He knew it would happen, sooner or later. "I think it's just that life moves on, one day turns into a different day and months and years turn into different months and years, and so do we. I'm sure I'm not what you need, Maggie."

Maggie, who had been staring into her lap, lifted her head, jutted out her chin and fixed him sorely in her gaze—all done with what seemed to be some sort of pride—then said, "And I suppose I'm not what you need."

There were few things that he could be sure of when it came to Maggie, but one was that she was sure to pick apart every single word. He knew that if he had to respond to what she said—and he certainly had to—it would have to be exact. So he gathered a deep breath and let it out as he said, "Maggie, what it is, really, is that you are so much like my mother. And I'm dealing with some real stuff with her right now—stuff that goes back long before you and I met."

Maggie gazed, dumbfounded and with her mouth agape, at the ceiling as she replied, "I'm confused. I thought it was a good thing to be like a man's mother."

Aaron leaned forward in his chair determinedly. He bore his eyes into her, hoping she would allow herself to fully understand what he was about to say by fixing her eyes onto his. So he softly said, "Maggie, look at me, please." And only when she did, with tears welling, did he say, "You should always know that it's a very complicated thing, because even in the best possible situations, it's a blessing and a curse for a woman to be like a man's mother."

"Well, that's good to know, I suppose" was all she said before the tears fell.

And when Aaron saw a familiar figure headed toward his office from the side of just one eye, he turned his face fully to see that it was just who he thought—his father. Never had Aaron been so glad for the distraction of someone, yet so trapped at the same time. The chore of trying to choose between bad and worse was bearing down on him with every step his father took toward him. He did the only thing that made sense in that moment that had him tightly ensnared as Maggie's tears fell silently. He asked, "Dad, what are you doing here?"

Junior stood in the doorway, holding his hat in his hand in a most downhearted way. He looked at Maggie sitting next to where he stood, as she wiped tears and greeted him with a smile that seemed strained. Junior tipped his hat like an old-fashioned gentleman and said, "How are you, Maggie?"

"I'm fine, Dr. Jackson, just fine," she said as she stood, pecked Junior's cheek with a hurried kiss, and moved past him until she was out of the office.

Junior turned to find a stone-faced Aaron with troubled eyes. Junior gave his son a smile that tightened his lips and showed a bit more teeth than usual. Most unnatural. Then he replied, "I thought we could go to lunch. My treat."

Aaron regarded him skeptically, then said, "Poppa, don't you think lunch would be just a little bit awkward right now?"

"Awkward how?"

"Awkward, Poppa, in the sense that you come in here one day after I find out I have a brother in New Orleans and you expect me to just say, 'Okay, let's go have lunch where we can ignore the big gorilla sitting at the table with us.' Do you have any idea how shocking all of this was to me and Ellen?"

"That's just the thing, son. I *want* to talk to you about Thyme. I have no intention whatsoever of acting as if yesterday didn't happen."

Aaron tentatively rose and grabbed his jacket hanging on the back of the chair. As he got his overcoat from the back of the door and put it on, he turned to his father and asked, "So you really want to do this?"

"I really want to do this," Junior said firmly.

Just as Aaron was about to follow his father's lead out the door, he stopped. He stopped because he couldn't imagine feeling comfortable enough out in public—where the public only knows *Aaron Jackson*—to have a conversation with free emotions. Whatever he and his father had to discuss—and he couldn't begin to fathom what exactly that might be—would seem belittled and insignificant under the roof of a restaurant. So he said, as his father was nearly halfway across the newsroom, "Poppa, on second thought, why don't we stay here and order something?"

"Why?" his father asked, cocking his head sideways as he ambled back toward Aaron's office.

"Well, because I really never go out for lunch since I don't even get to the studio until around lunchtime. I always bring something in with me or I order something from takeout. This is an awkward area, you know, because there's no place near enough to go and sit down and eat." He slid off his overcoat and hung it on the back of his door, then took his father's coat and hung it next to his. As he peeled off his suit jacket, he said, "We'd do better ordering takeout," he said as he settled into his chair. But he would say no more until his eyes had left his father, to find the crammed and cluttered bookcase in the corner. It was a most insufferable thought for him to have to acquiesce, but he did so as he continued in a lifeless tone, "That way we can close the door and talk about this if we have to. Is Chinese okay? That's what I normally order. Or would you rather have subs?"

"Chinese will do just fine," Junior answered in a tone that said it didn't much matter to him. He listened to Aaron order the beef and snow peas and the chicken with broccoli. It was only when Aaron got off the phone that Junior gave his son a most expectant look—as if he were waiting for the answer to some sort of question.

So Aaron leaned his chair back and stretched out his legs underneath the desk. He folded his arms across his chest, then told his father, "Poppa, you do know that this thing is not going to unfold so neatly with me saying 'Oh, this is my brother. Welcome, brother.'"

"I wouldn't expect it to be that simple, Aaron. This is a deeply complicated situation, and frankly I've been stunned since the day Thyme was born that I'm actually in this position. That I played a part in setting it all in motion."

"I do believe that," Aaron said as he sat up and pulled himself closer to his desk. But the question that stayed in his mind like a skipping record was quite a hefty one. "How do you see this whole thing playing out between your two sons?"

Junior crossed one leg then uncrossed it and shifted to cross the other. As he shook his head and shrugged his shoulders, he said, "I guess I see you two getting along. You're alike in some ways. He's got your sense of humor."

"So you see it as being that banal, huh? Two brothers getting together to tell each other jokes. Well, what I see are two men, each hating the other for their station in life, except one will hate the other more and that would be him hating me more because I've always worn the crown of the coveted son. But then there's still me, Poppa, the coveted son, who now knows that for all these years behind my back there has been this other son. And so I say, who cares that Thyme is not as special in terms of not being the well-born son; he's just not supposed to be there. So given all of that, you still think that he and I are going to come into a room and pretend the animosities aren't there and show each other scrapbooks of the years we've missed of each other's life?" Aaron didn't know if it even made any sense to go on, so he put his elbows on the desk and cupped one fist into the other hand, as if gearing up for a fight. He rested his chin on the fist-in-hand pedestal and said, "Well, you want to know something, Poppa, if

Thyme is anything like me, like you said he is, I'm telling you right now that it's not going to be that easy. It's my guess that everybody's most likely *not* going to just get along."

Junior looked tensely at Aaron, then slouched in the chair, seemingly in defeat, then said, "Well, I don't know what to do here. I mean, if none of this had come out yesterday I wouldn't have to try and set everything right so fast."

Aaron blinked several times at his father, because he wasn't at all certain he understood. It seemed to him that his father actually thought there could be a right time to tell them. But how could he think such a thing? Thyme was quite a well-formed man; a well-formed son and a well-formed brother. He wasn't some concept of a sibling in a perfect world that Aaron and Ellen waited a giddy nine months for. So Aaron gathered his thoughts, then said, "So you mean to tell me that there would have been a better time than yesterday for this whole thing to come out?"

"I-I guess—" he said, stammering to a halt with what seemed to be an incomplete thought. As if there was something better to say. Then he continued, "Look, I don't know, Aaron. I haven't known anything since that boy was born."

Aaron folded his arms stubbornly. "Well, I'm not all that sure I want to meet him. I just can't do it right now."

Junior stood, with a dolefulness that showed in his entire bearing. He went to the door, pushed it nearly closed to get his overcoat from the hook. He threaded his arms into it, then shrugged it the rest of the way on, and as he opened the door as widely as it had been, he turned to Aaron and said, "Well, I guess there's nothing to be said here. I thought I was doing the right thing because I'm sure I would need to know my brother if I were in your shoes—for better or for worse. But maybe that's just me. I'll see you, son. Enjoy the Chinese food."

And as he watched his father move farther away, Aaron knew he couldn't let him get too far. So he stood, and, moving with a quickness that would not let his father get away, he said, "Poppa." When Junior turned around just before he turned the corner that would have made Aaron run after him, or at least move even quicker, Aaron replied, "Would he come to Baltimore?"

With hope in his voice and a perked-up face, Junior offered his son a slight smile and replied, "He can. He can come here and he'd want to come here, I'm sure."

"Okay. Then Thyme and I will meet here in Baltimore."

Antonia mixed her cake batter to her own beat, which had been her own for practically her whole life. No electric mixer for her, and as she mixed and mixed her mind wandered to where her electric mixer just might be. It only saw the light of day when she needed to whip potatoes. Then she remembered that there was someone there in the kitchen with her, eating dinner like it was the first food she'd ever eaten and that it had come from a real kitchen where love and goodness soaked into every dish. Antonia looked over to the table and felt a deep comfort that she could trace back to a time when she was mothering her own children—plying them with food that, she was certain, made them know their house was a home.

A satisfied smile grew across her face as she said, "Jackie, honey, do you want more? There's plenty more of everything—more of the fish, more potato salad, more string beans, and more kale. Just come on over here and help yourself."

"Aw man, thank you, Miss Antonia," she said as she scooped the last bit of potato salad up and ate it. Then she rose, still chewing, and headed for the stove. "I've told you before, Miss Antonia—nobody I know can cook like you. I guess it's that New Orleans magic that puts good cooking into your blood, huh."

Antonia laughed diffidently as she said, "I guess it's something like that. One thing for sure I know, when you're from the south it's just un-southern not to know how to cook."

As she spooned more kale onto her plate, then more fish, Jackie replied, "Well, then you must be as southern as southern can be, 'cause you sure can cook." Jackie stood on the other side of the island where Antonia worked on her cake and said, "I mean, it just blows my mind that you make dessert. With my mother, you got dinner, and that was it. We knew what dessert was, we just never had it." Then, Jackie headed back to the table. When she set down her plate, she stamped her foot and said, "Aw doggone it! I forgot the potato salad."

"All right," Antonia said as she poured the cake batter evenly and beautifully into two round pans. "I'll get it for you. You just

sit." And after she put the cakes in the oven, she went to the refrig-
erator and pulled out the bowl of potato salad. She moved with
haste, stopping only to pluck a spoon from the drawer, and went
over to where Jackie sat at the table, because she didn't want anyone sitting in her kitchen having to wait for food. She put the bowl
right in front of Jackie's plate and took off the plastic wrap. "Just
take what you want, honey."

"Thank you, Miss Antonia," Jackie said as she dug right in,
pulling out a big glop of a spoonful. Before Antonia could turn to
leave, though, Jackie said, "Miss Antonia, I know this is none of
my business and all, but is everything okay between you and Dr.
Jackson? I mean, did you ever ask him about that broken
locket?"

Antonia stepped behind the island, where she could busy herself while coming up with just how she would tell Jackie everything that happened. After all, Antonia reasoned to herself, Jackie
did not need to know that Ellen and Aaron dragged her off to a
psychiatrist. So as she wiped the counter she said, with a certain
reserve in her voice, "Yes, I did ask him, Jackie. And it was just as
I knew. Junior and Cora had been carrying on an affair. And it's a
good thing you're sitting down, otherwise what I'm about to tell
you would lay you out on the floor." Antonia put the sponge
down so that her hands would be free to grip the counter as she
leaned toward Jackie, and she continued, "Not only had he been
having an affair with Cora, but they have a son together."

Jackie put her fork down and looked at Antonia with shocked
anger. She sat back and folded her arms with a clear stubborn-
ness, much like a pouting child, then replied, "Miss Antonia,
there's no way you're telling the truth. Dr. Jackson is such a family man, and you're telling me that he had a son with this woman!
I just can't believe this."

"You?" Antonia responded with an incredulity that had nothing to do with Jackie's disbelief. It was about how she had turned
the notion of Junior and Cora upside down, right side up, and
sideways and still she could not make sense of the two of them in
any way or form. So she continued, "Let me tell you, I still can't
look at him without seeing Cora all over him. Mostly, though, I
can't believe that my life with this man in the past, in the present, and in the future has become something else. Something

that I've never known, so I just can't say what it is; but it's all different now."

"What do you mean different, Miss Antonia?" Jackie asked as she swallowed a forkful of kale.

"I mean that I can't believe in anything that's happened, is happening, or has yet to happen in my family anymore because Junior has changed the reality," Antonia said as she wiped the counter back and forth for something to do.

Jackie set her fork down as if there was nothing, not even Antonia's good cooking, that could get in the way of what she was going to say. She wiped at her mouth so as not to disturb the layered-on lipstick, then said, "Miss Antonia, I'm not trying to hurt your feelings or nothin' like that, but I've got to be the one to tell you that you're wasting good time in a good marriage worried about an invisible woman."

Antonia stopped the busywork of wiping down a counter that was already spotless. She said not a word to question Jackie because it was all said in the crevices of her puzzled face.

"Cora was and still is invisible to him, Miss Antonia," Jackie said, smacking the back of her hand into the palm of the other, as if each slap would make her point clearer. Then she continued, "And if he can even see her a little bit now it's only because he's a decent man who fathered her son. That's all. Could you love a man who couldn't see the mother of his child even a little bit? A man who could look at her as if she were nothing?"

"No, I guess I couldn't," Antonia whispered in response to this dose of wisdom coming from the darnedest place.

"I didn't think you could. But trust me, she's no more visible than just a little bit, and I would bet that he never has and still can't see her in as full a color as he sees you." She picked up her fork then put it down. Jackie puckered her lips and furrowed her forehead in a contemplative way—a way that seemed to show an indecision of what she would share with Antonia in that moment of truth-telling. But then she looked at Antonia who was wrestling with a conflict that showed in every part of her, and continued, "Miss Antonia, when men lay with me, I'm invisible. I'm not even a little bit visible. But that's okay, see, because they're invisible to me too. It's all about the moment, and sometimes that moment is what they need to get through to the next moment where they can see clearly. If you don't believe that, then you're going to throw a hell of a good life away, and that's just crazy."

As if things had been timed, Jackie finished her last bit of food when Junior's key slid in the door. Not even Antonia heard, but Jackie did, her head snapping to attention like a hound's. She gathered her jacket in a hurry and said in a whisper, "I'll see you Miss Antonia. I need to get out of here so Dr. Jackson doesn't see me." As she opened the back door, she turned quickly to Antonia and said, "Please remember what I said."

"Oh, believe me I will, sugar," Antonia promised in a low voice as she blew Jackie a kiss and picked her plate up from the table.

Antonia listened as the sounds of Junior coming home made their way down the hall and through the cracks around the door. She could hear him drop his keys in his coat pocket. She could tell that he shrugged off his coat by the way the keys jingled three times. So now she knew that in any second he'd push through the swinging door and there'd be nothing before them—no distraction like breaking water and rushing to the hospital and the birth of a baby—to keep them from what she knew had to be faced. Junior, she knew, would be no less resolved to talk about it than he was the night before on the way to the hospital, in the hospital waiting room, and before he left the hospital all droopy-eyed and dragging once his grandson burst into the family. Even though the news of his Uncle Thyme still had Antonia, Ellen, but mostly Aaron, wobbly-legged and weak and wondering where firm ground might lay.

Antonia was taking dishes from the cupboard when Junior did finally push through the door and into the kitchen. Without a word of greeting or any sort of sentiment passing between them, Antonia said, "We're having red snapper, kale, and potato salad for dinner." No matter how mad she could get at him, she thought, he still had a right to know his meal.

Junior went to the table right where Jackie had sat not even minutes before, then made a plaintive sigh that accompanied a graceless plop into the chair. "How's the snapper fixed?"

She didn't look at him full on because she felt some part of her curling up into a hard intransigent knot of resentment that had

made its way into her from some other place in her heart where
the darkness of Junior, Cora, and Thyme danced mockingly.
Antonia couldn't begin to fathom why it mattered because he
should have simply considered himself lucky if she slapped a red
snapper on his plate still wiggling to breathe. But she gave him
the simplest answer she could that required the least amount of
words. "Pan seared."

It was just as she knew. How that fish would end up on his
plate didn't seem to matter one wit to him, and she knew this as
she watched him, as she had most of her life, from across the
room. And as he fidgeted with his fingers, massaging each tip one
at a time, she took him into her heart in the only way she knew;
she'd loved him for many more years than she didn't. It seemed to
her that for as long as she had a memory of love, there was Junior.
So there he was at the table waiting for dinner while she stood at
the counter preparing it. Across the room, Antonia thought, was
her one true and only love, and as her heartbeat was set on tremor,
she knew that there was nothing in her life that would have prepared her for the time when things simply weren't right. And if
things were never going to be right, how would the rest of her life
unfurl without Junior?

So she met his eyes when he looked at her and asked with a
quiver in his voice that nearly made him inaudible, "What do you
want to do, Antonia?"

"About what?" she asked while simultaneously wanting to
kick herself for that bit of ridiculous coy southern-womanness.

Junior took Antonia in with narrowed eyes that were at a complete loss for understanding. Then he replied, "I've betrayed you,
Antonia. I've got a grown son by another woman, and you want
to know 'about what?'"

Antonia picked up the dishes she'd just put on the counter
from the cupboard, then she began, "You know, Junior, I *could*
leave you. For my pride's sake, I could leave you as if I were some
twenty-five-year-old ingénue whose innocence makes her certain
she'll love as deeply again, but I'm not." She clasped the plates to
her bosom as she crossed the room. When she reached the table,
she put a plate in front of Junior and the other directly across from
him. As she sat, she handed him his knife and fork while she put
her own on either side of her plate. She looked up at Junior with a

shadow of a smile that lingered, then said, "I know that if I were to leave you for something that was fresh over thirty years ago but is as stale as can be now, I'd have a big ball of pain right here in the pit of my stomach that would be my own damned fault." She had pressed four fingers into her belly and did not relax them into her lap until she continued, "And that big ball, Junior, would kill me." The thought of Ellen flashed before her as she wondered how her daughter could endure a stench, merely a few years old, that was still so fresh its power to offend was nonetheless quite potent.

Junior reached out across the table for Antonia's hand. And when he took it, she stared at the two hands clasped, remembering as if it were one big memory, all that their two hands had gone through over the years sometimes clasped like this, but most of the time only metaphorically so. Then she looked at Junior and said, "I just never knew that our life was so profound. I always thought we were simple people."

Junior laughed heartily, and though she didn't quite see the humor, she joined him.

His laughter ebbed to a slight smile as he replied, "Antonia, you've never been simple. You remember the first time I ever laid eyes on you? There they were, those boys throwing those mushy tomatoes at that little half-wit dwarf who used to scoot around town on that rickety old cart, and there you were throwing stones at them with your little fifteen-year-old self and with all your might to get them to leave that dwarf-boy alone. You were all by yourself carrying that silly old yellow cat, and it was you against those big bullies, but you had no fear. Wrong was wrong for you, and you cussed up a blue streak throwing those rocks and stones from one hand and holding on to that basket full of cat in the other till those boys ran on their way. You were tenacious then and you're tenacious now. You weren't a typical girl with a typical girl's life, and you're not a typical woman with a typical woman's life. I know it's too much for some, but for me it's always been what's made you larger than anyone I've ever known, and why I love you larger than anyone I've ever known."

She blushed in a way she had no memory of ever doing since she was the girl Junior once courted. She smiled quite shyly while squeezing Junior's hand and said, "Today, someone made me see that to you Cora is nearly invisible, and would be completely invisible if it weren't for Thyme. And that's just the way it should be. Thyme is your son. Cora is his mother and there's no changing that." Though she could clearly see in every crevice in his puzzled face that he did not understand, she stood and continued: "Thyme has a right to know his brother and sister, so he will meet his other family." As she went to get their meal, she turned swiftly with an immediate ingenious thought as shown by her one raised finger, "*And* he'll come to the baby-naming ceremony! I'll tell Ellen."

As she put the fish and the kale in their serving dishes, she thought of what name she might want for the baby. There was Michael, which she thought was a nice enough, even downright lyrical name, but who wasn't named Michael, she thought. Then she thought of all the *J* names she could think of—Jason, Jacob, Justin, Jerry, James, Joseph, Jonathan, John. But then she stopped herself because none of the *J* names would be suitable for her grandson, who was, after all, someone quite special. So she asked Junior, "Have you thought of a name for the baby?"

Junior distractedly answered, "No. But listen. So yesterday I get this call from the emergency room to come down because there's a patient there asking only for me. So I get down there and it's this pianist who teaches down at Peabody and he's broken his wrist. Anyway, he tells me that he was told by somebody that I'm the best orthopedic surgeon. He said the name of the person who told him this, but it didn't ring any bells."

But before she would give him a chance to finish, Antonia cut Junior off when she exclaimed, "Oh my goodness! Now that's just a great thing, that somebody recommended you so highly to him. It doesn't surprise me, though."

"Well, thank you, sweetheart," Junior said with a quickness that said he simply wanted to get on with the story. "Anyway, I set his wrist because it was a simple break, you know. Nothing at all that would need surgery, so I put it in a cast and all. Nice, clean, neat. But today, he comes back to the hospital to see me with all this gratitude for saving his career and invites us to a soiree at his house. Now, he has all this gratitude over me tending to his simple break that only needed a cast, and I told him it was just a simple break, but all he can think is that I've saved his career. And all I know is that it won't be broken anymore."

"So, did you accept the invitation?"

"Oh yeah. It's for Friday afternoon around four."

Antonia stared off into space as she tried to imagine what she might wear. Then she looked desperately to Junior and asked with equal eagerness, "Should I go out and get something new to wear?"

"No indeed. You don't need to do all of that. There's plenty in your closet to choose from. Besides, you know, this really isn't our kind of thing, but I accepted out of courtesy, since this guy is so grateful and feels he must do something for me."

"Yeah, well I know it's not our kind of thing, and especially not our kind of crowd," she said pensively. "Still, it came up so out of the blue, and something that puts us in the position to know more about the world of a pianist that it makes me feel as if we almost *have* to go. That it's fated that we go."

"I guess," Junior said. "I don't know, though. I haven't thought about it that deeply. It is what it is—an invitation."

Antonia didn't say anything for several weighty seconds, thinking that perhaps she had put far too much meaning into an afternoon in which she and Junior will most likely merely honor their invitation with a fleeting appearance—because they were nothing if not well-mannered. So because she did not want to walk into the man's house to hear his name for the first time the moment they'd be introduced, she asked Junior, "What's his name?"

"Larson Fletcher."

CHAPTER

19

•

"Give me a chance to get there," Antonia snapped at Junior as she hurried down the hall, straightening the twisted chain on her fancy purse. "What if he opens the door and you're standing there by yourself? Don't ring the bell till I get there."

Junior waited for her to get into her place beside him, then rang the bell. "There now, are you satisfied? Besides, nobody could open the door that fast."

Just then, the door flew open as if on some kind of command from Antonia that would show Junior just how wrong he could be. Someone could, indeed, open the door that fast.

"Well, hello, Dr. Jackson," Larson said. Then he looked at Antonia, extended a hand, and replied, "And you must be Mrs. Jackson. Please come in. I'm so glad you could come."

"It was so nice of you to invite us," Junior said. "All I did was set your wrist into a cast."

Larson stepped back as if to see all of Junior, then said in a tone that seemed meant to set Junior straight, "All you did was save my career. Do you know how many hacks out there set broken bones wrong? This here just feels right." And he held up his arm for Antonia to see.

"Well, I've always known he was talented" was all she said.

As Larson took their coats, he started down what seemed as if it would be quite a long and winding road of explanation, telling them that the party started out as a friendly little get-together.

After all, he proclaimed with the flailing of his one good arm and hand, he and his wife give these soirees frequently. But as their list of invitees grew and grew, Larson said with all the drama in his intonation and hand-waving that would normally accompany an interesting story, it just made sense to turn it into what it had been screaming to become.

So as Antonia stood there staring at him, she knew without very little doubt that Junior wouldn't be on the page with her. He had, to her, no other sense besides the five with which he was born. And when she felt the questioning eyes of Larson, she covered quickly when she asked, "So you say you and your wife give these parties frequently?"

"Oh yes. As far as I'm concerned, what's the point in being a musician in the most non-New York City city in the world if you don't make your own excitement for yourself and others in your own home?"

"Well, I guess that's one way of looking at it," Antonia said with a most feminine laugh that didn't completely resonate with this man. So without a response, she said, "Tell me, then, how will you give this party its New York City excitement?"

"Well, in different ways," Larson said, as he handed Antonia's and Junior's coats off to some man who had come to him obviously at his implicit command. "For example, Antonia, you have an accent that has the sweetest, most lyrical southern lilt at the end of every single thing you say. But it's not a twang, so I'm guessing that you're from somewhere way south of here, but have been up here for quite some time. Am I right?"

"Yes, you are," she said, dragging out that last syllable as if it had far too much heft to simply say it and then leave it be. Then with widened eyes that said she just might have had something to declare, she smiled at Junior as if she had just been mystified by some sideshow conjurer. She took the glass of champagne Junior handed her from the waiter's tray who was passing slowly by. Then she continued, "We're both from New Orleans. But no one ever guesses that."

"Well, if you had given me a little more time, I would have," Larson said, sharing a laugh with Antonia and Junior.

Junior sipped from his champagne, then said, "So, I guess you're not from here since you're trying to recreate New York City in the most—what is it you said, 'the most non-New York City city in the world'?"

Larson smiled with a certain arrogance that was nearly unde-tectable, then said, "Why of course not. I'm from NYC. But this place, in its way, has things to offer, just not on the same scale. What drives me crazy about Baltimore, I have to say, is that the city's sidewalks roll up somewhere around eleven. If you don't have a nine-to-five schedule, it can feel very limiting."

"Yes, I can imagine," Antonia said as she took a swallow of champagne, knowing full well that not only couldn't she imagine, she really didn't care.

Larson moved closer to Antonia, then said, almost apologeti-cally, "But don't think for a moment that these sort of genteel par-lor games are the limit here. I've turned this party into a reception for a former student of mine who's moved back to Baltimore and is giving his first concert here. I'm so excited, and so proud of him. He's living, in a way, the life that I wanted. But what is it they say—'Those who can, do. Those who can't, teach.' "

Antonia knew that this was her turn, either because she was the only woman in the group or because someone needed to salve such an indictment, but all she could do was stare into the face of fate. Stare as if she had been struck in such a way that words would not bond with her voice for any readily understandable thought. If this wasn't one of those serendipitous moments, then they simply didn't exist. In a voice smaller than she'd ever heard come from herself, she asked, "Clayton Cannon was your student?"

"Yes, he was, and in a way still is," Larson said with a prideful grin. Then, as if it had suddenly hit him, he said, "Oh, and you must know all about him, being that he's from New Orleans."

"Yes, he's the pride of the Big Easy," Junior said as he finished his glass of champagne and looked across the rim of the glass with desperate eyes that were so alive with some sort of passion they could nearly speak.

She understood that language, the one his eyes spoke. And boy, did she ever want to give in to their command, because she knew what they wanted. The problem for her, though, was that there was not one miniscule part of her reasoning that believed this was merely a bizarre coincidence into which she and Junior had just miraculously tripped. No, this was akin to a tap on the shoulder by God; except God didn't just tap to get her attention. With this, she believed, He had just thrown a massive hard red-clay brick smack into the center of her forehead in a gesture meant to stun her so that from that point on she would have to know that if she were going to bring her nephew home, only her tenacity could make it happen. Antonia handed her empty glass to Junior as a waiter neared. Then she said to Larson, "I would love nothing more than to meet Clayton Cannon again."

"You've met him before?" Larson said with surprise.

And because Antonia knew she didn't necessarily have to, but if she did, it would certainly take that look of wonder out of Larson's eyes, she elaborated. "I met him not so long ago down at Harbor Place. We were both there for lunch, and he invited me to share his table when he saw me looking for one."

"Oh, that's just like him," Larson said, smiling as if he were bragging about a son. "He's a good person."

"Yes," Junior said desperately as he put his and Antonia's empty glasses on the passing tray. "That's exactly what I told Antonia when she told me the story. Would you excuse us for a minute?" he said, taking Antonia's arm firmly and moving them away from Larson's earshot. And as soon as they were far enough away, Junior started, "Antonia, now I know what you're thinking."

"You have no idea what I'm thinking," Antonia said with a particular edginess as she grabbed her arm away to make herself clear.

Then taking a half-step back, Junior looked determinedly at her. "Oh, I don't, huh? Well, how about this. You're thinking that this is a moment God must have sent to you. Only mere fate brings coincidences, is what you're thinking. But God, He sends you what's meant to be." He stepped closer to her again, then asked, "Am I right?"

"Well, if you know, then why ask? What's the point of all this close, quiet talk? Let's just let God send what's meant to be," she said plainly, yet with a clearly resolved passion. She gazed around the room as the doorbell rang, then she turned to Junior and said, "I really don't know what's going to happen here tonight. I really don't." And she didn't. She only smiled as she watched Clayton Cannon step across the threshold into the room. Behind him was

Susan, his wife, she knew, and next to Susan was Agnes. But even with both of them in his presence, all she could see was Clayton because in her mind he was positively glowing, bringing a light into the room that only the deserving, like she, could come close enough in which to bask. In that room, Clayton was all that really mattered.

As if he'd just seen gold across the room, Larson's eyes lit when he saw Clayton, nearly at the same time Antonia saw him. So Larson walked over to the Jacksons and said, "Please come with me, Antonia and Dr. Jackson. I had no idea that I would have at this party the present for Clayton of two, count them, two people from New Orleans. He'll be tickled. Nobody will be able to tear him away." So Larson grabbed Antonia's hand and snaked his way through the crowd, with her hanging on in tow. Junior had no place else to go but to follow his wife over to where Clayton stood.

When Clayton turned around toward Larson, he saw Antonia as if he could see only her. "Miss Antonia?" he asked as he walked closer, moving farther from his wife and mother.

"Yes, it's me," Antonia said quietly. Then she reached for Junior's hand and pulled him closer, and said in a diffident manner, as if she was expected to explain, "This is my husband, Dr. Jackson. He fixed Larson's broken wrist, and Larson was kind enough to invite us here tonight. We only found out just about fifteen minutes ago that this reception was for you. What an honor it is for us to be here."

"And what a coincidence!" he said, bending to kiss her cheek and lightly hug her. When he stood straight again, he took Junior's hand firmly and said, "It's a real pleasure, Dr. Jackson."

"Please call me Junior," he said smiling as if he were struck in some way.

"I sure will. Thank you," Clayton said humbly. Then, heading toward Larson for a hug, Clayton said, "So, Larson, I can't tell you how nice it is that you'd do this for me."

"For you, Clayton, it is never going out of my way," Larson said, hugging Clayton as if he were Larson's personal pride. "But I have an even bigger gift, which, since you already know Antonia, you may already know. But Junior and Antonia here are from New Orleans."

"Oh yeah! I do remember you told me that, Miss Antonia,"

Clayton exclaimed with an ebullient laugh that seemed to linger
sweetly. "Boy, Larson, this is such a treat, having New Orleans
natives at a party for me. This has got to be good luck. And Miss
Antonia, you know my mother, too, don't you?"

Antonia's smile faded to something that only slightly resembled its former joy. But she answered, "Yes, Clayton. Yes I do
know your mother."

"Mama, come on over here. There's somebody here you know,"
Clayton said, turning to look for his mother.

And when he found her, her face slowly fell so low that it
wasn't quite clear if she were truly surprised or simply wished
she had not been found. And since it was not clear at all, when
Clayton called for her again, she walked slowly to Clayton, and
Larson, and Junior Jackson, *and* Antonia. When she reached them,
she looked only at Antonia and said in a way that tried its best to
sound heartfelt but just couldn't make it, "This has got to be the
biggest surprise of my life, seeing you here." Then she hugged
Antonia and pulled back but still holding on to Antonia's shoulders while looking her squarely, unblinkingly in the eye. "What
on God's green earth are you doing here?"

"Mama," Clayton answered instead of Antonia, "Dr. Jackson,
here, Miss Antonia's husband, took care of Larson when he broke
his wrist. That's why it's in a cast."

Larson held his arm in midair to display his cast. Then said,
"It'll be back to new before I know it, thanks to Dr. Jackson."

The conversation seemed to be lulling until Larson asked, "So
Antonia, do the two of you ever get back to New Orleans much?"

"Junior does," Antonia said, sure she would stop right there,
because even though it stayed on the edge of her mind and the tip
of her tongue nearly every minute, she wasn't going to announce
to them all that Junior had been unfaithful with that awful Cora.
So she continued, "I don't go back there terribly often—haven't
been back in almost twenty-five years."

"My goodness!" Larson said. Then gawked at Antonia as if
she'd been living with some kind of mental lapse. "A great city
like New Orleans. Heck, I'd be back there whenever the wind
blew south."

"Well, it's not so easy for me," Antonia said, plucking another
glass of champagne from a passing tray. She took a sip, then

looked at the floor, then up at no one in particular and continued, "I had a twin brother who was killed in a car crash when I was seventeen." She took another sip to get through the rest of the story, then said, "We were so close. Knew each others' minds, you know. Anyway, when he died, I had one more torturous year in the place before I went off to college, and when I did, I never looked back. It just didn't seem to make sense if Emeril wasn't there."

"Well we can all understand about not wanting to go back to a place, or even talk about it once you've left," Agnes said with every word soaked in a desperation that seemed not to want to talk about New Orleans. "That's how I feel about New York. I'm so relieved that Clayton moved his family away from that place. Thank God I don't have to visit New York anymore."

Larson looked sideways at Antonia, then cut a quick eye over to Clayton, but went back to Antonia. His forehead creased with the wrinkles of a man whose mind was thinking and crunching and figuring out, then Larson said, "Wait a second! Your *brother's* name was Emeril?"

"That's right," Antonia confirmed. "Emeril Racine. And the most amazing thing is that my Junior here was almost in that car crash with Emeril and Junior's cousin. Junior just decided not to go with them that day. But I could have lost everything. Thank God I have Junior."

"That is unbelievable," Larson said quietly.

"What, about Junior and how I could have lost him, too?"

"What's that?" Larson asked. "You almost lost Junior too. That's unbelievable," Larson said haltingly as if he didn't completely know to what he was responding. Then he turned to engage Agnes in idle chat, asked how she'd been, and how the trip was. He listened to those responses until there was quiet air between them. That's when he wanted to know if she was excited about Clayton's concert that night. But when that was talked into a natural death, he turned to Clayton, smiled anxiously, then said softly, almost in a whisper, "Listen, I'd like all of us to go into my study over there. You'll all understand why when we get there," and he began to cross the room headed for his study.

When he reached the door, he looked behind him to find his train of four following, with Clayton seeming to have to shove his mother forward. As soon as the last one, Clayton, crossed the threshold, Larson closed the door behind him, then joined them all where they stood in a loose circle. "Listen, I have something to say and I have a feeling it won't get said by any of you, especially not tonight, but maybe not any night, or even day."

They all looked with the same tension at Larson, and with questioning eyes of equal roundness. Larson looked at each of them with the same round eyes, but they asked a different question. So he said, "I'm wondering if I should bring Susan over from her conversation to include her."

And almost as soon as the last word was said, Agnes fretfully replied, "Somehow, not knowing what you're about to say, I feel safe in saying no, leave her be."

"Okay, then," Larson said, shifting a little from foot to foot. "I'm not sure if many of you know the relationship between a pianist and his teacher. If you don't, you should know that since Clayton came to me here at the Peabody twenty-seven years ago as an unsure eighteen-year-old haunted by so many bayou memories, he has given me the privilege of a good part of his conscious and subconscious mind. I was his therapist, I was his mother, I was his father, I was even his whipping boy on his most frustrated day when all I was ever supposed to be was his teacher.

"Now, in this circle of us, right here in the present, which is attached so completely to Clayton's past, there's a name that I think all of us know, and that name is Emeril. Emeril is Antonia's dead twin brother from New Orleans. Emeril is also the name in a dream Clayton had when he was twelve, he told me, coming from the funeral of his so-called father, and he has never been sure if it was a dream or what he actually heard with an awakened mind, but it's a name that cast some doubt on the identity of his father."

Larson stopped and put his hand on Antonia's shoulder while looking into the faces of each one of them as if to make certain they were all still following him. When he seemed assured, he continued, "Now, who wants to go first to explain this lyrical name Emeril. I may be wrong about this, but if I am wrong and have no doubt made a room full of enemies, or at the least people who think I'm nuts, so be it. But I'm doing this for the clarity of Clayton's mind that has been unclear for far too long."

Larson looked first at Agnes with expectation, but Agnes said nothing. She only stared intensely at Larson with eyes that seemed cold enough to cut.

But Antonia knew that it was now Agnes's time, and so she bore a hole into Agnes. But when Agnes remained silent, Antonia finally admitted what that bane of her life refused to say. "Emeril was my twin brother who carried on with Agnes when they were teenagers. Only Emeril died on the very day Clayton was conceived. And I know it was the day he was conceived. I believe in every bone in my body that she married Douglas Cannon, had my brother's baby, and passed him off as Douglas's because Clayton looked so white. With everything in me, I know it happened."

Clayton turned as slowly as a man trying to hold back some errant emotion could to face his mother so that it was only the two of them in that space. He stared into eyes that wouldn't look at his. And he stayed there, staring, with a stance that had dug in its heels, but when her eyes never met his, he said, "Mother, you have a very small window of opportunity to hold on to my respect for you by telling me the truth right here, right now. This sounds too real to be untrue. So you have to tell me, is this what happened? What Miss Antonia says, is it true?"

Agnes, still without looking at her son, but only at Antonia, said in a voice far smaller than she, "Yes, cher. That's exactly what happened. Emeril Racine is your father."

Antonia stood in her place, but staked her claim nonetheless, because he had to know for sure. "So you realize that this makes you my nephew. It makes you my brother's son. It makes you the finest black man my brother could have ever hoped to father."

Clayton swung around to face Antonia in what seemed to be a searing rage. Despite an anger that seemed intense, his voice was not slathered in deep red, but rather more of a cool crimson when he said, "Miss Antonia, or Antonia, or Aunt Antonia, whichever, I am just as white as I am black, unless there's something my mother wants to tell me about *her*self. What difference would it make if I continue to live as a white man as long as I know my true father? Why is there a need to go and shout it from the rooftops? I don't go around shouting from the rooftops that I'm a white man. And what is race, anyway? Is it a perception we have of ourselves, or is it a perception we have of ourselves that we've allowed other people to inflict on us?"

Antonia clenched her jaw with equal fervor to the arms she folded stiffly in front of her. This had fallen so short of her dreams, yet now the words, which she wasn't sure were hers even as they formed, flowed. "Oh that was some very fancy philosophical thinking you just threw out there. But the truth is, you don't have to go out shouting from the rooftops that you're a white man, because that's what people see until you tell them differently. Anyway, I guess I see how it works. It's okay for you to know, as long as it's kept a secret and no one ever gets to know what kind of man my brother—my black brother—created because now that you know who you are, you believe that you're Canaan, the son of Ham. Canaan, the son of Noah's son, Ham, cursed as slave from whom slaves would forever descend. What is it the Bible says? 'Cursed be Canaan! The lowest of slaves shall he be to his brothers.' And you, Clayton, believe and bear the shame that all of us with black skin deserve as the fate of the children of Canaan. Cast out and marginalized. Isn't that what racism is, Clayton—scornful vengeance against falsely placed pride?"

Clayton found his way to a dimly lit corner of the room. Agnes followed him, and Antonia, following both of them, stopped just as Clayton said, "Momma, the last thing I need is you here with me now. I need to be alone with everything I've just learned."

"Cher, please let me explain. Please let me tell you everything."

"Why should I let you, Momma? I'd be giving you way more respect than you've given me since the day I was born."

"That is just not true, Clayton. Since you've been born I've done nothing but loved you. And I've loved your father through you," Agnes said as she hung her head.

"You know, Momma, I have had moments in my life when I sensed, somehow, that you were lying about something. But I thought to myself, 'No, that can't be true, because what kind of mother would she be to lie to you.' Well, now I know what kind of mother you actually were. The kind of mother who would set her child's life up as one of deceit. A disgraceful mother who could only think of her life and what she wanted."

Agnes moved closer to him, shaking her finger at him in anger. "Now, you listen to me. That is just not true. I thought of nothing but you. No, I didn't want to admit that I was the mother of a bastard baby; the mother of a black, bastard baby because I knew how difficult that would make *your* life. But there was no way I was going to sneak off and get rid of the only part of Emeril that would still be living."

Just then, Susan opened the door enough to peek inside the room. When she saw Clayton over in the corner, she stepped into the room and closed the door behind her. "I thought I saw you all come in here. What's going on?"

But no one answered her, as Agnes continued, "And your life didn't turn out so bad, after all, did it? If you had known the truth about whose blood really flowed through you, you wouldn't have had the confidence or the opportunity to rise to the heights you've reached in an America that would have constantly put roadblocks in your way. At that time, I would have been raising you up in an America that would have told you that because you're a black man, you aren't qualified to reach your dreams."

Susan, blinking her eyes rapidly as if it reflected the rhythm of her heart, said again, "What's going on? Would someone please answer me and tell me what the hell has happened."

Clayton turned to her and said harshly, "I've just found out that my father, my real father, was a black man, Emeril Racine. And over there is his twin sister, my Aunt Antonia."

Susan looked puzzlingly at Antonia, then gave the same gaze to her mother-in-law, as she said, "Momma, that's the woman I saw you having lunch with, isn't it?"

"It sure is," Clayton said, straightening his jacket. "Yeah, that's just one of Momma's many secrets, apparently. Why don't you ask her what else she might be hiding?" And he moved brusquely past his mother, then past Susan and, opening the door, he said, "I have to be at the Meyerhoff for a live television interview before my concert. I'll see you all later." And with that the door was closed and he was gone.

Antonia only stared behind him at the closed door before she shot an angry bolt of a glare at Larson and said, "It wasn't such a grand idea to drop the bomb that his mother is a lying, sneaky snake in the grass right before his concert." Then she went to where Agnes stood, set her jaw firmly, and pulled herself in tightly, otherwise she would have been in her first fistfight since she was eleven years old. She unclenched her jaw long enough to tell Agnes, "I hope you're happy. I hope your lying and scheming and low-down, bug-level baseness has paid off in some way for you. You ought to be ashamed of yourself."

Junior asked Larson for his and Antonia's coats. And as Larson went for them, Junior went to Antonia and said softly, "Come on, honey. It's time we get going."

"I need to get away from her, because there's no telling what I'd do if I was around her two seconds longer." And she turned from Agnes and moved with haste toward the door. Once she'd gone through, she slammed the door with all the anger she'd meant for Agnes.

CHAPTER

20

•

As Aaron went past a store inside the mall, he was struck by its name—5-7-9—and couldn't fathom what it could possibly mean. Then an ensemble of low-riding high-cropped skinny pants and a top that was more a band of fabric that showed mostly midriff caught his eyes. It made him think of Tawna and what she might have worn ten years before, and he wondered what that would have been like, to have known her back then. She would have been that tiny, he imagined, because she wasn't much larger than that now. And she would have had the same confident walk but minus the life experience that gave her such elegance now.

Before Aaron knew it, he had made his way to the food court. He looked for a spot where they could sit, far enough for privacy from all those who would definitely want to know what he'd have to say to a woman who was not Maggie Poole. When he found a place and sat, he looked around to see if Tawna was nearby, perhaps already sitting or just getting there. Across the tables a man smiled and nodded at him just as he was about to dig into the mound of food. Aaron couldn't identify him but the man looked familiar. It wasn't until a woman passing by the food court saw the man and yelled his name, "Tom!" with such enthusiasm that Aaron got it. Each time he had been in this place, he'd seen this man. As Tom, who was short in stature, but colossal with charisma, spoke to the woman, he had her, in no time whatsoever, giggling like a schoolgirl and doubling over with laughter that didn't seem to let her catch her breath. It made Aaron smile, because Tom was just the kind of man Aaron wanted to be. And even though he didn't know the man, he knew for sure by just watching him that Tom was the kind of man who could put a total stranger at ease just as he had this passing friend.

Just then Tawna snuck up behind Aaron, who was smiling like a teenage lover, and whispered in his ear, "Lost in thought?"

She startled him, but he recovered immediately as he said, "About you." Then he kissed her cheek that was right there until she turned her face to kiss him full on the mouth.

As she sat, Tawna asked, her eyes narrowed with worry, "So what's up? What is so important that you wanted to meet here, out of your way and mine?"

Aaron chuckled with boyish embarrassment and said, "I know this isn't the classiest place I could possibly pick to say what I need to say. I actually meant the food court at Owings Mills mall—not that that would be any classier than any other food court—but by the time I called you back you had already left, so here we are." Aaron looked up at her with earnest eyes that were also afraid of rejection, but he continued. "In a way, this is perfect, you know, because the simplicity of this place is like the simplicity of the way I want my future life to be with someone."

"Okay, so the beginning of our relationship is making you hope for the comforts of a mall food court. Go on," she said drolly, and in such a goofy way that she couldn't help but giggle.

Aaron laughed nervously for a second, then said, "Okay, I'll get to the point. Would you like to come with me to my sister's baby-naming ceremony? She hasn't named him yet because she wants the whole family to do it."

"That's really lovely, and it lets the baby know that he was brought into a world with a family that will cherish him and support him. That's great. I would love to go with you." Then she turned questioning eyes at him. "That's why you wanted to meet me? That's what you wanted to ask me? I love seeing you and being, even here, with you, but honestly you could have asked me that over the phone."

"Well, it's only part of what I wanted to ask you," he said, catching a glimpse of Tom standing at the Cinnabon counter as dapper as if he'd just stopped by the mall on his way from a fashion show. Tom would just say it, Aaron thought. So Aaron held

Tawna firmly in his eyes and said, "If I were to ask you right here in the food court to marry me, just because when I look at you, and talk to you, and listen to you, and hear your laugh, I know that I want everything that's you walking beside me, and sleeping beside me, and sometimes just doing nothing but sitting deep in thought beside me, what would you say?"

Tawna looked at him as if she had just shifted, right there on the spot, into another woman's life—as if she had no idea what she'd done or when she'd done this to him. And then she giggled with uncertainty, a seriousness that made the air seem ripe for her to flatly say no. Then she said, "I would say to you to ask me again in six months after we've crammed both of our attitudes up in a car and taken a five-hour road trip. That'll tell us something."

Aaron relaxed into himself enough to laugh easily, then said, "You're probably right about that." And so now he was loose enough. He could unclench all the muscles in his back, and that knot in his stomach could just go on its way. So he went to get up as he said to Tawna, "I guess we should get some lunch since we're here. What would you like to eat?"

Tawna gazed at him with widened eyes and said, "Are you kidding? After what you've just said to me you think I can eat something? I'm way too excited for that." She leaned across the table for a kiss, and once she got it she continued, "I have to get back anyway. I'll talk to you later."

As he watched her leave—and it brought with it the same sadness and beauty of watching a once-brilliant sun fade—he wondered just how ridiculous it might be to a sober mind that he would feel and say such things after this woman had been in his life for such a brief time. But he watched her until he couldn't see her, and then got up to head, not for the fried chicken, but for a coral hat and matching purse and maybe even a sheer scarf flung carelessly across them both in the store with numbers for a name.

Later that afternoon, Aaron walked through the newsroom from makeup and it seemed to him to be pitched at a calm that was immediately disturbing. Yet he knew there was nothing specifically different in the place at all since the room was still filled with the drone of coursing news. There was just an evenness to the whirr, and it put him in mind of one particular day during a childhood summertime visit down to Plaquemine, in Louisiana. That day, life stayed in constant momentum, taking the form of a marble game in the dirt with cousins—some blood, some not—and string beans Ellen and Grammy snapped on the porch. And as Aaron remembered that day, he recalled the stillness of the leaves, the birds that seemed as if their songs were forgotten, and the air that would no longer move. Still, there came a gust of wind that blew straight up out of hell with Satan riding on its back that turned Aaron's world upside down only to bring it back to earth to lie wounded on its backside. That's when he became cautious about the unnatural calm of things, whether in plain sight or obscured by the unchanging flow of life.

It was this other awareness that was speaking to him now, telling him that there was an unnatural calm around him, as news buzzed true to its own form. He looked across the room into Mark's office, and there was nothing different. Mark was on the phone using hands and arms to tell as much of his story as words, which is how he seemed to go through most of his day. The writers were hacking away at their keyboards. None of the monitors on the other stations were reporting anything outside of the mundane misdeeds of varying shades and sizes. Everything was the same, yet something peculiar had sidled up next to him and wouldn't go away.

When he knew he didn't have the time on his side to ponder it a second longer, Aaron turned to head into the studio. That's when he found Maggie coming toward him, and something wasn't right. And suddenly it struck him that it may have had something to do with the natural death their relationship had died, and the funeral she reluctantly and he willingly gave it. Still, with all that had taken him from her and into the arms of his tawny Tawna, there were moments, he knew, just as now, when it seemed as if he couldn't take another breath without Maggie's smile, and it wasn't there. So this was it, whatever it was; and what was he to do? He listened to the pumping of his heart, and held on to the last breath he took as he waited and watched her come closer with a questioning countenance. So when she got right to him, his mouth opened by the force of his instinct, though no words came out.

But Maggie only looked sideways at him with narrowed eyes

and said with an edginess in her tone, "Are you coming? They want to light you."

"Oh yeah," Aaron said with a relieved half-laugh. As she moved past him, he reached out and touched her hand propelled by a guilt he wished would go away, but actually had no idea when it would take its leave. "I'm on my way in right now."

As he stepped into the studio, the peace of mind Aaron had found from Maggie in that fleeting respite from his disquiet—a relief that made him believe that his extra sense was off kilter—was trumped by the wonder of why her face was so dragged down with some sort of concern that seemed larger than their breakup. That, he knew, was something he didn't imagine. And he knew Maggie in all the colors of her moods, and this look was something more than the mere disconsolate temperament of a jilted lover. Whatever it was involved him personally, intimately. So as he fit the IFB onto his ear and clipped the microphone onto his lapel, he willed Maggie back into the studio, because he wasn't going to wait until the first break of the show to find out what he could have said, could have done, didn't say, should have said, should have done, or didn't do to put that look on her face. Aaron had gotten himself settled behind the news desk when she finally came back to the studio. He didn't even let her get halfway to him before he said, "Maggie, is everything cool?"

Her jaws were set tightly until she reached Aaron and sat down next to him. Then as she slowly turned to face him, she said in a whisper, "No, Aaron, everything is not cool. Quite honestly, I'm worried about the third segment into the newscast. The one where we go live to that interview with Clayton Cannon. I just have a bad feeling about you doing the lead-in to that interview."

Aaron reared back his head, swollen with the arrogance of his pride and said, "Maggie, how can you say something like that to me? I'm a professional, and I've never behaved in any other way on the air. Off the air, that man is the bane of my life. On the air when I'm doing the intro to his interview, he is a piece of news."

She regarded him skeptically, then looked away to her news copy. And when she looked up, it wasn't into his eyes. Still, she said, "I just don't know, Aaron. I'm not so sure, for some reason. You've got a real tender spot when it comes to that man, and when it comes down to him or your professionalism, I don't give your professionalism a fighting chance of surviving against Clayton Cannon."

"Thanks for the vote of confidence," Aaron said tersely as he turned from her with a definite edginess in his comportment. As he studied his news copy, he could feel the heat of her stare deep into the side of his face, but he had not one other word for her. In his ear he heard the Channel Eleven theme music that he often heard in his mind, like a psychotic moment, at times outside of this place. Then the stage manager cued to Aaron in five, four, three . . .

So he read the headlines of the lead stories. "A triple murder in Pikesville leaves the quiet community gripped in fear as police try to solve the crime that has left behind very few clues as to who the killer might be." Then he paused for two seconds waiting for the video to change from Pikesville to the blazing row house in West Baltimore. "Two people are in critical condition after being overcome by smoke inhalation when fire breaks out in their West Baltimore home." He paused again to make certain the video was caught up, but also to shore up his foundation as he said, "And with just hours to go before his sold-out concert, the first since moving back here to Baltimore, Clayton Cannon talks to Keith Pettiford live from the Meyerhoff."

Then it was Aaron and Maggie, sitting together, smiling only halfway in their greeting because you just can't smile when you're about to talk about a triple murder. And a house fire. And Clayton Cannon, which was no smiling matter, hovering right up there at the same level of misery for Aaron. So Aaron said, "Good evening, I'm Aaron Jackson."

"And I'm Maggie Poole. Tonight we're going directly to Pikesville where we have Derek Dodson on the scene of a gruesome triple murder. Derek, what can you tell us?"

So Aaron watched the monitor intently as he listened to the details of three lives taken in an Upper Park Heights home, only three blocks down and around a corner from his house. And he wondered about those people's last moments. But there was one thing he knew without a doubt—even though the police now knew that there had to have been two killers, most likely men, Aaron knew they would not be looking for two black men. On Upper Park Heights, two black strangers would have to do a lot of huffing and puffing to blow down the door of any one of those homes where Jews lived quietly, guardedly in their wealth, he thought as he remembered his days of jogging past those impressive homes as the focus of nervous stares and barren smiles. But it was still such a shame, those murders.

Then Maggie said, "You say the police found no sign of forced entry, yet there's no indication that the victims knew their killers. Do they have any idea who they might be looking for?"

And just as Aaron knew the truth to be, he listened as Derek said, "Now the police say neighbors reported seeing two neatly dressed white men in the neighborhood, walking aimlessly up and down the street an hour before the murders. While the police are not labeling them as suspects, they are looking for them for questioning."

There are some crimes, Aaron thought with a wry smile meant only for himself, particularly since he was off camera, that are simply sociological impossibilities.

When Maggie finished with the triple murder, Aaron paid only narrow attention to the West Baltimore fire. But what did capture his thought was that one of the people overcome by smoke was blind, which made him think of Maggie's opinion of the most awful way to die. He recalled how, ever since he'd known her, she'd told him that her worst fear was to go blind and burn up in a fire. So now she's sitting right there talking about what would be the most horrible course she could possibly take to leave the planet. He let that thought go when he had to prepare for his cue. And when the camera was on him and he heard the break music in his ear, he said, "When we come back, we're going downtown to the Meyerhoff where Keith Pettiford will talk with Clayton Cannon just hours before his first concert in Baltimore since he moved here." And they were out.

Aaron put his scripts down and looked over at Maggie, and only when she turned to him did he say, "So that was your worst fear, right? That blind lady in the fire."

Maggie gave him a self-conscious smile that pressed her lips together to turn them only slightly upward at the corners, then replied, "She didn't burn up in the fire. She was blind, but she didn't burn up."

"You mean she would have had to actually burn up in the fire for it to be identical to your fear?"

"Yes. Breathing in smoke and burning flesh are two separate things, and burning flesh is a lot more horrifying, not to mention excruciating, than dying a smoky death."

"Oh yeah?" Aaron said with a sardonic laugh, before continuing, "Well, ask someone who's nearly died from breathing in smoke."

Maggie laughed thinly, then asked, "Are you ready for the next segment?"

"I don't think I should have to answer that, Maggie," Aaron said, only showing the uppermost layer of his irritation. She didn't mean to, he knew, and it was just her style, but with her plain-speak, she had a way of going right to the center of him with only one word and setting off a firestorm, to which he could pay no heed at best and beat down at worst.

"And we're back in five, four, three . . ." the stage director said.

Aaron prepared himself and looked straight into the camera, and when it was time, he said, "In less than three hours, Clayton Cannon will walk onto the stage at the Meyerhoff and play his first concert for the city as a resident. This has been a much anticipated concert for most of Baltimore, and now Keith Pettiford is with Clayton Cannon down at the Meyerhoff as he prepares for tonight. Keith, can you tell us a little about how he feels being back here to live and what it will feel like to take the stage tonight as a resident of the city?"

Aaron listened with more interest than he could recall ever having in anything that went through their airwaves as news, but reflexively leaned forward to rest on his forearms, as if he needed to hear or see better, and shook his foot with equal reaction to his anticipation. There was no telling what he'd hear, and he had no idea why he'd even want to hear it. But this phantom that had invaded his imaginings for as long as he'd had memory was now right in front of him, so to speak; and whatever there was for Aaron to glean from a few minutes of talk through a television monitor, he'd take. He had to understand Clayton Cannon on some level, for this man had a power that Aaron was desperate to know. And that power had been able to steal enough of his mother's heart away to make him long for the missing part of her in some way nearly every day of his life. Was it in Clayton's smile, which Aaron had to admit, was seductive and warm? Or was it in his eyes and the way they stayed focused with every word he said to Keith, as if he were forging a deep and lasting connection? There had to be something that would make an otherwise sane woman—that he now knew his mother to be—want to lay claim to this piano-playing thief of hearts.

But so far, all Clayton talked about was the excitement of Baltimore, the connectedness of Baltimoreans that made the city a small town, and an inexplicable pull he had felt to come back. And yes, he loved the crabs, and the harbor, and the bay. Oh, and Fells Point! What a difference all these years gone by have made. So what else? He's going to play Beethoven's Sonata in F Minor, crudely, Aaron heard him say, referred to as the "Appassionata." Crudely to music snobs who spoke intimately of arias and concertos and sonatas, Aaron supposed, since he'd never heard of it anyway; this Clayton said he'd play in memory of his audition at the Peabody Conservatory.

And so Aaron kept his interest tuned as Clayton went on to explain how the second half of his concert would be Chopin's Nocturnes since it was right in Baltimore, during his tender years at the conservatory, that he grew to fully understand the complexity of Chopin's piano pieces as something other than cleverly placed backdrop meant to mingle dramatically with carnal lust in European films. And Aaron studied the man with narrowed eyes, as Clayton went on to say that it was in Baltimore that he learned the intimidating process of bringing more to Chopin than just a large and awe-inspiring technique that only played the notes. Only played the notes? Aaron wondered. What else would he do, and would anybody else know what was missing if all Clayton did was play the notes?

But what dug viscerally into Aaron in a way he couldn't fathom was Clayton saying that it was when he discovered how to play more than just Chopin's notes that he fully embraced his power to bring the world together through his music. Bring the world together through his music. This haunted Aaron, and it was this understated passion, that Aaron couldn't begin to imagine having for anything, that made him now regard Clayton with a fascination that came quite close to the awe with which he regarded the man when he was ten years old and first laid eyes on him.

Then Clayton said something that Aaron knew he could only

possibly understand if he had the slightest inkling of the world in which Clayton lived. Clayton claimed that there was something pulling him to play the Nocturnes only in minor keys for the concert. There was something soothing to a brooding soul about minor keys. And then what Aaron heard next was of particular curiosity to him. Clayton claimed that even though a lifetime of brooding had come to an end just a few hours before, he would still play his concert in minor keys as a tribute to his release.

And this release, Aaron thought, what it could be he did not try to guess. All he knew for certain was that there was something about the man's newfound peace that made Aaron's stomach curl up inside his chest and sit there as if it did not belong someplace else entirely. He didn't know how, but Aaron had readied himself for what would come when Clayton said,

"There seems to be something fitting about this news coming today, the last day of Black History Month. But I just learned today that my father was not who I'd always known as my father. My father was a black man named Emeril Racine, and his twin sister, my Aunt Antonia Jackson, lives right here in Baltimore. And in some way, I believe this just may be the sort of psychic energy that brought me back here to Baltimore, almost against my will. And you know what else? My aunt's son is Aaron Jackson, your anchorman. We're cousins, Aaron and I."

And then Clayton did something Aaron simply could not abide when he waved into the camera and said, "Hey, cousin!"

So Keith, seeming not to know what else to say, said to Aaron, "Aaron, did you know about this? Did you know he was your cousin?"

In that moment, Aaron knew his life had been solidly divided into before and after—before the day he found out that his mother had been right all this time, and after he found out that he had been sitting for years in his wrongness. He stared without life, without motion into the camera and only said, "And so it's just like that for him. Just that easy." Then he stood without speaking another word, and almost without knowing what he did, walked from the set. He simply left, forcing Maggie to hold down the news on her own. He kept walking, and he didn't even bother to look behind at whether she would simply go on or stare after him in utter shock. There was the appropriate silence in the studio, except for Keith's controlled anxiety as he called, "Aaron. Aaron can you all hear me?" But nothing was said by Maggie or Josh, and Aaron's shock needed the empathy for the scarce seconds it lasted. And in those seconds he didn't care whether the air would be dead or filled with a station break. In that moment, he could be nothing but focused on the blow that had just knocked him from the seat to which he thought he would always be so firmly anchored.

There was a chair that sat by the door, and it was into this chair that he calmly and reasonably placed his IFB and the microphone from his lapel just before he passed through the door. He went down the hall at a clip, but before he could get to the newsroom, Mark was walking toward him even faster. Aaron had somehow found a sober part of his mind that was able to steel him for the lambasting that was sure to come from Mark. So he slowed only to meet Mark, who looked mad enough to flatten anything in his path.

"What the hell was that, Jackson? What are you doing walking out in the middle of my newscast? Are you out of your mind?"

"I just might be, Mark," Aaron said flatly as he stepped around Mark to continue on his path to a destination of which he wasn't even certain.

But Mark followed him, saying, "Jackson, you owe me some answers. But before you give them to me, you'd better get back in there during the next station break and do your job."

Aaron waited until he got to the door of the newsroom before he turned to Mark and said, "My job. And what would that job be today, Mark? Tap dancing like some white boy's fool just because he's so good to acknowledge that I'm his cousin to all of Baltimore who's listening? Is that my job, Mark? Because if it is, I'm sorry, but I'm going to have to call in sick today."

"You get paid a hell of a lot of money to be what you call a fool." Then Mark put his head down, as if with empathy. And, with his manner considerably softened, he said, "Look, Aaron, I don't really understand what just happened in there, but I suppose I can safely guess that you didn't know that Clayton Cannon was your cousin."

With a caustic laugh that gave even Aaron a chill, he replied, "Mark, not only did I not know, but it was the very last thing I wanted on this earth to be true." And he walked through the newsroom with his eye squarely on his office. He felt the silence, the tentative stares of all those who could not possibly know what was appropriate to say. Nothing was appropriate to say, and he was glad they had somehow understood, without truly understanding, the tenderness of the matter.

When he got to his office, Aaron went with haste to his chair and plopped himself angrily down into it. From where he sat, he could see Mark talking to Will Gittings, and could tell by the glee Will seemed to be trying his best to subdue that Mark was sending him in to fill the empty anchor's chair. That pasty-faced punk, Aaron thought. He's been dying to get in that chair since he first landed at Channel Eleven, Aaron said so loudly in his mind that he almost actually heard it. Let him go on, because who in hell cares, anyway? Surely Aaron didn't, and surely not now.

Aaron had been focused for minutes on the picture of his family atop his desk before he realized it was fixed in his gaze. When he finally took his eyes off of it to look up, coming toward his office trotting as fast as a fat man can hurry was Tim, and his face was in full pissed-off-general manager mode. Aaron knew what was coming, because Tim's face was red with the same flame that was in his eyes. But Aaron decided to head him off before Tim could get fully into the office. "Okay, look Tim, I know I was wrong. But I just don't want to hear it right now."

"Oh, but you're going to hear it," the man said with his voice filling every single space in Aaron's office and most of the newsroom. "How do you have the balls to just get up out of that chair and walk off the set with the cameras rolling? I don't give a damn about what's going on with you and that man and how this all took you by surprise, you have a job to do and we don't have room in here for you to be acting out your personal feelings through this kind of drama."

Aaron lowered his head with contrition, then said softly, "You just don't know."

"You're right, I don't know, and I don't want to know. I just know that you did something that was absolutely inappropriate. The only way I would be able to understand what you did was if you saw your mother get shot live, and even then I would expect you to excuse yourself appropriately."

What if someone has just stolen my mother away? Aaron thought. It's not as bad as shooting her, still she'll be no less gone. Wouldn't that be cause enough? Aaron put his focus back on the picture of his family and tried to imagine another face in it, because there was no doubt that his mother would want it that way. So they'd all have to go back over to Ellen's and call in a photographer whose job it would be to fit not just one more, but four more people into the picture in front of the fireplace, because it would not be the whole family, he knew his mother would say, without Clayton's wife and twin boys. Yet the day would be filled with nothing near the lightness of being it had been with the taking of this picture propped proudly on his desk. The way Ellen and Rick heard the photographer, who had not a trace of any kind of accent except a Baltimore one, say *"bootiful"* enough times to know that it wasn't meant as a joke, yet they just could not stop giggling long enough to smile. Then there was the way his mother playfully scolded him each time he, in some sort of five-year-old regression, turned his two fingers into ears behind her head. She delighted in his silliness. And his father, who had started off the most sober of them all, began asking the photographer about airbrushing his image to make him look like a G.Q. model. Then Aaron thought of the new picture—and Agnes. No way would Agnes be allowed within a mile of Antonia's newly cast family.

Suddenly Aaron became aware of Tim's eyes still pressed hard into him, so he slid himself away from his thoughts of a new family portrait and plainly said, "I'm really sorry, Tim," as he listened to his phone ring, and ring, and ring.

Ellen cradled her boy in her arm, patting his little bottom gently with her hand while she dialed the phone again. Either Aaron had left the building altogether or he simply was not answering his phone. But she was calling his cell phone too, getting only his voice mail. At least now they know, she thought as she worried herself through all the tragic scenarios each time she remembered the look on Aaron's face when it became clearer than crystal that their mother had been right all these years. At least now they know. And what a way to find out! That's why Ellen couldn't be sure if it was the news itself that had devastated her brother, or the delivery of it; but one thing she knew without one doubt—her brother was truly distraught.

The baby began to squirm with the threat of waking up, so she watched and tried to stay stark still considering that the other side of her was rumbling with fear for her brother. But the baby was only sleep-shifting, she discovered, as he settled back into his new position—which looked to her to be no different than his old one—in her arm. He was out like a drunk. And that, she figured, was most likely the baby equivalent of such a state—drunk from her milk and comfort, she thought he must be. And she wondered if she'd ever get over the birth of her child. What a magical moment, she thought, smiling at the thought of him drifting from her womb into her arms, and then looking at her as if he had been waiting all ten months of his entire life to meet her. She never got over the birth of her children, Ellen remembered Antonia saying, and her mother fell far short of being the emotional, giddy, sappy mother Ellen could already feel herself becoming. So if her birth, and Aaron's birth could make a mother like theirs so sentimental all these years later, she supposed she *would* never get over the birth of this little boy.

By the time the bell rang, Ellen had already heard the muffled footsteps of someone at the front door, so she had started the process of trying to get on her feet with an armful of baby. Once she was standing, she repositioned the baby and went as quickly as she could move toward the door; because it had to be the answer to her prayers—Aaron. When she got up the three steps to the aperture of the living room and front hall, she could see the side of Aaron's coat through the side window of the door.

So she flung the door open and said with the relief of a mother, "Thank God. I've been worried sick about you. You weren't answering your phone at work or your cell phone. I didn't know what to think."

"Yeah, I got your messages." Aaron closed the door behind him and began peeling off his coat. He followed Ellen into the living room and threw his coat across a chair as he descended the steps. "So, I guess you saw the newscast tonight. The one I didn't finish," he said as he sat on the opposite end of the sofa from where Ellen and the baby sat. He leaned over and looked at the sleeping baby, then said, "My God what a boy! He is so beautiful, Ellie."

"Thank you, Aaron. He is wonderful," she said with a grin stretched so far across her face it barely let her speak. She was so full of pride. But her face grew sober when she continued, "Yes, I did see it."

Aaron looked at his sister despondently and said, "The difference is, you weren't right in the middle of reporting the news. You didn't have a meltdown on live TV."

"No, I didn't," she said, watching her baby move again. "And neither did you. You reacted like any normal person would react, I think, under the same circumstances. These people out here watching you every night, the patients I see, none of them have any idea what it's been like for us from the moment we found out that this man existed." She stood again, went to the bassinette, and gently put her boy down. Then she quietly tiptoed back to the sofa and sat. "I don't love Clayton Cannon and I don't hate him—same as before. I'm just glad it's over. I'm just glad we know the truth."

Then Aaron slid a little closer to Ellen and said in a low voice, "And what about that truth, huh? In a million years I didn't think this would—could—be true, but it's true. And this is the thing—I'm not so sure if I simply didn't think it could be true, or if I wanted so badly for it *not* to be true."

"Oh, Aaron, come on," Ellen said with the tiniest twitter of laughter, but with just a bit of the real impatience she was actually feeling dangling on the edge of each word. "That's an easy one. Of course we didn't want it to be true. If it wasn't true and Clayton Cannon was absolutely no relation, then we'd get our mother back. After all these years, we'd get our mother back."

Aaron settled himself back on the sofa. He looked across the room, as if he could see his thoughts over there, then said, "So she really was gone, huh? I mean, you saw it too?"

Ellen leaned sideways toward her brother and slid her hand the rest of the way across the sofa to take his hand. She squeezed it with all the love—motherly, sisterly or whatever kind he needed—and comfort she could send him, and said, "Of course she was gone, Aaron. She was as gone as can be."

Ellen's little one chirped with a cacophony of his baby sounds, and it was the sweetest thing that had been in the air in the last hour or so. She watched Aaron as he got up and went haltingly to the bassinette. He peeped in, then looked over at Ellen and asked if he could pick him up. "Sure," she said. "He's awake, so go ahead."

Aaron picked up the boy with all the awkwardness and uncertainty in the hunched shoulders and nervous eyes of a childless man. Then Aaron said to him, "One thing you'll never have to worry about is your mother ever leaving you in any way. She's not going anywhere because you're the beginning and the end to her." He looked up at Ellen and said, "So, I guess the question now is what will we say to her."

Ellen first watched the sight of her brother holding her son, and it filled her up enough to make her tear. A baby, she thought, with an uncle he'll know who will never have to go out chasing after him to prove he's family, and a mother who will always tell him the truth—even, she thought in this extreme moment, about Santa Claus, the Easter Bunny, and the Tooth Fairy. Why should he believe in anything but God, and her, and his father. And then she narrowed her eyes and looked at Aaron when she said, "No, the question, baby brother, is what will she say to us."

CHAPTER

21

•

Aaron could still feel the sense of Ellen's baby in his arms as he stood outside the stage door of the Meyerhoff late that night. A new life was a powerful thing. A force pulling you toward your responsibilities at the same time as it fed you with the limitlessness of its innocence. If Aaron could possibly look at this newborn baby boy and feel, as the boy's uncle, the strength of that pull, he could only imagine what it must feel like to Ellen. And he had to wonder how on earth it would be possible for anything to compromise that feeling, even a mystery that only a few hours ago came to its conclusion.

Aaron was wondering if Clayton Cannon was feeling any "new life" tonight or if things had already gone back to normal for him after he'd turned everyone else's upside down. The only thing more unimaginable to him than his mother being right after all these years was that he would find out about it in the way that he did.

Clayton certainly had his admirers, Aaron noted. There were dozens waiting along with Aaron and who now swarmed around the pianist as he came out the door, as though he were some kind of enormous celebrity. Aaron couldn't imagine how anyone who did what Clayton Cannon did for a living could be considered a celebrity, but he was obviously the only one in this crowd who felt that way. For the next quarter of an hour, Clayton signed autographs and listened with what Aaron was certain was measured humility to songs of praise and adulation. He wondered how many of the people heaping this praise actually knew anything about classical music and how many of them were just drawn to him because he was some kind of transplanted local hero.

Finally the sycophants dispersed, leaving Aaron alone with Clayton. Maybe twenty paces separated them. Aaron knew right away that Clayton recognized him. Just as he knew right away that Clayton was a little apprehensive about seeing him in this setting. Clayton wasn't waving at him now, maybe because the distance between them wasn't nearly as great, and Aaron wondered if the man had any idea what a furor he'd set off in the newsroom with his little greeting. Considering how slow and small his steps were, Aaron thought that he might have.

"I'm not going to hit you, if that's why you're so hesitant to come closer to me," Aaron said.

Clayton laughed. "No, I don't think you're going to hit me. Although with the way I put you on the spot earlier in that interview, I wouldn't blame you at all if you wanted to."

Aaron was surprised at how easily his own smile came to his face. Had he expected Clayton to act in some way that would justify a firestorm of vituperation? If he had—and only now had he begun to realize that he had no idea what to expect when he confronted him—it was pretty obvious that he wasn't going to get anything of the sort. "Good," he said. "Because I do want to. It's just that I won't."

"Fair enough."

The distance eventually closed between them and Clayton reached out his hand to shake. Aaron knew it would have not only been rude, but pointless to refuse, so he took the man's hand. The hand didn't feel particularly special, even though it was half of a pair of the most celebrated hands in all of Baltimore.

"I have a place over at Harbor Court, which you probably know already," Clayton said. "There's a restaurant over there where we can have a drink and maybe talk some of this out."

"I think talking might be a good idea right about now."

Clayton nodded and walked toward the limousine that was waiting for him. The driver already stood with the door open.

"I'll meet you over there," Aaron said, turning toward his car.

Clayton stopped, which caused Aaron to stop as well. "I was thinking the driver could take both of us."

Aaron had no intention of accepting a limousine ride from Clayton Cannon. Their relationship, whatever it might turn out to be, was not going to start that way. "That's okay. I'll take my car."

"Can you give me a ride, then?"

Clayton was grinning and Aaron wasn't sure what to make of that, but he nodded and then watched as Clayton signaled to the driver that he wouldn't be needed. They walked silently to Aaron's car and when Aaron looked across his hood, Clayton still had the faintest hint of a smile on this face. It didn't as much seem that he was being smug, just that he seemed more entertained by this situation than he had the right to be.

"Look, I'm just going to say this right off," Aaron said. "I found you flip and arrogant and thought you had a hell of a lot of nerve the way you just claimed me and my family in such a public way without making it a private matter first." Now that the words had started coming, Aaron found that he had no desire to stop them. "It was like it couldn't have meant to you what it had been building up to mean for us for at least all of my life, and my sister's life too. And my mother, please. She knew this day was coming just as sure as my grandmother's arthritic knee could predict rain. But for you, it was just something to say. You just said it, and it wasn't as simple as me just accepting it. You did it wrong. You did it wrong, and in a callous way."

If Clayton had been chastened by Aaron's outburst, he gave no indication of it. He just nodded, as though to acknowledge that he'd heard something and then said, "Do you think we can get into the car?"

Aaron couldn't be sure if Clayton was being arrogant or was just embarrassed by the scolding. Not feeling like he had much of an alternative and feeling a little embarrassed himself about just spewing out words like that, he opened the car doors and they drove off to Harbor Court in silence. It was no more than a five-minute drive, especially at this time of night, and Aaron was beginning to think they'd get there without talking at all when Clayton spoke up.

"Look," he said, "I'm a concert pianist. It seems very simple and in its way meaningless because it's so esoteric. I'm not a rock star. I'm not a movie star. I'm this guy who plays this incredible old-world music for high-minded people that tend not to be very mainstream. So I get to these concert halls filled with these high-minded people and I play as brilliantly as I can play that night, then I go home and wait for the next concert. Except it's not that simple. When crowds form backstage or at the stage door or some guy like yourself sticks a microphone in my face to ask about who knows what, I do the very best I can to keep a part of my most honest, my most personal self close to me. Make no mistake, though, eighty percent of what I do and who I am when I lift up from that piano stool is persona. When I waved hello into the camera at my cousin it was the only thing I could do to keep everybody out of my true heart and true mind."

He turned to Aaron at that point. "I would imagine it's no different for you," he said. "I would guess that when you're on the air, we're only seeing about twenty percent of the true Aaron."

"Well, that's true," Aaron said, not sure he liked the fact that this instant cousin of his was trying to establish a professional bond as well. "It's just that earlier today, in that moment, it was way too personal, and persona became an unbearable pretense."

"Trust me, it wasn't premeditated. And I don't think I'd gotten all of the day's revelations into my head when that interview started. I know that the way you got the news was shocking, but it wasn't much more than an hour before that, I had also been shocked by the same news."

As Harbor Court came into view, Aaron allowed himself a moment to look at things from Clayton's point of view. The man had to be reeling, at least a little bit. There was no way you could learn the things that he had learned today and not be seriously affected by them. Maybe even affected enough to do something foolish, completely out of character, and hurtful to others. It didn't justify what he did, but it did go a long way toward explaining it.

They pulled into the garage and got out of the car. The attendant there made no effort to help them. In fact, he seemed to be actively avoiding doing so.

"Hey, DeWitt," Clayton said to the attendant. "This is my cousin Aaron Jackson, and this is his car. We'll leave it here for you to take care of."

The man turned in the other direction. If there was any doubt in Aaron's mind that the attendant was actively slighting them, it was erased when he heard the man mumble, "You don't get the same privileges for guests, or cousins," he spat the word "cousin" as though it was a vile thing, "as you do for yourself. He'll have to park it on his own."

Clayton turned toward Aaron and offered a confused smile. Then he turned back to the attendant and said, a little more force-fully "DeWitt, you've parked the cars of many of my guests down here. What the hell are you talking about?"

DeWitt might be a lot of things, and Aaron was thinking of a few of them right now, but one was clearly not confrontational. He wouldn't make eye contact with Clayton and he began to walk off, even as he kept speaking. "I'm talking about the rules, Mr. Can-non, or Racine, or whoever you're supposed to be. Either follow them or have your cousin take his car someplace else."

Clayton again turned toward Aaron, but this time there was fury in his eyes. He was very obviously not accustomed to being spoken to like this. He stalked off toward DeWitt, grabbed him by the arm, and got in his face.

"You work for me, or have you forgotten that? Maybe we need to go get your boss, who also works for me, to tell you this. Park my cousin's car and do it now or tomorrow you'll be going back to New Orleans to pick chickens instead of staying here long enough to eventually take your fiftieth piano audition at the Peabody."

DeWitt was definitely not capable of dealing well with hostil-ity. As Aaron watched the attendant's eyes darting back and forth, he was pretty sure that the kid was wondering if these two men— these two black men—were going to get violent with him. At that moment, Aaron had little or no desire to ease his mind. He brought his keys over to where Clayton and DeWitt were standing and pushed them into the attendant's hands.

"That's my car right there, and these are my keys, and you will take these keys and put my car safely away. But you will not bury it, since I won't be here all night. That is your job. You know how to do your job, right?"

DeWitt tried to project what must have passed for insolence in his mind and tugged his hand away, heading over to Aaron's car.

Clayton seemed flabbergasted. "I don't have any idea . . ."

"It would be my guess that this chicken-picking car-parker, professional piano tryout here treated you with much more respect before your interview tonight, huh?"

Clayton seemed to understand what was going on all at once and glared at the attendant. For a moment, Aaron thought he was going to charge after the man, but then the air seemed to come out of him and he glanced up at Aaron with a face full of questions.

As they made their way out of the garage and up into the restaurant, Aaron realized that their conversation was going to go a lot differently than either of them might have imagined when they got into the car at the Meyerhoff. Aaron hadn't come here tonight to help Clayton Cannon make his transition into a world that could hate you on sight—though in Clayton's case that was never going to be much of an issue.

But regardless of why he'd come, and he'd never made those reasons entirely clear to himself, it would be the parallels that would be on his mind as they sat there in the Explorer's Lounge. The parallels between Clayton the public figure and Aaron the public figure. And the parallels between Clayton the man, who had unintentionally cast a huge shadow on Aaron's life, just as Aaron had most assuredly cast a huge shadow on the life of the brother he'd only just come to learn existed.

•

That the boys were still asleep in this early morning was a mercy. Because if they were hearing what their mother was saying right now, they'd most assuredly be even more indelibly marked than they were going to be by the changes in their family history. Clayton could barely believe what he was hearing, even though Susan was doing her best to make him believe it.

"What I can't understand, even in the light of a new day," Susan said to her mother-in law, "is how you could be so completely and utterly inconsiderate of the people who would be affected by this elaborate charade of yours."

Clayton had never known his mother to be contrite and it was not so much contrition that he saw on her face now as resignation to the consequences of being found out. "Susan, dear, as a mother you have to know that I was doing what I truly, in my heart, believed was best for my son."

Susan glanced over at Clayton then with the first expression in their years of marriage that he'd been completely unable to read. He could swear he saw contempt in her eyes, but he couldn't fathom anything he'd done that might be considered contemptible. "This isn't only about *your son*," she said.

"Yes, of course there is the Jackson family. I'm going to need to make amends to them, but . . ."

"*Or* the Jacksons," Susan said with an intensity that Clayton was certain he'd never heard before. "Do you have any idea what this means to me?"

Clayton had kept quiet until now, allowing his wife to blow off a little steam and certainly feeling like his mother had it coming. But this was altogether different and in his mind more than a little bit unwarranted. "What are you saying, Susan?" he asked, crossing the room to stand between the two women.

"I'm saying that my entire world caved in on me yesterday afternoon."

"In exactly what way does this affect you?" Clayton said, trying to keep from his voice the rising sense that his life was about to shift a little farther off its center.

"I'm saying . . ." Susan paused to gather herself. "I'm saying that because of your mother's lies, I have been stunned to discover that I have been married to a black man without my knowledge."

As sucker-punched as Clayton felt by DeWitt's actions in the parking lot the night before, he was entirely unprepared to hear these words from his wife's mouth. "Susan, you can't possibly—"

"*You* can't possibly understand what this is like, Clayton."

"I think I might be able to. After all, just yesterday I learned that half of the blood in my veins is black."

"Which you seem to have embraced as proudly as if you'd just discovered that you were the bastard son to royalty. I, on the other hand, see no such cause for celebration. This changes everything. It changes the way our children will be raised. It changes the way society perceives us. And most importantly, it changes the way *I* perceive us."

"Are you saying that this information changes what we have between us? What we are to each other?"

"I'm saying that it changes everything. I never imagined myself married to a black man." She hesitated, looked down at the floor and then up again at Clayton. "And I don't want to be. I can't be."

"What are you saying, Susan?"

"I'm saying that I'm going back to New Orleans."

Clayton's eye caught his mother standing across from them, absolutely dumbfounded. This image of his mother, who always had something to say and never had any qualms about saying it, would have struck him as comical if the conversation he was in the middle of wasn't so tragic.

He turned his attention completely toward his wife. She looked entirely different to him now. In the past minute she had become a foreigner, someone from a land a million miles away.

"I'm not letting you take my boys away from me," he said firmly.

And then Susan said something that topped everything else she'd already said. "I'm not planning to."

"You intend to abandon your marriage *and* your children?"

Susan's lips quivered and her eyes began to fill. Relying on a strength that might have been grossly misdirected but was nonetheless powerful, she regained her composure. "I don't know how to raise two black boys in this world."

"You raise them the same way you have been raising them."

"No," she said, shaking her head briskly. "That way isn't possible any longer."

"What are you going to say to them?"

"I'm not going to say anything to them right now."

She retreated to the bedroom and returned a minute later with a suitcase. She must have packed it while he was having a drink with Aaron last night. Clayton was still finding it hard to believe that this wasn't some kind of elaborate and unfortunate joke.

"You can tell them I've gone to visit my family," Susan said when she came back. "We'll decide on a more permanent story later. I'll send for the rest of my things once I'm settled."

Clayton thought about fighting her, maybe even doing something that would wake up the children. Once she saw them, surely her resolve would break. But he realized in that moment that he didn't want her resolve to break. He had no real complaints about their marriage, nothing that amounted to a desire to escape it. But if Susan could even think about ending it over something like this, it couldn't have been much of one.

"You can make whatever arrangements you need to make through my lawyer," he said.

Susan nodded. How could he possibly do something so casual at a time like this? "Good luck with all of this, Clayton."

Then she picked up her suitcase, opened the door, and exited his life.

CHAPTER
23

•

The first complication that Aaron found himself faced with after they picked Thyme up from the airport had to do with the seating in the car. Aaron certainly didn't want Thyme sitting up front with his father while he and Tawna were stuck in the back. But at the same time, he couldn't very well make Tawna sit with Thyme; and having the three of them in back while his father drove alone up front like a chauffeur wasn't even worth considering. So Thyme sat in the front seat, proudly perched—or so Aaron imagined—next to a father that he knew in a completely different way than Aaron knew him. *Welcome to the rest of your life, Aaron Jackson. The compromises have only just begun.* In his late-thirties, Aaron had only a short time ago believed that most of the major adjustments in life were ones he had already made. This thinking now seemed to him like a tired and not particularly funny joke.

Aaron didn't know much about Thyme's mother, and what he did know was from his mother and therefore highly suspect, but he could certainly see a whole lot of Junior in his new brother's expressions. Their eyes wrinkled up in the same way and there was a strong similarity around the mouth. But what reminded Aaron most of his father was Thyme's easy, talkative manner. Aaron had every expectation that there would be a series of awkward silences on the drive to Ellen's baby-naming ceremony. The way he figured it, after hello just about everything else was shaky ground. But if Thyme had any such concerns, he had a foolproof way of covering them up. He had talked practically nonstop since they got into the car—about the flight, about Baltimore, about the road they were driving on—a whole lot of nothing, but it certainly filled in the spaces. Even the loquacious Junior Jackson couldn't get much of a word in edgewise. After about ten minutes, Aaron just turned to Tawna and she reached for his hand and melted him with a smile. If she was going to look at him that way, Thyme could just prattle on the entire day for all Aaron would care.

For a moment, Thyme stopped talking and Aaron wondered if perhaps he'd exhausted himself. Maybe he'd used up his store of nervous energy. But then he turned nearly completely around in his seat and said, "Baby-naming ceremony, huh? This whole day is just one first after another. Dad told me about it, but I'm still not sure I understand what goes on at one of these things."

Aaron felt a little twinge when Thyme referred to his father that way. It wasn't like he assumed that he was going to call him "Mr. Jackson," but it still felt strange to have someone use that term when they were talking about the man who raised him. It must have shown on his face because Thyme tilted his head and said, "Does it make you feel a little weird to hear me call him 'Dad'?"

Junior was shaking his head and chuckling to himself in the front seat and even Aaron had to laugh a little at Thyme's boldness. "No," Aaron said. "I guess it could, or maybe should, but it doesn't. I'll admit that hearing it come out of your mouth that first time, and so casually, seemed a little odd. But I'm pretty sure that it was just a one-time thing."

Thyme nodded, and it looked less like he was acknowledging what Aaron was saying than that he was offering his approval over what Aaron said. His body still swiveled toward the back, Thyme looked off at the traffic for a moment and then made eye contact with Aaron again. "Well, if I'm being honest here, I have to tell you that it makes me feel odd, kind of left out and jealous, hearing you call him 'Poppa.' It's like you've called him that your whole life knowing for sure you were the only son calling him that, while I was down in New Orleans and from the time I was ten I knew that some other boy called him something like Dad, or Daddy—or Poppa."

Aaron wasn't sure how to react to this and he could feel Tawna squeezing his hand, though he wasn't sure what she meant by *that*. Was Thyme trying to suggest that he had some kind of prior claim on sibling jealousy? But as much as he wanted to get riled up by this, and maybe deliver a little sharply worded speech that made it entirely clear whose world had been more shaken by this situation and how, he had to admit to himself that Thyme probably did have a point. While Aaron had an enormous adjustment to make in getting used to sharing his father with another son, in Thyme's eyes he'd been enjoying a privileged position all along. For the first time, Aaron made himself think about the value associated with being the first son rather than the only son.

"Thyme, that's the nature of this thing, you know?" he said. "And neither one of us had a say in deciding it. So we either live with it and pretend we don't feel it, or feel it completely and make it help us bond as brothers. I don't know which will work."

Junior, who had been silent for some time now, chose that moment to speak up. "I have some thoughts about that."

"And I'm sure they're good thoughts, Poppa," Aaron said. "But they're not very relevant to this discussion. The only thoughts on this subject that matter are Thyme's and mine."

Thyme smiled at him then. Through the glance he caught of his father from the rearview mirror, he could tell that he was smiling as well. And when Tawna squeezed his hand this time, he was pretty sure he knew exactly what she meant by it.

Aaron had never really been opposed to change in his life, though there were plenty of times when he thought he was. The simple fact was that he'd always handled change well, maybe even thrived on it. If he was going to be entirely honest with himself, he might even say that his mother, who constantly dangled the name of Clayton Cannon in front of him, had made him perpetually prepared for change. He would never have invited this latest change into his life, but now that it was here and it had a face and a name and a body full of kinetic energy, Aaron knew that he'd find a way to incorporate it into his life and maybe even enjoy it.

Thyme turned to face forward. "This baby-naming thing, it's kind of a bourgeois thing, huh? 'Cause we don't do nothing like that down where I'm from. Never even heard of it."

Aaron laughed out loud. There was no one in the family who talked like Thyme, and he had a feeling that he was going to be continually surprised by him. "Well, it's not exactly meant to be bourgeois, or anything like that. It's just my sister's big idea of trying to get some kind of tradition going in this family. She feels we have no tradition, though I have a feeling this is the first of many she's going to introduce in the coming years."

Totally spontaneously, Aaron reached forward and clapped his brother on the shoulder. "And now you're a part of it."

Antonia needed to stand back for a moment, just to observe this family of hers. It certainly had grown recently, both in ways she knew in her heart it would and in ways that she would never have expected in her entire life.

She was so glad that Clayton had come with his boys. He had been dealt some surprising blows in the last few days, and though she didn't know the boys as well as she was going to in the future, she was pretty sure she saw a bit of confusion in their eyes. She would never understand Susan as long as she lived. How any mother could turn her back on her children, no matter what she discovered about the blood that ran through their veins, was far, far beyond her comprehension and happily so.

They were such handsome boys. Smart, too. And if the way they gurgled and cooed over the baby was any indication, there was real warmth and kindness in them as well. It wouldn't be easy for them to have only one parent to truly care for and nurture them, but they would be surrounded by family. Antonia would make sure of it, even if it meant spending more time with Agnes Cannon than anyone should ever have to.

And then there was Thyme. He certainly had a lot of Junior in him. The young Junior, especially. This impression of him was a little bit disconcerting when Antonia first caught sight of him, but then again just about everything about him was likely to be a little disconcerting for a while. Junior seemed hesitant about bringing him over to meet her—how ridiculous to think there should be any hesitancy between them after all these years—so she'd walked right over and introduced herself.

"I'm not sure who on earth I am to you," she said to Thyme, "but I'll welcome you to my daughter's house all the same."

"Well, ma'am, you've been the woman who's kept my dad happy all these years, so I would say that makes you a terribly important person to me."

Antonia laughed. "I see your father has taught you some of his tricks over the years." She took him by the arm. "How come no one has gotten you anything to eat yet? You do like catfish, don't you?"

Now Thyme was chatting it up with Rick, though she couldn't imagine what it was that the two of them had to say to one another. Antonia hadn't been able to look Rick squarely in the eye since Ellen told her about his indiscretion, but she figured she'd come around eventually. He certainly seemed to love that baby. And whatever it was that had caused him to stray on her daughter when he did, he seemed to love Ellen an awful lot now. Probably always had.

Aaron had come out of his car ride with his new brother without a mark. She'd been worried about her son and how the news flashes of the last few weeks were affecting him. He'd had a lot of assumptions turned around, and she wouldn't have blamed him at all if he'd done some serious acting out as a result. But other than that episode at the television station—and who could really blame him for that?—he seemed to be bearing up surprisingly well. He'd even managed to mend fences at his job, though Antonia had a feeling it required much more humility than Aaron had ever intended to express in his life. Times like these tested a man, but it seemed that Aaron was more than up to it. It had to have a lot to do with that new woman of his.

Tawna was about as different from Maggie as Antonia could imagine. Certainly not as homespun and settled. And nowhere near as easy to get a fix on. From the moment she'd met Maggie, Antonia knew who she was and knew what she wanted and knew that she'd treat her son with respect and make him feel needed. These were important things, but they weren't the only important things. And while Aaron had never really explained his reasons for leaving Maggie behind, Antonia had a feeling that the thing she couldn't give him was first and foremost a sense of wanting a future together. That was probably more important to her son now than it had ever been in his life. Whether Tawna could provide it or not, and whether she could provide all of the other things that were important in making two people work together, Antonia didn't know. But one thing that was absolutely certain was that she had never once seen her son look at a woman the way he looked at Tawna. That had to account for something.

Aaron must have seen her looking at him because he got up from where he was sitting, kissed Tawna on the side of her head, and walked over to her.

"Have you decided to be a bystander rather than a participant?" he asked when he stood next to her.

"Now when have you ever known me to be a bystander?"

"I thought maybe you were thinking about turning over a new leaf. This would be the day to do such a thing, wouldn't it?"

"That might very well be the case, but I'm not turning over anything. I was just giving myself a little time to behold my family, that's all."

"It was a nice thing you did with Thyme."

Antonia took Aaron's hand and held it with both of hers. "He'd traveled a long distance. He didn't need some crazy lady getting up in his face an hour after he set foot in Baltimore."

"No, he certainly didn't need that."

"You know, I must tell you honestly that it feels so strange looking over there and not seeing Maggie. She was such a presence here. Belonged right away."

Antonia could feel Aaron's hand tightening around hers and she looked up at him. He was getting ready to defend his position, to state his case, to declare his independence for the thousandth time in his adult life.

"But things change, huh?" she said softly. "They have to. And families change. Even with this whole thing with your sister's need for tradition, things eventually have to change in some way."

She felt her son's hand relax and the warmth return to his eyes. He didn't usually settle down so quickly after he got his back up.

"Have you thought of a name for the baby?" he asked.

"Nothing that's good enough for him."

"Well, I certainly hope someone has a good one, because I've drawn a complete blank. You won't believe the most ordinary names that have come into my head." He shot her a sideways glance and said, "I guess we could always name him after an herb. Or maybe Ellen could start a new family tradition and name him after some kind of leafy vegetable. Do you think Turnip Green is too much of a mouthful?"

Antonia punched him playfully on the arm. "I think you might want to keep that one to yourself." She looked over at the crowd gathered around the tiny boy. "He'll have a fine name. No matter what it is, it'll be a fine one."

Aaron leaned down and kissed her on the cheek. "I should get back. Will you be joining us or are you still beholding?"

"I'll be over in a minute."

Aaron moved to let go of her hands and she pulled him back for one more moment. "Tawna is lovely and elegant and smart. She'll fit right in."

She watched Aaron head back toward the couch and noted the smile he received from his girlfriend upon his arrival. Right then Clayton's twins ran past her in the middle of some game they were playing and she smiled down at them.

This was a ceremony, all right. Much more of one than Ellen could possibly have imagined when she came up with the idea. It was time for Antonia to join it.

EPILOGUE

•

Antonia wondered if her first real memory of Agnes Cannon would always be her strongest. They were working together in the same house arguing about the best way to make monkey bread. As was so often the case with Agnes and her notions, she had some ridiculous ideas about monkey bread, like using pecans in the recipe, and Antonia tried to make it clear to her that no one who had any measure of self-respect whatsoever would put nuts in their monkey bread. Emeril had just been hired to do some odd jobs around the house and chose that moment to come into the kitchen. When Agnes and Emeril met, Antonia knew without a doubt that something was going to happen between them. What that something was was hardly a mystery, considering Agnes's reputation. But as she watched Agnes study her brother with those green eyes of hers, Antonia felt a twinge of trouble—a twinge that told her that Agnes would somehow steal her brother away. It left her feeling horribly unsettled. The day got worse after that, with the woman of the house choosing Agnes's monkey bread over Antonia's and Antonia just feeling miserable about everything.

Agnes was Agnes Marquette back then, of course, but as far as Antonia was concerned she had always been exactly the same way, regardless of the name. She would never understand what Emeril saw in her, other than the easy availability. But Emeril should have understood that other women would make themselves available to him. More honorable, worthier women. Women who would provide Emeril with something beyond just base pleasure.

But in a sense maybe it was time to accept the fact that Agnes had given Emeril something that he would not have gotten any-where else before he died. She gave him a legacy. And even though it had taken her decades to own up to that legacy, it was an awfully impressive one indeed.

It had been more than a week since the revelations at Larson Fletcher's party. Calling them revelations wasn't really appropri-ate since for Antonia the events in the parlor that day were much more about confirmation than anything else. But regardless of what anyone called them, it seemed that enough time had passed afterward and that the only proper thing to do was to open a line of communication between the mother of Emeril's child and that child's aunt. And so Antonia did what she seemed to be making a habit of doing these days—she took a deep breath and rose above her fundamental instincts. She invited Agnes for a visit because they had to begin their future somewhere.

The doorbell rang, pulling Antonia away from a past inhabited by Agnes Marquette. The Agnes who stood outside was not in any way recognizable as that woman. She seemed to have fallen lower than Antonia ever thought Agnes was capable of falling. It wasn't that Antonia hadn't given any thought to what Agnes had gone through in the last nine days, what with everything she had to explain to her son and the fallout that led to the end of Clayton's marriage. It was just that until she saw her at this moment, Anto-nia couldn't put a face on the experience. But she was staring at that face now and it was a sunken and almost unimaginably world-weary one.

The very first words from Agnes's mouth while she stood in the doorway were, "You must hate me," and Antonia realized that Agnes had no way of knowing what to expect when she accepted the invitation. Their phone conversation had been brief and Anto-nia could imagine how easy it would have been to get any number of impressions from it.

She opened the door and let Agnes in from the cold. The woman stepped tentatively into the room, as though she was pre-pared for some kind of onslaught.

"I could see how you might think that," Antonia said as she took Agnes's coat. "But I don't hate you. I feel deeply for you."

Antonia saw a flash of confusion cross Agnes's face.

"I saw Clayton's eyes when he looked at you. And I saw your heart break in half when you looked at your son and told him what you did."

"You have no idea," Agnes said sadly.

Antonia took a moment to gather herself. She hadn't planned on getting this honest with Agnes this quickly, but the moment was presenting itself and Antonia knew better than to ignore the signal.

"Actually, I can. I had never been able to see it or accept it until that moment with you and Clayton, but I had put that same look in my own son's eyes more than once—when he was young and when he was older. I guess in thinking about it, the memories of that look are worse when he was younger, because I know he couldn't understand anything that could help him know why he had so much sadness with him to begin with."

The admission drained Antonia a little, maybe the more so because she was making it in front of someone who had represented so many negative things in her life for so long. But looking across at Agnes now, she didn't see a rival, but someone with whom she had a surprisingly large amount in common.

"It's hard for a mother to know what to do," Agnes said, and Antonia simply nodded at the undeniable simple truth of the statement.

They sat after that and talked for a good long time. They shared memories of Emeril. Antonia delighted Agnes with stories about her brother as an awkward boy before he matured into a strapping young man, and Agnes told Antonia stories about his tenderness and how he paid attention to her like she was the only other person in the world. They talked about what Clayton was like growing up and about the hundreds or maybe thousands of times that a gesture or an inflection would remind Agnes of Emeril. They talked about the brief period of time they worked together in the same kitchen and Antonia was polite enough not to mention how much she despised Agnes back then.

And as they talked, Antonia came to accept that there was a lot more about Agnes to like than she ever would have imagined.

She had never believed that Agnes really cared about her brother, but Antonia would have had to have been unforgivably hard-hearted not to believe it after hearing Agnes speak about him now. And when she told funny stories about raising her son, Antonia just knew that motherhood had bestowed many of the same gifts upon Agnes that it had upon her. If she was truly going to understand family in a new way—and with Clayton and Thyme in the fold now, there was little choice but to do exactly that—she was going to have to find a way to include Agnes in the definition.

"You know," Antonia said, "if we had been in a different place than we were and in a different time, maybe you'd be my sister-in-law right now."

Agnes reached across to touch her on the arm and Antonia was pretty sure that this was the first time they'd ever touched each other. "I would have been, Antonia. You'd better believe I would have been or I would have died trying. I dreamed in every spare minute I could about a different life for me and Emeril. Some-where far away from New Orleans. Maybe New York where I could have been something else, something better, and Emeril could have been whatever he wanted to be. He was so smart, you know? And we would have raised our boy to be just who and what he is now."

It was a dream that could have come true, maybe even would have come true, if fate had been kinder all those years ago. "It wasn't until I met Clayton and we both knew that he was Emeril's son that I realized you took a hell of a bold chance to bring my nephew into the world," she said. "Douglas Cannon could have ruined your life if Clayton hadn't looked the way he looks."

"I didn't care," Agnes said, her head down. "I really didn't care or think about it until that child came out of me. I just knew that I had to have a part of Emeril to keep, and if Clayton had come out looking black and Douglas had set me out on my behind for trick-ing him the way I did, well, then my boy and I would have found our way somehow." She looked up and Antonia could see that Agnes's eyes had misted over. "I had Clayton and so I still had Emeril."

It was Antonia's turn to look down now. "I didn't," she said. "I didn't have either one after Emeril died."

Agnes wiped at her eyes. "And I'm sorry. I am so deeply sorry that I let things get to a place where I couldn't turn it around."

There was nothing said for the next couple of minutes, but it didn't feel uncomfortable or strange, just like both of them had a lot of thinking to do.

"You know," Antonia said at last, "I've been chasing after Clayton and what he represents to my family for most of my adult life. But just now I realized that I might have been chasing after you as well."

Agnes shook her head skeptically. "I think you might have been just as happy if I disappeared off the face of the Earth."

Antonia laughed. "Well, I might have thought that on any number of occasions, but somewhere deep inside, I think I might have known something different. After all, you were the only woman my brother ever loved."

"He did love me."

"I know that. He told me in lots of ways that I didn't want to hear. But I hear it now. And I believe in some ridiculously roundabout way, it wasn't my will that got us to this place at all. It was Emeril's will to make this patchwork into a family."

Agnes looked like she was about to add something when the doorbell rang. It was Aaron and Tawna.

"I just wanted to come by to tell you that I'm going to be gone for a few days," Aaron said, smiling at Tawna.

"Where are you going?"

"To New York. We're going to cram our attitudes into my car and take a long drive. And if we don't kill each other on the way," Aaron leaned over and kissed his girlfriend on the temple and she playfully pushed him away, "we're going to eat some very expensive food and see a couple of shows."

"Is anything else dramatic going to happen on this trip?" Antonia asked.

"You never know," Tawna said with a grin that absolutely split her face in half.

Antonia glanced over at her son. She had never seen him so eager to be with a woman before. This Tawna was going to turn out to be very good for him.

"Oh, hey, Mrs. Cannon," Aaron said, noticing Agnes sitting in a chair in the living room and waving.

"Agnes," Antonia said, taking Tawna by the arm, this is my future daughter-in-law, Tawna."

Antonia looked up to see her son rolling his eyes at the way she made the introduction, but he didn't protest it.

"Well, it's very nice to meet you, Tawna," Agnes said, walking toward them and shaking Tawna's hand.

"Nice to meet you, Mrs. Cannon," Tawna said.

"Call me Agnes. And you too, of course, Aaron."

Aaron nodded, then reached over and kissed Antonia on the cheek. "We gotta go. We'll be back after the weekend."

He took Tawna's hand and they headed out the door and down the walk to the car. They waved and Antonia and Agnes waved back.

"It's Aunt Agnes," Antonia said, calling after them.

Aaron glanced at her with a confused expression on his face and then opened the car door for Tawna.

He'd figure it out.

They all would.

Let's Talk

•

Hot discussion topics for Reading Groups

1. The nature of family is the centerpiece of this novel. Antonia risks the family she has to seek out the nephew she desperately wants to claim. Was it a risk worth taking? Why was this so important to her?

2. Clayton's life turns on the realization that he is half-black. Why is this true when he's been living in the same skin his entire life? Would things have been different for him if the public wasn't also aware of it?

3. Why do you think Agnes denies Clayton's parentage for so long? Does she do this because of race or because of some battle for "ownership" of Emeril and Emeril's legacy?

4. Why does Susan find it so impossible to accept the truth of Clayton's heritage? What is it about the world she grew up in that makes her feel this way?

5. Food plays a significant role in this novel. In what ways is food used here as an expression of family?

6. Ellen plans the baby-naming ceremony because she feels her family lacks tradition. Why is this so important to her? Do you think she's right about her family?

7. Why does Aaron have such a difficult time making a commitment to Maggie when he easily does so with Tawna? Does it have to do with the women, or does it have to do with the changes in Aaron's own life?

8. The relative nature of celebrity plays a function in several relationships here. Do you think Aaron would have had as much trouble dealing with his family connection to Clayton if Clayton wasn't a bigger star than he was?

9. Junior's love for Antonia seems very strong and his commitment to her absolute. Why do you think he feels the need to keep the existence of Thyme a secret?

10. Why do you think Antonia feels the need to "take in strays" like Jackie the prostitute when her own family longs for more of her attention?

Tribute to Patricia,
A Woman of Courage

•

My sister, Patricia Jones's soul left her body on May 30, 2002. It has taken two years to finally accept that she is no longer here with me physically, but I continue to be warmed by her memory. She will always be for me, the most courageous and spiritual woman I have ever known. She filled my life with love, laughter, excitement, fun and adventure. Patricia's zest for life could be infectious and one always listened with amazement as she told stories about her various exploits.

> "I was riding the subway from work and the subway stopped. It broke down and we had to walk through the tunnel to get out"; "I was standing on line in the bank and the guy in front of me seemed to be taking such a long time. I was becoming impatient when he turned to leave, seemingly in a hurry, and then the teller rang an alarm. This man had just robbed the bank."; "I was on the subway and a man sitting beside me fell asleep. He leaned over on me and I pushed him off. He fell on the floor and didn't move. Someone checked him and found that he was dead. I was so upset. I said, 'I just pushed him off of me, how did this happen?' All I knew was that I wanted to hurry and get off of the train."

Patricia loved helping and doing for others. Once a homeless youth asked her for money and she took him into McDonald's and bought him a meal. She took groceries to a family in need, even though she had very little money for her own expenses. Pat's spirit had a way of inspiring people, such as the many people of Christ Church in Riverdale, who talked about how she had helped to change their lives. There was also her friend who had found a lump but was afraid to see about it. Pat persuaded her to get a mammogram, making the appointment for her and accompanying her to the appointment.

Pat was nothing less than passionate about various issues. She wrote articles for many magazines, addressing issues of race, interracial relationships, homosexuality, politics and more. In a speech she delivered she says:

"I must admit that as I stand here tonight, I am wearied. I am wearied with what I consider the tedium of all the hoopla over counting down to January first. But as I think about the year 2000, I think that all the fuss is really not about the number. It's about one question that none of us ever really think about consciously, but it's a very basic one: Does the passage of time really matter? Of course we know it does, particularly when we look into the faces of our growing children that came into the world seemingly yesterday. But that doesn't stop any of us from taking the passage of time for granted. When I think about the passage of time, I'm reminded of the old maxim that is trite, but nonetheless true: The more things change, the more they stay the same. . . .

. . . Four months ago, my first novel, Passing, was published. While I knew that the title of the book would make people assume they knew what the story was about, I wasn't prepared for what ended up happening because of the title. Because many thought the book was about a black woman passing for white, letters I received through the mail, and through the publishing company's website, all showed that many people bought the book for the story of a black woman passing for white. Fortunately, they still enjoyed it in spite of it not being what they thought it would be, but it really made me stop and think. Aside from the fact that I think a story about a black woman passing for white would be such a dreadful cliché, passing for white is a term I simply disavow because of the connotation of the superiority of one race over another. Yet, there are so many who still find the topic pertinent. I

was actually shocked that in 1999, I got the number of letters I got from people telling me of how they originally picked up the book because they have a black aunt, or uncle, or cousin, or some other relative living in a distant place and living as a white person. But to be the devil's advocate for a moment here, wouldn't that be a choice that everyone should feel free to make in terms of how we define ourselves? I mean, if there's a woman standing next to me looking as white as I look black, even if she does have more black blood than white, why shouldn't she define herself in a way that makes her feel more comfortable in her own skin? Perhaps this term, passing for white, is another one of those labels that other people have placed on black people with white skin, and this is why I disavow the term. Because in trying to give it shame, the language has imposed on it something that was possibly not intended. At the turn of the last century, blacks with white skin passed for white for survival. Nowadays, survival is arguable, but what no one can contest is that it could quite possibly be done to spite the labels of color that are still so prevalent in an America headed for the twenty-first century.

So in closing, I must say, the discussion of the term passing in all those letters I received has made me think of a question I am most often asked about my own child: "What will you tell her she is?" The first impudent thought that comes to my mind when asked this is to say: "Well, if for some reason she ever forgets, I'll tell her that she's a human female." But my better judgment tells me that this answer would only make matters worse. So my pat answer is this: I say that I have made my daughter aware of all the parts of her heritage that make her so special. And when and if the subject of how she should define herself comes up, I will let her know that if this is supposed to be the land of the free, then she should feel free enough to define herself in whatever way makes her feel whole. However, I would set her up for serious hurt and disappointment if I were not to tell her that there will be many, many in this country who will look at her, and look at me, and not allow her the freedom to define herself as she so chooses—case closed. She can fight it, she can accept it, or she can choose to simply not be touched by it, but she will ultimately need to know that even with the passage of time, color still matters in America."

Pat was loved by so many. Her passing affected us all, but what is more important is that her life affected us all. Her family and friends pay tribute:

To my friend—
  "You are the image that you seek
  You are the message as you speak
  You are a lamp the light shines through
  Infinite Energy expressed as You"

Your friend forever,
Debbie Derella Cheren

•

My very best friend, your sister, Bettye, introduced us when you were in elementary school. I remember her having to pick you up from school. Boy, would she be mad. We were teenagers in high school and didn't think looking after a little sister was the highlight of our day.

Even though we were not sisters by birth, you were that little sister to me. I watched you grow from a little girl in pigtails to a beautiful effervescent woman. My memories of you will always be your radiant smile and your quick sense of humor. In fact, you could always shock me with your vivid language (especially if your mother was present). I would laugh and laugh and love you more for being you.

There are many memories I have of you, Pat, and they will always be with me. I will not speak on your illness because it took you away too soon. I am at this moment filled with sorrow and yes, tears as I am trying very hard to put my thoughts in writing.

My memories will always be happy ones. Bettye and I were talking about you several nights ago and we started laughing when we remembered her son Keith and Chenelle's wedding. You were a riot. You and I sat next to each other and no one could understand why I was laughing because you kept a straight face. If only they could hear what you were saying. Let's just say it was a "colorful" conversation.

If someone should see me smiling and chuckling out loud, they

will think, this person is strange. If they ask, I will say I am thinking of my "little sister" who is no longer here with me. She left
behind many wonderful memories.

I love you and will always miss you.

Cynthia

●

Her inner and outer beauty, her smile lit up everyone's heart. Her
laughter, her warmth, her genuine personae is what I miss
most. . . . Pat you are always in my heart. . . .

Love you, Millie.

●

Patricia! A great sister!!

Love, Dave Miller

●

I'd been to other funerals—uncles, grandparents, young cousins
with short trajectories, too weak to escape the gravity of black
life—but only the death of my father hit me like the loss of Pat.
Some deaths are unexplainable, tragic; others ultimately make
sense. Mama Della, my grandmother, was a kind of sacred and
perpetual being, always old, always there, a deep dish apple pie-
baking life constant. I assumed, and in a way really believed, that
after hitting 100 Mama Della would get another century free, but
when she passed just shy of 102, I merely felt grateful for having
had her around for so long. Pat, however, was a baby. In some
ways, my baby. And I was her best girlfriend. And when it was my
turn to pay my respects to the family at the church, after having
held up fairly well through the service, I collapsed into her sister
Velma's arms and cried, clinging to her like a lab-raised Rhesus
monkey to a mother-shaped towel.

Tears and a Tyrannosaur. For a moment, I felt guilty. My mind
flashed to my seven- or eight-year-old nephew Austin watching
Jurassic Park for the first time. The T-Rex, a delightfully engineered
animatronic terror, made quick work of the lawyer in two chomps
and Austin was rolling on the floor. Samuel L. Jackson was reduced
to a severed arm and Austin was seized by an almost obscene gid-

diness. But when the two kids were being menaced by a pair of overachieving velociraptors he steadfastly refused to watch, their faces a mirror of his fear. In that moment, held in Velma's arms, I wondered if I was being Austin. But the moment passed. I wasn't. I was desperate because a woman, a friend I loved, was no longer.

Boston University, 1982. Pat sat across the room in Soviet Political Dynamics, a slender and stunning curve of deep chocolate intelligence and grace with a southern flavor to her voice when occasionally it was raised to articulate some high-level cold war shadiness. To many folk, brown and otherwise, the brilliance of her smile, the "good" hair—big and home grown—the poorly masked high IQ, the Tanglewood-coached fingers coupled with her reticence, pointed to a chocolate-dipped white girl variety of conceit, but to my eyes she was all shyness and vulnerability. I adored her, but shy myself, I never spoke to her.

Manhattan. Eight years later, Madison and 42nd, and there she was, as stunning as ever and walking directly toward me. I tried to imagine the course of our paths since our divergence, perhaps as a stabilizing device, to keep my now rapidly vibrating molecules from losing their cohesion—imagine running into her after all these years only to go poof in a gentle fog of cowardice. No. I would not cave in. I resolved to speak to her, and further, I *willed* that she would be delighted to see me, give me her number and invite me to a picnic somewhere in New Jersey. And so it was.

I said *girlfriend* earlier. I said it because at her New York memorial, her female friends indicated that they were delighted to meet me after hearing about me for so long. They were the ones to tell me that she referred to me as her best girlfriend. But I'm not a girl. Not at all. Nor was it my intention to ever be so dubbed.

I never made it to the picnic, but I did invite her over to my place for brunch, which I prepared myself. She was a delightful guest and we talked for hours. And again. Hanging, talking, laughing. One afternoon, in her St. James Place studio, she sat on a bentwood rocker, crossed her legs, took a sip of something cool, set it down, opened an original manuscript and began to read. Observations about life on the left coast, Los Angeles to be specific. Funny. Sharp. Artful. Perceptive. Her voice sweet and confident, her cadence enchanting, her deep brown legs long and generously exposed. It was all I could do to keep from throwing myself to my knees and pressing my lips to her thighs. When she finished reading she rose, sat next to me on the couch, without speaking put her foot on my knee, and without speaking I took it into my hand and kneaded, stretched, caressed—heel, ball, arch, toes and between, and then the other, all my budding desire finding expression in the gesture.

Valentine's Day. I've re-known Pat for more than a few months. Spoken to her almost daily. Never really stopped thinking about her. And felt some reciprocity—I'm sure of it. A trip to Balducci's. Three large chocolate-covered strawberries in a ribbon-bound box and a bike ride in the pouring rain. She opens the door with a smile and invites me in.

"I can't come in."

She stands in the doorway. I remain on the stoop. "I need to talk to you." I hand her the box. She smiles again. "I want you to have them because I'd love more than anything for you to be my Valentine, and I don't even like Valentine's Day." I can feel her breath catch. "But I also have to tell you . . ." The smile ebbs. ". . . that I have a girlfriend."

I think she might have cried. I think I did. She didn't speak to me for a while. When she did, I caught more than a little hell. But while a measure of romantic trust was irreparably eroded, our rapport was intact and we became close. Very close. And so we'd remain. One of my proudest moments was being one of her bridesmaids, or as written in the program, her bride's dude. There's so much more I could tell, good and bad, fun, silly and sad, but I think I'll end it here. As she put it one day as we headed to a book signing at the Studio Museum in Harlem, she's the writer, I'm just the pretty thing on her arm to keep her drink refreshed.

(Is this okay, Pat? You are, will always be my darling Sha Sha, and you know what I'm thinking, right? Yeah, you know.)

Daryl N. Long
May 25, 2004

•

Memories

Even at three years old, Pat demonstrated a remarkable maturity. I took her to see the movie *Mary Poppins.* She was a perfect little girl, focusing on the movie like a child beyond her years.

She was always so very friendly and developed special relationships with people. My husband, Sylvan, took off from work one day to go to her junior high school for career day. The two of them had a special bond because of her outgoing nature. During her illness, she visited Maryland many times. We visited her often at her mother's house.

One time, while she was undergoing chemotherapy, she was pulling out her hair and Sylvan told her to stop. She said that her hair was going to come out anyway and that she would just wear a wig. They both laughed. Her sense of humor was always present. Sylvan drove himself to visit Pat before she returned to New York. They were both courageously fighting cancer. Pat had a book reading at Enoch Pratt Library, the main branch in Baltimore, and recited several passages beautifully. Once again she was courageous, friendly, outgoing and professional at this event. I remember the last time I saw her at a book signing in Owings Mills Mall in Baltimore. She wasn't feeling well, but with her usual sense of professionalism and friendliness, she kept her obligation. Pat had a dream of being a writer. She accomplished her dream when so many don't. She couldn't be stopped. Pat did it her way, and she was a success. Words that describe Pat are friendly, persevering, joyful, outgoing, professional, stylish and very humorous.

Love you,
Sylvia, your cousin

•

My Dearest Pat,

What words can I say to express my love for you? I live every day with fond memories and regrets. Memories of your visits to Baltimore, my trips to New York, letters written, pictures taken; regrets of never spending enough time with you, and choosing to hang with my friends instead of my family. My greatest regret is never saying goodbye. On your final visit to Baltimore, I knew it was going to be your last, but for some reason, I couldn't let you go. I relied on faith to pull you through again. I was selfish. I was angry when you died. There were so many things I never got to tell you.

I have always admired you for your free spirit, your charisma, your dedication and commitment to your family, and the way you never hesitated to speak your mind. I will never forget the life-altering decision I made in the eighth grade. I never told you this, but you were a very intricate part of my healing. You always made me feel pretty when I felt ugly. I will always remember when you told me I had to love and accept myself to love and respect others. I will never forget that. When I was lost and confused, it was you who told me to write down all of the goals and aspirations I had for myself, put them in my favorite Bible verse and never open to that page again until I accomplished my missions in life. For that, I am eternally grateful. For that, I never gave up and I always persevered.

On my twenty-third birthday, I confidently opened to that Bible verse, as I had finally met the ideals set forth for myself. This Bible verse is the center of my wedding and will always remain close to my heart because of you. I love therefore I can love. I miss the crazy healthy food you always made, your timeless sense of humor, your remarkable smile, and the clothes that you made me, but above all, I miss you. You helped me to realize that my family should always be my #1 priority. As far as Alexandra is concerned, I will always be there for her, just like you were there for me. I will never leave or forsake her. I thank you for watching over me and protecting me, for helping me through hardships and for your angelic visits. I hope you are proud of me for the woman I have become. You are truly one of a kind, you are timeless, priceless, and I will never forget you.

Love,
Miss Kelley, your loving niece

•

To my Aunt Patricia in the skies above,
Looking down upon us, with your sweet, sweet love
This is a tribute to you, and your effect on me
Years and years of bringing happiness and glee
From your bright smile to your unique fashion
To the literary works that you write with passion
From the beautiful child you brought into this world
To your personality that glows brighter than a pearl
The jokes and witty comments that made me laugh so hard

Your devotion, dedication, and faith in GOD
Your energy, focus, and motivation
You always seem to rise above any complication
I thank you for all that you have done
As a tribute, I gave part of your name to my son
Here's a toast to you—Aunt, Author, and Friend
I miss you and I will definitely see you again

Keith Pettiford

•

Dear Pat,

I wake up some mornings and I hear your sweet voice, then I look at my son (Justin Randall Patrick) and remember what an inspiration you were to all. This is why my son has your name. I didn't get to spend a lot of time with you but the times that were shared were cherished ones, like talking about shoes and the new books that were out. Then there is Kayla who asks about you and how your boo boo is doing. I tell her that Aunt Pat is OK and she's better than she's ever been.

Love, Chenelle, Kayla, and Justin

•

If there was one thing I remember about Pat, it was her energy. She loved to EAT and it never slowed her down. When she would visit, you had to make sure you had enough snacks for her because she would eat all night. She always told it like it was, very real and straight to the point. Never had any qualms about telling a person how she felt. She's had life experiences like none other. She told some hilarious stories about her life in New York. Pat also was a dynamite clothes maker who wore her own creations. She made children's clothes for her daughter to wear as well. Writing was her love and putting out three books was just the tip of the iceberg for her. If only she had the time to enjoy her success. I was so honored to be at the signing of her first book, and to see the crowd that gathered around her to have their book signed is something you could only dream about. And that was her dream. She was a talent.

Pat I love you and I miss you.

Derek (your loving nephew)

•

"Me and my Pat—went to the zoo—we saw so many animals it wasn't too soon . . . with my Pat, my Pat, my Pat and my Pat. . . ." That was our song Pat. One of my favorite parts of growing up was spending every summer with you in New York. It was like hanging out with my big sister, best friend, and mother all in one. We shared so much—my first Broadway play, the Zodiac Killer, subway rides in the dark, and all of Central Park's weirdoes. I miss you so much. Sometimes it feels like you are still in New York and I will see you at Christmas. Then Christmas comes and reality sets in that you are gone. But I know you are still the same ole Pat, crazy, fun, and colorful as ever—just in a different place. You will never be forgotten and I love you.

Love always,
Your Beanie (Kenya, your loving niece)

•

A Vision of Loveliness
by Erin Dodson
You came to me in a vision, so beautiful to see.
You came to me in a vision and spoke so gently to me.
You assured me you were ok and that everything was alright.
I never shall forget just how you looked that night.
You came to me in a vision so beautiful to see.
That vision of loveliness left me with such peace.

•

Dear Pat,
    You came to me in a vision the night before I went to see you at the funeral home. A light shined through my door that was so bright. You were wearing orange, your favorite color. You spoke to me and said, "Erin, it's ok." The very next day, I went to see you at the funeral home. You were wearing the same orange outfit you were wearing in my vision. It didn't scare me. I was honored that you chose to come to me. All I can say is you are greatly missed. Your humor, your charm, and definitely your unique style are all a part of what make you so special. It is hard to accept that you are gone. Always know that you will forever

live on in my heart and my memories of you. I love you, though we didn't say it much.

Love forever,
"Lady Erin"

•

Thoughts on a Life

Asked to reflect upon my Aunt Pat's life by delivering some words, I ran across a quote I squirreled away by a woman named Gail Sher. She said: "Writers write. Writing is a process. You don't know what your writing will be like until the end of the process. If writing is your practice, the only way to fail is not to write." While I'm not a professional writer, this quotation's relevancy for me and my life is fast. Whatever it is you do, your biggest failure is to fail to do it. To make excuses. The bravery my aunt showed to do what she loved, despite difficult circumstances, represents the inspiration that my aunt has had on my life through living her own.

Writing this reflection is difficult. It feels like going through an old trunk of pictures in an attic of filed away thoughts, sorting, distilling, editing, organizing, and eventually, composing a story, an account, that one could follow to a better understanding of the inspiration that Pat represents. I can only imagine what writing a novel is like. There's so much bravery in simply putting pen to paper, but much more in living. Despite having all the issues that make her a normal human being and some many never experience, Pat both lived and wrote very well. In defiance to her tragic living circumstances, she continued to pursue her writing. As a part of her family, it does not matter to me whether she sold five books or five million. I'm simply happy and inspired that she did something that she really wanted to do. So many people go through life without a book to publish, leaving their families to store only the old "photos" of their memory in each person's own personal attic sometimes never to be sorted through. Her real accomplishments are her growing daughter and the wonderful memories I have of her.

The eastern tome, the *Tao Te Ching*, says that "If one fully understands the present moment, there is nothing else left to do and nothing left to pursue." Forty-two years, two months, two days is indeed a lifetime; for some, less and for others, more. No one on earth is guaranteed another day. O how important it is to live life—I mean, really live it. When looking back on the wake of a soul one can only hope to have lived the present moment fully by being one with the things that really matter. My aunt did. She loved her family. She told her story. She raised her daughter. She made her way. She dealt with life. She did so much. And . . . she did it all graciously.

The way I'll always remember Pat is that when she walked down the street her smile and her inner beauty would illuminate the way.

Love,
Chris, your nephew

●

My memories of Pat are many, but one stands out more because it reflects the person Pat was. I was supposed to pick Pat and Alexandra up from the train station. I got there early so I would be able to be down on the tracks to help her with the bags. I went down as the train came in and Pat did not get off. I went back to the station to find that there were two trains coming from New York but only one listed. The other train appeared on the board. I ran to go down to the platform and saw Pat, dragging the bags and holding onto the railing. She looked so helpless but was still climbing the stairs. I finally got a wheelchair and took her to my car. That was an experience that I will never forget. She was such a courageous woman. I love you.

Love,
Tom, your brother

●

My Pat

How do I begin to put into a few words just how wonderful and special she was? She was beautiful, inside and out. She was caring, loving, witty, whimsical, and wise. She was a daughter, a mother, an aunt, a cousin, and a friend. She was my sister and her name was Patricia.

Patricia was on loan to us from God for forty-two years. He put her here as his special angel to touch the lives of the people whose paths she crossed. Everyone who knew her loved her. Everyone who met her saw the beauty in her heart. They saw the beauty that was Pat. In the short time Pat was with us, she accomplished so many wonderful things. She traveled the world by herself, never giving it a single thought. She met many interesting people. She wrote numerous articles for various magazines and three novels. She was never afraid to try something new. Pat did things that many of us would only dream of doing. This is what made Pat so unique and special. I admired Pat for her whimsical nature. When she decided to move from Baltimore to New York, we all were amazed. In her 15 or so years in New York, she moved so many times that I never entered her address in my book in pen, because I knew she would suddenly decide she needed a change and move.

Her most endearing quality to me that I will always remember was her wit. We would be dying of laughter, as she would regale us with stories of her many adventures in New York. She always had a story to tell. She would say such funny things that, at times, we could not stop laughing. I remember one instance where we were all sitting around the kitchen table and Pat was telling us about a celebrity whose house caught fire and burned to the ground. I kept asking her how the fire started. Finally, after the third time I asked her, she swung around in the chair and retorted, "I don't know! Her cat was smoking in bed!" We laughed for hours about that. That was classic Pat.

I miss the fun we always had when she was in Baltimore or when I was in New York. I miss her beautiful smile. I miss the Saturday mornings when I would pick up the phone and hear, "Annie, what are you doing?" Simply stated, I miss Pat.

We watched Pat suffer through her bouts with cancer three times. Each time was so very difficult for us all. It was hard to see someone so wonderful suffer the way she did. But each time she went through it, she never let it break her spirit. She faced it head on with the confidence that she would beat it. This third time, however, was the most difficult for her. No one knew, but it was evident in the end that Pat had made her peace with God and accepted her fate. As for the rest of us, we were totally in denial. We couldn't face the reality of the situation. Just the thought of living our lives without Pat was frightening.

I will always remember the day she left Baltimore to return to New York. As she was sitting in the car, I leaned in, kissed her, and told her to hurry up and get better so Bettye and I could come up to New York and go shopping with her on Austin Street. She never spoke, but looked at me as if she were looking at me for the last time. Sadly, it was. That look on her face is ingrained in my mind. Sometimes people leave us so quickly that we miss the chance to say the things we always wanted to say. If I could speak to Pat right now, I would tell her how very much I love her. I would tell her how proud I am of her and the things she accomplished in her short time here on earth. Finally, I would tell her how very difficult it is to be here without her.

Pat's spirit will live on in my heart forever. It will also live on in her daughter, Alexandra. I believe Alexandra will continue the work her mother was put on earth to do—to touch as many lives, even in a small way, as she can. That is what Pat did. There is a void in all our hearts that will never be filled because she is no longer with us. I will forever love, admire, and cherish her. She is, my sister, Pat.

Annette "Annie" Dodson

•

To Patricia My Sister, My Friend:

When I think about making a tribute to you my lovely sister, I think back to the time when you were a little girl and it was my responsibility to take you to school and pick you up. So sweet and so loving, you made sure that I always said good-bye to you as I left you on the school steps and that I made sure you had everything you needed. When I fell short of my commitment to you, you had the school call me at home to come back to say goodbye and to put your mittens in your book bag or pin them to your coat sleeve. Yet through all the things I had to do for you, as you grew up I can't begin to thank you for all the things you did for me. You always said things to me to make me laugh when I was sad. You helped me to understand my daughter in ways I couldn't at times.

For me, Gospel music has always been very soothing when I was troubled or sad. So, when I was troubled while you were struggling with the cancer fight, I always found songs to help me through. I remember giving you the tape with the song "My Help Cometh from the Lord." It was this song that I felt would help you to hold on and know that God would bring you through. Although in a way he did take you out of your suffering, it was not the way I wanted it to be. So sometimes when I hear this song it brings tears to my eyes because I had only hoped and prayed that the outcome would be different. However, we are so very blessed that we have a part of you still with us through your writings.

You have always been the center of this family. We always looked to you to make us laugh, and you always did. Even when you were very sick, you still said things that made us laugh. I admire your achievements: your strength, your resilience, your spirit and your ability persevere.

I regret never saying all the things that were in my heart on your last visit to Baltimore. You were so very concerned for Velma on that visit, and I can't help believing that you knew your fate even though we were hopeful that you were going to get better. I love you so very much and will always be here for your lovely daughter Alexandra; for she is so much like you and for us she will carry on your spirit. I miss you so much and know that I will see you again someday.

Love,
Bettye Pettiford
Your loving sister

●

"I don't know anyone with the same purity of heart and soul as you. Thank you for being my nephew. Thank you for being my friend. But mostly, thank you for being you.

Love forever,
Pat"

This was how she autographed her book *Red on a Rose* for me. I cherish this sentiment with all of my heart because she was like a sister to me and she knew I felt the same about her. Within Pat was a never ending magnitude of infinite strength, wisdom and will. She loved strong and always wanted the same strength of love in return. Pat was like a volcano set up on a mountain of dreams and goals cut short as she poured over the top with success. Because of her success, I try to live my life with a passion like she would have continued to do. Her philosophies in me will always live.

Love,
Mark (your nephew)

•

I was the last person to see Pat alive. That memory will stay with me for the rest of my life. I'd never been touched by death like that. I had to perform mouth to mouth resuscitation and heart massage before the medical people arrived. The only thing I could think of was "Could I have done more? Did I let her down?" Why was I the only one to have to do this?

From the time she came to live in New York, my relationship with Pat was one of reliance. Even though she was a very capable person, with extraordinary talent and drive, she came to rely on me to make things right. This was a comfortable relationship for both of us, because she made me feel larger than I was. Did I fail her in her final moments? I will always wonder.

Our last meaningful conversation before she started the sleep and pain regimen was about her wanting what other people took for granted . . . health and normalcy. I reminded her that if she received those things today, would she be what she had become? She smiled and understood that we are given what we are given and duration has nothing to do with contribution.

If I failed you Pat, I'm sorry. I did the best I could. Why was I the only one to do this? Because you relied on me to do what was best. I hope I didn't let you down.

Love always,
Ken Adams (your loving brother-in-law)

•

To my darling daughter Patricia:

When you were in middle school, you had the opportunity to travel abroad to Paris, and I knew then that you would be a world traveler. Then when you got to the 11th grade at Seton Keough, I was not prepared for what I had to face when you were diagnosed with Hodgkin's disease at the age of fifteen. Everything looked so bleak yet I stood by my faith that you would pull through. You were able to make it to your junior prom, right at the beginning of your Chemotherapy treatments, and although you were so very thin, you truly looked beautiful. I became so sad and felt that God was not listening to me when you took a turn for the worse. You missed most of your twelfth grade and your senior prom. However, once again you persevered and were able to complete your last year of high school in conjunction with your first year of college at Morgan State. I was never so happy because it was a sign that we had beaten this dreaded cancer.

As you transferred to Boston University, graduated, and landed your first job with *Black Enterprise*, my initial thought of you being a world traveler came to fruition. You traveled to various parts of Africa, France and Italy, writing articles for the magazine. Oh what a joy that was for you to have that great life.

With your marriage and the birth of your daughter (Alexandra), I just knew that you would be around to see this lovely child grow to adulthood. Unfortunately, the demon of cancer struck again. This time I could not be there to hold your hand, rock you when you were in pain and just take care of you as I did before. Not having my sight and being much older did not give me the ability to do that. However, I stayed on my knees in prayer that you would progress as you did before. I feel that if I could have been there for you, with all the proper medical treatment you would still be here today. The hardest thing a mother has to do in life is to bury her child. I definitely was not prepared for that, but I do believe that you are in a better place. Watching you suffer as you did was far too difficult to bear. I love you so much as I often told you through your good and bad times, and I truly miss you. Your humor was infectious and your spirit astounding.

Love,
Mother

•

Pat's daughter was the most important person in her life. Patricia took so much time with Alexandra, teaching her, guiding her, playing with her, correcting her behavior when needed. Alexandra is the child she is today because of Pat. Pat and Alexandra played word games, spelling games, math games. They did so much together. Alexandra remembers her mother saying to her "you are the most perfect thing I have ever made." Alexandra and Pat had such a bond, that Pat lives on for Alexandra. Alexandra always talks of her mother in the present tense. She was never gone for her. During the year of her mother's illness, Alexandra had a difficult time understanding why her mommy could not do all of the things she once did with her, but she always sat and talked with her mother and tried to help her. Alexandra could be found often rubbing her mother's back when it hurt or rubbing her legs when they were swollen and aching.

She wrote the following after her mother's death: *"My mom is nice. My mom helps me when I'm sick. My mom goes shopping with me. My mom plays with me. My mom gives me math. And she is special."* Alexandra had just turned seven when she wrote this, her mother having passed just before her birthday. Alexandra has a large collection of angels to remind her that her mother is in heaven and watching over her.

Today she writes:

My Mommy,

I love to write! I take a class called Creative Writing, and I wouldn't have taken the class if my mommy wasn't a writer. My mommy also came into my class when I was in kindergarten, twice. When she came I felt like blushing of happiness. When people looked at me, I smiled really big because it was my mommy up there, and not anybody else's.

My mommy was a really funny person, too, and it rubbed off in her writing. When my dad was reading *Passing* to me, I'll never forget her expression "ack, ack, ackalacky." I'm not really sure what "ackalacky" means, but I smile whenever I think of it. A lot of times when I think of my mommy I'm sad, because she's not here, but a lot of times I'm happy—and I smile when I remember the things that she said, or did with me.

Love,
Alexandra Bacchus, age 8

For me, her sister Velma, Patricia was my best friend. It has been a difficult journey learning to live without Pat, yet I know that is what she wants me to do. She always believed that life was to be lived. Patricia embraced life fully and tried to live each day with purpose. She was able to fulfill most of her dreams, some were left unfulfilled, but the larger dreams, the important goals were achieved. I do have the memories of the great times we shared as well as the sad or troubling moments we shared. Pat was so special because she had a deeper understanding of what is important in life than most of us ever have. She always believed that tomorrow was not promised so "live for today." I always felt that she was in a hurry to live and accomplish her goals. Now as I look back, I understand that she never expected to live a long life.

Well, Pat you may not have lived a long life, but you did live a full life. I miss you so very much, but I know you are in a place where you are at peace. You have left a great legacy behind in your writing, your friends and family, but most importantly in your daughter.

Love you,
Velma

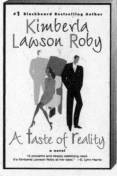